Ms. Mary Mack

Nicholas Panagakos

This story is a work of fiction. All events held within the story are the product of the author's imagination. Any similarities to persons, living or dead, places, small cats named Mr. Biscuit, or representatives from prestigious museums are purely coincidental. Except for the town of Winsted. That's a real place. There are some real museums in here too, but the goons are all made up. Wait. I do mention some other stuff. Song titles, mostly. Couple of actual hotels and restaurants. Every character in this story is fictitious and any real locations have neither endorsed nor allowed me permission to mention their places of business. Any events that occur in locations or businesses are fictitious and entirely for the sake of entertainment. For all litigation, complaints, involuntary spasms, dry throat, itchy leakage, discharge, or bad language, please contact my butt.
))=3 $

A carol from Kenneth Grahame's The Wind in the Willows was used to open chapter 8, "I Am A Bird And I Eat Little Worms". If you haven't read The Wind in the Willows, I would highly recommend it.
It's neat.

Ms. Mary Mack

For Yanira

Index

1. It's Like A Game .... pg. 9
2. Where Are Your Shoes? .... pg. 28
3. You Haven't Found Me Yet .... pg. 38
4. Nothing Unreal Exists .... pg. 48
5. Someday You'll Understand .... pg. 63
6. Don't Look At Her Eyes .... pg. 73
7. I Haven't Got A Card .... pg. 87
8. I Am A Bird And I Eat Little Worms .... pg. 98
9. And What About The Bears? .... pg. 113
10. Let's Go Mets .... pg. 126
11. I Like Stupid Hats .... pg. 138
12. I Can't Do This Anymore .... pg. 157
13. You're Gonna Be Ok .... pg. 171
14. Didja See It? .... pg. 186
15. The Glitter Ghost Fun Factory .... pg. 201
16. Thank You, Loose Lips .... pg. 215
17. Welcome Home .... pg. 234
18. I Need To Know You .... pg. 252
19. I Love A Good Nightmare .... pg. 267
20. You Wanna Meet My Folks? .... pg. 279
21. CASH ONLY .... pg. 301
22. It's Complicated .... pg. 316
23. Two Sheep Were Grazing In A Field .... pg. 330
24. I Don't Wanna Go Down To The Basement .... pg. 344
25. Not Much Further To Go .... pg. 358
26. Is This Real? .... pg. 371
27. I Found You .... pg. 384

Epilogue: How Showing Up Is Overrated .... pg. 397

1. It's Like A Game

Ms. Mary Kirkland was born in the second-floor bathtub of the house that her great grandfather had built. The house had the charming inconsistencies often found in the work of those afflicted with an overabundance of rugged individualism. Half of the roof was peaked with a tall-rounded tower, belfry, and spire rising from the eastern corner of the house while the rest of the roof was only slightly slanted. This was meant to create a drainage incline for rain and melting snow, but an unfortunate result from this was an inexplicable attraction from the local birds. With a continuous pattern of cause and effect, birds would try to build nests on the roof only to find that its slant would cause them to slide off and down onto the ground below. Thankfully, there was never enough time for the birds to lay eggs. But these were stubborn birds that did not know how to take a hint. Mary's father would often translate to Mary what the birds were saying in frustration, but he had enough sense to leave out the curse words.

The windows of the house were a combination of rounded, rectangular, square, and triangular. Some of the windows were even octagonal. There were two doors to the house, one in the front and one in the back leading out from the kitchen. Both doors were painted slate gray, sporting brass doorknobs, and were taller than they were wide. The foundation to the house was strong, and the beams well fitted. From a distance the house looked a little strange. It made even less sense up close.

Mary's home was in a small clearing surrounded by woods that expanded a great distance on all sides. The house stood at the end of a long dirt path that stretched roughly a mile from the road leading into town. Mary used to wait for cars to leave the driveway and run through the dirt and dust that the tires kicked up in the air. It was one of her favorite games where she would pretend that she was flying through a cloud and that she could safely jump back down to earth as the dust dissipated. Sometimes she would ask her parents to drive up the road just so that she could play in the clouds.

Ms. Mary was just Mary at the time. Those kinds of titles were reserved for grown-ups that received mail and knew who they were. Mary had received birthday cards and Valentine's Day cards before, but they had always been addressed to her as "Mary", "Mary Moo", or "Mary Rama-Lama-Dingdong". She did not like being called "Mary Rama-Lama-Dingdong", and although it was a popular choice among her relatives, she thought it was undignified.

On one occasion, a letter addressed to a Dr. Philip Garbanzo had accidentally arrived with an invitation to a dental conference in Los Angeles. That was an exciting day, but Mary did not feel as though she could claim the prefix of "Dr." because Phillip Garbanzo was a different person altogether. If she started walking around claiming to be a doctor, then maybe Phillip Garbanzo would have to stop being one. She did not have the heart to take that away from him, even if he was named after a bean.

Once Mary received her first correspondence with the prefix "Ms." then she could claim it as her own. Until then she would just have to be satisfied being Mary. This was not an immediate concern, but she did check the mail frequently for the day when she could grow up.

Mary lived with her parents and her grandmother. Her parents were not intentionally neglectful, they were busy. That is what you tell a child when you cannot spend time with them. You are busy. A child accepts this to be true with limited follow-up questions. Mary's parents spent most of their time working and when they were not working, they were distracted by trying to impress other people. Her mother worked as a paralegal for a prominent law firm in town and her father worked for a company that designed graphic images for the tops of pizza boxes. They had several social and professional connections that required a certain amount of involvement outside of business hours.

Sometimes her parents went to the movies or a friend's house for dinner. They seldom entertained others in their own home but if there was a friendly gathering to which they had not received an invitation, they would privately sulk. There was no sense in public sulking because what does that get you, really? Those nights were when Mary would put forth the most effort to entertain her parents.

In the slow evolution of an evening, with her mother and father becoming fuzzy by alcohol and social resentment, Mary would pretend that she was on television and would sing and perform comedy for her family. Sometimes she would read passages from her favorite books or make up her own stories. Her parents watched her through their haze of liquor and self-pity saying, "That's nice, dear."

Mary's grandmother would sit in her large, brown vinyl living room chair and applaud with vigor at each performance. She would often nudge her son to bring him to attention and suggest that he join her in cheering his daughter. He would provide his enthusiasm not so much for the support of Mary, whom he did love, but more for the fear of his own mother. This was a cyclical process in Mary's home. The concept of fear and love each held a duplicitous nature for the Kirkland's.

The mornings would be buzzing with fast paced action at the breakfast table. Eggs and buttered toast would fly through the air as fragments of conversation blended together to create such a cacophonous row as to put your early morning teeth on edge. Mary would try to ask her mother a question but she would be interrupted by her mother asking a different question to her father who would ignore his wife and begin to compliment Mary until he would stop half-way through his compliment to answer her mother's question while her mother would shout at the news on the radio as Mary repeated her question to her mother before her father would notice the time and then swallow his hot coffee whole (which would later give him indigestion) and jump up to kiss his wife and ruffle Mary's hair all around (which she hated).

Her mother would be two steps behind him out of the door to begin her own workday so far away forever. Mary would then either catch the bus to school or be left on her own under the supervision of her grandmother, depending on the day.

She loved her grandmother very much but was also sometimes frightened by the things she said and did. Mary's grandmother would yell at the television, even when it was off. Sometimes she would stand in a corner of the room and stare out with a fixed gaze on the opposite wall. She would stand there stiff as a post for a few minutes before going about the rest of her day as though nothing unusual had happened. Every night she would drink whiskey and soda out of a big red plastic cup. If Mary ever tried to drink from it, she would get smacked and told, "No!"

Mary's grandmother also had moments of incredible kindness. It would not be unusual for her to return home from running errands with a selection of fine candy for Mary to enjoy. She would also bring coloring books, crayons, and special pencils back from her shopping. It was difficult to tell when her kindness would turn. When it did, it was clear that Mary's grandmother misunderstood children. She was often in a serious mood that would distract her from playing in a real way. Mary spent her most formative years playing by herself.

Mary was playing in the backyard on the kind of autumn afternoon where you get to wear your favorite sweater and walk through the smell of the damp world. She was building a small house with sticks and leaves when she noticed two little eyes watching her from behind a flowering dogwood tree. The suddenness of its appearance startled Mary to where she almost fell over.

Mary had always maintained a curious mind and was beginning to recognize her fear not as a negative emotional response, but as a natural reaction that she could name. She still became frightened, certainly, but she was becoming aware that the world was filled with circumstances that were beyond her control. Her father had told her once that being brave was not the absence of fear but being terrified and having the courage to do the damn thing anyway. The curse word at the end made it particularly impactful on Mary and it became one of the few pieces of advice from her father that she would try her best to keep.

Mary slowly approached the dogwood with her hands shaking. As she got closer, the eyes she saw became a face, the face became a head, the head then grew a neck, and by the time Mary had arrived at the tree, there was a little boy, around her age but slightly younger, staring at her through a pair of serious hazel eyes.

"Where'd you come from?" asked Mary.

"I don't know," said the little boy, "I just got here."

"Well, do you have a name?"

"Yes," the boy made a face like he was about to sneeze, but it passed, "what's your name?"

"My name is Mary. I live here." Mary pointed to her house and the little boy peeked out from around the tree. "Where do you live?"

"I don't know," said the boy, "I like your tree."

"It's my favorite," said Mary.

The little boy came out from around the dogwood and sat in the grass. He wore brown corduroy pants and a light blue shirt with buttons on the front. He was not wearing any shoes, which Mary found to be odd, but there were many things in this world that Mary felt were odd. Mary sat down next to the boy and they both began pulling small clumps of grass out from the ground.

"Where's your mom and dad?" asked Mary.

"They're away," said the boy, "but I don't know where they are. Do you have a mom and dad?"

"I think I do," said Mary, "sometimes."

Mary had often fantasized about being an orphan. She could have so many different adventures and would not have to listen to anyone. All sorts of dangers and victories awaited her on the open road. She thought on this for a while before deciding to change the subject and practice her hospitality.

"Do you want to play a game?" she said.

"I'm already playing a game," said the boy, "I'm playing hide-and-seek. I was hiding, but I ran away."

"Did they find you?"

"No," said the boy, "I'm faster than they are."

"Are you hungry?"

The boy's eyes grew wide and became filled with a soft white light that Mary had never seen in another person's face.

"Yes," he said, "I am *very* hungry."

Mary brought the boy inside the house and into the kitchen. She was not sure where her grandmother was and wanted to be quiet. There was a very real risk in making too much noise if her grandmother was in an angry mood. The world outside of her house was much more appealing than the home where she lived. She found peace out in the woods while home felt too oppressive. There was a movie she had seen with her parents recently that showed what a minefield was, so Mary stepped carefully around her house.

Mary gestured to the boy to be quiet as they both moved slowly through the kitchen. There were still slices of bread, meat, and cheese left out from lunch, so Mary did her best to make a sandwich for her new friend. She may have added a little too much mustard, and there may have been an incident involving the jar of mayonnaise and the floor, but soon enough there was a sandwich prepared for the boy who watched all that Mary did with solemn fascination. He was smiling and did not ask any questions when Mary handed him the plate.

She had barely put the plate on the table when the sandwich disappeared and was all eaten up in a series of three large bites. The boy had said he was hungry, but Mary had never seen anyone eat like that before. He smiled and wiped his mouth on the back of his hand. They both jumped when the sound of heavy running footsteps interrupted the moment and Mary's grandmother dashed into the kitchen wearing her big brown boots. She scoffed at the mess that Mary had made while her hard fingers curled around the doorframe.

"What the hell are ya doin', Mary?" she asked.

Mary was so frightened that she dropped the plate and it smashed into pieces on the kitchen floor. The boy did not move from his chair, but a strange look overcame him. His skin became pale, and his lip began to quiver; just as a child's would, had it been caught doing something wrong.

"Oh, now look at that," shouted her grandmother, "I step out for ten minutes and just look what you did. Go to your room!"

"He said he was hungry," said Mary.

"Who? Who's hungry?"

Mary pointed to the little boy sitting at the kitchen table, but her grandmother looked at the chair as though it were empty. She looked all over the room but found no satisfaction with Mary's claim of a boy being in the kitchen with them. Mary began to whimper as she looked at the boy. He was watching how her grandmother moved and would follow her with his eyes wherever she went. There was a frightened look on his face, but his eyes followed her all the same. He looked like a scared cat watching a large and unusual bird through a window. Mary was about to expand upon an explanation when her grandmother picked her up by the back of her shirt and carried her like a suitcase up the stairs and into her room. She dropped Mary on her bed and slammed the door behind her as she left.

"I don't want to hear another sound out of you," said her grandmother through the door, "And you can forget about dinner since you've already had two lunches, you fat little thing!"

Mary listened to the sound of her grandmother's boots descending the stairs that would lead her back to her living room chair. She was worried about the boy, but she was also angry at him for getting her in trouble. Soon she would be listening to the rhythm of her grandmother's deviated septum rattling half the house with deep snores. Mary would not dare to leave her room again for the remainder of the night. Her grandmother's wrath was something that Mary had seen enough of to know that it would be mighty.

There was the sound of the television, muffled and indiscernible through the wall, and then the sound of her grandmother snoring in her chair. Sometimes Mary would wake up in the middle of the night to the sound of her grandmother snoring in her bedroom down the hall. Mary felt frightened and angry, captive as she was in her own home. Without another option, she laid her face against her pillow and began to cry. She cried for so long that she fell asleep with her face buried in her pillow as it softly took her tears.

It was dark outside when Mary woke up. She was feeling the delirium that tends to follow a nap that lasts too long. The fuzzy feeling where you cannot tell what day it is or whether you are supposed to stay asleep until morning could remove any understanding of thought. A person's sense of identity might even slip under these conditions. Mary could see the hallway light coming in from beneath her door. The sound of her parents speaking softly downstairs in the living room had her guessing that it was probably time for dinner. The Kirkland's never really ate at the dinner table except for special occasions. They liked to watch television while they ate.

Mary sat up in bed and rubbed her face. Her eyes were still stinging and puffy from having cried and she was very thirsty. She opened her door and poked her head out into the hallway. The television was on, and she could hear her parents and grandmother talking about the president. Mary did not care about presidents, but she wanted to see her mother and father after having experienced such a difficult day. Mary walked down the stairs and her parents smiled at her warmly.

"Hey there, sleepers," said her father, "you had a good long nap!"

"Are you going to be able to sleep tonight?" asked her mother.

Mary nodded and rubbed her eyes. "I'm thirsty," she said.

Mary's father got up and went to the kitchen. He returned with a big glass of water, a small glass of juice, and a bowl of creamy lemon chicken soup with a large crust of sourdough bread hanging off the side of the bowl. Mary's mother set up a standing tray so that Mary could watch television with them while she dipped her bread and ate her soup. This was her favorite meal and was usually served on special occasions. There was a fleeting moment where Mary thought that it may be her birthday, but this was quickly dismissed as she remembered that they had only just celebrated her birthday in August.

Mary's grandmother did not say anything, but she smiled plainly as she watched Mary use the bread to soak up every drop of soup. Mary remembered the boy in an instant and fought against the impulse to search the kitchen. There was no reason he would still be sitting at the table, but she did not know what else to do and she wanted to be sure that he was ok. The suspicious fear that Mary had towards her grandmother was growing more each day. This was a point of confusion for Mary as she wanted nothing more in the world than for her grandmother to love her.

Without knowing how to make that happen, or what it was that she was doing wrong, Mary continued to try her best to win her grandmother's favor. Mary decided to stay on the couch for now and not mention the boy. She would look for him later.

There was a movie about a submarine on the television and Mary's thoughts traveled to what it would be like to live underwater. She had been giving the idea more attention each day, and it was becoming an appealing fascination. Mary liked small spaces and was convinced that she could happily live in a deep-sea submarine. She was just beginning to acquire an interest in sea life, especially whales.

To Mary it seemed as though each time she would learn about a new kind of whale, two more would pop up out of nowhere and leave her searching for more information. The possible combinations of whale species made Mary giddy. If it were raining outside, and if Mary was not allowed to play in the yard or the woods, then her favorite indoor game was Submarine. She would confine herself in the smallest enclosure she could find in the house and spend most of the afternoon on deep sea expeditions fighting creatures like giant squid off the shores of large islands. The game would usually end with Mary becoming friends with whatever creature she was fighting. It was easier for Mary to make friends in her fantasy world than in her real life.

Last year Mary had found a little panel door built into the wall of her grandmother's room that she tried to sneak into when no one was looking. She thought it perfectly resembled a submarine hatch. It was a small square door with no handle, but it fastened with three latches bolted into the wall. Mary thought it might have led to a secret treasure of pirate's gold, but when her grandmother caught her trying to open the locks, she erupted with rage. This terrified Mary so severely that she never entered her grandmother's room again. In fact, she avoided that end of the hallway altogether. Mary loved her grandmother very much, but she did not like to flinch.

Watching the submarine dive in the movie had Mary thinking of how far down a person would have to go until they arrived at the bottom of the ocean. Her mind created deep sea monsters that were ferocious and some that were friendly. Mary thought of great big fat monsters that only ate cakes and tiny skinny monsters that would disappear completely if they turned to their sides. They would all live in giant underwater cities with stores and traffic lights, restaurants, and offices. There would also be parks and rollercoasters where other monsters could play or be eaten or both. Mary considered many things as she fell back asleep in her father's arms and dreamt of submarines.

Mary woke up in her bed with the morning sun slowly warming her face. It had been three days since she had seen the boy in her yard, but she still had not mentioned anything to her parents. She had made the mistake of talking about him with a classmate, but the secret disclosure was received with ridicule and accusations that Mary had become even stranger than she already was. Mary tried to play it off as a joke, but now half of the school would ask about her ghost at any given opportunity.

Nobody enjoys being made to feel crazy, but Mary was also beginning to question her own sanity. Although she wondered who he was and where he had come from, she knew that she must be careful not to talk about him. She was not sure why, but she had a suspicion that it was a dangerous topic. Mary's morning thoughts were interrupted by her mother calling her to breakfast before the school bus arrived.

Mary did not like breakfast, but she knew that her refusal would only lead to an extensive lecture about how important it was. Mary's mother would give vague examples of less fortunate people who would be grateful to have anything at all to eat. This made Mary feel confused because she did not think it was her fault that so many people in the world could go hungry just because she found scrambled eggs to be repulsive. If anything, she felt compelled to give her breakfast to someone who wanted it more than she did.

Mary was about to raise this option to her mother when her father stumbled into the kitchen with one shoe in his hand, the leg of his pants tucked into one sock, and half of his shirt tucked into his waistline. Her father quickly buttered a piece of bread, rolled up the scrambled eggs, and nearly swallowed his breakfast whole. Mary thought of a nature show on television where a snake ate a whole rat without chewing. Her father's dangling tie became his extended tail and it wiggled beneath his jaw. Mary wanted to ask her father a question about snakes, but he was already out the door and off to work with one shoe still in hand. Mary thought of asking her mother questions about snakes, but she was not wearing a tie so she may not have the right kind of information. Although her mother did know about eggs. Snakes laid eggs. There may have been some overlap between neckties and eggs. Mary decided to see just what her mother knew about snakes.

"Mom," asked Mary, "do we have snakes?"

"What, dear?"

Mary's mother was applying lipstick using the large mirror centered inside the kitchen cabinet. The black walnut cabinet was an heirloom of Mary's great-grandfather and had been placed in the kitchen when the house was built. To anyone's knowledge, it has stood unmoved since its installation. Mary would often find small treasures in the variety of drawers that lined the front and sides of the cabinet. When Mary was six, she found a brass thimble that she was convinced had been made of pure gold. Mary had just read Rumpelstiltskin and wondered if he could be living in the basement or in the walls where nobody could find him. There were many hours spent when Mary would walk up and down the house running her hand against the smooth wallpaper to feel for hidden doors and secret passageways.

She kept the thimble in her pocket for a long time until it inevitably became misplaced somewhere for someone else to find. Mary was sad for exactly two days before she began to recognize the impermanence of the material world. Age six was such a long time ago.

"Do we have snakes?" asked Mary.

"Oh, you don't want snakes," said her mother, "They're not good pets."

"No, not for a pet," said Mary, "just normal snakes. Outside snakes."

Mary's mother looked at her with confusion.

"Did you see a snake, honey?"

"No."

"Why are you asking about snakes?"

Mary shrugged and moved her eggs around her plate. She knew all along that her mother was unaware of the habits of snakes. This was to be cataloged in Mary's memory as one of her great disappointments. Against her better judgment, and with mysteries weighing heavily on her mind, Mary decided to fish around her mother for any clues she might have about the little boy she had found in their backyard.

"I saw a little boy in the yard the other day," said Mary, "he was weird."

"In our yard?"

"Yep," said Mary, "just behind the little tree in the back."

"Where did he come from?"

"He didn't know."

"He didn't know where he was from?"

"I asked him, but he said he didn't know. He said he was hungry, so I brought him inside and I made him a sandwich."

"Oh, *that* boy," said Mary's mother, "your grandmother told me all about 'him'."

This made Mary nervous. If her mother had known about the little boy from the backyard, why had she not said anything to Mary up until now? Was she also trying to learn what Mary knew? This was becoming dangerous again, and Mary had a suspicion that she was already in trouble. Mary began to defend herself the best way she knew how: explain that it was not her fault.

"I tried to tell grandma," said Mary, "but she just got mad and hurt me."

"Mary, don't exaggerate."

"I'm not exaggerating!"

"Your grandmother came home and found you making a mess all over the kitchen. Now you're getting a little too old for imaginary friends, Mary. We just want you to show some accountability. If you make a mistake, then all you have to do is apologize and try harder. Ok, sweetie?"

"He's real," shouted Mary, "he's real and I'm not exaggerating!"

"I don't want you talking to 'strange boys' anymore," said her mother, "And I don't want you making up stories. If you do see a stranger around here, you tell me right away. Ok?"

"OK, *mom*."

Mary sank into her chair and made up her mind to never tell her mother if she saw the boy ever again. She regretted bringing him up in the first place. The feeling of betrayal and contempt that was welling up within Mary was involuntarily squashed down until she began to feel nothing at all. After a few minutes of silence, a wave of calm washed over her.

"Listen dear," said her mother, "I'm going to be working late tonight and then your father and I are going to see a show. Be good for Grandma, finish your homework, and don't stay up too late watching movies. And no scary movies, you get nightmares."

Mary loved scary movies almost exclusively. She was only eleven years old, but she had begun watching the classic Dracula and Frankenstein movies from the nineteen-thirties when she was much younger. They did give her nightmares, but she enjoyed those as well. She would wake up terrified and sometimes she would cry, but she also thought of her nightmares as continuous chapters of the films.

Her favorite was the Invisible Man. The idea that someone could exist and not exist at the same time was appealing to her. The ability to move unnoticed through groups of people while playing practical jokes was too good of an idea for her to ignore. Sometimes Mary would try to become invisible simply by closing her eyes and repeating *I'm invisible* to herself over and over. These were unsuccessful trials, but she still had hope.

Mary finished her breakfast and rode the bus to school with her mind swimming in snakes, submarines, the strange boy, and becoming invisible. *What if Dracula was invisible*, she thought.

This would later become another nightmare which she would inevitably forget after waking up. She was thinking about invisible Dracula when Elizabeth Brandt sat next to her.

"Hello Mary."

"Hi Lizzy."

"Can I see your math homework?"

Elizabeth always copied Mary's math homework. It was not that Mary was particularly good at math. She was passing, but just barely. Mary let Elizabeth copy her homework because Elizabeth was terrible at math and no one else would let her copy theirs. Mary only tolerated Elizabeth, and even this had its limitations. Then again it was more than what most people could do.

"Did you see the new boy that just transferred to our class?" asked Elizabeth.

"Ugh," said Mary, only half paying attention, "who cares? Boys are gross and mean."

"I think he's cute."

"You think every boy is cute."

"So what?"

Elizabeth stood up to see if she could spot the new classmate further up the bus, but she just saw the face of Addison Spinoza staring back at her. Addison Spinoza was equivalent to a social death sentence. He was another recent transfer from an unfortunate homeschool environment and had no real ability to interact with people.

Addison had been court mandated to be removed from his parents' custody after a series of intentional malfeasance fell upon him from their hands. None of this was his fault, but it planted within him a severe discomfort and general fear of other people. After his parents relinquished custody of Addison to one of his aunts, she was unwilling to commit to homeschooling. She said that having Addison spend so much time at home would be too much of a strain on her dogs. They had been purchased from a farm to be put out for breeding and the very presence of

Addison caused enough anxiety to jeopardize their fertility. She considered it a liability to have him hanging around the house, so homeschooling was not an option. Having had little to no social interactions outside of the mailman, talking to Addison was uncomfortable, to say the least. He smelled like old apples.

It was no surprise then that Elizabeth jumped back down and covered her face with her hands when she saw him staring back at her from the front of the bus.

"Oh, god," she said, "Oh, god, oh, god!"

"What happened?" asked Mary, still lost in thought about Dracula.

"He saw me," said Elizabeth, "Addison saw me, and he was staring at me."

"What, you don't think he's cute?" Mary said, smiling to herself.

"NO! I hate him."

Addison came to the back of the bus where Mary and Elizabeth were sitting. He took an empty spot on the bench across the aisle and continued to stare uncomfortably at Elizabeth. They were five minutes away from the school, but time is always a funny thing when you do not want to be somewhere.

"Go away, Addison!" said Elizabeth.

Addison looked at Elizabeth through his dull eyes. He sent a puzzled look to Mary, but she just shrugged and made an ugly face back at him. The bus jostled along with the two girls doing their best to repulse Addison back to his seat, but he continued to stare at them with his blank expression. After a few painful seconds of torture, Addison stood up and returned to his seat at the front of the bus utterly defeated. Mary continued to look out the window and thought about dropping Elizabeth from the top of Dracula's castle. Resigned to her limitations, Mary sighed at another of life's seemingly endless disappointments.

"I can't stand him," said Elizabeth.

"You're one to talk."

"What?!"

"You only talk to me because no one else will let you copy their homework."

"That's not true!"

"No one else will let you copy their homework because they don't like you."

"Liar!"

"You and Addison are gonna get married someday."

Elizabeth jumped from the seat and ran up the bus aisle in tears. There was no lie in what Mary had said, but the truth can be devastating to most people with no self-awareness. Elizabeth never felt the need to have that kind of introspection, so these were truly shocking observations.

Mary continued to look out of the window until the school could be seen just up the road. She wondered if Dracula ever had to go to school.

The day was relatively uneventful, but Mary had difficulty focusing on her classes. She was caught daydreaming twice in Mr. Zaposta's science class and was given extra homework as punishment. Now on top of her regular assignments, she was responsible for writing a three-page biological description of three different kinds of frogs, single spaced, and with pictures. Despite the aggravation of additional work that would cut time out of Mary's leisure, this was a fortunate assignment because of her love for all reptiles and amphibians. Mary was always chasing frogs and salamanders in the ravine behind her house. There were days where she could not begin to count the frogs, for their numbers were sometimes unfathomable.

Mary would always do her best to be very careful when she walked among the frogs, toads, and salamanders. If she accidentally stepped on a frog, she would always prepare a modest and tasteful funeral. Mary would select a plot beneath the bushes that lined the banks of the river running through the ravine. It was important that she found the plot to be appropriate, depending on the personality of the frog. There would be a small service, very dignified, and she would bring dead flies that she collected from her windowsill as refreshments, should any mourners stop to pay their respects. She considered her funerals to be the social events of the season, but she took little joy in them. The ends never seemed to justify the means.

On most days when Mary returned home from school, on her best days, she would set her homework on the kitchen table and get it out of the way as soon as she could. That is, if she decided to do her homework. She was a fine procrastinator. This would afford her the luxury and freedom to play outside before the night would become too dark to see. Her father had a flashlight that he kept in the kitchen junk drawer, but Mary's grandmother would get angry if she went to play outside at night. She would tell Mary that there were things in the woods. Darker things that she never could know about. Mary had been hearing stories like this for her entire childhood, but she was beginning to feel bolder in her years. She was eleven, after all.

There were nights when Mary would stay awake until well after midnight because she was looking out into the woods from her bedroom window. She would sit in the dark and watch for the slightest movement, hoping to see something leap out from the trees. As much as she wanted to see monsters, she dreaded the possibility at the same time. Those nights would end with the blankets over her head, startled by the slightest sound.

The afternoon was a different story. The afternoon meant freedom. Mary would walk into her back woods in the daylight hours and sit among the secret world moving around her. There were songbirds out of sight and insects that she could hear buzzing through the flowers and trees. Her hands would sink into the dirt and moss that lay around her. It all produced a unique tactile sensation that she would be unable to fully replicate as she got older, though she would often try. Pulling her hands from the earth, she would bring them up to her face and inhale the smells until she could draw no more air into her lungs. It was a deep smell, deep and honest, and it did her heart well to have it. There were days when the sensation was the only thing Mary had to look forward to. She had tried tasting it once, but it disagreed with her palette.

Further away from her house there was a clearing that Mary had found the previous year. It was a small, circular patch of grass that was just a little wider than her height in diameter, if she were to lay down. On the most pleasant days, Mary would quietly lay in the center of the circle for hours, just staring at the blue hole in the sky that was bordered by the tops of trees above her head. She dreamt about the world she wanted to know and made up silly little songs. For Mary was tied to the woods as the fish to the sea, the birds in the sky, and the subterranean mole-men that she was convinced had been living in a cave behind her house for some time. She had no tangible proof of their existence but would swear on a stack of bibles that they were there, burying the bones of their dead and protecting their happy home from the rest of humanity.

The rhythm of life around her brought an enormous sense of well-being and she only felt a little afraid to be in the woods alone. The rewards were worth her apprehension. Sometimes if she was feeling particularly brave, Mary would stay out until it began to get dark. Her walk back home at dusk would be peppered with incandescent fireflies and the deep croaking bullfrogs that were more active after the sun had descended over the hill behind her house. The trees would cast strange shadows and the ground felt as though it could swallow her up if it wanted to. Mary had to be careful where she stepped for fear of discovering an animal's burrow or even just a small sinkhole.

She had recently seen a movie where a cowboy was caught in quicksand and disappeared beneath the desert sun. Only his hat remained as the music swelled dramatically. Mary felt at home in the woods. It made her feel better about being alive, but she was mindful of quicksand.

It was boot weather that day when Mary got home from school. It had rained earlier, and the backwoods had become slick with mud and moss. Mary took a running start from the middle of her yard and sprinted as fast as she could in her heavy boots. When she got to the border between her yard and the woods, she bent her knees, kept her feet straight, and slid along the top grass and mud. She barely made it three feet when the toe of her boot snagged a root poking up from the ground and it sent Mary flying face first into a milk thistle bush. Its nettles had been softened by the rain, but not enough to graciously receive Mary with comfort.

She was upside-down in the bush with her legs sticking up in the air when she saw two bare feet in brown corduroy trousers walking towards her. Mary kicked as hard as she could to dislodge herself from the pricker bush. She was freed when two large hands grabbed her by the waist and pulled her straight out. Mary's grandmother was holding her upside down and laughing at her predicament. There were thistles stuck in her hair and a few scratches on her face, but she was otherwise unharmed.

"What are ya doin' in the bushes, Mary?" said her grandmother.

"I got stuck."

"No kiddin'. You goin' for a nature walk?"

Mary looked at her grandmother's legs and saw that she was neither barefoot nor wearing corduroy pants. This struck her as suspicious, so she began to look for her friend. She felt a new sense of sinister intention on the wind.

"Yeah," said Mary, "I need to look for frogs."

"Frogs, huh," Mary's grandmother rubbed her hands together and looked at the sky. "Won't be dark for another hour. Mind if I join you?"

Mary nodded and took her grandmother's hand. She did not have the hands of an old lady. They were neither soft nor dainty. Her hands were firm with work. Even as she had been getting older, she had not stopped performing physical labor when it was needed. Mary's grandmother had been a plumber, an independent contractor, a bus driver, and a volunteer firefighter well into her fifties. She had accomplished a myriad of other jobs as well, but many of them were not for the likes of a sensitive company.

There was a family rumor that Mary's grandmother had once murdered a man with whom she worked in a slaughterhouse. The motive changed depending on who was telling the story, but Mary was unaware of this rumor. She was thought to be too young for those types of stories. What she did remember hearing was when her father would talk about a time "when mom went away".

Mary and her grandmother walked in the afternoon light as a transparent late day moon hung in the blue sky, cut with wisps of cirrus clouds. The fleeting daylight became less pronounced as they walked deeper into the woods, giving a certain glow to the trees against the sunset. Mary's grandmother stepped as though the ground itself had no choice but to flatten beneath her boots. Her footing was so confident that it was all Mary could do to keep up with her as she held her giant hand.

It was becoming clear to Mary that they were no longer walking to the ravine. She was instead being led towards an unknown destination. The walk had lost its casual tone and the pace had become guided in that non-negotiable style that her family felt was the only appropriate way to handle decisions. Mary did not live in a home of compromise. She was beginning to feel a pain in her wrist as her grandmother led her with a firm grip. There was a moment's panic as Mary fantasized the image of her grandmother chopping her into pieces with an ax, but her grandmother was not carrying an ax so that concern quickly rescinded.

They were deep in the woods now. With no trail ahead or behind them and her sense of direction jumbled, all the light was evenly dull to Mary's eyes. The world around her now was a grayscale collection of thin birch trees and large stones. Her grandmother let go of her hand and walked a little way ahead while Mary sat on a boulder to catch her breath. Mary only realized how tired she was from the walk when she sat down. She began looking for frogs, but there were none that she could see. In fact, Mary had been so focused on the journey into the deep forest that she was just noticing how quiet the world around her had become.

There were no birds, no insects. There was no movement in the world and even the wind was absent. Mary had never experienced stillness like this, and it began to frighten her. The area in which she sat was beyond the tree line and the dirt that had laid across the ground was now a carpet of sleek stone where no grass could be found. The stone spread out flatly with small craigs which connected to the point of a cliff some fifty yards above a quarry.

Looking back from where they had come from, she began to see figures moving behind the trees; tall and dark featureless beings that made no sound and cast no shadow. Mary would blink and they would be gone, but she knew them. She had seen them before in her room late at night, but never outside. If she were to take the time to focus her eyes and try to clearly see one of their intangible shapes, the figures would disappear back to wherever they had come from. This gave Mary the courage to face them if she began to feel scared, but it was only a small comfort.

"Mary," called her grandmother, "you ever been out this way before?"

Mary shook her head without taking her eyes from the woods behind them. She knew that she had never been that deep into the woods, but there was the nagging feeling of familiarity. It was an unexplainable sensation apart from how it made Mary feel increasingly uncomfortable. There was something about the cliffside that frightened her. Her grandmother kicked the heel of her boots against the stone ground, knocking loose some dirt that had caked beneath them.

"Come gimme a hand," she said.

Mary stood up and brushed some dust from the back of her pants. Her grandmother had moved a little way from where she had been sitting, but when Mary walked towards her voice, she saw her standing beside a tall wooden shed. To any other adult, it was not very big, but it was taller than her grandmother and certainly much taller than Mary. To Mary it was enormous. It had once been painted white, but the years of seasonal exposure had done a number to the paint which had by this time become peeled and worn thin. There were no windows, and a large padlock was fastened to the latch on the door.

"Come over here, Mary," said her grandmother, "this is a very important thing we have to do, but we can't tell anybody about it."

"How come," asked Mary.

"It's a secret. We can't let anybody know where this is. It's like a game."

Mary's grandmother was knocking on one side of the shed and pressed her ear against the wall. Her eyes looked serious and very pointed as she knocked and listened. She gestured to Mary to stand beside her. Mary pressed her ear against the shed, hearing only the occasional rap of her grandmother's hand against the wood. All was still.

"Ok," said Mary's grandmother, almost relieved, "that's alright. Mary, can you hear anything?"

"No," said Mary.

Then she did hear something.

Mary could hear a small scratching sound coming from inside the shed. It was a very faint sound, like someone was sliding their finger across a piece of paper. Her grandmother tensed up and grabbed Mary's shoulder so hard and so suddenly that Mary yelped and jumped with fright. Mary and her grandmother began to back away from the shed as the light scratching grew louder. The speed of the noise became desperate.

What had begun as the smooth suggestion of friction had now become the frantic clawing of an animal trapped. Mary hugged her grandmother and buried her face into the side of her thick canvas jacket. The smell of stale cigarettes and body powder had become absorbed by the material of her coat, but this was a familiar scent that Mary liked.

Her grandmother began to shout words that Mary did not know, but she recognized the rage in her tone. The sounds falling out of her grandmother's mouth were similar to what she launched towards the television on any given night, only more severe. Whatever was in the shed was matching the volume of her grandmother's screams with its own. The pitched howling carried a shrillness that cut through Mary's heart and made her feel cold. It brought a dull, metallic taste that began to linger in the back of her throat.

Mary's inability to comprehend what her grandmother was saying also brought a freezing terror that stopped Mary's mind from processing information. The language sounded powerful. After a few moments that felt as though they would never end, it stopped. It all stopped and returned to stillness.

"I knew it," said her grandmother, "I knew it. That son of a bitch!"

Mary's grandmother turned away from the shed and began marching back through the woods, leaving Mary to clumsily trail behind her. She practically had to sprint to keep up with her grandmother's stride. They were approaching the ravine where Mary was hoping to stop, but her grandmother kept marching with a purpose.

"Grandma," said Mary, "we have to get frogs!"

"Get what you need," said her grandmother, "I need to take care of somethin'. We all need to take care of somethin' sometimes."

Mary reluctantly stayed at the ravine, but the night was selfishly approaching. Wishing that her grandmother had stayed behind for company, Mary started looking around the ground for frogs. She was frightened from what she heard in the shed and imagined whatever was inside to be sprinting after her, hot on her trail. She thought of glowing red eyes and thick black hair with gnashing, blood-stained teeth. Sharp and stabbing claws that shined in the light would have remnants of skin hanging from the nails while pink and bloody foam coated the bottom of its mouth. All of this would come from the other children it had killed and taken back to eat in its shed. She thought of everything she knew about werewolves which she realized was very little, in the grand scheme of things.

There was an image in Mary's mind of violence. Violence so terrible that death would be seen as salvation. She knew that the monster must have been just over the embankment, swallowing the last rays of the sun. Mary watched the horizon for fifteen minutes until she became so frightened by her own imagination that she started to cry.

Mary had no frog research when she returned home. Her head was heavy with doom, and it hung limp between her slumped shoulders. Her family were in the living room watching television, talking about some war happening someplace that Mary had never heard of and had certainly never been to. Mary thought of war as a game where the good guys and bad guys fought in someone's backyard. Bang, Bang. You're dead. You have to wait on your side for the next game to start. Mary refused to play war because she did not like to die.

From the dim phosphorous light of the television set came the sound of a popular song advertising the latest advances in home furnishings. Mary's grandmother was quietly sipping from her plastic cup and looking at Mary without expression while her mother and father stared blankly at the television screen. The doorway from the kitchen across the hall to the living room held Mary's little frame, covered in dirt and grit, as she leaned her shoulder against it. She watched her parents for a few minutes before removing her coat and boots.

"Put your coat on the hook, dear," her mother said flatly, "and put your boots in the alcove."

Mary did as she was told without saying a word. She thought of telling her parents about the shed and the monster and the woods and the frogs but decided against it. Mary felt too tired to talk to anybody ever again. With new tears filling her eyes, she walked up the stairs to her room. Closing the door, she sat in a little chair in front of her desk and started to draw a picture of the shed. It was surrounded by wolves.

2. Where Are Your Shoes?

  The following morning found breakfast to be quiet as Mary's parents had to leave especially early that day. Mary had barely slept through the night and her dreams ran in circles around what possible horrors could be living in the white shed. These were not her usual Frankenstein nightmares where she could find some small amount of joy in the stylized terror of old Hollywood. These nightmares were all speed without sound, with the quick motion of twisted facial expressions filling the sky around her. Ageless, and with no gender or features to attribute definition, the shifting forms of torment suffocated the dark gray atmosphere around her.
  There were flashes when Mary could almost recognize some of the faces as people she knew, but there was never enough time for these nightmares to keep from slipping. If Mary tried to run, then her legs were always slower than her fears, which were no less than one step behind her. She tried to run away from everything, but whichever way she tried to escape she would be met with the shaking, screaming phantoms that moved around her in silence. Their long open mouths drew in sorrowful breaths but still could not produce any sound. The frustration on these faces shifted quickly between rage, fear, and misery. She thought she could hear a voice shouting something to her, but it sounded far away; as though the voice was wrapped in cotton, stuffed in a bottle, and sinking to the bottom of the sea. The ground beneath her feet became black and unstable as thin, greasy hair came up from the dirt and tried to drag Mary underground into the shadows of despair.
  The sound of her alarm ripped Mary out from her nightmare and back into her bed. A fog of morning confusion swam through Mary's head as she tried to remember parts of her dream. She could recall an idea of faces and a feeling of immeasurable guilt, but that was all. Her legs hurt as she tried to leave the bed.
  Mary went to the bathroom and filled the sink with cold water to dunk her face and let it soak for a while. She found comfort in this on especially hot days or when she began to feel overwhelmed by the world around her. Keeping her face submerged helped Mary understand what

was important and what was incidental, but everything is important when you are eleven years old. With her face submerged in the bathroom sink she felt slightly removed from the world that she knew, as though there was a universal understanding that she wanted to be left alone. It brought a kind of serenity that left her feeling consoled and alive again. She reached for a towel hanging from a hook on the bathroom door and began to pat her face dry as she looked at her reflection in the mirror.

Her grandfather had often told her stories about a time when he had gotten stuck inside of mirrors. The worlds inside were like ours, except everything was backwards and no one was ever nice or kind. Mary would listen to these stories in awe and believe every word that her grandfather said. He once told her of a time when he had to fight his evil twin on the other side of the mirror and when Mary asked how her grandfather managed to escape, he winked and said, "Maybe I didn't".

Then he would scream and snatch her up while he rubbed his rough beard against her face. Mary would laugh as her grandfather would chase her around the house. He would threaten to put lizards in her eyes, among other gruesome events, but he would always stop teasing Mary if she got too scared. Mary was not afraid of mirrors anymore, but she still watched herself suspiciously and would sometimes wait for her reflection to blink.

Mary walked into the kitchen to find two single packets of instant oatmeal next to a juice box on the table. Mary did not want to go to school, but she did want to get out of the house before her grandmother woke up. The events from the day before were still frightening but she was torn between her fear and her curiosity. Still, she felt complicit in the event and was now tied to whatever consequences may follow. Her fear was real, but her intrigue was unmistakable. She knew that she would have to find some way to return to the shed. It was still all too fresh and too strange to be approached lightly.

Mary stuffed the oatmeal packets in her coat pocket and walked to the bus stop with the juice box in hand. The sky was gray and lifeless as a subtle breeze barely managed to move the bangs that fell upon her face. She wished that today would just be over so she could somehow remain uninvolved with the world, if only for a little while.

Mary took her usual seat in the back of the bus as Elizabeth and Addison took the empty bench across the aisle.

"Hello *Mary*," said Elizabeth, "how's it goin', *Mary*?"

Mary briefly looked at the pair before bringing her attention back to the world zipping past the window. So much of what she had known felt much smaller now.

"I don't need to copy your homework anymore," said Elizabeth, "*Addison* is helping me now."

Elizabeth hugged Addison's arm tightly and looked up at his half-open eyes. He presented the smallest example of a smile and released a noise that could be mistaken for a giggle.

"You two aren't even in the same class," said Mary, "how's he going to help?"

"Addison is a genius," said Elizabeth, "he knows everything about...well, everything."

"I'm very happy for you," said Mary, "I'm sure you'll both have weird lookin' children that fart too much."

"What about you," said Elizabeth, "there's a rumor that you've been seeing ghosts in your yard. Now who's the weirdo, Scary Mary?"

"He's not a ghost," Mary had her own doubts as soon as she said this, "I made him a sandwich and I saw him eat it. Ghosts don't eat sandwiches."

"Well, I think you're crazy. You're going to go live in a loony bin, and you'll never get married or anything."

Mary had no interest in getting married, so the insult fell flat. The opportunity to shut Elizabeth up was too tempting for Mary to ignore, however. Nobody that she had previously trusted was able to help her, much less believe her. Mary decided at that moment that she would have to investigate these mysteries on her own. The best way for her to do that would be to remove anybody that could potentially cause her to be distracted.

"I'm going to send my ghost to come eat the skin off your bones," she said, "or maybe you'd like some lizards to lay their eggs behind your eyes."

Mary hissed and stuck out her tongue while she screwed up her eyes. Elizabeth and Addison both looked upset. This suited Mary just fine.

"You're so weird," said Elizabeth, "You're weird and you're crazy and nobody is gonna like you again ever!"

Elizabeth left in a huff back to the front of the bus while Addison trailed behind her like a busted dog. Mary brought her attention back to the window and continued to think about the shed. Elizabeth had hurt Mary's feelings, but she would think about that later at recess. There was too much going on for Mary to worry about Elizabeth and Addison's future life together. She thought about bringing them to the shed and making them pee their pants with fright. They would never bother her again after that.

When Mary arrived in science class, Mr. Zaposta was unhappy with her inability to produce the extra assignment he had requested. She had not finished her regular assignment either, which Mr. Zaposta took more personally than the absence of her additional work. Mary did not have an explanation for it because she was afraid of becoming even more of a laughingstock. She knew better than to tell him about the shed. People already thought she was talking to ghosts, so a monster in a shed did not need to be their business. Mary was given detention and she sulked back to her seat to continue the morning lesson. hell of a way to start the day.

    During recess Mary left the cafeteria and walked across the playground to one of her secret spots. The playground was a large, fenced area surrounded by a section of deep wood that expanded well past the property line of the school. The playground area had a variety of underwhelming amenities that were expected to stimulate children of all ages. The jungle gym generally lost its charm after the age of five. Mary knew where there was a hole in the fence that she would use to sneak out into the woods so that she could be left alone for a while. There was a stone path just past the hole which led to concrete steps buried beneath bushes and unkempt brush. The stone steps led to an open foundation with high segments of walls that connected to a disintegrated ceiling. Different sections had all partially eroded over time.

    Mary called it The Mummy's Tomb and would play around the structure, laying in the sun coming through the overhanging trees. Sometimes she would read or pretend that she was a hermit and that this was her house. She would curse at the squirrels and birds to leave her alone. She told them that she was not interested in buying any of their vacuum cleaners and would complain about the noise when they drove their little cars down her street at all hours of the night.

    There were fragments of dirty magazines with pictures of naked ladies and empty liquor bottles that she would line up along the stone walls to throw rocks at. Sometimes Mary would find the remains of campfires and the ends of cigarettes strewn across the ground. These were much more interesting than the old, rusted monkey bars. It was easy for her to lose track of time while she was there so she tried to remain within earshot of the recess monitor's whistle which would signal when to return to class.

    There had been times when she had missed the whistle and had been left behind, only to return to her classes well after they had resumed. This would lead to the small chitter of laughter and ridicule from her classmates and chastising from her teachers. If she were asked why she was late or where she had gone, Mary would just shrug and return to her seat. There was no way, not even under threat of torture, that she would divulge the location of The Mummy's Tomb.

    She was lying on one of the broken stone walls thinking about how grateful she was to have some time to think when the sound of footsteps through the leaves broke her harmony. It was the new boy in class that Elizabeth had told her about. Mary had seen him around the school, but she had yet to be impressed. He was smart looking, but in an unremarkable way. She thought he looked like everybody else. He walked over to Mary, waving hello as she sat up on her elbows. She did not return the gesture.

"Hi," he said, "I'm Jimmy."

"I know who you are," said Mary, "I've seen you around."

She quickly became very defensive of her secret playground. Jimmy was new and Mary had no way to tell whether she could trust him. In the interest of self-preservation, and for the sanctity of The Mummy's Tomb, Mary decided that she did not.

"I like your fort," he said.

"It's not a fort," said Mary, "it's The Mummy's Tomb."

"Is there a real mummy?!"

"There is and he only listens to me. Now get out of here before he kills you."

Jimmy remained but looked hurt by Mary's remark. She stood up and grabbed a large stick, holding it over her head in a threatening gesture. Jimmy took a step back.

"Get out of here!" shouted Mary.

"You really are crazy," said Jimmy, "I just wanted to say hi."

"So? Say it and go. I'm busy."

Jimmy looked like he wanted to cry. There was a moment of guilt that came over Mary in an instant, but she had to stand her ground. If Jimmy were to come back to The Mummy's Tomb, then he might claim it as his own, or worse. He could tell someone about it and then Mary would be forced to share her secret space. This was unacceptable.

"Who are you supposed to be," said Jimmy, "king shit, or somethin'?"

Jimmy turned around and ran back up the hill to the playground, restoring the secret peace of The Mummy's Tomb. Mary tried to mentally return to where she was before Jimmy had interrupted her, but her mood had shifted. She did not know why she was suddenly so mean, and Jimmy had not really done anything wrong. She did not like being mean. After trying to forget about it and finding no return to her meditation, Mary decided to apologize. She cursed under her breath as she walked back to the school, the words "king shit" kicked around in her mind.

Mary was walking across the playground when a clump of dirt hit her hard in the back of the head. It stunned her and she froze in place, standing in the moment of pain and panic that makes you stupid for a second. Mary wiped the dirt out of her hair and spun around just to have a second clump of dirt hit her in the mouth. She fell backwards onto the ground and heard the unmistakable cackle of Elizabeth from a few yards away.

Mary spit out what she could of the dirt, but there had been a small stone in the clump that had cut her lip. She was not bleeding terribly, but there was enough pain and embarrassment to send her into a blind rage. The collection of events from the week flooded Mary with feelings of shame, anger, and fear. She quietly stood up, brushed the dirt from her hair and clothes, spit more blood and mud out from her mouth, and calmly walked towards Elizabeth and Addison.

"It wasn't me," said Elizabeth," maybe it was your ghost."

Mary did not say a word, but instead pounced on Elizabeth and began to punch her face repeatedly. Mary had never hit another person before. She would later admit to not liking it so much, but in that moment, she felt angry and invincible.

It can be easy to run a scenario in your own mind where you have the strength of ten people. The fantasy starts and you imagine that you could easily fight off a whole fleet of trained assassins, but there really is only one way to find out. Luckily, Mary seemed to be a natural.

Elizabeth went down with the first punch, but Mary did not stop hitting her until a teacher separated the two and led Mary back inside to speak with the principal. They walked past Jimmy who was talking to a group of boys from the class and their eyes met in a moment of awkward understanding. Mary tried to spit blood on the ground dramatically but instead it just dribbled down the front of her shirt. The last thing Mary saw was Elizabeth sobbing on the ground while she looked for her own teeth. Addison, reluctantly, tried to help.

The hallway outside of the principal's office was that brown and yellow color scheme that worked perfectly in nineteen seventy-six but had somehow lost its flair over time. Mary had been given an ice pack and a piece of gauze for her bleeding lip, but her eye was beginning to bruise over into a respectable shiner. Elizabeth had managed to get one good shot in, but it was not enough to stop Mary in her rampage.

Mary had only been to the principal's office once before when she had been caught holding a lit cigarette in the girl's bathroom. She was not smoking it, but another girl had asked her to hold it while she used the toilet. Naturally, that excuse did not work, and Mary had been given a three-day suspension. The suspension consisted of Mary performing every household chore you could think of in her home. Mary cut the grass, washed the floors, vacuumed the stairs, cleaned the gutters, did the laundry, washed the car, cleaned the windows, painted the doors, installed new kitchen floor tiles, and spent one particularly difficult evening cutting her grandmother's toenails. Mary had made up her mind then and there that she would never set foot in the principal's office again.

But these things happen.

There was a younger boy sitting in a green plastic chair quietly reading a book across from Mary. He was wearing brown corduroy pants and a blue button-down shirt. He was not wearing any shoes. Mary had not noticed him at first, but she let out a groan and held her face in her hands when she realized who it was.

"God, what are you doing here?" asked Mary.

He did not acknowledge Mary but continued to read his book. He kicked his bare feet against the legs of his chair and turned the next page.

"I'm waiting for my shoes," he said.

"Are you a ghost?" asked Mary.

"No."

"Where are your shoes?"

"They got wet," he said.

"Oh," said Mary, "how'd they get wet?"

He did not look up from his book, but he nodded his head to the left where there was a poster of a cartoon cat on the wall. It was lying on a hammock, drinking lemonade and wearing sunglasses, underneath pink bubble letters that read CAMPING IS IN TENTS. Mary stared in disbelief and looked around the room to see if anyone else might have been experiencing this. Nobody seemed to pay either of them any mind, so it was difficult enough to gauge the reality of her own existence.

"You got me into trouble, you know," said Mary.

The boy looked up from his book with genuine regret in his eyes. They sat in a clouded milk hazel that seemed to know every answer to any possible question, regardless of what he chose to tell Mary.

"I'm sorry about that," he said, "thank you for the sandwich."

"Aw, it's fine," said Mary, "What are you reading?"

"It doesn't matter," said the boy.

"Is it any good?"

The boy shrugged and kept reading while Mary kicked her feet against the legs of her chair and stared at the ground. The boy did not say anything more as the assistant principal called Mary's name and escorted her into the office. She looked back at the boy, but he never raised his head.

The principal was a large, round man with small glasses that sunk into his face. There were red indentations around his eyes and temples when he took them off. He was mostly bald on top with the theoretical existence of hair and big bushy eyebrows that swept over the tops of his glasses. They would twitch when he was beginning to get angry. The principal silently motioned for Mary to have a seat in front of his desk as he shuffled some papers into a folder. He looked at Mary through his glasses and she thought she might have seen a slight twitch in his eyebrows.

"Hello, Mary," he said, "do you know why I've asked to see you?"

Mary shrugged and held the ice pack against her lip.

"Elizabeth had to go to the emergency room. Did you know that? We found some of her teeth, but a lot of them were broken. They'll put caps on what they can, but she'll probably need dental implants for what they can't fix. She's very scared right now."

Mary tried not to laugh at this, but a small smile betrayed her face.

"This isn't funny, Mary," said the principal, "Elizabeth is very badly hurt. Do you understand what you've done?"

Mary nodded and brought her ice pack down from her mouth. She licked her split lip and it stung, but she did not want to show them that she was in pain.

"Now I know that it can be difficult to express…big feelings. Believe me, I know. But we cannot have these violent episodes in our school."

Mary nodded again, but she had stopped listening. In her mind, she had already begun to plan her great escape away from this place.

"We think you could stand some time to think about the consequences of your actions. You will be suspended for a week, your assignments will be sent to your home, and you will have to write an essay on the dangers of violence in a civilized world. We have informed your parents about what happened today. They're coming to pick you up now."

Mary began to gently cry in her chair. Expressions of emotions outside of anger made the principal uncomfortable, so he asked the assistant principal to escort Mary to one of the "Quiet Rooms" for students experiencing emotional distress. Mary wiped her eyes as she was brought back out to the hallway. She looked at where the boy had been sitting, but he was not there anymore. All she could see was the smiling face of the cartoon cat telling her that camping was cool. The fact that it was wearing dark sunglasses had been meant to invoke trust from a familiar source of joy, but Mary did not appreciate the presentation. She felt like the cat had become disingenuous.

After spending half an hour in the Quiet Room, Mary was led to an uncomfortable bench bolted to the wall that was designated for students waiting to be picked up. This bench was only used by students who were sick or in serious trouble. Another girl was sitting next to Mary with a plastic bag in her hand. Her face was a pale green, and she would sometimes gag and spit into the bag that was already a quarter filled with the remnants of a half-digested breakfast. Mary tried to ignore the smell that hung around her companion. It was Mary's turn to feel sick when she saw her grandmother's large frame enter the school. She did not say anything to Mary but spoke briefly to the secretary before taking Mary by the shoulder and walking her out of the school.

The ride home was quiet and felt as though ages would pass before they came to the entrance of their driveway. Mary's grandmother drove an older Chevrolet that rattled when she turned the wheel and always smelled like cigarettes and gasoline. Mary's face was flushed red and puffy from having cried. Her black eye was showing green around the edges, her lip was sore and warm, and she wondered how many more tears were left inside her. All that she felt was the numb understanding that it would be a long while before something good would happen. Her grandmother did not speak for the whole ride. As soon as Mary got into the car, her grandmother turned on a quiet talk radio station that gave a detailed report of a student uprising in Myanmar. Mary did not understand any of the subject matter, but it was difficult for her to concentrate on anything. She thought that everything would be ok if they never arrived home and just drove on forever.

Her mind traveled further than she ever would, but she did not know that just yet. The images of lush jungle ruins and island pirate coves flooded her imagination as the alternative reality was closing all around her. She remembered seeing a painting in a magazine of well-dressed people lounging beneath a length of shady trees that ran beside a river. The painting was blurry, but it was a peaceful scene that she found appealing. Mary wished that she could be blurred sometimes.

Anywhere but here, she thought, *please let me be anywhere but here.*

The car pulled down the driveway and slowed to a stop halfway to the house. Mary's grandmother put the car in park and took the keys from the ignition, leaving Mary alone in the passenger seat. She watched her grandmother begin to walk into the woods, leaving her in the silence of the world. It did not take long for Mary to begin feeling anxious and overwhelmed. Quick as a flash, she unbuckled herself and leapt from the car, sprinting into the woods after her grandmother. She found her crouched beside a tree, pulling bits of bark off and smelling them. Some pieces she would put in her pocket, but some pieces she would smell and throw away. Mary watched her do this for a little while before she found the courage to speak.

"Grandma?"

"What is it, Mary?"

"What are you doing?"

"Might build a fire later. This is good starter wood, but some of it's wet."

"I'm sorry I got in trouble today."

Mary's grandmother stood up from her crouch and stretched her back dramatically. She twisted her waist from side-to-side and let out a satisfied groan.

"You didn't do nothin' wrong," she said, "that little girl is shaping up to be a real cunt anyway. You can always tell 'round this age. Kids start to wake up 'round this age."

"You're not mad at me?"

"Naw, Mary. C'mere."

She embraced Mary in her big arms and held her tightly against her rough canvas coat. One of her grandmother's brass buttons was pressing into Mary's face, but she could tolerate the pain so long as her grandmother loved her and recognized her as a person instead of a nuisance child. This was to be saved as a good memory for Mary in the years to come.

Her parents came home late that night and did not mention a word of Mary's suspension. The messages sent by Mary's school had never reached either of them so there was no need to explain something that they knew nothing about. The question of Mary's split lip and black eye was palmed by an all too familiar story of Mary simply falling out of a tree. Mary's grandmother also told them that the school would be closed for a week due to fumigation and that Mary would be receiving her assignments at home so as not to fall behind in her studies. Mary's parents found this to be an exemplary display of preparation on the school's part and decided to have a celebratory drink for Mary's surprise vacation.

Before anyone could tell what was happening, the house had erupted into an intimate party between Mary, her parents, and her grandmother. Food was prepared in quantities that would suggest a dozen guests, at least. The refrigerator was cleaned out and the variety of delights that were made surpassed the quality of those provided by the finest hotel restaurants. Mary and her family sat at the dinner table away from the television and she was regaled with wonderful stories from her parents' youth. Her grandmother filled in the gaps which unraveled some of the mysteries that surrounded her parents and the likelihood of their ever having been children themselves. In all Mary's years of being alive she could not remember a more spontaneous and satisfying event. Her parents were progressively becoming more intoxicated at an impressive rate of speed while her grandmother played rock and roll records on their stereo system, singing along to every word. Mary danced with her family in wild rhythms, and the party lasted long into the night.

3. You Haven't Found Me Yet

So, it was vacation, then. At least that was how Mary decided to approach her suspension. The only person who knew the truth outside of Elizabeth, Addison, and the principal was Mary's grandmother, and she had already expressed her thoughts on the matter. It had been less than twenty-four hours since Mary had walloped Elizabeth, but it was already becoming a memory. Mary woke up before her alarm, which she had forgotten to turn off, and lay in her bed surrounded by the morning. Lying in bed with no reason to leave became a new feeling of luxury that Mary decided to revisit frequently in the future. But she was hungry, which was itself unusual given her disinclination towards breakfast. Maybe this was the beginning of a new era.

Mary yawned and winced as she accidentally reopened the cut on her lip. She faintly tasted blood in a warm spot on her mouth and resolved herself to be more mindful about it. The house was quiet as she left her room and stood in the novelty of an incidental existence. There were the remains of last night's party around the house with some items left in unusual places.

A tablecloth had been draped over the television and two empty bottles of wine were wedged into the couch cushions. The stale smell of cooking and alcohol lingered in the air, which Mary found to be displeasing but not as repulsive as her classmate's barf bag. She wandered around the house with no specific destination in mind and casually ran her hand across the shelves, touching the bric-a-brac which rested undisturbed beneath a thin layer of dust. For a brief instant, maybe less than half a second, Mary felt invisible and smiled to herself. This was the first time in a long time that she was not held to a morning routine, so the thought of what to do came sporadically and without ambition. After a brief internal debate about how she would spend her time, she decided to go to her tower.

Sometimes when Mary was feeling shy and wanted to hide away for a little while, she would climb the stairs that led to the rounded tower that stood on the eastern corner of the house. Mary called it a tower, but it was more like a rumpus room. It was round with one large bay window facing the east. This allowed the morning sun to enter and chase away all the shadows.

The flood of good natural light that filled the room made it a prime location for her grandfather's painting studio when he lived with them. Along with being an avid fibber, Mary's grandfather was also a vivid painter. It was rumored that he had shown real talent in his youth but refused to follow an academic career in art after the cost of school became too daunting for him to afford. As a self-taught artist, her grandfather pressed beyond the boundaries of contemporary training, which he already considered to be too old-fashioned. His portraits were impressive, and he had a skill for capturing features that were less obvious than the model's presented expression. His search for the Mona Lisa smile would sometimes reveal an even darker tone than playful whimsy. Mary had been in the room at night and the strange collection of family memorabilia looked bigger in the darkness. Her grandfather's paintings of objects and distant relations stared out of their frames in a state of perpetual judgment.

Boxes that were half covered in tarps became hiding places for the darker shadows that seemed to whisper and breathe in their own unnatural way. These were the same shadows that Mary had seen on the silent edge of the woods, where the white shed stood with its own imposing silence. Knowing that the shadows were not held specifically to her tower raised an understanding that Mary may have underestimated their capabilities. She had known them for most of her life and was developing a familiarity with how they operated. She hated them.

The daylight brought unassailable security to the tower. Although a room is often just a room, some are more ordinary than others. A person can fill a room with the hopes and dreams of an ambitious future, a room for life and living in uncertain times. A room can be utilized as a place of prayer and reflection in the need for sanctuary. Rooms can hold secrets with locks, doors, bolts, and latches. Some rooms lay empty for years without purpose, not knowing when someone will make them their own. Some rooms can be deceptive. Most rooms remember.

Mary had resolved herself to only climb the tower in the daylight hours, if possible. There were no electrical outlets in the room, so there was a long series of power strips and extension cords snaking their way up the stairwell banister, connecting to an incandescent halogen floor light. This was helpful, but not nearly as effective as natural sunlight when it came to maximum visibility. The floor light cast more shadows than it eliminated.

Mary climbed the stairs leading up to her tower and could feel the humidity rise ten degrees warmer than it was downstairs. It was always hot in the room, but it was nice in wintertime. When she was little, Mary would fall asleep on an old couch in the center of the room while she waited for Santa. She did not wait for Santa anymore, but she would sometimes fall asleep on the couch. It was too early for a nap, so Mary walked around the room in a wide circle, running her hand over the tops of the items that surrounded the couch like sentinel guards. There were boxes of books and old national geographic magazines. Stacks of newspapers from fifty years ago were slumped against other boxes marked "FRAGILE" and "KITCHEN". There was a tin suit of armor mounted to an iron base that was too small even for Mary to wear. Dozens of upholstered chairs were stacked atop each other and covered in beige painter's tarps. There were a few old rugs rolled up and leaning precariously against the curved wall. She made about four laps around the room before she stopped in front of a large wooden clock.

This was her favorite object in the house. It had an ivory white face that was in the belly of an intricately carved wooden owl with large blinking eyes. The hands of the clock had little mice carved in the metal ends that pointed to each number. Mary liked to think that the mice were in love and chasing each other at night. Back and forth they would go throughout time in the game of chance and pursuit. As close as they would get, the owl would always intervene and never allow them to be together. Owls and time can be dangerous things, but neither could stop the mice from their destiny.

Mary would look at the clock for a long time and create a small fantasy world within its mechanisms. She had memorized the numbers in-between the numbers. Sometimes she would make ugly faces at the owl in defense of the two lovers lost in time. Even though Mary herself was not interested in finding love, she did admire those who searched with pure intentions. She gave the owl one last sneer before returning downstairs.

There was no breakfast left for Mary. This was upsetting in a strange way that Mary had not anticipated. She was hungry, to be sure, so finding nothing left for her to eat made her feel a little sad. With breakfast having been such an important and unmissable event, having nothing felt like she had been lied to for most of her life. She imagined the usual morning scene of shouting and haphazard dressing with butter and eggs and toast being consumed, but not enjoyed. As there would surely be a time in the future when Mary could think back fondly at the chaotic breakfast routine, there was no sentimentality or nostalgia for the present. If the importance of breakfast had suddenly become irrelevant, then what, if anything, could really matter in life?

Mary already had suspicions that school did not matter. Every time she was faced with a problem or a conflict in the classroom, it never seemed to work out in her favor. School had become an unnecessary waste of time that took her away from what she cared about. This revelation suited Mary just fine as her priority had become investigating the mysterious shed. The lack of support in the morning and the complete lack of supervision had emboldened Mary, leaving her feeling particularly brave, especially after having won her first fight. She lightly pressed her tongue against the cut that split her lip and the sting was a reminder that it had not closed. When she thought about the fight and played it back in her mind, there was not a whole lot of bad that came out of it. Sure, Mary had gotten dirt in her mouth, a black eye, and a cut on her lip, but Elizabeth lost some teeth and Mary got a vacation. Not a bad trade, to be sure. It had been some time ago when Mary learned that the fear of getting hit was often much worse than actually getting hit. This had left Mary feeling emboldened for any future conflict that would undoubtedly come and go in her life.

Taking an apple from the kitchen counter as a modest breakfast, Mary returned to her room and emptied her backpack onto her bed. Once all her schoolbooks and papers were out of the bag, Mary went to work collecting what she thought would be necessary for any possible danger waiting for her on the walk back to the shed. First, and most importantly, Mary found the compass that her grandfather had given her just before he left. She held it in her hand and gently opened the metal casing, exposing the balancing needle floating under glass. Mary stood in place and slowly turned in a complete circle to see how the needle would react. It wobbled a bit but stayed pointed in the same direction until she returned to where she started.

Mary missed her grandfather and often wondered where he was. She thought of his kind eyes and thick black beard that he would sometimes fold up over his face. He would say that he was a fiercely hungry bear and that he was especially fond of gobbling up little girls. Sometimes this was fun, but sometimes Mary would get scared and cry. If this happened, her grandfather would give her some of the melted caramel that he was regularly preparing for toffee. He would heap a large dollop on a wooden spoon and speak softly to Mary and apologize for scaring her. Mary remembered this vividly and could almost taste the caramel when the sun hit her face just right.

Her grandfather had unexpectedly disappeared one night, leaving Mary and her family to wonder where he had gone. All that was left was a small note scribbled with strange, cryptic words. It was mostly nonsense about the Yukon. It had been a known passion that he carried so the choice was not remarkable, but the sudden departure was difficult to understand. There was optimism towards his return home for a little while, but after a few years without communication, Mary's parents had come to terms with the fact that he must have died somewhere, either up north or along the way. Her grandfather had carried himself with the adventurous spirit of a man who knew he was not long for this world. He also had several health complications that would not have guaranteed him a life much longer than the one he had already lived.

Burying the compass within her inside jacket pocket, Mary collected the remaining supplies that she would need for her journey. She filled her bag with a small flashlight that she had recently bought from a book fair, batteries, two water bottles, a ten-foot length of rope that she found in the hallway linen closet, a turkey sandwich, another apple, a pocketknife that she had found outside of The Mummy's Tomb three weeks ago, a smaller canvas bag just in case, and a small wooden baseball bat that she had been given upon entry to a Red Sox game on free bat day. Mary laced up her boots and looked at her reflection in her closet mirror. She felt like a grown-up preparing for an expedition and hoped that she resembled her grandfather. She looked like a little girl playing dress up.

Mary was nervous about returning to the shed and what she might find there, but this did not discourage Mary from her mission. She double checked her backpack and her pockets, leaving her room with caution so as not to raise her grandmother's suspicions. Mary crept down the stairs to find that her grandmother was not home. Or at least, she was not in the immediate vicinity. She could still be sleeping, but it was hard to tell without the confirmation of snores. With the patience of a burglar, Mary hugged the wall and only stepped on carpeted areas of the floor. She tried to step where the boards did not squeak or groan under the lightest feather weight. There was a moment's breath when Mary's shoulder accidentally nudged a picture frame out of place. The lightest scrape against the wall would have been nearly imperceptible under different circumstances, but the sound still went through Mary's heart like her great betrayer. She stood very still until she was certain that God was not listening.

Opening the back door washed Mary in an early morning light that she was unfamiliar with under the day's theme of passive expectations. The journey to school would often cloud her perception of the natural world. Through the chaos of an undesired breakfast and the disappointment of routine, her mind could only focus on getting through the day without incident. Her freedom brought a new sense of adventure, as well as new anxieties. There was a different air cutting through the trees that surrounded the house. For the first time in her life, Mary considered the fact that the tree line dividing her backyard from the woods was more than a simple doorway to an exotic world. It was also a perimeter set to keep the wild out of her family's presumed security. There are only so many guarantees in the reality of natural existence and very few of them are pleasant. Most absolutes can be downright scary;

educational, but scary, nonetheless. Mary took a deep breath as she left her back porch and crossed her backyard to where her securities ended.

There was very little that Mary could remember from her first trip to the shed. She was convinced that she had never been to that part of the woods before, so returning would prove to be more difficult alone. Mary considered asking her grandmother how to get there, but she thought that may lead to an interrogation. She plotted a course for the hill that rose on the other side of the ravine and walked towards the horizon. Mary was having a grand time, despite the anxiety that bloomed with anticipation. There were fluctuations of joy and wonder, fear, and apprehension. She almost turned back as she crossed the ravine, standing before the hill that separated the land that she knew from the possible dangers that lay ahead. She removed the small baseball bat from her bag and held it like a sword against the unknown. There were no frogs to be seen that day, or at least none that she could notice. The world seemed to be holding its breath along with each of her steps. Every one of her senses was on alert and working overtime.

At the top of the hill a seemingly endless collection of trees were interwoven together with such density that there was no way of telling how deep the forest could go. She strolled casually, trying to be brave as she smacked her bat lightly against the side of every tree she passed. The action had the brief gratification of feeling like royalty. Mary was a brave adventurer of the wild and the forest would have to part to let her through. This lost its charm after a few minutes when her courage began to falter. The trees left Mary outnumbered and her bat could only do so much.

The woods were so big that Mary felt like she was shrinking each minute. For all that she knew, this could have been the end of the world. She paused for a moment and tried to find a familiar marker; some kind of sign to remind her of the path that they had taken before. She was so focused and alert in her investigation that a flock of birds flying out from the top of a tree nearly made her jump out of her skin.

Mary held the compass tightly as she looked at the needle pointing south-west. She turned a little way to her right until the needle read west and she crossed the threshold of the unknown. West felt right, as far as directions go. Mary remembered the setting sun on her face as her grandmother took her to the colorless stretch of birch trees. To where the shed stood. She thought that if she could plot a course in the general direction then she would be able to sneak around the site from a distance and plan a clear course of action.

Mary wished she had thought of bringing binoculars. She knew that her father had a pair, but they were off limits to Mary. They were a serious adult tool and not to be played with by children. Mary did have an old collapsible spyglass back in her room, but there was a crack in the lens, and the metal scope had bent past the ability to collapse. Clearly this was meant for a child because it was useless, but Mary was now an explorer, like her grandfather. She made a note to use this argument the next time she asked to borrow her father's binoculars.

The noises of wildlife in the woods were still present, so Mary knew that she had some ways to go before she could reach the quiet edge of the cliff. A shiver ran through her body as she remembered the silence that awaited her at the edge of the world. There was a metallic taste in the back of her throat that always seemed to present itself in moments of intense fear, so she decided to take a break and eat a little something to cover the flavor. The fresh air had made her appetite more pronounced than it had been when she had first left her house.

Mary found a dry boulder that jutted up between a moss-covered tree stump and the remains of an old stone retaining wall. She rested on the stone and took a moment to observe her new surroundings. This area was unknown to her. Taking the apple out of her bag, Mary looked over the terrain and marveled at the difference between her beloved ravine and the wild woods.

Mushroom caps the size of tea saucers spread across the ground and made trails that led towards unknown destinations. Having time to listen allowed Mary to notice the sound of what must have been a river close to where she was sitting. The pace of steady water running off towards the inevitable sea laid the backdrop of possibilities and journeys yet to be taken. She smelt the old world in the absence of an invasive human presence. Mary did not count herself because there were times that she barely felt present at all, much less human. She ran her hand across the stone on which she sat and read the surface gradations with her fingertips. Her apple even tasted sweeter.

A rustling from a nearby bush caused Mary to jump and broke her from her contemplations. She dropped her apple, grabbed her bag, and pulled out her pocketknife. Panic caused the knife to fall from her hand and it landed without a sound in a patch of autumn leaves. She could not find it fast enough as the padded sound of running came towards where she was searching. Mary closed her eyes and froze, waiting for her death to spring upon her with sharp teeth and the hunger of a thousand years.

Nothing happened.

The passing moments grew insufferable as Mary slowly opened her eyes. She raised her head to see the little corduroy boy standing just a few feet in front of her. He held her apple in his hands, and he was cleaning the dirt from it. Mary wanted to laugh and cry but her frustration caused her to shout instead.

"What is wrong with you?!"

"Nothing," said the boy, "are you ok?"

"No, not really! You scared the hell out of me. Why are you following me?"

"I'm not following you. You're following me."

Mary dusted herself off and continued to look for her pocketknife. It had landed between the boulder and the retaining wall but had been obscured by the leaves knocked about by Mary's fumbling hands. She put the knife in her front pocket and turned to collect her bag. Slinging the bag over one shoulder, she looked at the boy with an attitude of frustration and exhaustion.

"What are you doing out here?" she asked.

"I'm looking for my shoes."

"Oh, piss on your shoes," said Mary, "I have more important things to worry about."

"Are you going to the shed?"

Mary stopped and stared at the boy. He stood casually without expression and looked back at her with his strange eyes. She tried to get a read on his intentions, but there was something blocking her. It was uncomfortable and the harder she tried to search for his reason, the further it slipped away. Still, if he knew about the shed then he must have known how to get there.

"Is this the right direction?" she asked.

"Sort of. Not really. It will be."

"What do you mean?"

He scratched his head and looked up at the sky. This was when Mary noticed how dirty his hands were; as though he had been digging in the dirt for days on end. His clothes were clean, and his face was tidy, but his hands and neck were smudged with dirt.

"You'll find it," said the boy, "it might not be what you think, but you'll find it. And maybe not right away. C'mon. I'll show you."

The boy took point and walked past Mary into the forest. They walked deeper into the woods without speaking for what seemed like hours. After a while, with a few brief stops to rest and to enjoy a rare black squirrel sighting, the sounds of the forest became less pronounced and then dwindled down to nothing. They had reached the edge of where the silence would begin, and the ground became large sheets of gray stone. Crossing from where the dirt floor became sheets of rock brought an abrupt end to the sounds of the natural world. There was no shed in sight.

Mary found the rock where she had been sitting the day before, but there was nothing where the shed had been standing. Just the rock floor that sloped to an abrupt cliff overlooking a quarry. The midday sky that was once a vibrant blue had become gray with cloud cover and it brought a shaded mist which lingered above the land. A silent breeze lightly blew across their hair and they both stood quietly, watching the world stand still.

"I don't understand," said Mary.

"I told you," said the boy, "you were going in the right direction, but you were going the wrong way."

"Where did the shed go?"

"It went to where it is. Then it will go where it will be."

"I don't understand," said Mary, "it was here the other day. I saw it."

"And now it's not here anymore," said the boy, "but it's somewhere. Probably."

Mary sat on the boulder she had found and took the turkey sandwich out from her bag. She needed to have a good think and the quarter of an apple she had earlier was hardly satisfying after their hike. The boy's eyes grew large and bright when he saw the sandwich and he made a small noise from the back of his throat. Mary looked at the boy and separated the sandwich in half, holding a share in front of him as an offering. He reached for the sandwich, but Mary pulled back her hand.

"Tell me who you are." she said.

"You haven't found me yet."

"What do you mean?"

"Give me some food and I'll tell you."

"Tell me who you are, and I'll give you some food."

The stalemate grew amidst the silent atmosphere. Neither would yield favor to the other and in a moment of spiteful malice, Mary chucked half of the sandwich over the edge of the cliff without compromise. When she turned back to the boy, he was gone. Mary was becoming less surprised by his frequent arrivals and sudden departures, so she sat in silence and finished her half of the sandwich.

It was late afternoon by the time that she made it back to the house and her parents had already returned from work. Mary was tired from her failed expedition and wanted nothing more than to sit on the couch and watch television. When she entered her house, she dropped her bag on the floor and took off her boots, leaving them in the alcove. Soft voices were speaking in the kitchen, and it sounded like someone was crying. Her father was sitting at the table with his face in his hands and her mother stood with her back to him at the kitchen sink, smoking a cigarette out of the open window. Mary had never seen her father cry or her mother smoke cigarettes before. The whole scene scared her a little. She made a small noise that was meant to sound like "Dad?" but it barely left her throat. Both of her parents turned to her and embraced her in their arms. Her father sobbed into Mary's shoulder and her mother pressed Mary's face against her stomach.

"Oh, Mary," said her mother, "where have you been? We have the police out looking for you!"

"I was playing," said Mary, "I just went to the ravine."

"Well, you shouldn't have gone out by yourself," said her mother.

Mary's mother choked on her words as she started to cry. Her body shook as she pressed Mary's face against her warm stomach and squeezed the back of her head with her thin fingers. There was nothing that Mary could do as she stood there caught between her parents. Her anxiety only grew as her father wiped his nose and walked towards the liquor cabinet, reaching for a bottle of bourbon. There was no time for ice or a glass with the mood he was in. Once Mary's head was released, she looked at her parents with confusion.

"Honey, I'm sorry," her mother said, "your grandmother passed."

"What?" said Mary.

"She's dead, honey," said her mother, "she died in her sleep this morning."

"What?" said Mary.

She felt her face tighten and wanted to cry, but she held her breath, distracting herself with another discomfort. She felt embarrassed to cry in front of her parents. It can be difficult for a person to immediately understand the death of a loved one, especially at eleven years old. Your brain registers the words, and they sit with you for a little while. You repeat them silently to yourself and stand with the frozen expression while you try to decide what to do next. You have to do something, anything to distract yourself from what has happened. Memories cross your mind in blurred expressions of love, joy, sorrow, and goodwill. Holidays and presents, food and old jokes circle all around you with the freshness and intensity of now. Facing death head on is almost too overwhelming for some people to believe. The reality of the situation is that there is nothing more you can do apart from hold the ones you have a little closer than before.

4. Nothing Unreal Exists

Francis Jane Kirkland, nee Linquett, b. 1938, died in her home on Thursday, October 12th, 2013, at the age of 79 years. Francis was a loving wife, mother, and grandmother. She is survived by her son Marcus Kirkland, his wife Loretta Kirkland, nee Coggeshall, and their daughter Mary Kirkland. Francis Kirkland had been married to Bartholomew Albert Kirkland for thirty-two love filled years. Bartholomew Kirkland passed on in 2015. Services will be held for friends and family on Tuesday, October 24th at the Finster Family Funeral Parlor on Maple St. At the request of the bereaved, in lieu of flowers please send a generous donation to the Charles Barkley Foundation Fellowship.

The few people who attended the wake of Francis Kirkland were friends of Mary's parents, a few distant relatives, some of Mary's classmates, and their families. It was a modest event, but Francis Kirkland had never been one to entertain guests with outstanding generosity. Because of her personality and general identity, she had garnered the reputation of an irritable and intimidating person. She was a grand and terrible example of intense behavior and attitude. Francis Kirkland was never known to be subtle. Even when she was quiet, a powerful sense of character would emanate from within her, and it was not always pleasant. She was a woman who demanded satisfaction in all things, settling for nothing less than what she needed.

Some knew her as an outwardly hostile and eccentric person whose sense of humor bordered on sadism. Others had made a conscious effort to never know Francis Kirkland at all. Rumors filled the town with what she had done in her life, and conflicting accounts of the same stories phased into each other in conversations at parties. These stories were always delivered in hushed tones. Her accomplishments became condemnations depending on who you were speaking to. Some people came to the funeral to pay their respects while a few who knew her well enough came to be sure that she was dead. Some still refused to believe it was true, but this was not coming from a place of mourning.

It was too warm in the funeral parlor and Mary was uncomfortable. The thick and hanging aroma of flowers mixed with a noticeable collection of colognes and perfumes. The smell of dust burning from old heat radiators kept the air dry and made everyone clear their throats for want of a drink. Mary's dress clothes were stiff, they were making her itch, and she wanted to be left alone. Unfortunately, everybody wanted to talk to Mary. She had not cried yet, but she was still feeling embarrassed to show that much emotion in front of her parents. A room filled with strangers was even worse.

Too much had happened over the past few weeks, and this had left Mary feeling especially hollow. Losing her grandmother was a feeling like seeing someone walking away from a conversation while you were in the middle of a sentence. No one had prepared her for such a sudden absence. Mary stood still at the foot of her grandmother's coffin as she received their guests with resentment, forcing a new kind of composure that she would have otherwise chosen to ignore. This was performed more as a defense mechanism than politeness.

Mary would look at her grandmother's body periodically waiting for her to breathe, move, say something. Anything. But nothing. Her grandmother's face was slightly sallow and pitted, with a frog-like expression. This did bring Mary some odd solace, but she took little joy in it. She wanted to go to her ravine. It was a thought which helped her remain calm in her discomforts. The knowledge that her patience would be rewarded with eventual privacy brought a new sense of discipline to which Mary was otherwise unaccustomed. Even so, the clock on the wall above a fake fireplace was broken.

As though her anxieties had not suffered enough, there was a tense moment when Elizabeth and Addison walked through the line to pay their respects to Mary's family. Thankfully, nothing substantial developed from the brief encounter. Their pace was consistent with the other mourners in line. Each person moved in that slow waddle that came from a self-conscious attempt to walk in time with the person in front of you. A sort of shuffle-stop-shuffle-stop. Elizabeth and Addison each shook the hands of the Kirkland's instead of providing an embrace. They were cordial and polite, but there was a silent conversation between Mary and Elizabeth. They gave each other a look that said, "This isn't over". Addison, of course, did not say anything as his sad eyes were glued to the dead body of Mary's grandmother.

Mary was happy to leave the funeral parlor as her family all crawled into the back of a rented black limousine. Mary had never been in a limousine before. Her parents had rented it to take them to the cemetery and it had become the most luxurious thing that Mary had ever experienced. The driver wore a funny hat, which Mary admired, and the smell of leather made her feel very sleepy. The cemetery was not a far drive from the funeral home, but they were moving slowly down the road in a procession to pay communal respect to the dead. Mr. Kirkland reached into the small bar that was built into the side and pulled out two little bottles of whiskey and a can of cola. He drank one of the whiskeys by itself while he handed the cola to Mary.

"Here, Mary," he said, "drink some of this for me. Not too much, though."

Mary was happy to comply with her father's request as she took the cold can from his slender hand. She had been so thirsty in the funeral parlor, so the cold soda coated the inside of her mouth with the flavor of a good dream. She also liked how it felt as the bubbles leapt up and tickled the roof of her mouth.

"Thanks, Mary," said Mr. Kirkland, "we'll get you some more when we get back home."

Mr. Kirkland opened the other small bottle of whiskey and poured it into the half-filled can of cold soda. Mrs. Kirkland cleared her throat in disapproval as she turned her head and watched the people on the sidewalk move faster than their limousine. The car continued down the street while the world went about its business.

They arrived at the cemetery where the family had arranged a small service. There was no body to bury as it had been stipulated in Francis Kirkland's will that she be cremated. A headstone was placed in the family plot as a marker for future mourners to pay their respects. The group gathered around a small clearing beside a row of more weathered headstones while the brisk October winds whipped around their black coats. A local priest had been asked to say a few words and he was more than happy to oblige, on the stipulation that the Kirkland's make a small donation towards his congregation. He stood before the small group of mourners and raised his hands in a request for silence.

"Francine Kirkland, a loving mother to her son Marcus, a gracious mother-in-law to his wife Loretta, and grandmother to their daughter Mary, has left this earth, as God intends for us all to do. For we all must return to that which we had first left at the time of our birth. From that instantaneous shock and awe of perfect life to the inevitable peace of a well-deserved rest. We know that God has embraced sister Francine into the warm and loving arms of heaven, where she will surely find comfort in his kingdom."

The priest then returned to his seat and said nothing more of her passing. There had been an expectation that something a little more substantial might be said in favor of Francis Kirkland, but nobody else was sure what to say. A woman that Mary did not know stood up and began to sing, but no one else felt enough enthusiasm to contribute. The woman continued in anticipation that someone would join her, but after a few awkward moments, her voice faded into mumbles, and she sat down without finishing the song. A tall man standing behind the mourners shaded beneath a tree still full of orange leaves laughed out once from behind his dark sunglasses. Everyone looked back at him with equal parts shock and annoyance. He raised his hand in apology and rubbed the back of his head. His shock of salt and pepper hair ruffled underneath his fingertips. Mary's father said a word that she did not understand, but she knew that the word was exclusively bad.

When the services ended and everybody left the cemetery, the Kirkland family returned home with enough time to finish preparing the house for visiting mourners. They were not expecting more than the usual small funeral crowd. There would be the friends and family that only came around when someone had died, a few people from work who would come for socially political purposes, and the collection of town residents who had nothing better to do. A free lunch is a free lunch.

The family would tell old stories and talk about how it was always such a shame that this was the only time when they all got together. There would be agreements to make plans under happier circumstances, but they all knew that it would never happen. It had to be said, but they would have to wait for the next funeral. There will be extended relatives who you never really remember all that well, but then familiarity allows you to recall why it is that they remain extended and not permanent fixtures in your life.

Good to see you! How've you been? She's getting so big! Who is this handsome young man and what happened to little Mikey!

Then there are the people who cannot tell the difference between a wake and a party. They are respectful and poised for a little while until they are not. When this time comes, they do not make very much room for anyone else to speak.

Mary's father was already drunk by the time they had returned home. He had been suffering from emotional nervousness and turmoil for the past three days as the funeral grew closer. He found no respite in his family's attempts to comfort him. Instead, he found sedation in the form of bourbon. The limousine ride back from the cemetery found Mr. Kirkland repeating his whiskey ritual from earlier in the day. Instead of giving Mary a can of soda to drink, Mr. Kirkland circumvented the ritual by emptying both bottles of whiskey into his mouth, one after the other. Once the whiskey was gone, Mr. Kirkland shook his head in a reflex to the alcohol and reached for a fresh can of cola. He popped the top and tilted back his head, allowing the soda to fall into his mouth like a faucet. Mrs. Kirkland had said something under her breath, but it went unnoticed.

The drive home was a little quicker than the funeral procession, and it was all for the better. Once they arrived at the house Mary went up to her room without speaking to anyone. She did not want to go back downstairs, but she knew that it was an expected obligation for her familial duties. She told herself that it was necessary, if only for a little while, and a means to an end of getting back to her ravine.

She changed out of her uncomfortable funeral clothes and into a more casual outfit. Mary chose familiar jeans and a T-shirt with a picture of a dinosaur on the front. She put on her sneakers with the mismatched laces and laid on her bed with her eyes open, looking out the window and holding her grandfather's compass. The next half an hour was spent opening and closing the metal casing of the compass, watching the little needle dance as she turned it this way and that in her hands. She thought of her grandmother in every capacity.

Recalling the moments of ecstatic joy and traumatic discipline led Mary to the revelation that people were complicated. Her grandmother did very bad things, but she also did good things, too. Mary began to recall all the good things and bad things that she had managed to accomplish in her eleven years of being alive. How many good things or bad things will she do in the coming years? Hurting Elizabeth felt good in the moment, but now it felt a little less good after some time had passed. Will she ever hurt anyone so badly that she could not take it back? Mary was experiencing her first existential crisis. This would be cataloged as a pensive memory and one that she would often return to in moments that followed critical action.

There was a light knock on the door before Mary's mother poked her head in and asked a favor in the form of a question. These questions usually had one correct answer.

"Sweetie, do you want to come downstairs?"

"I will," said Mary, "I'll come down in a little bit."

"You changed out of your clothes," her mother said, slightly slurred as she herself had also begun drinking, "you look so pretty in your nice clothes."

"It was itchy."

"Well get dressed, we have company."

"Why do I have to?"

"Mary, don't do this to me now," said her mother, "we have people downstairs."

"I don't think they care what I'm wearing."

"Well, I care what you wear."

Mary huffed and started changing back into her funeral clothes. Her mother stood in the doorway until she finished changing and then smiled at Mary.

"See," said her mother, "doesn't that look better?"

"It's itchy," said Mary, "how long are they going to be here?"

"Don't be rude, Mary. They're our guests and we're all upset."

"I don't want to go downstairs. I want to go outside."

"Mary, if you're not downstairs in five minutes then you're going to be in serious trouble."

"I don't care."

"Five minutes," said her mother, "and then I'll take you downstairs myself. And I don't want to hear any made-up stories. Please, just try to be normal today."

Her mother shut the door and held onto the banister as she shuffled back down the stairs. She only began to stumble once before catching herself and making sure that no one had seen her trip. Mary stood in the middle of the room with clenched fists and her teeth grinding against each other. Her knuckles were white, and her hands were red as she stared out the window and thought again about running away. There must have been a train somewhere that could take Mary to a place without school or her parents. A place without Elizabeths and Addisons and strange little boys without shoes. A place without people. A place without death.

"Let's get this over with," Mary said to herself.

The party downstairs was in full swing. There were a fair amount of people milling about and nibbling on the type of food that is served at a funeral reception. Some people brought their own casseroles and sandwich platters, finger foods, cheeses, crackers, cured meats in different shapes, and a neglected bowl of fruit salad that had already begun to gather a few flies. There was a table set aside for beer, wine, whiskey, vodka, gin, rum, and one dusty bottle of Campari from three Christmases ago. Diet caffeine-free soda was kept in the fridge for the kids.

Several children of different ages and relations were running throughout the house. Mary recognized a cousin from Indiana that she did not necessarily want to see. He had always been a bully and Mary did not wish to speak with him. In fact, Mary did not want to speak with anybody.

"You're Mary, right?"

Mary turned to see the tall man who laughed at the funeral. He was still wearing his sunglasses and smiled in a strange way. There was no reason for him to look outright familiar, but there was something nagging at the back of Mary's mind that they had met somewhere before. It was just a passing moment, but it struck her with compelling notice. Mary nodded back to the thin man that towered over her.

"My name is Patrick," he said, "I was a friend of your grandmothers."

"It's nice to meet you," said Mary. Although she did not feel nice meeting him.

"Your grandmother ever mention me?"

Mary shook her head. Patrick ran his hand through his hair and looked down at Mary as though he were trying to answer his own question. Mary was growing increasingly uncomfortable as he knelt to her level and put his hand on her shoulder.

"I'm sorry about your grandma," he said, "she was a lot of fun, wasn't she?"

"I guess so," said Mary.

"We used to have a lot of fun," said Patrick, "she loved to play games. What's your favorite game, Mary?"

Mary shrugged and looked at her shoes. She wanted to leave the conversation. The easiest way for her to depart was to turn around and walk away, which she did in an awkward and clumsy way. Patrick cleared his throat, stood up, and walked towards the food table to see what was available. Mary watched him move down the line until he started talking to another man in a corduroy suit. They both started laughing and Mary began to feel sick.

Mary walked into the kitchen to get a glass of water when she found her father sitting at the table. He looked disheveled with a fresh mustard stain on the front of his white dress shirt. A glass of neat whiskey was resting in his hand. He smiled at Mary gently and gestured for her to come sit with him. Mary took her glass of water and sat next to her father, leaning her head on his shoulder and closing her eyes. Neither one of them spoke for a few minutes, until her father cleared his throat. It was meant to be a subtle cough to help him speak more clearly, but what started as a light dilation of his esophagus had evolved into a full-on coughing fit. He covered his mouth and his face turned white as he brought up so much residual phlegm that he ran out the back door to vomit in the garden. Mary was feeling too angry to be frightened, but instead drank her water in the solitude of an empty kitchen. She sat and wondered if anyone would notice if she were there. With any luck, nobody would.

Aunt Colleen was the sister of Mary's mother, and she was a large woman without the social handicap of good manners. There were very few quiet features about her and there was no question in anyone's mind as to whether she was in the room at any given time. You knew when she was in the room, just as Mary knew when Aunt Colleen had entered the kitchen. The door swung open and audibly smacked the side of the refrigerator as Aunt Colleen announced her presence.

"Oh. My. GAWWWWWD! THERE SHE IIIIIIISS!" cried Aunt Colleen as she threw her big arms around Mary and pulled her head violently into her chest.

Mary was almost stabbed in the cheek by a large rhinestone dragonfly brooch on Aunt Colleen's jacket, but her face had been so deeply absorbed into Aunt Colleen's breasts that they acted as impenetrable shields. Mary was suffocating. She flailed her arms violently trying to push Aunt Colleen away.

"Look at you!" continued Aunt Colleen, while she ruffled Mary's hair, "Oh! I can't! You have gotten so big! I remember when your mother was pregnant with you. We were all convinced that you were going to be a boy because your mother carried you so low, right? I told your mother that you were going to be a boy, one hundred percent. To think we almost put money on it! Oh! And now here you are, a beautiful young woman! I'm sure your mother had a hell of a time getting her tummy back to normal after all that, but that's the price of motherhood."

Aunt Colleen released Mary from her grip and began fanning herself with her hand. Mary collapsed onto her chair with a red face, grateful to be breathing fresh air again. Aunt Colleen's perfume had fused to Mary's skin, and she did not like how it smelled. She sat next to Mary and continued to fan herself with a napkin that she pulled from her purse. Aunt Colleen took off her wide-brimmed black fascinator to reveal a mass of thick, red, curly hair. It slowly began to spring up higher as she removed her hat.

"Now tell me," said Aunt Colleen, "How. Are. You." She emphasized each word with a light pat on the table.

"I'm ok," said Mary.

"Poor Mary-Moo," said Aunt Colleen, making a face, "You miss your grandma?"

Mary shrugged and said, "I guess so."

"Well don't you worry," said Aunt Colleen, "your grandmother is up in Heaven right now. She's with grandpa again and they're both looking down at you with all the love in their hearts."

Mary recalled a time when her grandmother nearly shot her grandfather with a pistol over a game of horseshoes. They both called each other bad names that made Mary's mother clamp her hands over her ears. Her grandmother pulled a small handgun out of her bag and pointed it towards her grandfather with the kind of confidence that let everybody know that she was a skilled shot. Her grandfather made a rude gesture, and her grandmother knocked him in the mouth with the butt of her gun. Maybe there had been less blood than Mary remembered, but at the time it was substantial. Somehow Heaven seemed a stretch.

"Poor thing," Aunt Colleen continued, "your father must be a wreck. He's always been so sensitive. I'll never know why your mother went for him. Don't get me wrong, I like him fine, but that is not my type of man."

Mary started moving her glass around the water ring that had formed on the table. She tried to spread the water evenly into a circle, but it would always bleed over to one side.

"Now George Fagan, he was a man. We used to go together in high school, and he was," Aunt Colleen paused and began to fan herself a little faster than before, "he was good."

The murmur of company from the next room filled the kitchen as Aunt Colleen's memories of George Fagan began to occupy her attention. Mary walked to the kitchen window and placed the glass gently in the sink next to a few small plates and a plastic fork. Half of a ham sandwich was dismantled on a plate beside a handful of potato chips. Mary had already had a sandwich but there was an impulsive thought to reach into the sink and eat the remains. Instead, she looked out the window and saw her father lying face down on the lawn. A few of the children took turns running and jumping over his body while he would occasionally try to swat them away with his limp arm. The kids were always faster than his swings and this added comedy to their game.

"Horrible thing, dementia," said Aunt Colleen, "watching someone you love just drift away."

Mary looked at Aunt Colleen with a blank expression.

"What's that?" asked Mary.

"Dementia, dear. Hasn't anybody talked with you about this?"

Mary shook her head and sat back down. Aunt Colleen continued:

"Your grandmother was sick, Mary. She was very sick. She had a disease called dementia. Do you know what that is?"

Mary shook her head.

"Dementia is...well, it's when your brain doesn't work that well when you get older. Your grandmother would get confused. She'd see things that weren't there or hear things. Your mother told me that she found your grandmother in the bathtub once wearing all her clothes and holding some giant doll. She didn't have the water on, thank God, but when your mother asked her what she was doing, your grandmother just said she was playing. What a sin."

"Did she see a doctor?"

"Oh, yes. She saw a lot of doctors."

"They couldn't make her better?"

"It's not really something you can cure, Mary. Your parent's tried to keep your grandmother comfortable, but after that there's not a whole lot you can do."

Mary thought hard about this. Was the boy, the shed, everything a hallucination? If that were the case, did she dream up her school, too? Was she in fact having this conversation right now? She quietly pinched her arm with enough force to break the skin and made a face as she started to bleed.

"Oh my God," cried Aunt Colleen, "honey, you're bleeding! Come here."

Grabbing Mary by the wrist, Aunt Colleen led her to the kitchen sink where she ran Mary's arm under cold water. Aunt Colleen's grip hurt

Mary more than the cut did, but Mary's protestations were misinterpreted simply as a child being difficult.

"Now, now, it's not as bad as all that," said Aunt Colleen with a sigh, "you certainly are your father's daughter. I think I have a band aid in my purse."

Mary's mother came into the kitchen holding an empty water pitcher and a small pair of shoes. She put the shoes on the kitchen countertop and began to complain to herself as she filled the pitcher with ice. Aunt Colleen forgot about the bandage and embraced her sister while Mary's mother continued to pull ice from a bag in the freezer.

"Loretta, I am so sorry you have to deal with all this," said Aunt Colleen, "do you need anything? Anything at all?"

"Mary, go get your father," said her mother, ignoring Aunt Colleen.

"I know that this must be a difficult time," said Aunt Colleen, "and dealing with Marcus can't be any easier now."

"Mary!" said her mother, "Now!"

Mary stood up from her chair and left out the back door in a huff, letting it slam behind her. She walked to where she had seen her father lying on the ground but stepped over him without stopping. There was no attempt made on Mary's part to get his attention and she could still hear Aunt Colleen continue to offer half-hearted support for her mother through the open kitchen window. Mary's walk became a jog which then turned into a full sprint as she tried to outrun the tears that began to stream down her cheeks.

Running past the flowering dogwood tree, Mary reached out and tore off a small branch, throwing it to the ground. She made a straight shot for the woods without looking back. They embraced Mary, welcoming her into their damp and dark world without threats, promises, or expectations. Their only request was that she would just be herself. However, at that point for Mary it may have been a sizable request. Existence had not been very kind.

The sounds of the party then drifted behind her as Mary walked deeper into the forest. It had become a warm enough afternoon to where there was no need for a jacket, but Mary was still in her funeral clothes which were persistently itchy and uncomfortable. She took off her shoes and left them on a tree stump, reminding herself to pick them up on her way back. The thought of returning was then shot out of her mind like a lightning strike.

Why should I go back, she thought to herself, *I could go anywhere I want to.* But she would need supplies. She could not leave without her compass. *I'll wait until the party is over*, she thought, *as soon as mom and dad go to sleep, then I'll run.*

The ravine was quiet as Mary stepped on the slope that led down to the water. She slid backwards with her chin tucked against her chest, almost in pure spite, as the mud caked against the back of her dress. Sitting beside the easy running water brought the peace to carry off unwanted circumstances and bad dreams. All the frogs, toads, and salamanders were present, but quietly recognized that today was a day of mourning. After all that Mary had done to pay her respects for their fallen, so now must they return the favor. Because of this, Mary would love them forever.

Her tears began in earnest now, for the shame and embarrassment of showing emotion had caused Mary to forget how to experience true sorrow. Without anyone to bring her unwanted attention, Mary openly wept for her grandmother on a riverbank of quiet frogs.

The walk back home was exhausting not because of the distance or the terrain, that was easy enough, but because Mary knew what was waiting for her upon her return. Coming back to the edge of the forest and just before her yard began, Mary walked to where she had left her dress shoes. They were gone. She looked around the ground and thought that a squirrel or a racoon could have possibly knocked them off the stump, but they were nowhere to be found. If she thought she was in trouble before, now she would really be in for it.

"Thank you," came a voice from behind her.

Mary turned around to find the little boy standing only five feet away from her wearing the shoes she had been looking for.

"Thank you for the shoes," he said.

"Those are girl's shoes."

"Well, I like them anyway," said the boy, "are you ok?"

"No," said Mary, "not really."

The boy looked down at his shoes and rocked back and forth on his heels. They really did look good on him. They even looked clean; all things considered.

"I know you're not real," said Mary, "why don't you just go away."

"How do you know I'm not real?"

"Because I have dementia. I see things that aren't real and that means you."

"You don't have dementia, Mary," said the boy as he sat on the stump, "I think you may just be confused. You're definitely tired."

"What are you talking about?"

"Maybe nothing," said the boy, "but I'm not *un*real. Nothing unreal exists."

"What are you?"

"I told you," said the boy, "you haven't found me yet."

He rose from the stump and took a moment to admire his new shoes.

"I was mad at you for throwing away the sandwich," said the boy, "I was very hungry, but I'm not hungry anymore and I'm not mad at you. And thank you for the shoes. I'm sorry about your grandmother. I liked her very much. I trusted her."

"What happened to my grandmother?"

He looked at Mary with his milk hazel eyes and started to say something before he stopped and corrected himself.

"The same thing that happens to everybody," he said, "she died."

The boy looked at Mary sympathetically, like he was about to say something painful. He cleared his throat twice before he spoke.

"I have to go away for a while," he said, "I'm not sure when I'll be back. Might be soon, might be never."

"Where are you going?" asked Mary.

"Not sure yet."

"Fine," said Mary, "get out of here, then."

"I'm sorry," said the boy, "If you want to look for me, then I would think about it carefully. I hope that you do, but it might be…difficult."

"Why would I want to look for you?"

The boy chose his words very carefully.

"Sometimes it's not up to us."

"I don't want to look for you," said Mary, "I don't want to do anything ever again. I'm going to run away and become a fighter pilot. Or a painter. I can do whatever I want and nobody's gonna stop me."

"It doesn't work that way all the time," said the boy, "sometimes you find things without thinking about it. Other times you can spend your whole life looking for something and never find it. Things are funny like that."

"Well, that doesn't sound very helpful," said Mary.

"I found you, didn't I? And I found my shoes. I found you by accident, but I was looking for my shoes."

"No," said Mary, "you found my shoes."

"Most things were someone else's at one time or another."

Mary had run out of arguments. She had very little energy to keep talking in circles and she was becoming very annoyed. If the boy disappeared forever, it would be no worry to her.

"Goodbye," said the boy, "if I don't come back soon, I hope you're ok. It would be nice to see you again, but I don't want it to be hard. Goodbye."

Mary did not blink, but the boy was gone, shoes and all.

She stood overwhelmed, knowing nothing more than what she already had from the start of her troubles. Walking back to the house with her head in a fog, she did not care to feel about much anymore. She knew she would be in trouble when she returned home. So what? What else was new? She held no capacity to care about Elizabeth or Addison. They did not have any friends anyway, so they could go sit on a pin. They could go sit on a hundred pins, for all that Mary cared. It was at that moment when Mary realized how alone she was. There was not a soul in her life with whom she could discuss these phenomena. With her grandmother gone there was no guiding hand to assist in her navigating what was next to be done. Her parents would just think that she was making up stories and her friends already thought she was crazy. For the first time since all this started, she wanted the boy to return.

The party was winding down by the time that Mary got home. Her father had been removed from the lawn, most likely by a combined effort between Mary's mother and Aunt Colleen. Mary imagined there was a lot of adult cursing and maybe the release of some of her father's bodily fluids. This was suggested by the trail of darker grass that led up to the house. Mary did not feel any shame as she walked straight through the kitchen barefoot, muddy, and looking a mess. Her mother and Aunt Colleen were standing in the living room drinking coffee while the last lingering guests enjoyed a final piece of cake.

Mary did not say a word as she walked past her aunt and mother and began to climb the stairs leading up to her room. There was an audible gasp from Aunt Colleen that brought a smile to Mary's face, but her mother was silent as she watched Mary walk up the stairs. Someone was vomiting in the upstairs bathroom at the end of the hall and Mary could only assume that it was her father in mourning. She chose to leave him with his grief and closed the door behind her as she entered her room.

It was night by the time that the final guest left the house. Mary's father had been put to bed and her mother was sitting on the living room sofa with Aunt Colleen. Mary walked down the stairs in her jeans and dinosaur T-shirt with old mud still caked on her arms and face. She sat in her grandmother's chair and quietly watched TV.

"Mary," said her mother, clearing her throat, "we need to talk to you."

Mary paid them no attention as she continued to watch a movie about two people in love. It was in black and white, and nobody's hair moved, which made everything look a little more romantic.

"*Mary*," emphasized her mother, "look at me."

Mary turned to her mother. Her lips were pressed tightly together, and it looked as though her face was turning a darker shade of pink. She could tell that her mother was angry, but Aunt Colleen blankly stared at the carpet, looking uncomfortable and hypnotized.

"Mary, we know that you were suspended," said her mother, "the school called to make sure that you had access to your assignments. They told us what you did to Elizabeth, and her mother refused to come today because she expects us to pay for her daughter's medical bills. We feel, your father and I, that with your recent behavior being what it is, we have to make an adjustment."

"What kind of adjustment?" asked Mary.

"We've decided, your father and I, that it would be in your best interest if you were to go to a different school."

"What kind of school?"

"There's a school in Connecticut that would be beneficial to your needs. Now, you would be staying there for the remainder of your education until you graduate high school, but we'd come to visit all the time. Do you understand what I'm saying?"

Mary understood what her mother was saying, but she did not understand the implications of traveling to a different state just to go to a different school. There were plenty of schools in Massachusetts.

"How would I get there," she asked, "is there a bus?"

"No, darling," said her mother, "you would be living there in a dormitory. You may have to share a room with another student, but you would be living there every day."

This frightened Mary and made her angry. She had wanted to run away, but on her own terms. Good kids did not go to sleepover schools.

"When can I come home?"

"You could come home for Christmas," said her mother, "maybe for a bit in the summer. We'll send you letters every week, and I'm sure that you'll make all sorts of new friends."

"I'm not going," said Mary, "I don't want to go. I want to stay here."

Now this really was a pickle for Mary. She had a chance to leave and a place to stay if she did, but what she wanted was to live in the woods. She wanted to build her own house, like her great grandfather, and eat tasty food and have adventures like the animals in her books. A twenty-four-hour school was the last thing she wanted.

"We've already made the arrangements," said her mother, "you'll be leaving on Friday so you can get used to the school over the weekend. This way you can catch up with your class. We had to make special arrangements for you to enter after the semester started so I want you to be grateful that we could get you in as soon as we did."

Aunt Colleen began to sniffle as she pulled a napkin out of her purse. A few small packets of jelly fell to the floor, and she grumbled to herself as she began to pick them up. Mary wanted to hit something hard.

"I'm not going," said Mary, "I hate you and I'm not going anywhere!"

Mary ran up the stairs to her room and slammed the door. A loud moan from her parents' bedroom could be heard as her father regained consciousness to his affliction.

"Who's slamming doors?!" he groaned from the room. This question was met without reply as he continued to manufacture unfortunate sounds to himself.

Mary wasted no time as she began to fill her backpack with the essential things required for a long journey. Many items were worth leaving behind, but she found her favorite book and a few necessities that she could never part with. Her bag was getting heavy, so she looked around her room for a few final items. The packing was nearly finished when she realized that she had almost forgotten her grandfather's compass. Panic washed over her as she looked around her room, but it was nowhere to be found. She looked beneath her bed, behind her bookcase, in every drawer that she had in her room. She even unpacked her bag completely to see if she had already thrown it in without noticing. It was gone. Standing in the center of her room in disarray, and with practically everything that she owned strewn about, Mary collapsed onto a pile of her clothes and cried herself to sleep.

5. Someday You'll Understand

It was a beautiful day, dammit. It was not raining or mucky. There were no blizzards or hurricanes, and no flaming apocalypse was falling from the sky. It was a beautiful day and Mary wanted to disappear. It was Thursday, the day before Mary would be leaving for St. Philomena's School for Girls, and Mary was laying in her ravine, watching the frogs. She let her hand float in the shallow edges of the water as it lazily traveled around her fingers. Her arm had fallen asleep from having been laying on her side for so long, but the pins and needles added a unique sensation to the feeling of cold water running around her hand.

Both of her parents had already left for work when Mary had woken up that morning, but at this point she hardly noticed when they were home. Mary moved through the house like she was a ghost to herself. She barely ate or slept, and her dreams had become afflicted with confrontational visions of terror, death, and violence. But this was only when she slept. Her daydreams had all but disappeared. She tried to watch her favorite movies with Dracula and Frankenstein, but the stories had become lost to her. Not even the antics of Abbott and Costello could provide enough of a distraction to forget about the uncertainty of her assigned future.

The sun was warm enough to cut through the air and it fell upon Mary's face as she lay on the ground. She had not spoken out loud since she had woken up, but this was a game that she would sometimes play. Her personal record for not speaking was nearly forty-eight hours. The challenge became advanced during the school day when she would be called upon to answer a question only to stare blankly at the teacher and be sent home with a note for her parents to sign. Several of Mary's teachers had sent enough notes home that she had developed a talent for forging her mother's signature. Her parents would be confused when Mary's report card arrived with four full sheets of paper reporting several of Mary's behavioral discrepancies. Maybe this was what got Mary jammed up in the first place. She saw the quiet game as an exercise of her mental faculties, but in this instance, it was pure melancholia. The game was not fun anymore.

A cloud passed across the sun and the world became tinted in that afternoon way where the greens become a little bluer and the water looks murky and dark. The day seemed to stand still alongside Mary's inactivity, but there were a few frogs and toads flipping about in their business. They waded in the shallow water along with Mary's hand. She had not moved in some time and the residential amphibians had accepted her as part of the natural terrain. Mary had become another mound of indifferent mud that was neither hostile nor affable. She wanted the earth to rise around the edges of her form and swallow her up until she looked like a proper hill. Given enough time, if the earth would then claim her and split her body down the middle, it would be possible for Mary to become her own ravine. No one would find her, and no one would send her away to frightening places. Hills and mounds have it good.

Mary thought about this for some time, barely thinking of anything else. Clips of other ideas would intrude upon her state, but these flashes of plans and regrets flew in and out of her mind like small knives set to cut her life into ribbons. Laying on the ground, with her hand in the water, doing her best to be a hill, she quietly told her thoughts to go away.

Her grandfather's compass that she had been desperately looking for was found the next morning, buried beneath the pile of clothes upon which she had fallen asleep. After it was found, Mary made a vow to keep it on her person and to never part with it. The treasure sat in her jacket pocket with her hand gripping the metal casing. It felt heavy and cool, in a pleasant way.

A light rain began to fall upon Mary's face as she lay on the ground, doing her best not to exist. The air had turned colder than she was prepared for and after a brief internal argument, she convinced herself to return home. Being outside and away from the house was all that Mary wanted. Having her plans for a passive day suddenly change to that of action made her mood drop even lower than it had already been. Mary decided to spend the rest of her miserable day indoors and go to her tower.

The frogs came out in abundance now that she was on the move. Little voices spread across the ground like daisies and their heads popped out of the water with so many bubbles floating around them. Wiping the dirt from her jacket and pants, Mary started back to the house in a foul and frustrated mood. She stopped at the flowering dogwood tree in the backyard and thought about the boy, wishing for him to return. There was no one around that Mary felt comfortable talking to about her feelings. As annoying as he was with his vague advice and observations, she wanted to talk to him.

Mary closed her eyes tight and spoke low to herself as if she were praying for him to come back. Her hands held onto two thick branches and squeezed them in the hopes that he would appear like a genie from a lamp. She gripped the tree until her hands hurt and still no one came. The only response to the ritual was the sound of distant thunder and a darker roll of clouds coming in from the west. It would appear as though the forest itself had begun to push Mary away. She suddenly became very frightened as everything she had ever known had rejected her. She ran back into the house, slamming the back door and locking it behind her.

 Mary kept her boots on and proceeded to track mud across the house. She knew that her parents would be upset, but there were few punishments left that would make her life much worse. Opening the refrigerator, Mary removed the half-filled gallon of milk and put it in the oven. She did not turn the oven on, but she imagined what it would be like the next time her mother began to preheat it for a meal. What a surprise that would be. Considering how infrequently the oven was used, that may be an even bigger surprise after enough time had passed. Mary then took a permanent marker from the countertop and went throughout the rest of the house, writing curse words on the backs of furniture and knick-knacks that would not be touched until they were dusted. She wrote terrible things and even made up a few words that she thought sounded sinister. "King Shit" had stuck in her mind ever since Jimmy had used the expression and it was growing on her.

 After she felt satisfied with her domestic vandalism, Mary took an apple from the kitchen and bit it three times before rolling the rest beneath the living room couch. It was not a particularly good apple. Knowing that her parents had just installed a new carpet in the living room, Mary thought that it could use a little more character. After a few more misplaced items and a few more choice expletives, Mary walked up the stairs to her tower so she could be miserable there for a while. At least it would be warmer.

 The rain had become increasingly heavy and was striking the house in a steady beat. Small rivers ran down the windowpanes and glass that showed the world outside to be a gray and dreary place. It was almost too dark to see anything clearly outside of the house. Sporadic rolls of thunder followed brief flashes of lightning that were set apart enough to let Mary know that the storm was quickly approaching. It would soon be fully upon the house. The smell of the room was damp, and the humidity was thick when Mary opened the door. She flicked the switch for the industrial floor lamp that sat beneath the window of the room, but when the light broke through the darkness she froze with immense fear. An enormous white shed was standing plain as day in the middle of the room.

 Mary froze in terror. The shed stood as though it was always meant to be there. Doubt filled Mary's mind as she questioned whether the shed had always been up in the tower, and she had just failed to notice. It looked as natural as any other artifact or piece of furniture that had been placed and forgotten under a tarp. The couch that had once occupied the center of the room had been moved against the rounded wall behind some paintings that maintained dust collected over the years. It was evident that they had not been touched in a long time. Sprouts of grass and dirt that came up around the bottom edges of the shed gave the impression that the earth itself could also travel wherever it went. The only sounds to be heard were the distant thunder that was making its way towards the house, and Mary's ragged, shuddering breath.

Beneath the glow from the industrial lamp, the shed cast shadows that stretched across the ceiling and made its existence that much more imposing. It stood as the largest thing that Mary had ever seen, and it commanded a certain authority that refused to be ignored. Mary turned her back to the shed and tried to open the door that led downstairs, but it had become stuck on the thick rubber cable that ran power to the floor lamp. However hard Mary tried to pry the door open, the bottom would only jam the chord into an increasingly uncompromisable position. Panic gripped Mary by the throat and she could recognize the metallic taste.

With her back against the only exit, she could not blink for fear that something would spring upon her. She crept along the wall until she found some miscellaneous debris and boxes that she could hide behind. There were plenty of obstacles that lay between her and the shed, but there was no way out of the room. The air seemed to be getting thicker and it was becoming difficult for Mary to breathe as she began to hyperventilate. A blinding flash of lightning cut through the room and the house shook beneath the hammering thunder from the collision of atmosphere, making Mary scream and shake with fear.

Everything went dark.

The electricity to the house had been knocked out by the storm and the light was sucked out from the room. It was as though the darkness had been waiting between the slats of the wall for an opportunity to escape. Cupping her hands over her mouth to stay quiet, Mary was finding it harder and harder to breathe. She fought against the sensations that ran beneath her skin telling her to run.

Run for your life, you idiot, run!

But there was nowhere to run to. The best she could do was to remain hidden. Mary tried to stay still, tucked in a crawl space between two large boxes and beneath a third box, all covered by a thick plastic tarp. She had often camped out in the room beneath this tent to quietly read or just disappear occasionally. It smelt of old pages and dust, which were normally smells that Mary could enjoy. Under these circumstances, they felt suffocating. Once or twice, she would bite her own fingers just to feel anything else.

As the moments stretched into minutes, she bit herself more and more. It became the only action she had any control over. Mary strained her ears to recognize any sound other than her own heart or the storm beating against the house. The thunder was rolling steadily, bringing rain that hammered the windows and roof. There was another sound in the room that had gone otherwise unnoticed. At first Mary thought that she was imagining it out of fear and panic, but as time continued, painful, and slow, it became clear that she was not alone in the room. Someone was whispering.

The whisper she heard was low and from a singular source, as far as Mary could determine. It was a sound that crept across the floor without footsteps. It moved without legs and feet, but still it moved. From each corner of the room came a voice that shriveled and crept across the floor. She could not understand what was being said, but then a second voice cut through a little higher than the first. Before long, it became a conversation between two different entities that Mary did not understand. The two voices sounded viscous and had the quality of a throat gargling thick mud. Laughter filled the air until Mary made an audible gasp. She had forgotten to exhale this whole time and was now gasping for air. Both voices cut out instantly and Mary started to panic.

A scraping sound began to move something towards her hiding place. There was no way for Mary to see what was happening without giving up her secret location, so she lay on her stomach and buried her face in her hands. The small footsteps dragged along the floor in different directions and the sound of shifting boxes began to fill the room. One voice became three and then four and five voices. There was no real way for Mary to determine how many things were in the room, but she thought it was more than three and less than a hundred.

Dear God, she thought, *don't let them find me.*

Now maybe it was because this was the first time that Mary had tried to speak to God directly and he took it personally, or maybe it was just bad luck and coincidence, but that was when she started to hiccup.

She promised to be good.
*hic
She promised to be kind.
*hic
She promised not to hit anybody ever again.
*hic
She promised to clean up all the messes she made today.
*hic
She promised to go to the stupid girls' school.
*hic
She missed her grandmother and that,

*hic

Stupid ghost kid.

The tarp was ripped up from over her head and the box covering her was lifted and tossed aside. Mary screamed and hiccupped at the same time, which was a very strange and silly noise that would rob anybody of their dignity in their final moments. Most people try to think that their last words would be something substantial or deep, something poignant worth writing down, but most people just scream when they die. She kept her eyes shut tight until she heard her father's voice.

"Sweetheart, what's wrong?"

Mary opened her eyes to a well-lit room. Her father was standing over her with a concerned look on his face and a coffee stain on the collar of his white buttoned shirt. Sitting up, Mary looked around the room to find it was just as it should be. There was no shed in the middle and the couch had been returned to where it had always been. The paintings and boxes remained undisturbed, displaying their years. Even the rain had stopped.

"Mary," said her father, "I know you're upset about the school, but your mother and I feel that this is really what's best for you right now. And you can be angry and hate us, but we know in time that you'll look back and see this was the right thing to do. Hopefully...someday you'll understand."

Mary had no words for her father but continued to look around the room for any sign that something was wrong. Something must have been wrong. She looked for the slightest clue that would prove that she was not going crazy and what she had experienced was real. She found none. Mary looked at her father and started to cry before he embraced her in his arms and lifted her off the floor.

He said many things to comfort Mary about the school, but that was not why she was crying. The bravery that she required to face these new phenomena was a level of courage that Mary was so far unprepared. She was trying to be brave, but she was also concerned for her parents' safety, should these things return after she left. Or worse, would these things follow her all the way to Connecticut.

The rest of the evening consisted of Mary cleaning the messes that she had left in the wake of her rampage. She even retrieved the apple that she had rolled beneath the couch because she knew that it would go unnoticed. The lecture from her parents that followed the house cleaning was carried through tones of exhaustion and resignation. Mary was not listening at all but that was also part of the problem, according to her parents. Her mother thanked her for cleaning up after herself but continued to say that her behavior was not normal and that she had a lot of growing up to do if she was expecting to do well at her new school.

"This isn't just for you," said her mother, "this is for your future. You have an obligation to this family to honor our name and a responsibility to do right by it. We do not act like this, Mary. You need to start being proud of who you are and where you come from."

Mary shut down and decided that if she could not hear what her parents were saying, then none of it would happen. This was a great hope that she held for her survival, but hope is rarely kind at times.

"I know it's scary," said her father, "it's new, it's far, and it's scary. But if you don't try scary things every once and a while, you can't grow as a person. Remember what we talked about being brave?"

Mary nodded her head.

"It's like that forever," her father continued, "the work never really ends, Mary. If we're lucky it just gets a little easier."

This did not help Mary feel better. She wanted to believe her father, but she was so tired. The thought of taking on so many new things at the same time was an overwhelming sensation which made giving up an attractive option. She did not know how to express her frustration without talking about the strange things she had been seeing. If she did that then they might send her to a worse place. Mary resigned herself to keeping these events to herself.

"Now, have you started packing?" asked her mother.

Mary shook her head, waiting for another lecture.

"Ok," said her mother, "let's go pack."

Mary's mother helped to clean up her room and they spent the night going through the difference between what Mary would want to bring with her and what she would need. Her grandfather's compass was still sitting in her pocket. She had already made up her mind to keep it forever, and the feeling of weight was helping her nerves. Other necessary items were three large sweaters and a winter coat for the coming months, a scarf and wool hat, new shoes to replace the ones she had given to the boy (although she said that they had fallen into the river and floated away), a small album of family photographs, and a stuffed duck that she had had since she was born. His name was Duck, and his beak was permanently crooked from Mary teething it as a baby.

When Mary began to pack some of her favorite books, her mother thought it impractical for Mary to bring any with her. It was stated in the acceptance letter that there would be no need for students to bring their own books for leisure because the school had a substantial library. Mary agreed with her fingers crossed behind her back and made sure to sneak a copy of The Wind in the Willows, which was her favorite book, into her suitcase. Her father would stay up with Mary if she were sick and read out loud from the book until she fell asleep. He even did the voices right. Mary would fall asleep and dream of life on the river with Mole and Rat.

Her dreams would be interwoven with so many wonderful adventures in Toad Hall and harrowing dangers from the crafty weasels. There were always happy endings and last-minute miracles until she would wake up in her bed in her room in her house in her life; only to be called to a breakfast that she did not want. Mary almost preferred her nightmares of Dracula and Frankenstein. Waking from a nightmare is a relief. Waking from a good dream is almost always disappointing, especially if you're not allowed to fall back asleep.

Mary had two large suitcases that she would be bringing with her to St. Philomena's. They were packed strategically and waiting at the front door so they would not be forgotten when it came time to leave in the morning. It would be a three-hour drive to the school so they would have to leave around four-thirty in the morning to make it there in time for Mary's eight o'clock orientation. No one was looking forward to this, but it was what adults referred to as an "obligation" and a "responsibility". These were two words that would continue to imbue feelings of anger in Mary whenever she heard them. Considering that this was her first exposure to the world outside of her own, who could blame her?

It was getting to be late in the evening and everyone was tired. Mary was becoming more nervous about her life being ripped out from under her and the strange things she had been seeing. There was no way anyone could convince her that they were hallucinations. The boy even said that she did not have dementia so that removed Mary's only explanation.

Without the capacity to understand or comprehend what it was that she had been experiencing, Mary would have to find some way to communicate the dangers without having her parents think she was crazy. She wanted to tell them as much as she did not, which was a lot. There would be three hours in the car to talk it over with them, should the opportunity present itself. But would she be ready to talk about it if the opportunity presented itself? It took all that Mary could muster just to clearly remember the events in order. Even then, she felt as though she may have been forgetting the details and getting some parts mixed up.

Mary's parents set up TV trays for supper that night and the three of them watched reruns of I Love Lucy. There was something about the sound of old television shows that made Mary sleepy. It was sedative and made Mary feel as though she were absent; like nothing else existed around her and it was impossible for anything to touch her. Dinner consisted of pizza and salad prepared and delivered by Captain Nemo's Pizzeria. The restaurant was owned by a man named Roberto, but everyone called him Nemo. He kept an antique diving suit hanging on the wall of his restaurant and would tell his customers that it had belonged to his brother.

"The navy killed my brother," he would say, "lost forever at sea and they could only recover his empty suit!"

This was a polite lie. Roberto's brother had been a drunk that drowned in the swimming pool of the Flamingo hotel and casino in Las Vegas. Roberto would rather his brother be remembered as a mysterious hero instead of reprobate.

Roberto had always been fond of the Kirkland's after Marcus had given him a sizable discount on some graphic design work for his sign and pizza boxes. Every time the Kirkland's came into Captain Nemo's, Roberto would ask Mary when she would start working at the restaurant. Mary liked the idea of working in a pizzeria and she liked Roberto very much. He never ruffled her hair when he saw her, and she liked the funny way that he said her name. He sang it rather than spoke it. Sometimes he would hold out his hand and give Mary a secret portion of fresh mozzarella cheese. This would make Mary very happy, and it would become her favorite part of visiting Captain Nemo's.

Mary thought of a life where she could have pizza every day and all the fringe benefits that would come from it. She would not have to go to school ever again unless there was pizza school. That was a school that Mary could thrive in, she thought. She pictured giant chef hats and lots of pepperoni flying along to loud Italian music that she would never understand. It was all magic to her and she loved Roberto very much. When Mary's mother opened their box of pizza there was a small portion of mozzarella tucked into the corner. It sat in the center of a heart drawn with a permanent marker.

Mary's mother put her arm around Mary and squeezed her tightly, kissing the top of her head. Her father joined in on the other side and the three of them held each other in a quiet embrace. Mary felt sad, but mostly numb. Everything was happening so quickly that she had not allowed herself any time to appropriately process each event. She felt that as soon as she was able to comprehend something as it occurred, something else would come along and push the other out of the way. It was an overwhelming process that left a lot of holes in Mary's ability to receive information. She gently squeezed both of her parents' arms and continued watching I Love Lucy.

After dinner was over and the rest of the pizza was wrapped up, Mary's mother set some aside for the next day's trip. They would have to drive with very limited stops to make it on time, so bringing food with them was the practical solution to the question of breakfast. Apart from gasoline and bathroom breaks, they would be driving directly to the school. Mary's father began loading the car with supplies for an additional trip along with their own suitcases.

Instead of driving there and back on the same day, Mary's father had booked a few nights' stay in a hotel at a small resort in the Catskills. Mary's parents would make the most of the trip as best they could in the rustic luxury of distraction. And if they happen to enjoy a fine meal and a few bottles of good wine in their grief, then all the better. The car was packed, loaded, and ready for the road before Mary's parents sat on her bed and tucked her in. Mary was waiting for a speech of some kind. It felt like a ceremonial occasion and her father had a penchant for making long extrapolations on hopeful futures and inspirational thoughts, although his deliveries were often clumsy, at best.

"Well," he said, "goodnight."

Her parents each kissed her on the head and smiled as they shut the light and closed the door. Mary was left alone in her childhood room for what would be the last night before she set out into the unknown. She felt like she should have something to say, but she did not know what that would be. She watched the shadows dance from the tree branches outside of her bedroom window as the moonlight spread across her floor like nightsilk.

There was a different kind of stillness around her that had the feeling of a hanging pause; not quite the end of something or the beginning, but something like a deep breath awaiting further instructions. She turned to her side and faced the wall against her bed. Curling her fingers around her mouth, she lightly bit down until it started to hurt, and she smiled to herself. During her cleanup that night, no one thought to check for the half gallon of milk that was still sitting comfortably in the oven.

"King shit," she said to herself.

6. Don't Look At Her Eyes

    The drive to St. Philomena's was a slog. Attempting to do anything at four in the morning is a complicated process, and none of the Kirkland's had any desire for this obligation. It is hard enough to get yourself up and moving, but to have three people organized and coordinated just to see straight is downright laughable. Even with the car being packed the night before, there were still a few snags in the departure. Mr. Kirkland's irritable bowel syndrome was flaring up as it usually did before long trips in the car. The upstairs bathroom had become compromised by his predicament, so Mary and her mother were forced to utilize the bathroom downstairs, although it did not have a mirror. Mary was up, surprisingly, and ready to go despite her desire to be difficult. Her mother and father argued through the bathroom door and continued to argue as they prepared to leave. The Kirkland's were deliberately silent for the first hour of the drive. Four in the morning can be a curious time that signifies either the end of something wonderful or the beginning of something terrible. Sometimes it can be both, but one can never tell. They all thought it best not to discuss perspective.
    Mary slept for most of the trip. Not having slept well for her last night at home, the gentle hum and vibration from the car rocked her back to her dreams, although she would later forget them. She woke up in the back of the car sprawled out across the seat. Her father had stopped at a gas station for fuel and a bathroom break, so Mary decided to stretch her legs and investigate the area.
    She had not really traveled much in her life up to this point, so the journey was enough of a distraction to keep her mind from wandering towards thoughts of where she was going. She looked at the strange cars lined up along the wire fence that divided an unfamiliar stretch of trees and wondered what was on the other side. In an effort to search this small section of undiscovered geography, she told her father that she needed to use the bathroom, just so she could go behind the gas station and see what other anomalies could be found. Behind the white painted brick building was a silver gas tank that was used to fill empty propane canisters. It was old and overgrown with weeds and long grass with spiderwebs delicately

connected between scattered blades shooting up from the ground. An impressive amount of cigarette butts and small plastic liquor bottles were scattered across the ground and the tank itself was covered in graffiti. Mary immediately thought of The Mummy's Tomb, and she sighed a little sigh.

She may never see it again, but she hoped that Jimmy would still play there now that she was gone. It would be her way of an apology for how she had threatened him. There was something about him that Mary initially found distrustful, but since he was the only other soul that knew about her secret house, she hoped that he would keep it a secret. Without any way of knowing, she was sure that he would understand.

Mary walked back to the car to find her mother sitting in the passenger's seat with a small bag of snacks and a comic book for her. It was not a particularly interesting comic book, but it was something for Mary to read while they were on the road. There was a pink fluffy bunny on the cover underneath the title of Pooches and Smooches. Mary thumbed through a few pages of a story where three bubbly-looking woodland friends with large eyes had to share four pieces of pie. An argument began as to who would be allowed to enjoy the fourth piece, but all was resolved as another big-eyed woodland critter came along. The power of friendship persevered over adversity and the four animals joyfully went swimming after they finished their pieces of pie. Mary thought it was lazy writing. She would have preferred some kind of fight-to-the-death scenario between the doe eyed critters over the last piece of pie. Or better still, should the pie become sentient and destroy the animals in self-defense.

Does anyone ever defend the life of the pie, she thought to herself.

She then thought about the sun exploding in the story's climax, making their arguments irrelevant. Mary continued to read the rest of the comic, but without expectations.

The family rolled along the road between dense stretches of woodland expanse that blended in a blur of brown, green, and gray. Mary was looking through the car window and into the woods as they went speeding by. She imagined packs of wild animals running alongside them and strained her eyes to see if there were any monsters that could be lurking between the trees. She wanted to at least get a glimpse of one, but with no luck. Still, it was more entertaining than Pooches and Smooches.

The radio was playing soft rock and roll that sounded familiar but was unplaceable in Mary's memory. The singer was talking about what happened on different days of the week and how none of it really mattered, except for Friday. Apparently, on Friday he was in love. Mary thought this to be a funny thing because how can someone be in love for just one day? Mary wondered whether she had been in love. To the best of her recollection, the event had not yet happened. She thought about what love meant and in what context. She loved her grandmother and her parents. She thought that they might love her. She loved her ravine and everything in it. She loved Dracula, the Wolf Man, and Frankenstein. Her mind continued down the constraints of love and whether there were contingencies that allowed love to exist for specific periods of time. Mary decided that she had never been in love before. The whole process seemed confusing and unimportant. She continued to look out the window in search of monsters while trying not to become increasingly bored.

The Kirkland's arrived at St. Philomena's School for Girls at approximately seven forty-seven am. Mary's orientation with the headmistress was scheduled for eight, so there really was no time for a substantial goodbye. They drove through a large wrought iron gate and began to climb up a winding driveway that stretched through green open grounds peppered with black birch and pignut hickory trees. There were five buildings on the grounds that they could see. One large building that resembled a cathedral stood centered between two pairs of smaller buildings on either side.

The center building was massive in its ornamentation and sported stone gargoyles across the cornice molding and carved stone lintels with swirling detail. Four towers rose to pointed steeples from each corner with a larger, taller steeple rising from the center. A clock face was embedded in the center of the bell tower. Above the wooden front doors of St. Philomena's was a carving that read, "Astra Inclinant, Sed Non Obligant". The neighboring buildings were plain, but still detailed with imbrication around the facades. Each of the side buildings had names above their own doors that read "Pasce Spiritum", "Bonum Nuntium", "Sperare", and "Felix Domus". These were the dormitories set aside for the students.

Children of varying ages were roaming the grounds in clean white shirts and navy-blue pants. Some of them were quietly reading beneath the shaded trees while others who had not yet received breakfast were making their way towards the main building to the cafeteria. Mary had never seen anything like it before in her life and she went from feeling obstinate to intimidated. The fear that comes from the unknown can either be squashed or amplified, depending on the circumstances. Everyone looked so happy and clean, so carefree and healthy, that Mary wanted to go home. The driveway rounded up to the doors of the main building and Mary attempted to keep the car moving by sheer force of will. Once the engine was turned off, she realized that there was no hope.

Her father carried her two suitcases up the stairs of the main building while Mary's mother opened the giant brown doors with some difficulty. They entered a cavernous hallway that stretched the length of the building and led to a large wooden staircase which split both to the left and the right. The second-floor landing circled back to the front of the building above where Mary and her parents stood. Both sides of the second floor offered rooms running the full length of the hall. Portrait paintings of former headmasters and headmistresses, deans, professors, nuns, and priests were spread across the walls in what was meant to be a welcoming emanation of good will. In turn, the display left more of a resemblance to a cortege for the release from carefree adolescence and wonder. Mary thought it all to be far too serious, but she did like the smell of the room.

A clean looking man in a light gray suit opened one of the doors in the hallway and greeted them with a smile.

"Ah," he said, "you must be the Kirkland's."

"Yes, thank you," said Mary's father, fumbling with the bags "sorry if we're a little late."

"Not at all. In fact, you're right on time. This way, please."

The man introduced himself as Franklin Lewis, the caretaker for house business. His responsibilities were coordinating the general upkeep of the main building and managing the essential facilities that kept the school operational. Mr. Lewis led the Kirkland family on a casual tour of the grounds while providing a brief history of the school and their philosophies.

"St. Philomena's was built in nineteen-sixteen as a hospital for veterans returning from World War One. Although it was initially built for the recovery of those suffering residual effects of psychiatric crises, the surplus of wounded soldiers returning home required the construction of two additional wards. These were built for soldiers with more physical injuries and contagious diseases. A group of sisters led by Father Bertrand Armadillo established St. Philomena's as a place of rest for soldiers who may have otherwise been seen as cowardly or traitors for being unfit to continue fighting. Naturally the advances in medicine and understanding of mental health were not as advanced as they are by today's standards, so there was a significant period of trial and error on the part of the faculty."

"Sounds like a bummer," said Mr. Kirkland.

"Yes," said Mr. Lewis, "quite a terrible 'bummer'."

Mr. Lewis continued to expand upon the development and changes that had occurred over the years at St. Philomena's. The school had gone from hospital, to convent, to seminary school, and then to boarding school. They had attempted to integrate a co-educational program in the nineteen-seventies, allowing both men and women to attend the school, but this had proven to be more problematic than progressive. By the nineteen-eighties, St. Philomena's was declared to be a school exclusively for girls and young women, ages nine to eighteen; with an option to remain a student till the age of twenty in special cases.

Mary was half listening to Mr. Lewis, but her focus was on the landscape. It was beautiful. The forest surrounding the grounds was an invitation to adventure, albeit a particularly crowded adventure with the other students. These trees were new to her and would require further investigation. She wanted to run into the woods at full speed and spend the rest of her days living on the outskirts of humanity, happily picking food out from garbage cans, and building nests underground. St. Philomena's was beginning to feel less tangible and more surreal as she continued to look things over. It resembled an attractive painting that could change with intention.

The school made her feel more grown up, but she was scared. Mary brought her finger up to her mouth and lightly bit the side of it until her mother took her hand away. She gripped it in her own hand, giving a light squeeze. She looked at Mary from the corner of her eye and Mary looked at the ground.

"The dormitories are kept in these side buildings," said Mr. Lewis, "each building has its own compact kitchen for the older students to practice their domestic culinary skills while they cook for the younger students. They provide breakfast for our youngest up to the age of ten, while lunch and dinner are served in the main building there. The dormitories have their own bathroom facilities and sleeping quarters which are the students' responsibility to keep clean and disinfected. Room inspections are performed on a rotation and all students are expected to be in bed by nine pm each night. They may stay up until ten on Saturdays, but that is an earned privilege."

Mr. Lewis brought a handkerchief out from his inside jacket pocket. He sneezed twice but kept both suppressed to maintain his composure to an involuntary act.

"Excuse me," he said, "hay fever. We have a gymnasium built behind the main building with exercise equipment, a running track, a heated Olympic sized swimming pool, and a half basketball court for our more active students. The media room in the main building is a place for students to engage in the development of their technological inclinations regarding digital art, global business, communications, etc. There is also a library with both physical and digitized editions of classical literature, history, mathematics, science, and of course, biblical texts. Although we maintain alignment with the Catholic archdiocese, we do not discourage the students from learning about other religions of historical value. Strictly for research, of course."

"That sounds neat," said Mr. Kirkland.

"It most certainly is 'neat'." said Mr. Lewis, "could I offer you all coffee or a light breakfast?"

"We really must be going," said Mary's father, "we have to check into a spot in the Catskills."

"How lovely," said Mr. Lewis, "well let's get Mary settled in her room then."

"What do you think, Mary?" asked her mother.

Her mother squeezed Mary's hand tightly which caused her to wince. Mary looked up and smiled at Mr. Lewis who then smiled in return, although without much enthusiasm. They entered the building marked Sperare and opened the door to another hallway lined with small, numbered rooms on either side. They walked past closed doors with portraits of Jesus and the saints between them and Mary felt as though she were under surveillance. Each painting had a different saint looking serious with strange objects in their hands and golden glowing rings around the tops of their heads.

"What does 'Sperare' mean, Frank?" asked her father.

"It means 'Hope', Mr. Kirkland."

There was a subtle twitch in the corner of Mr. Lewis' mouth which suggested his discomfort towards the informality of Mr. Kirkland. He was grateful that his own genial training and obligations would not permit him to openly express this feeling.

"The houses are primarily organized by age to provide our students with a sense of companionship, although all students are encouraged to engage with each other freely. Each dormitory is assigned a matron to observe and supervise the safety and well-being of each student. Your matron, Ms. Kirkland, will be Ms. Tristan. You will have the chance to meet her later."

Mr. Lewis opened door number seven and escorted the Kirkland's into a sparsely decorated room with two beds, two dressers, a washing sink, a window, and a crucifix. Each bed had a bedside table with a drawer containing the King James Bible. One of the beds had clearly been slept in and made up that morning. There was a wrinkle in the blanket and a pink stuffed rabbit on the pillow, signifying the presence of a roommate. There were also two pairs of shoes tucked neatly beneath the bed frame along with a framed picture of what looked like someone's parents placed on top of their bedside table. Mary looked at the powder blue walls and thought about what her roommate would be like. She would rather not have one.

"Welcome, Ms. Kirkland," said Mr. Lewis, "make yourself at home."

Mary sat on the bed and looked around the room. There were three pairs of navy-blue pants and three white shirts folded on her bedside table. Mary looked back at her parents and tried to communicate silently with her eyes.

Please don't make me do this, she thought, *please don't make me stay here.*

Her mother knelt beside Mary and ruffled her hair while she smiled and reminded Mary to behave herself, to pay attention, make lots of new friends, and to have fun. Mary could feel the tears begin to form but refused to give her parents and Mr. Lewis the satisfaction of seeing her cry. Instead, she just hugged her mother and father before they left for their trip to the Catskills. The goodbye was all too brief, as most goodbyes are, and as Mr. Lewis began to escort her parents back to their car, he turned back to Mary.

"Ms. Kirkland," he said, "once you are settled, please change into your uniform and join me in the main hall, room three-thirteen, to have some tea and meet with the Headmistress."

He turned back to her parents before turning to Mary once more.

"Do your best to reach us in less than half an hour."

With a final wave goodbye from her parents, the main door at the end of the hall was closed and Mary was left alone. She sat quietly on her bed and looked around the room, even though there was not much for her to see. She sat like that for a few minutes before she opened her suitcase and removed her copy of The Wind in the Willows. Opening the small drawer beside her bed, Mary removed the King James Bible and replaced it with her book. Mary opened the bible and began to read some of the passages in no special order. She had never read the bible before so her curiosity had her scan some pages to see what she could pick up.

There were many words that Mary did not understand, and the print was so small that she would often lose her place as she was reading. She left the bible on top of the bedside table and continued to unpack her suitcases. Mary neatly placed her belongings in her designated dresser and took a step back to see her new personal space. The room was sparse, but it was hers. She hated it.

Mary stood on her tiptoes to look out of her window that opened out over a portion of the grounds. The morning sky was clear and presented a feeling of cautious optimism despite Mary's general suspicions. The children had all returned indoors from play and the vast yard that lay before the main hall looked mythical in its design. A deer walked slowly across the grass and paused for a moment to tilt its head towards a sound that Mary could not hear. It quickly ran back into the woods and vanished.

The door to Mary's room opened and a girl around Mary's age walked in carrying a textbook under her arm. It was a book on introductory geometry which she tossed carelessly on her bed. Noticing Mary, she stopped and laughed to herself, half startled and half cynical.

"Well, they didn't waste much time," she said, "didn't even let the bed get cold."

Mary held out her hand stiffly and introduced herself. It was received enthusiastically, and Mary felt a little more relaxed.

"Hi," she said, "I'm Mary."

"Ruth," said her roommate, "Ruth Rubenstein."

Ruth flopped onto her bed and took out a candy bar from beneath her mattress. She opened the wrapper and offered a piece to Mary who took it gladly. The candy bar was ordinary, but it made Mary happy that her roommate was nice.

"We're not supposed to keep food in the room," said Ruth, "Mr. Lewis does inspections sometimes. He's a pain in the ass. If it's Ms. Tristan, then you can relax a little bit. I don't think she knows where she even is half the time. If Lewis comes in and finds any food, you get written up."

"Like detention?" asked Mary.

"I wish! No, if you get three write ups then you're stuck cleaning the dorm bathrooms twice a day for five days. And that's with going to school. You can kiss your free time goodbye."

Mary ate her chocolate in nibbles as she wanted to avoid looking greedy, but she was very hungry.

"The last girl they had in here, the one you replaced, had so many write ups that they kicked her out."

Mary hoped the expulsion would mean being forced into exile from the school and being sent to live in the surrounding woods. She imagined packs of wild children attacking hikers and cars that had broken down on the highway. Mary smiled at the thought of being feral and hoped to get kicked out some day.

"What was her name?" asked Mary.

"Caitlin. She was alright. She knew a lot of dirty jokes, but she snored. Do you snore?"

Mary shook her head no. She did not know if she snored because she was always asleep at the time. Mary tried to think of a dirty joke, but nothing good came to mind.

"Pretty sure all white people snore," said Ruth, "my dad snores real bad, but not my mom. How old are you?"

"Eleven."

"Well, I'm twelve."

Mary sat on the bed and took her stuffed duck out of her suitcase. She was a little embarrassed to have a stuffed animal, but Ruth had one of her own which brought some confidence. She put Duck on her pillow and tucked her suitcase beneath her bed.

"Where's room three-thirteen?" asked Mary.

"You gotta go talk to Dracula?"

Mary's eyes grew big at the thought and Ruth began to laugh.

"That's the headmistress," said Ruth, "she's a mean bitch. Her and Mr. Lewis. I think they're related or something. One of the older girls said she saw them kissing but I also heard Mr. Lewis is, like, a homo or something."

"He likes boys?"

"That's what a homo is, dummy," said Ruth, "you never met a homo before?"

Mary lied and said that she had known lots of homosexuals, but this was not true (at least none that she had been aware of). Ruth had also never met any homosexuals, (at least none that she had been aware of), but she doubled down on the lie just the same, claiming to have several gay friends. After taking turns adding to the number of homosexuals that they knew, both girls came to an agreement that they were experts on the subject and decided to focus on the task at hand.

"What's her name?" asked Mary.

"Who, the headmistress? I don't know," said Ruth, "I don't think she has one. Everybody just calls her Headmistress."

"Do you think she's really a vampire?"

"...maybe," said Ruth, "maybe...I'm a vampire, too."

Mary was not in the mood for games.

"Maybe," said Ruth, "we're all...vampires!"

Ruth hissed and leapt at Mary who shrieked and covered her head. She yelled at Ruth to stop and that the joke was not funny, but Ruth persisted. Only when Mary punched her arm with sincerity did Ruth step back in frustration.

"Jeez," said Ruth, "I was just joking."

"It's not funny," shouted Mary, "I don't like it here and I don't like that."

Mary held onto Duck and pouted on the side of her bed. Ruth was torn between being annoyed with Mary and feeling guilty for upsetting her. She handled the situation using her best judgment. She condescended. Ruth did not have very good judgment at the time.

"Girl, you have to grow up," she said, "come on, I'll show you three-thirteen."

Ruth led the way across the yard and into the main hall. She pointed out certain rooms that were off limits, which rooms were classrooms, and which rooms were supposedly haunted. The two girls climbed the staircase at the back of the hall and took a left onto the second-floor landing. In the middle of the landing was a door marked:

313
HEADMISTRESS
PLEASE KNOCK

"There you go," said Ruth, "just don't look at her eyes. She doesn't like it."

Ruth was running down the hallway and back down the staircase before Mary could ask what she meant. Not wanting to go in so soon, Mary stood in front of the door for a few seconds before lightly knocking on what she imagined to be her final moments of life. Mr. Lewis opened the door and smiled thinly at Mary, waving her inside. She walked past him and wondered if all homosexuals looked like him.

The room was very warm and thick with atmosphere. Heavy green velvet curtains covered tall windows, allowing just enough space for minimal sunlight to break through. Tall standing lamps provided soft yellow light to fill in the spaces left untouched by the sun while full bookcases built into the walls brought a feeling of influence and authority about the room. A series of taxidermied birds and small animals were placed strategically on several small tables across the floor as well as several display boxes on the walls showing colorful beetles in pin and pose. The room looked clean, but there was an old feeling about it, like it had remained untouched for decades. Mr. Lewis walked to a small tea cart that was next to a large mahogany desk. It would have looked just as natural in the captain's quarters of a clipper ship. No one sat behind the desk, but the high arched chair hinted that this was the desk of a very important person. The absence brought a certain disturbance to Mary's already shaken calm.

"Tea, Ms. Kirkland?"

"Yes, please."

Mr. Lewis poured a cup of tea for Mary and asked if she wanted milk or cream with sugar, which she graciously declined. Mary was anxious about making a strong impression and she did not trust the offer. She decided to be suspicious of all things from now on. Mary accepted the cup of tea and made a face as she took a bitter sip. Mr. Lewis smiled to himself at her reaction.

"The headmistress should be with us momentarily," said Mr. Lewis, "how do you like your room?"

"It's fine," said Mary, "Ruth's nice."

"Ah, yes. Ms. Rubenstein. She certainly is a character."

The two sat in silence for a few awkward minutes until a tall door along the wall slid open and in walked the oldest woman that Mary had ever seen. She carried her age in her face, as the rest of her moved with the confidence and grace of a much younger person. It was clear, however, that the headmistress had no sense of self-doubt. Her composure was paramount to her character. She wore a dark maroon dress, almost black, that nearly grazed the floor with each step. Her hair was tied in a tight bun on the back of her head, and it resembled a helmet that could be removed if necessary.

There was nothing remarkable about the eyes of the headmistress as far as Mary could tell, but she also wanted to avoid some accusation of a well-known act with diabolical implications. Mary only stared for a moment before she forced herself to look at the ground. She attempted to glance at the eyes of the headmistress a few more times to figure out what could be wrong with them. Not-knowing was becoming frustrating. She resigned herself to staring back at the ground. Mr. Lewis stood to greet the headmistress, so Mary stood as well.

"Good morning Ms. Kirkland," said the headmistress, "welcome to St. Philomena's. I hope you take the time you need to adjust to our ways, but you'll find that we are no more difficult to navigate than the rest of the world. Of course, you will be held to the same standards as your fellow students regarding behavior and academic success. For the time you are here, you will refer to me as headmistress and I will refer to you as Ms. Kirkland, is that understood?"

Mary nodded to the affirmative.

"Say 'Yes, headmistress.'"

"Yes, headmistress," said Mary.

Mary wanted to go home.

"Good. Please sit down."

The headmistress opened a drawer in her desk and removed a large file with what Mary assumed to be her life story. Mary was beginning to see the resemblance to Dracula when she looked into her eyes, but her's were nearly more sinister.

There was the uncomfortable moment where the headmistress glanced up in time to make eye contact with Mary who then went completely red in the face and turned her head to look at a stuffed pheasant on a table beneath a lamp. The headmistress smiled to herself at the obvious anxiety that existed within Mary. Those were her favorite kind of students because they were already afraid. The work had started early, and the students would be more easily manipulated as time went by. If she could find a way to grind them down just a little bit more, then the transformation could be made from a petulant child to a young, respectable citizen well suited to the expectations of proper society.

The headmistress saw it as her part, her mission, to level the playing field away from all the radical thinkers and sexual deviants that managed to survive despite her prayers. She opened the file and shuffled some papers around until she found the specific page she was looking for.

Reaching into her pocket, she removed a pair of small glasses and put them gently on the ridge of her nose.

"Now we have agreed to take you in on our lottery scholarship. This will cover most of your tuition, but you should know that this was a difficult decision based on the transcripts from your previous school. There are concerns to me regarding your performance, but we also felt it was our Christian duty to aid those who are most in need of redemption."

The headmistress' long fingers slipped as she tried to turn the page. She ran the tip of her finger across her tongue which made a wet and scraping sound that made Mary squirm in her chair.

"In looking through your scholastic history, your performance has been mediocre, at best. You regularly produce incomplete work in class and with your home assignments. You have a penchant for daydreaming, telling fabrications to justify bad behavior, and you have a history of violence against your fellow classmates. You are also quite a skilled forger, from my understanding."

Mary thought of a movie she had seen once where a judge sentenced a prisoner to death by hanging and it was beginning to sound appealing. She discreetly pinched the skin on her arm between her fingernails.

"I appreciate a challenge and we have a lot of work to do, Ms. Kirkland," said the headmistress, "if I find that your performance in any way does not meet our expectations, or if you choose to persist in problematic behavior, then you will lose your scholarship."

The headmistress slowly rose from her chair and glided across the room almost effortlessly. The closer she walked towards Mary, the larger she became. The towing presence of the headmistress made Mary instinctively shrink into her chair.

"'Astra inclinant, sed non obligant'," said the headmistress, "do you know what that means?"

Mary shook her head no.

"It means, 'The stars incline us, they do not bind us.' It means that although we may be pushed by fate towards the events of our lives, it is ultimately up to us to decide what it is that we do. Free will, Ms. Kirkland. It is your choice that determines what decisions will form the tract of your life. Just as fate and free will have brought you to us."

The headmistress walked back to her desk and opened two drawers on either side from where she was sitting. Two small glass jars, each containing a single beetle, were brought out and placed on the desk where Mary could see them. From a different drawer she produced two dark glass bottles, which she opened and dabbed individually on two cotton balls. She opened the jars containing each beetle and dropped a cotton ball in both. The headmistress continued:

"Despite the illusion that a decision can provide many different outcomes, there are only two. You can do the good thing," she held up the glass bottle containing a beetle that was suckling on the liquid that had been absorbed by the ball of cotton, "or the bad thing." she held up the other jar which now contained a dead beetle; having been poisoned by whatever it was that she had dabbed onto the cotton ball. Mary's hands began to shake as she tried to gently place her teacup on the table in front of her. She did not want any more tea.

"Most people will complicate their decisions with blame. There is no need to take responsibility for one's actions if it is always someone else's fault. This is a weak habit that we do our best to break here at St. Philomena's. Only you are accountable for the consequences in your life. Ideally this revelation comes quickly with age. Although there are still a fair number of people who refuse to recognize the harm that their perverted understanding of choice inflicts on the innocent. We pray, of course, for their salvation, but in the end all we have in life is choice...and faith. Do you pray, Ms. Kirkland?"

Mary thought for a moment. She prayed to God in the tower back home and that did her no favors, so she was not in a big-time rush to make that mistake again. But she suspected that saying no would also lead to consequences. The choice metaphor was becoming clear to her in real time.

"Sometimes," said Mary.

The headmistress smiled to show two rows of straight teeth that were abnormally white. They looked brand new.

"That's a good answer, Ms. Kirkland," she said, "I know that your family is not of the Faith, but I don't blame them. The unenlightened are legion and they surround us. We are blessed to live in a time where our beliefs...our truth, is under constant attack from all sides. It is in these times of opposition that the warriors of the cross can rise and strike down those who work towards the destruction of mankind. There is still time for your own redemption, however. I intend to be a guiding hand in awakening your faith through penance and sacrifice. Do you know the scriptures?"

Mary cut her losses and shook her head no.

"You've no doubt found the bible in your room. Upon arrival at St. Philomena's, every student is expected to find a verse that speaks to them personally and have it memorized. Think of it as a promise to our Lord. Come back to me in three days with a memorized verse but be mindful of your selection. Remember, it's your choice. Mr. Lewis?"

"Yes, headmistress?"

"See Mary back to her room and be sure that she knows where her bible is."

"Yes, headmistress."

Mr. Lewis gently took a flat palm to Mary's back and guided her to the door. Their steps made polyrhythmic clicks across the hardwood floor, but all sound had become dampened by the amount of hanging cloth and books. In this brief introduction, there were three revelations that had become clear to Mary. She was not safe. She was alone. She wanted to leave. The last thing she saw was a taxidermied mongoose about to be killed by a cobra. The door closed behind them, and Mary was brought back to Sperare. It was then she realized that by some indeterminable force, she had received the prefix of "Ms."

Mary had officially grown up.

7. I Haven't Got A Card

When Mr. Lewis escorted Mary back to her room, he found her bible sitting on top of her bedside table. When he opened the drawer and found it empty, he smiled to himself in an oddly satisfied way. Panic and confusion hit Mary when she saw that her copy of The Wind in the Willows was missing, but she refused to say anything or show fear in front of Mr. Lewis. He reminded Mary that lunch would be served in the dining hall behind the main building at eleven forty-five. With that he left to allow Mary time to begin studying her bible. As soon as her door closed, Mary tore through the room and began searching for her favorite book. After looking in every conceivable place for a book to hide, she lay on her bed and began to cry. Her tears came quickly and with great force as she found herself stripped of her last hope for happiness in a strange and scary place. She had already been upset about having been sent to the school, and with her only comfort now missing, Mary was certain that she would not survive. Ruth entered the room and sat on her bed across from Mary with a flower in her hand.

"Was it that bad," she asked, "did she do the beetle thing?"

"Where's my book?!" Mary snapped through her tears. She did not have the strength to pursue a threat, but she was hoping for mercy.

Ruth stood on the edge of her bed and removed a loose brick from the wall. She placed the flower in the space, reached her hand deeper inside, and retrieved Mary's book, safe and sound. Mary became so overjoyed that she snatched the book from Ruth and held it tightly against her chest as she wiped her face with her hands. Ruth smiled and shook her head.

"You really are just a baby," she said, "we gotta toughen you up some."

"Why did you hide my book?"

"Contraband," said Ruth, "the headmistress has to approve everything in the school. If she found that then she would have burned it."

"Why," asked Mary, "it's a good book. What's wrong with it?"

"Talking animals," said Ruth, "sign of the devil. Didn't you know that? Jeez, everything is the sign of the devil around here."

Mary held the book even tighter. If anything were to happen to it, then she would not know what to do. Ruth reached her hand back into the wall and retrieved three of her own books. She had copies of To Kill a Mockingbird, A Light in the Attic, and Harriet the Spy. Mary had never heard of any of these books before and it felt as though she had discovered a new country. The two girls sat on the floor of their room and told each other their favorite stories.

Ruth came to St. Philomena's from Brooklyn, so having the school in the middle of the woods was not an ideal situation for her to be in, as far as she could figure. She shared her experiences growing up in the city and how much she missed it. She told Mary about the Portuguese bakery beneath her apartment and how she woke up every morning to the smell of freshly baked pastries and bread. She talked about the flavor ice man who pushed a cart through the street with a big block of ice that he would scrape into paper cones and flavor with all kinds of syrup. Cherry and coconut were her favorite flavors, but lemon was good, too. She told Mary about how she was the best at all the games and how she was the Double Dutch champion of her block. Mary had never had the opportunity to play Double Dutch because she did not have those kinds of games where she came from. After thinking about it some more, Mary realized that she did not have those kinds of friends, either.

Mary talked about her ravine and the frogs and how the only real city she had ever seen was Boston. Ruth asked her if she was a Red Sox fan and proceeded to berate Mary in the classic spirit of the Yankees/Red Sox feud. Mary was becoming visibly agitated about being teased, so Ruth consoled her and told Mary not to worry. Ruth was a Mets fan, anyway. This conversation was becoming upsetting so Mary decided to talk about the things that she knew Ruth could never criticize.

She talked about her favorite movies and her grandmother. She proudly told Ruth about her epic battle with Elizabeth and the state that she left her in, but she did admit that she felt a little bad about it now. Ruth immediately took her side and promised that if Elizabeth ever tried to get revenge that she would be there to help Mary beat the snot out of her. Mary found this to be a comfort of great magnitude and decided then and there that Ruth would be her best friend. From that small glimmer of kindness, she felt as though a great weight was being lifted from the dread of St. Philomena's.

The conversation between Mary and Ruth was beginning to take on the tone of familiarity that usually comes with the meeting of a new friend. They were both surprised at how well they were getting along with each other and there was a fresh sense of developing trust. Whatever passed between them would stay between them. There were several promises made and lots of joyful fibs around their accomplishments.

Mary was beginning to feel emboldened by Ruth's worldly knowledge, so she decided to press her perspective for insight to her recent supernatural encounters. She told Ruth about the strange corduroy boy and the shed that was following her. Each scene was depicted to the best of Mary's memory, although she was first to admit that there were fuzzy parts mixing together. Mary would get flustered when she found holes in her story or sentences that trailed off into dead-end thoughts. Ruth listened to her seriously and patiently waited for Mary to finish explaining her experiences. Once Mary had finished, Ruth remained silent to the point where Mary began to feel self-conscious. After thinking about it briefly, Ruth nodded her head and stood up.

"I believe you," she said, "I've seen some weird stuff, but that's too weird to be phony."

Mary was overjoyed. She felt like crying again but did her best to hide it. She asked Ruth if she could keep her book and her grandfather's compass in the secret compartment and Ruth agreed that it would probably be for the best.

"Let's go get some lunch," said Ruth, "but if it were me, I'd keep that shed stuff to yourself. At least for a little while, anyway. Not everybody here is as sophisticated as me."

The two friends, for now that was what they were, left Sperare and walked across the yard to the main hall. They passed a group of girls sitting in a circle beneath a tree and Ruth stopped Mary so that she could be introduced. Mary felt shy when she walked up to the circle, but Ruth did all the talking.

"Hi gang," said Ruth, "this is Mary. She just got in. Mary, this is the gang."

Mary provided a weak hello and waved a little. There was a murmur of hellos from the group beneath the tree, but they returned their attention to the previous discussion. Ruth and Mary continued to the main hall while Mary kept her eyes to the ground. Other students were making their way towards the dining room and the chatter made Mary feel smaller. She was not shy back home, although she did keep to herself. If being the new kid in school is hard, being the new kid at St. Philomena's was an exercise in fear. Mary was out of her element and wanted to avoid any unwanted attention. She followed Ruth around like a puppy and quietly observed all that was happening around her.

The dining room was large and held several round tables that filled the center of the room like white lily pads. Each of the walls also produced at least five rows of long picnic tables that stretched across the floor. Ruth and Mary stood in line for food, and each took a white plastic tray that had separate compartments for different portions of food. Mary only realized how hungry she was when she smelt the lunch that had been prepared. The serving staff in the cafeteria were all large women wearing immaculately white aprons and puffy white caps. Mary thought they looked like clouds and she thought about her home.

The line shuffled in procession as Ruth and Mary made their way to the serving stations. There was spaghetti, meatballs, sausages, lasagna, cheeseburgers, hot dogs, pizza, roasted chicken, prime rib, garden salad, potato salad, macaroni salad, tuna salad, chicken salad, mashed potatoes, baked potatoes, french fries, steamed broccoli, steamed carrots, steamed cauliflower, creamed spinach, creamed corn, corn bread, corn on the cob, corn fritters, puff pastry, donuts, ice cream, vanilla pudding, chocolate pudding, butterscotch pudding, rice pudding, bread pudding, tapioca pudding, chocolate covered strawberries, fresh pineapple, cantaloupe, pears, oranges, apples, and three kinds of cake. Mary loaded her tray to capacity and continued in line with her eyes on her food. Her mouth was watering by the time she arrived at the little woman sitting on a stool next to a cash register.

"Swipe your card, dear," she said.

Mary became confused and looked to Ruth for guidance. The other students in line behind them started to grumble and complain about the delay.

"Haven't you got a card?" asked the woman.

"A what?" asked Mary.

"You don't have a card?" asked Ruth.

Mary had no card. She did not know what a card was. No one had told her about a card and her hands began to shake from hunger and embarrassment. The woman at the register sighed and gently took the tray from Mary's hands. Walking towards a barrel marked "compost", the woman dumped the food that Mary had selected and placed the tray in a bus-bin to be collected and cleaned later for another student to use. One who presumably could pay.

"If you don't have a card, then you can't eat from the hot line," said the woman, "go to that little window over there."

She pointed to a small station built into the far wall where a bored looking woman stood behind a half-door. She wore a stained gray apron and a paper hat. Mary looked once more to Ruth for an explanation, but Ruth just gestured with her head for Mary to keep it moving. Mary walked to the little window and stood there biting her finger and not knowing what to say. The bored woman just stared at Mary and began to look annoyed.

"What?" she said.

"I...I haven't got a card," said Mary.

"Did you lose it or are you waiting to get one?"

"I don't know."

"Did you fill out the commissary assistance pamphlet?"

"What's that?"

The woman rolled her eyes. She reached her hand beneath the counter and handed Mary a three-page pamphlet titled "commissary assistance form". Mary took the pamphlet and looked at the woman for answers.

"Fill this out and return it to the financial office in room five hundred," said the woman, "once your application is approved then you can be eligible for commissary assistance. Your parents should have filled this out before you arrived."

Mary felt more tears welling up as she stared blankly at the pamphlet. The woman looked at Mary with a growing understanding of her situation and disappeared behind the counter. The feeling of nausea and mortification had replaced the hunger that occupied Mary's mind only a few minutes ago. Mary's hands were trembling when the woman returned with a brown paper bag and handed it to her.

"This ones on the house," she said, "but we can't provide you with more food until you submit the form."

Mary took the bag. Her voice was shaking as she thanked the woman, and she stuffed the pamphlet in her pants pocket. Mary walked across the cafeteria looking for Ruth, but she had become lost in a sea of clean and happy faces. Not wanting to sit anywhere or talk to anyone, Mary left the dining room out a side door and walked across the yard to sit beneath a tree.

She opened the bag to find a white bread bologna sandwich, a bruised apple, a juice box, and a bag of chips. Mary devoured the food and looked in the bag twice more to see if there had been something that she may have missed. She was still hungry and was trying her best to make food appear in an ordinary paper bag with no history of magic. When no food came, Mary leaned back against the tree and stared ahead into the yard of St. Philomena's.

There were students lounging together and playing games, running, reading, and having fun. Mary would never admit to herself that she wanted to join them and enjoy herself, but she felt utterly alone and scared. She took the pamphlet out of her pocket and began to look it over. It was asking questions about her parents' bank statements, their personal income, equity, collateral, and a few other words that Mary had never heard before. There was a section for her name and address that she understood, but she needed a pen.

An older student reading a book was close to where Mary was sitting. After several minutes of finding the courage, Mary approached her. The older student looked up from her book at Mary and smiled.

"Hello," she said, "you must be new."

"My name is Mary. I just got here today."

"I'm Lucy," said the girl, reaching out a hand, "it's nice to meet you."

Mary's voice cracked as she asked for a pen to which Lucy nodded and reached into her satchel to retrieve one. She handed it to Mary who said thank you but stared back at Lucy without saying anything else. Lucy saw the crumpled pamphlet in Mary's hand and looked back at her with sympathy.

"Would you like some help with that?" she asked.

Mary nodded and sat down next to Lucy. They looked over the pamphlet together and Lucy did her best to help Mary fill out the information. There were a lot of questions regarding the finances of Mary's parents that she would have no way of knowing, but Lucy just smiled and told Mary not to worry. Lucy began to fill out the personal financial information of her parents and Mary thought that Lucy might have been a witch, psychic, or some kind of psychic witch. Mary liked her very much and she admired her confidence. Lucy finished answering the questions and handed the pamphlet back to Mary.

"Here you go," she said, "do you know where the financial office is?"

Marry shook her head no.

"Come on."

Lucy walked Mary back to the main hall and showed her where room five hundred was. She wished Mary good luck and went back outside to continue reading before her next class. The hall was bustling with students leaving the cafeteria and returning to their afternoon activities. Conversations hovered over their heads, mixed with laughter, gossip, and disbelief. Fighting against the current of her new classmates, Mary pushed through the crowd and did her best to find small pockets of space where she could slip past the students. It was not something so terrible as getting beaten up, but someone kept stepping on her feet and she did get poked by a few elbows.

After she had worked her way through the crowd, Mary opened the door to room five-hundred and found a little man with thick glasses sitting behind a small green desk. Mary thought he resembled an owl and almost expected to see a small nest in a corner of the room.

"Yes?" said the little man. He kept his eyes on his work, scribbling furiously on a piece of paper.

"My name is Mary," she said, handing him the pamphlet.

The man took the pamphlet and seemed nearly startled as he saw Mary for the first time. He adjusted his glasses while he looked over the form and made little snorts as he breathed, even though his mouth stayed open. He read it for some time and Mary began to worry that he would say that something was wrong. After reading the pamphlet over, he ripped off a serrated portion from the bottom of a page and placed the rest in a folder. The serrated portion was then brought to a copy machine, scanned, printed out, placed in another folder, and the original portion was removed, placed in an envelope, and filed in a long cabinet drawer. He cleared his throat and spoke plainly as though he was reading from a script.

"Please give us three business days to determine the eligibility of your request for acceptance into the commissary assistance program. Because today is Friday, the following weekend will not count towards the three business days. You can expect to hear a response from us by Wednesday, at the earliest."

He returned to the paperwork laid out across his desk. Mary just stood in place and waited for something to happen. The little man looked at Mary over the rim of his glasses and raised a bushy eyebrow.

"They said I can't get food until I fix this," said Mary.

The little man closed his eyes and nodded to himself. Folding his hands together across his desk, he leaned back and looked at the ceiling to think. He loved puzzles, problem solving, and making sure things were in their proper place. He was not trying to help Mary for the sake of her well-being as much as he was trying to feel better about himself by solving a problem.

"Do you have enough money to pay for the cafeteria until Wednesday?" he asked.

Mary shook her head no.

"Can you call your parents and see if they will send you money until Wednesday?"

"They're on a trip."

"Do you know their phone numbers?"

Mary shook her head no.

"That's ok," he said, opening another filing cabinet, "we should have their contact information on file. What is your last name, please?"

"Kirkland," said Mary.

"Let me see."

The small man retrieved Mary's file with all her application information, admittance forms, acceptance letter, and personal data. He made an uncomfortable face while he looked over Mary's paperwork, and shook his head as he put the file back in the drawer while opening a different cabinet. A different file was pulled, quickly read, and then returned to the filing cabinet. He repeated this action three more times before he stood up and walked past Mary. She could see sweat beginning to form on his face and parts of his clothes were starting to grow darker. His face was red as he closed the door behind him, leaving Mary alone in the room. He poked his head back through the door and asked Mary to follow him.

They walked to the end of the hall, up the stairs and to the left, and down the second-floor landing before arriving at the headmistress' office. The little man cleared his throat, adjusted his collar, and knocked twice. They heard the annoyed voice of the headmistress tell them to come in and they each gulped as they entered. She was sitting behind her desk reading and eating large cherries out of an immaculate marble bowl. These were the biggest cherries that Mary had ever seen. They were nearly the size of plums, but with bright red skin and long green stems. The headmistress ate them carefully and removed the pits from her mouth with a gloved hand. She did not look up from her book when they entered the room.

"What is it?" she asked.

"It's Ms. Kirkland," said the little man, "we don't seem to have her parents' contact information on file, Miss."

The headmistress looked up from her book and removed a cherry pit from her mouth, placing it on a small white plate.

"What do you mean it's not on file?"

"Just that, Miss," he continued, "I've looked in all three copies and photocopies of Ms. Kirkland's admissions paperwork as well as her intake forms. Neither has documented telephone numbers or email addresses for her parents."

"Ms. Kirkland, please wait outside."

"Yes, headmistress," said Mary.

Mary left the office and sat in a small chair against the wall in the hallway. She stared at the red and gold runner carpet that stretched the length of the landing, trying not to think of how scared she was. The carpet was laid with intricate gold patterns and symbols that Mary assumed to be keys and a secret language from another world. It was designed for someone else's world that she could not make any sense of.

Mary had often tried to invent her own language using shapes and squiggles, like the Egyptian hieroglyphics that she had seen in books. The red and gold symbols on the carpet looked nothing like Egyptian hieroglyphics, but she was sure that they told a story all the same. She looked up from the carpet and stared at a painting of St. Sebastian tied to a post and shot full of arrows. His face was looking up to the sky and twisted like a child whose favorite toy had been taken away. There was an expression of disappointment in a world that gave up little hope for optimism, especially when you are covered in so many arrows. Mary felt sick looking at it.

The door to the headmistress' office opened and the little man left, wiping his brow. He gave Mary a weak smile and gestured for her to enter the office. Mary stood up and walked into the headmistress' office to find fresh tea prepared along with an assortment of small cakes, cookies, and a bowl of cherries that were much smaller than the ones which the headmistress had been eating. The headmistress was sitting in a red leather armchair beside the tea table and the chaise lounge where Mary was invited to sit. She was smiling as Mary entered her office, which made the room feel that much more unnatural.

"Please sit down, Ms. Kirkland."

"Yes, headmistress."

Mary sat down in the chaise lounge beside the table, doing her best to ignore the assortment of refreshments that were certainly meant for someone else. The headmistress poured a cup of tea for Mary, added cream and sugar without asking, and handed it to her. Mary accepted the tea with a thank you and searched her cup for traces of poison.

"Please, help yourself," said the headmistress gesturing to the pastries on the table.

Mary accepted a single cookie, which she slowly nibbled and picked at. She felt like a crazy person and did her best not to stare at the headmistress' psychic eyes.

"Thank you for joining me for tea," said the headmistress, "it is not often that I get to enjoy the private company of my students twice in the same day. How has your morning been so far?"

"I tried to get lunch, but I didn't have a card."

"So I've been told. It is a terrible shame that your parents neglected that portion of the application. Would you like us to contact your parents on your behalf? They should be able to send you some money for food until your application is confirmed."

Mary nodded her head and took another bite of her cookie. It tasted like sweet almonds and was filled with a kind of paste that was deliciously unfamiliar. She looked at the other cakes on the table with suspicious hunger while imagining baited traps that would spring upon her and dismember her limbs. With all the fear and paranoia, there was still time to weigh the risk and reward.

"Now Mary, please think carefully. Do you know your parents' phone numbers?"

Mary shook her head.

"That really is very reckless of you, Mary," said the headmistress, "what if something were to happen to you while you were here? How would we be able to get in contact with your parents?"

Mary shrugged because she did not know.

"They had mentioned going on a trip," said the headmistress, "do you remember where they were going?"

Mary thought hard as she tried to remember any details that could be helpful.

"They said they were going to cats kill." Mary remembered this because she found the idea to be upsetting. She liked to think that her parents would not engage in the act, but she also had her doubts on the extent of their behavior.

"Ah, yes. The Catskills. Are they staying with family? Friends?"

"I don't know," said Mary, "I think they're in a hotel."

"Do you remember which hotel?"

Mary shook her head. She took another cookie from the table and ate it in a single bite. The threat of death was no longer important. These were damn good cookies.

"Ok, Ms. Kirkland. I will make an exception in your case. You are welcome to take your lunches and dinners from the commissary assistance program before your application is approved. There will be an itemized invoice to calculate the cost of your meals. This will be sent to your parents at the end of the semester. Once your application is approved, then they will receive separate billing for the commissary assistance program as it is calculated based on their income. You will have food here."

Mary was happy and began to reconsider her initial distrust of the headmistress. Maybe she was not such a terrible person after all. How bad could she be if she had such good cookies? Mary reached for a third, but the headmistress smoothly drew the tea table back out of her reach.

"Thank you for stopping by, Ms. Kirkland," said the headmistress, "if you would please return to your dormitory and continue to study your bible. I feel as though it would be to your benefit."

Mary left the office of the headmistress and walked back across the yard to her dormitory. Lucy was still sitting in the yard reading her book, so Mary approached Lucy to express her gratitude.

"Hi Lucy," said Mary.

"Hello Mary. How'd it go?"

"I think it went ok. She said I can get food from the little hole in the wall. Who's that weird lady there?"

"Her name is Marissa," said Lucy, "she's nice enough, but she can be a little prickly."

"She doesn't look like the other lunch ladies," said Mary, "they look like clouds. She looks like a bird."

"You better watch out for Marissa," said Lucy, "sometimes it's hard to understand her moods. I've seen her do good things and terrible things, all in the same day."

Mary nodded and considered this. It made sense to her that someone could be nice and mean all at once. Mary thought about her grandmother.

"Are you in Sperare?" asked Lucy.

Mary nodded her head.

"Well, I'm in Pasce Spiritum, room ten. If you need help with anything, come find me. I know this place can be a little scary at first."

Lucy held out a closed fist in Mary's direction, but Mary simply looked at her with confusion.

"Bump it," said Lucy.

Mary made a fist and lightly tapped Lucy's, to which Lucy began to laugh.

"Take it easy, Mary. Don't let 'em bring you down."

Mary smiled and left Lucy to return to her reading, feeling exhausted and overwhelmed.

What a weird place, thought Mary, *what a weird, weird place.*

She returned to her room in Sperare, but Ruth was not there. There was a great feeling of relief to have some free time after all that had happened already, and Mary wanted a distraction. She climbed on Ruth's bed to reach the hiding place. Upon removing the brick, she found a small parcel wrapped in a napkin and tied with string sitting on top of her book. She took it out of the compartment and read the note scribbled on the side with pen:

Mary! I'm sorry about lunch. Thought you might need this. -R

The back of the parcel was sealed with the drawing of a jolly roger in red pencil. Mary opened the paper to find three large cranberry walnut cookies wrapped in light pink tissue. She smiled at the gesture and took the cookies with her book down from the secret space. Sitting on her bed with the pilfered snack and her forbidden book made the place feel a little less crazy. There was still much to do and a great deal of adjustment to be made on Mary's part, but the unsolicited kindness from older students and those of her own age became a promising development. Mary opened The Wind in the Willows to a chapter titled "Dulce Domum" and was suddenly struck with a wonderful idea.

8. I Am A Bird And I Eat Little Worms

"Villagers all, this frosty tide,
Let your doors swing open wide,
Though wind may follow, and snow beside,
Yet draw us in by your fire to bide;
Joy shall be yours in the morning!
Here we stand in the cold and the sleet,
Blowing fingers and stamping feet,
Come from far away you to greet—
You by the fire and we in the street—
Bidding you joy in the morning!

For ere one half of the night was gone,
Sudden a star has led us on,
Raining bliss and benison—
Bliss to-morrow and more anon,
Joy for every morning!
Goodman Joseph toiled through the snow—
Saw the star o'er a stable low;
Mary she might not further go—
Welcome thatch, and litter below!
Joy was hers in the morning!
And then they heard the angels tell
'Who were the first to cry NOWELL?
Animals all, as it befell,
In the stable where they did dwell!
Joy shall be theirs in the morning!"

Mary looked up from the paper she was reading and waited for the approval of the committee that sat before her. Three days had passed since Mary's arrival to St. Philomena's, and she had just presented her first assignment. She was told to memorize and recite a passage from the bible that she found moving and spoke to her personal spiritual mission. Finding the bible to be too daunting, and given the time constraints that she was under, she decided to crib a song from her copy of The Wind in the Willows. She took time over the weekend to recite it in her room with Ruth, who helped Mary get the inflection right and make it sound more biblical. Standing in front of the committee made her nervous, but she also felt proud of her trick. The committee consisted of Mr. Lewis, the headmistress, Ms. Tristan who was the dorm mother for the Sperare house, a Ms. Canister who was the head of the history department, Mrs. Lipwitz who led the arts department, and Ms. Fingerblatz who was the dorm mother for the Pasce Spiritum house.

After explaining that she had been unable to memorize the passage, but had it written down, Mary was permitted to present it with the acknowledgement that she would automatically lose a few marks for incomplete work. When she finished reading her perfidious scripture, there was a muted conversation from the committee that barely registered above a whisper. The only committee members uninvolved in the deliberation was Mr. Lewis and the headmistress, who sat in the center of the group and kept a fixed gaze of silence upon Mary. The headmistress' face betrayed no singular expression.

"Thank you, Ms. Kirkland," said Ms. Canister, "that was indeed a beautiful passage. Now, which book from the bible had you selected this scripture from?"

"...Psalms," said Mary, after taking a moment to remember what she and Ruth had practiced. This was met with nods of approval from a few committee members and led to their writing small notes on pieces of paper.

"And why is this passage important to you?" asked Ms. Fingerblatz.

"...it's important to me because...my father used to read it to me when I was sick and it made me feel better," said Mary.

This was met with a few more nods and more little notes jotted down by the committee. The headmistress did not move from her focus, and it was making Mary sweat a little. The magnetic gaze had consumed Mary's attention and made it difficult for her to think about anything else. The three days at St. Philomena's had done very little to help her adjust comfortably. She still very much would have rather been home.

"How do you feel this passage will be helpful for your development here at St. Philomena's?" asked Ms. Tristan.

"...this passage will help me...it'll help me..." Mary was stuck trying to think of a good answer. Before she could think of the right thing to say, the headmistress slowly stood from her seat and asked the last question Mary wanted to hear.

"What is the title of this Psalm, Ms. Kirkland?"

"...it's the Christmas psalm."

"And who wrote this psalm?"

Time froze in a personal hell as Mary began to die a little inside. She was unprepared for this line of questioning, and she could not think quickly enough. The headmistress' face was immovable.

"How long have you been a liar, Ms. Kirkland?"

Now Mary was truly frightened. She could feel herself turning red as her body began to shake and her stomach turned itself into one big knot. The top of her head began to sweat. Considering the design of the school and its history of demanding strict obedience, Mary thought about what kind of torture devices they had in the basement for liars and heathens.

"I know that all children are liars," said the headmistress, looking down the line of the committee members, "we should *all* know that children are liars. It is part of their nature. What I did not know is how stupid and foolish this committee could be to believe the lies of a child."

The committee looked at each other and grew increasingly uncomfortable, except for Mr. Lewis who had not been paying much attention. He had managed to balance the rounded end of a pen upright on the table. The headmistress sat down and folded her hands in front of herself.

"Ms. Kirkland," she said, "in lieu of your ability to produce the assignment, and due to your deception for which this farce was performed, you will be assigned custodial duties in each dormitory for the next two weeks. After which time if you cannot produce a memorized scripture, then your custodial duties will persist for an additional two months."

The room was silent enough to hear the idea of a pin dropping. Ms. Tristan attempted to clear her throat, but it was still too dry. She took a sip of water, raised her hand, and turned to the headmistress.

"If I may," she said, "if I may make a suggestion..."

The headmistress turned her head towards Ms. Tristan in such an aggressive manner that her hypnotic eyes seemed to glow with rage. They had caught the light like a cat preparing for the killing stroke. Ms. Tristan lowered her hand and retracted her suggestion.

"Also," continued the headmistress, "for wasting this committee's valuable time and energy, you will lose your lunch and dinner privileges for today. You will fast until this time tomorrow, with the exception of water. If you do eat anything within the next twenty-four hours, then the punishment will reset until its completion. Consider your time of fasting to be an offering to the Lord. Please return to your dormitory and familiarize yourself with our facilities equipment."

Mary wanted to throw up. She looked across the faces of the committee members for any consolation but found that none of them would meet her plea. Having no voice to defend herself, Mary turned around and marched back to her dormitory, blinded by her own anger. She fell upon her bed and sobbed deeply from fear, from rage, and from the seemingly endless well of the headmistress's cruelty. So disturbed was she in the chaotic flood of emotions that she did not notice that both Ms. Tristan and Mr. Lewis were standing at her door. Mr. Lewis knocked on the frame three times before stepping into the room while Ms. Tristan lingered in the doorway.

"It is a nasty and necessary business, Ms. Kirkland," he said, "I would like to think that you would be able to understand why these consequences are unavoidable. However, it is unfortunate that you have chosen to become upset."

Mary buried her face in her pillow and did her best to stifle the sobs that were catching in her throat.

"Consider the suffering that our Lord had to endure in his time. For in his own suffering, he is responsible for our salvation," Mr. Lewis began searching through the room and opening drawers, "in our work, we work for Him. Just as we suffer, we suffer for Him. It is as though we are all on Christ's path, in our own insignificant way. Please stand up, Ms. Kirkland."

With her whole body shaking and unbalanced, Mary stood up and crossed the small room to sit on Ruth's bed. She felt sick and unable to stand on her own. Mr. Lewis lifted Duck from Mary's pillow, looked it over, shot a glance towards Mary, and gently handed Duck to her. Mary embraced Duck as though he would save her life or, at the very least, take her away from this awful place. Mr. Lewis then proceeded to undo Mary's bed sheets and turn her mattress over. After he had done so and failed to find satisfaction in his pursuit of contraband, he knelt to eye-level with Mary. Her body was shaking with sorrow and rage.

"I'm sorry Ms. Kirkland," said Mr. Lewis, "would you please stand up once more?"

Mary said nothing but crossed the room and sat on her exposed bed frame as Mr. Lewis then disassembled Ruth's bed just as he had Mary's. Ms. Tristan stood in the door frame staring at nothing. Her ability to dissociate at will was legendary at St. Philomena's. At that moment in time, she was a million miles away, sitting poolside in the hot sun and being fed seedless grapes by several large and mostly naked men who all happened to be covered in exotic oils that made them smell like warm cinnamon sticks. They all had the face of John Stamos.

Finding nothing consequential, Mr. Lewis turned to Mary.

"Where is the book, Ms. Kirkland?"

Mary sat on the frame of her bed squeezing Duck in her arms and wishing to disappear. She did not want to look at Mr. Lewis or Ms. Tristan and she did not want to exist anymore.

"Ms. Kirkland, we need to remove the book from your possession as contraband. I also enjoyed Kenneth Grahame in my youth, but it is not your place to plagiarize his work. Especially if it is from a book that you're not supposed to have."

Ms. Tristan started to say something about karaoke, but she trailed off, cutting her own voice before it made its way across the room. Mary could not breathe for the tears that she shed were causing her to choke on her own words. She pleaded with Mr. Lewis that it was a good book and how badly she needed to have it. Her admission to the book's existence was her undoing as Mr. Lewis began to calmly look around the room with more attention. His pacing was slow as he searched the room and his eyes moved with the calculation of a nocturnal predator. It was then he noticed that one of the taller points in the opposite wall had a brick that looked a bit crooked. He walked towards the secret compartment in the wall as Mary began to cry harder and scream "No" over and over. Mr. Lewis easily removed the loose brick and smiled as he looked at Mary.

"Ah," he said, "I've found it."

Mr. Lewis removed all the books from the space, as well as two chocolate bars, a deck of cards, a handmade slingshot, Ruth's flower, and Mary's grandfather's compass. He placed the contraband carefully in a plastic bag.

"These are a considerable number of possessions for someone who has only just arrived," said Mr. Lewis, "I couldn't possibly imagine that these are all your items. Would it be fair to assume that some of these belong to Ms. Rubenstein?"

Mary stared at the floor, unable to think or even consider speaking. All she could do was whimper and shake as she sat on her bedframe.

"We'll check in with Ms. Rubenstein later," said Mr. Lewis, "in the meantime it would be better to reassemble your room now before you begin your newly appointed custodial duties. I find that if I leave my personal housekeeping until the last minute, it seems a more daunting task."

Mr. Lewis left the room in disarray while Ms. Tristan lingered in the door frame. She shook her head and made a sound that could have been mistaken for an apology before following Mr. Lewis out of Sperare. Mary held Duck tightly while she lifted a finger up to her mouth and nibbled its side. Her life as she knew it was over.

The last remnants of her previous home had been taken from her, and for no good reason. There was a rage growing beneath her despair. A mixture of all possible negative emotions coated her stomach and rose in her blood, becoming evenly distributed throughout her circulatory system. Mary imagined that her blood had turned black and cold as it ran through her veins and poisoned her mind. She was more than happy to embrace the change and hoped it was permanent. Ms. Tristan returned with a bucket, a mop, gloves, and other cleaning supplies to ensure a thorough job could be performed by Mary. She knelt to where Mary was sitting and awkwardly patted her on the back. Mary wanted to spit in her face.

Cleaning had never been a priority for Mary in her previous life as a child. Now that she had officially grown up it was not shaping up to be much better. It was not that Mary was a dirty person, but the general order of things did not bring her any special joy. She certainly did not mind playing in the dirt and the mud. Nearly all her clothes were stained with grass and the life of the wild, but she bathed regularly and had a reasonable grasp of hygiene. However, excessive cleaning was seen in her eyes as wasteful in the grand scheme of things. Why would anyone want to spend so much time cleaning when there was so much of the world to explore?

Unfortunately, her personal opinions had little say in the matter as this new cleaning business had been administered as a punishment. To avoid further disciplinary actions, Mary set to work in her room and began to mentally prepare for the task of cleaning the rest of the public spaces in the other dormitories.

It took roughly an hour for Mary to put her and Ruth's room back in order. Flipping mattresses is not an easy task for any eleven-year-old, but Mary managed with a minimal amount of trouble. The drawers were stuffed back into their compartments and the bibles were neatly placed on the bedside tables. Ruth returned from one of her classes and asked how Mary's morning performance had been received. It was briefly explained to Ruth that the recital had not been successful. Mary explained her punishment through gasps of breath and the shivering voice of a broken little girl. At first Ruth thought that Mary was just being sensitive, but after she did a quick scan of the room, she realized that something had happened.

"What's going on?" asked Ruth, "why's everything so...crooked?"

"Mr. Lewis...he," Mary trailed off as she looked at the ground. Unable to meet Ruth's eyes, Mary glanced at the brick that had once protected their contraband.

Ruth jumped onto her bed and removed the loose brick from the wall. She dug her hand into the compartment but found that all her hidden treasures had been removed.

"Asshole!" she said.

"I'm sorry," said Mary.

"How did this happen?"

"I'm sorry," said Mary.

"It's ok," said Ruth, "this isn't your fault. We're gonna get it back."

"What?"

"All of it," said Ruth, "We're taking it all back and we're gonna get out of this monkey house."

Mary liked the sound of that, so they began planning. It was agreed that whatever happened next would be done in secret. Nothing was to be decided without discussion, and everything had to be calculated and agreed upon. First, Ruth would begin her reconnaissance work with some of the older students who had been at St. Philomena's the longest. The thought was that they could have some idea as to where confiscated items were kept. Time was a factor as well, to be sure that none of their books would be destroyed, if they had not been burned already.

"In the meantime, we should go about our business and stay out of trouble," said Ruth, "you have to clean the dorms and I'll ask the older kids about what they know."

"Ok," said Mary, although she felt like she was getting the short end of the stick.

"I'm going to get to it, then," said Ruth, "I'll try to bring you some food later."

Ruth threw Mary a peace sign before she left Sperare to run reconnaissance. Mary grumbled as she prepared her tools for the punishment that she did not know how to perform. Still devastated about losing her book and compass, invigorated by the heroic optimism of Ruth, Mary stuck her mop in the bucket and started wheeling it down the hall to fill it with water and cleaning detergent.

There are a multitude of terrible feelings that any one person can experience in a lifetime. Those with the least amount of good luck will experience the worst of them several times, sometimes all at once. The three worst feelings that Mary could not stand were being cold, wet, or hungry. If someone happened to deliver all three simultaneously, that would be about the saddest situation. The strangest thoughts will come around as your mind struggles to think about anything else.

Mary had made her way to the end of the hall to where a faucet was sticking out of the wall. The bucket and mop were cumbersome, and Mary had no real prior experience in mopping or proper bucket diplomacy. She had seen it done on television and thought that it could not have been that difficult, but she had no idea how to calculate the soap to water ratio.

The entire bottle of cleaning solution was emptied into the bucket because the hall that she had to mop was very long. It made sense that since she was cleaning the hallway once, it should only take one bottle of cleaning solution to do the job. If Mary had taken the time to read the instructions on the bottle, she would have seen that she only needed half a cup of solution per three gallons of water.

When she began to fill the bucket with water soap bubbles and foam began to flow over the sides and onto the floor. In a panic, Mary tried to pull the bucket out from under the faucet, but it was too heavy for her to lift. The whole mess slipped out of her hands and spilled all over Mary and the ground. The river of suds ran down the length of the hall and when Mary tried to move out of the way, she slipped and fell onto the floor. She landed hard on the tile and was soaking wet through her uniform. She tried to stand up but slipped and fell again just as hard as the first time. Crawling carefully on her hands and knees, she made it back to her room where the floor was dry and sat there for a while next to the radiator. She was beginning to feel warm again when she heard the voices of the other Sperare residents begin to file back to their dorm rooms.

What followed was the sound of several dozen students falling and sliding across the soaking wet floor. As they did not have time to warn each other, and before the next student had any idea what was going on, they would yelp, fall, and slide against the walls bouncing like marbles. The noises were tremendous as the yelps became screams and the screams became cries. Howls and wails echoed down the hall while Mary sat next to her radiator turning white as the blood left her face.

Ms. Tristan had arrived on the scene to find a pile of students lying on the dormitory floor. At first, she had thought that they were committed to some kind of non-violent protest, but it did not take long for her to understand the situation after she slipped and fell as well. She was fine though. She managed to instigate a dissociative state before she hit the floor. This allowed her body to go limp and evenly absorb much of the impact. It still hurt, but she was fine. Mary did her best to make herself invisible. So much for keeping a low profile.

The infirmary was busy that day after the Sperare incident. Five of the students had minor hairline fractures and a few others had some bad sprains, but nobody was seriously injured. After the dust had settled, there was a small unspoken understanding that they would have to miss a few days of classes. No one seemed to mind this outcome, but they were still very much annoyed with Mary. In the spirit of the school's legal accountability, a decision was made to remove Mary from custodial duties and find different work for her that would cause the least amount of damage to her classmates and the faculty.

Mary found herself once more in the office of the headmistress, but she was not frightened anymore. Mary was angry and no amount of cookies would be enough to bring back her good graces. The air in the room had a denser feel than the last time she was in the headmistress' office, but that may have just been the insurmountable rage that was bubbling within her. Mary was annoyed and felt like picking a fight. She felt as though she had been set up for failure and that she was being blamed for something that could have easily been avoided had she simply been left alone. There were no cherries or tea on this visit.

"I would like to think," said the headmistress, "that you did not intentionally mean to harm any of your fellow classmates."

"No, headmistress." Mary was trying to remain calm, but she could tell that she was making the face of an irritated octopus.

"Indeed. However, in the interest of your classmates' health and safety, as well as everyone else's, you will be reassigned from the dormitory custodial detail and be placed as a facilities technician in the cafeteria."

"Yes, headmistress."

"Your work will be focused on washing the dishes, pots, pans, and cutlery. I would almost be impressed if you could find some way to commit further harm with a dish rag."

Mary accepted this challenge and thought about snapping everybody on the butt with her mighty dish rag. Her rag would be mighty, and no butt would be safe.

"Yes, headmistress," said Mary.

"Report to the cafeteria immediately. They are nearly finished with lunch and will need the kitchen cleaned before dinner service."

Mary rose to leave before the headmistress cleared her throat, asking Mary to face her once more.

"Remember, Ms. Kirkland," she said, "you are still fasting for today. If I find that you have eaten one morsel of food, then your punishment will be extended and expanded upon. It would do you well to keep that in mind and keep your mind on your duties."

"Yes, headmistress."

Mary thought of new and interesting ways to have the headmistress's eyes removed. She could turn into a bat and pluck them out as the headmistress slept. She could dig a tiger trap in the ground and lay pointed sticks to catch her falling body. Maybe she could find that bottle of good beetle food and put a few drops in her eyes. Let the beetles take care of it.

All this and more filled Mary's mind as she entered the cafeteria and tried to ignore the gnawing in her stomach from her penitent fasting. Lunch was underway and everybody else was enjoying themselves. There were full plates and full bellies with full smiles and hearts filled with laughter and the promise of a future filled with love and fulfillment. The students were talking about their future wedding days and what their husbands would look like. What they would do for a career. How many children they were planning on having along with their names. Some girls explained how their horses were infinitely better than the other girls' horses. One student was complaining about their recent vacation to Rome and how their parents would force them to visit boring old museums.

Mary walked through all this and went to speak to lunch lady Marissa, who was idly chewing gum and blowing bubbles the size of her head. Marissa saw Mary approaching and popped the bubble with the pointed tip of her fingernail.

"You get that paperwork straightened out, hon?" asked Marissa, chewing all the while.

"Yes, ma'am," said Mary, "I've been sent to wash dishes."

"That a fact? You're a little short for a dishwasher, but we don't discriminate around here as long as you ain't afraid of work. You on punishment?"

"Yes ma'am."

"Ok," said Marissa. She shook her head and looked around, trying to figure out what to do. "Hold on a sec, hon. Hey Jen? Jen?! JENNAAY! Jesus, quit fuckin' around and show this, I'm sorry, what's your name?"

"Mary."

"Thanks, hon. JENNIFER! Goddammit, will you come show Mary what the hell she has to do?" Marissa pulled out a magazine and began to thumb through the pages. She snorted and laughed to herself saying, "They say they're punishing you girls, but then we're the ones that get stuck babysitting."

An alarmingly thin and frail looking woman whom Mary presumed to be Jennifer came shuffling out of the back onto the cafeteria floor. Her hair was long and hung down limply from beneath her hairnet. She held her hands together in front of her body as though they were likely to fall off if she were to let them go. There was a slouch to her back that caused her to waddle from side to side when she walked, but she did have eyes that were kind, if not a little sad. Jennifer spoke in a series of mumbles that were too low for Mary to understand completely, but she did get the gist of it with some of Jennifer's quick hand gestures. She followed Jennifer into the back through a pair of hard plastic swinging doors and entered the inner workings of the cafeteria.

Her first impression of the kitchen was that it was hot. It was very hot, and everything looked wet. There were giant machines with purposes that baffled Mary's understanding. So many different noises flew across the room from so many different locations that it was difficult to know what noise was coming from where. The room was filled with women and machines all shouting and moving in syncopation. She followed Jennifer into the back where a massive metal cube stamped HOBART spit steam and heat and noise in every direction out from its metallic seams. Mary had never heard such a racket, but she liked the energy.

She was about to ask Jennifer a question before she found herself being dressed in an apron that was about three sizes too big for her. Someone else was standing behind her tucking her hair up into a cloth cap and she was handed the smallest pair of anti-slip shoes that they had. They were still too big for Mary, so Jennifer took a magazine out from somebody's hands, ripped out a few crumpled pages, and used them to fill in the empty spaces. Jennifer took a step backwards and looked at Mary. It was not elegant, but it was the best they could do, given the circumstances. Jennifer mumbled something and gave Mary a weak thumbs up before shuffling back to her station. A large woman with thick white hair walked up to Mary and presented her with one of the warmest smiles that she had ever seen. She looked like Mrs. Santa Claus.

"Hello, dear," she said through a thick French accent, "my name is Therese. What is your name, little one?"

"Mary."

"Bonjour, Mary! So blessed to have the name of our holy mother," Therese took Mary's hand and shook it confidently, "will you be washing the pots with me today?

"Yes, ma'am."

"Allow me to introduce you to my friend Hobart."

Therese slapped the side of the dishwasher with the word HOBART stamped into its sliding door.

"Mary, this is Hobart. Hobart, meet Mary. Good. Now we are all friends."

Although Therese's intentions were playful and sincere, Mary was feeling too hungry and emotionally exhausted to appreciate the game. There had been too many sad days, and they were beginning to take their toll. She was feeling more grown up by the minute.

"But Madame," said Therese, "you have not yet grown tall enough to reach the sink. I will fetch a stool for you."

Therese shuffled off to a utility closet while Mary waited by the three-bay sink. No sooner had Therese left Mary than she managed to return from the opposite side of the room. An unfamiliar look crossed her face as Mary stood in confusion.

"Hello dear," she said, "my name is Louise. What's your name, little one?"

Mary was in no mood for these games. It was bad enough that she was feeling abused and exploited. She crossed her arms and looked away in defiance of this patronizing tone that she was receiving. With all that she had already suffered, she would not be made to feel small.

"I already told you. My name is Mary."

"But we have only just met," said Louise, "would you like to meet Hobart?"

Mary stomped her foot and pouted as she felt teased by this woman. This was by far the most infuriating punishment she had ever received.

The thought of spending her free time outside of class being teased and starved felt like an expulsion from humanity.

"Cet enfant n'a pas de sourire," said Louise.

There was a moment of tense silence as Mary and Louise sized each other up before Therese joined them with a step stool for Mary. Frustration turned to the absence of thought as Mary tried to process the two identical women that stood before her.

"I am Therese."

"And I am Louise."

"We are twins."

"Well, twin sisters."

"So to speak."

"Quite Literally."

Mary had never met a twin before, much less a full set. Embarrassment filled her heart as she realized that she had overreacted, but she was too hungry to think about it for long. From the movies she had seen Mary had to believe that there was always an evil twin. She wondered which one had committed the most atrocities.

"There is a third," said Louise, "but we have not heard from her in several years."

"It is true," said Therese, "one day we are enjoying a fine meal at home, the three of us, and the next minute..."

"Poof."

"Into thin air."

"Like a fart into a ceiling fan."

Louise released a loud example of flatulence that was so impressive that Mary could not help but laugh. Therese protested through her own laughter as she fanned the air away from her face. The art of gastrointestinal expression was lost on Therese, but Louise herself was quite proud.

"What happened to your third sister?" asked Mary.

"Well, I believe she has joined the army," said Louise.

"And I believe she has married a farmer," said Therese, "so, to answer your question,"

"We do not know."

Mary nodded with a growing understanding that people can suddenly flit in and out of our lives. She wondered how many people she would meet in her life and how many would stay. How many people would she lose? Her eyes had been resting on the floor while Louise and Therese continued debating their sister's whereabouts.

"Ok, mon petite," said Louise, "up we go."

Mary climbed the step stool to where she could reach the chambered sink and the levers for the Hobart dishwashing machine. The smell of discarded food waste and standing water made Mary wrinkle her nose and look away. It was a putrid smell that was so pronounced that she could almost taste it. It made her feel dizzy and a little sick.

"So," said Therese, "it is quite simple. Take the dirty plate. Give it a spray. Put the plate on the rack. Put the rack into Hobart. Drop the gate and let it work. That is all."

Therese clapped her hands twice to emphasize the simplicity. Mary nodded her head. It really did seem simple enough. Louise smiled down at Mary.

"You remind me of my youngest, Clarissa," she said, "she is the youngest of my five and the absolute best at committing mischief."

"Five?!" said Therese, "if you have five children, then what happened to your other two?"

"Those are yours," said Louise, "never in my life have I had seven children."

"You have seven, I have five!"

"If that is the case then what has happened to your ass? That does not come from five children. Six, maybe, but definitely seven."

"My ass has not changed in ten years!"

"And how old is your youngest?!"

This continued for some time as Mary did her best to keep up with the conversation. Having disappeared from the observations of the sisters, Mary turned her focus to the sink filled with foul mystery. She reached her hands into the water and immediately pulled them back because it was much too hot and burned her skin. She jumped and made a noise that broke the argument between Louise and Therese. The maternal instincts of a caretaker overpowered their feud as they both sprang into action. Louise produced two rubber gloves out of thin air while Therese made sure that Mary was ok. They fitted her with gloves and tightened the wrists with rubber bands so as not to fall from her smaller hands. Once they were convinced that Mary was alright, the two sisters jumped right back into their argument and left Mary to her work.

Mary did her best and it was an unremarkable day. Not ideal by any stretch of the imagination, but it was tolerable and much better than having to clean entire dormitories. She was perched above the rotten sink water for much of the night, which helped to distract her from the intense hunger that she felt. The hunger came in waves of pain that accompanied the quick strikes of deep need. They would come frequently but were becoming less and less pronounced as Mary began to grow accustomed to the sensation.

There was a kind of meditation that developed from the repetitive motion of monotonous work. The rhythmic beat and mechanical noises from the dishwashing machine created small melodies that Mary would write songs for in her head. She was grateful for a new way to pass the time while she tried not to burn her hands or die of hunger. The lyrics would be re-written several times, but the original composition went like this:

I am a bird and I eat little worms
No one knows where I live
But I'm brown and I'm good
I am up in a tree
And I know what I need
I am up in a tree
And I know what I need

The song continued like this for most of the night with a few alterations to the lyrics. Because she had spent so much time listening to the same rhythm play over and over from the dishwasher, the tune was then embedded in Mary's memory. It helped to distract her from hunger and the sorrows that had stood to greet her at St. Philomena's.

Mary was helping Jennifer carry bags of garbage out to the dumpsters at the end of the night when Marissa appeared from around the corner of the building. She was smoking a cigarette and sipping from a metal flask. She passed the flask to Jennifer who took a sip and handed it back to Marissa.

"How'd your first day go?" asked Marissa.

"It's ok," said Mary, "it was smelly."

"Yeah, it's not glamorous, but it's alright."

Marissa took another sip and then deposited the flask into the front pocket of her apron. She stubbed out the cigarette and let a long plume of smoke out of her lungs. It looked pretty when it dissipated into the night.

"You comin' back tomorrow?" asked Marissa.

"Yes," said Mary, "for two weeks, I think."

"Shit girl, you must have done something real bad. Wait a minute, did you eat anything today?"

Mary felt the hunger pains double as she was reminded of her fasting.

"No, I'm not supposed to."

"Jesus," said Marissa, "these fuckin' people. How old are you?"

"Eleven."

Marissa sucked her teeth and muttered something under her breath that Mary did not understand. She missed half of what Marissa said, but she was getting better at remembering curse words. The best ones were already cataloged in the back of her mind for later use.

"Hold on," said Marissa.

Marissa went back into the kitchen and emerged with a cheeseburger, a small bag of fries, and a slice of apple pie. Mary thought it may have been a trick, but she was too hungry to consider any consequences. She took the food and thanked Marissa as she walked across the yard back to Sperare. It was dark and Mary tried her best to remain hidden while she broke her fast, so she sat beneath a tree and ate her meal in secret. She tried to pace herself, but the food was consumed with such veracity that by the time Mary was finished she was too full to move. The stars were spread across the sky and before Mary knew it, she had fallen asleep in the warm autumn night beneath the pignut hickory tree.

What a weird place, thought Mary, *what a weird, weird place.*

9. And What About the Bears?

Mary awoke with the dawn. Her clothes were damp from morning dew, and she had a tremendous headache. The previous day's fasting had taken its toll on her faculties and a terrible thirst was what woke her. It was quiet in the lonesome morning with a thin translucent mist covering the grounds. She was cold, but unbothered as solitude had become a luxury to be savored in its rarity. A deer silently walked across the yard a little way off and Mary lay still as she watched it cautiously graze. She wondered if it was the same deer that she had seen the day she arrived. There was a feeling of peace in the early gray morning as all was quiet except for the doves that sang their morning song. For the first time in a long stretch of bad days, Mary fell in love with the world. Brushing the grass and dirt from her clothes, she trudged sleepily back to Sperare to try and get some proper sleep before beginning her very first classes.

She was still being oriented to the school and had not attended any of her assigned lesson plans yet, but today would be her first introduction to the academic curriculum. This did not feel like any first day of school that Mary had experienced before. There were still the lingering anxieties that came with being a stranger in a new place. With the indoctrination by the headmistress and a series of collected punishments, none of which Mary considered justifiable, any real mystery as to how St. Philomena's operated had left her mind.

Mary was nervous to meet her classmates because she had only experienced embarrassment in their presence. Between the misunderstanding in the cafeteria line, the mop incident, and the sense of alienation that came from being the only student working in the kitchen, it would be difficult for Mary to concentrate on her classes or even consider them to be important. There was a strong concern that she had already garnered a reputation without having spoken to anyone directly, other than Lucy and Ruth. Her mind was also focused on the retrieval of her and Ruth's confiscated items as well as the eventual escape from the school. There was a sense of urgency to these plans that felt more important than her classes.

The pain in her head was similar to the sensation of several hammers striking the inside of Mary's brain. It wore through her strength as she returned to her room and fell onto her bed. Ruth was gently snoring in the bliss of sleep as Mary closed her eyes.

Ms. Tristan was at the foot of Mary's bed in what felt like no more than a few minutes later. Mary had accidentally slept through her first class and was in danger of missing the start of her second. Ms. Tristan was emphasizing the importance of punctuality in one's responsibilities as Mary crawled out of her bed. She felt like a slug as she began to splash water on her face from the basin beneath her window. Mary brushed her teeth and went to her second class wearing the clothes she had on from the night before. The lingering smell of dishwater clung to her uniform and brought a slight nausea to accompany her headache. The warning bell rang for the beginning of class just as Mary took a seat among her fellow students.

Her teacher, Mrs. Hoarfrost, passed out copies of the book they had been reading. It was presented as an important piece of classic English literature, but it was a boring story about the problems of a wealthy family and the impending marriages of their children. There were only a handful of words that Mary understood as she struggled to piece the sentences together without falling asleep. Instead of asking for clarification or help, she scanned the words and tried to fill in the blanks as best she could. After twenty minutes of reading, Mrs. Hoarfrost asked the class to close their books and begin a discussion of the day's lesson. She stood in the front of the room and clasped her hands together with the kind of enthusiasm that would frighten most cats.

"Before we begin dissecting the thrilling times that were Victorian England, I would like to welcome and introduce Ms. Kirkland to St. Philomena's. She has only just arrived a few days ago but has already managed to leave an impression upon our headmistress. Ms. Kirkland, would you stand up please?"

There was a small wave of giggles as Mary stood up and looked at the ground shyly. Receiving attention from strangers made her uncomfortable, especially if it was not on her terms. She quietly said hello and stood still, not quite sure what to do. The girls sitting next to Mary made faces about how bad her clothes smelled. The combination of cotton and polyester fabric was still damp and felt thick against her skin. Mary was able to smell her own clothes, but she tried to convince herself that it must have been someone else.

"Ms. Kirkland," said Mrs. Hoarfrost, "would you please explain to us the underlying metaphor in today's reading?"

Mary stood in her anxieties with no idea what to say. She did not know what a metaphor was, and she certainly did not understand half of what she had read. She knew that three people had been sitting on a sofa arguing about dinner, but that was all that she could comprehend from the reading. She cleared her throat as it had suddenly run completely dry.

"What, um...what's a metaphor?"

The class began to snicker, and some students shook their heads in ridicule of Mary's ignorance. She started to sweat and regretted asking the question. Mrs. Hoarfrost also shook her head, but it was more from a place of pity.

"A metaphor," she said, "is a suggested meaning represented by a different phrasing. For example: 'Time is money' is a metaphor for the value of time. 'She's an early bird' is a metaphor for productivity. Do you understand?"

Mary did not understand but stood where she was and waited for the end of the world. Sadly, it did not come. More laughter and groans began to emanate from her classmates and her damp clothes were beginning to feel hot.

"She's really out of her depth," said a student.

"Her brain is a dishrag now," said another.

"She doesn't have a leg to stand on."

"That's an idiom, idiot!"

"I'm not an idiot!"

"No, you're just ugly!"

The ridicule between Mary's classmates had evolved into a slight riot as different students piped in their own insults and opinions. Mary slowly began to sit down at her desk and bit the side of her finger so that she could feel anything other than this mortification. She did not like where this was going, but she was glad to have the classroom's attention diverted away from herself. Mrs. Hoarfrost decided to end the discussion before it led to bloodshed.

"That is enough," she said, "that is enough! Now I can appreciate the fact that Mary is ignorant, considering her upbringing and her personal academic history, but you should all know better than to behave like a group of savages. You will all take out your workbooks and write five hundred words on the importance of high literature. Ms. Kirkland, if you would please join me in the hallway."

The jeers of her fellow classmates followed Mary and Mrs. Hoarfrost out of the classroom and into the hallway as the door closed behind them. Mary wanted to cry, but she thought she may need her tears for later. Everything about St. Philomena's had made Mary want to cry and she still had a headache from the morning.

"Ms. Kirkland I would appreciate it if you did not continue to disrupt my class. Now I enjoy a good joke as much as the next person, but there is no justification for impeding the education of your fellow classmates. You cannot expect the rest of the world to slow to your pace just because you're stupid. If you do instigate another disruption, then I will be forced to send you to speak with the headmistress."

No sooner had the words left her mouth than Mr. Lewis approached them with a dire, if not entirely too formal, look on his face.

"Good morning, Mrs. Hoarfrost," he said, "hello Ms. Kirkland. The headmistress has requested your presence immediately. Please join me in her office."

"Right now?" asked Mary.

"Right now."

Mrs. Hoarfrost pursed her lips in stifled frustration. She felt slighted from her opportunity to assert her castigating authority over Mary, but there was no room to argue with Mr. Lewis. She knew that no good would come from it.

Mrs. Hoarfrost did find some slight satisfaction in knowing that no one was ever summoned to speak with the headmistress in times of celebration. She gave Mary a smile, excusing her from the remainder of the class to which Mary made a mock curtsey and twisted her own voice as she said thank you. Mr. Lewis led Mary up the stairs and into room three-thirteen with the kind of pacing that suggested imperative. This was something which Mary was becoming quite familiar with; except this time, they walked without speaking to each other. Mr. Lewis had usually been keen enough to have a sardonic word to say on most topics, especially if it was something that Mary would much rather not discuss. This was different and Mary was already fed up. With a light knock on the door, they were both summoned inside by the headmistress.

"Good morning, Ms. Kirkland," she said without standing or looking at Mary, "I have received some information that we need to discuss privately."

The headmistress made a gesture to Mr. Lewis, who took his cue and left the room. Mary sat on the little wooden chair in front of the headmistress's desk and crossed her arms. She was over this shit. Mary did not care if she missed her first class. She did not care if the headmistress knew that she ate a cheeseburger the night before. Mary felt humiliated and angry at the world. She was angry with her parents for sending her to St. Philomena's. She hoped that they were having a terrible time on their trip, and she wished they were dead. Whatever it was that the headmistress wanted to discuss, Mary felt ready for war.

"Your parents have died," said the headmistress, "you have my condolences. You will be permitted to remain in our custody for the semester until a member of your extended family can be contacted. When the semester is over, and if a family member is unreachable, the state will become your legal guardian and place you in a suitable transient home until you can be processed and placed in the foster care system. You will be a ward of the state until a foster family chooses you as an appropriate candidate for adoption. You will be excused from classes while you are with us, but you will be expected to work off a portion of your stay in the kitchen for the remainder of the semester. Whatever debt or fees remain unpaid after you leave the school will be frozen and taken on by whatever family is deemed responsible enough to adopt you. There will be a small, garnered interest, depending on the amount of time that it takes for you to find a family capable of…raising you. Do you understand?"

Mary did not understand. Still after the headmistress kept talking Mary could not hear or understand anything at all. Her comprehension became deflated and was replaced with a void that began to fill her entire body. This was an absence so strong and absolute that in its depth lay the presence of form. This form of absence replaced any kind of feeling that Mary would recognize as reactive to the information she was meant to be receiving. She sat in her chair without moving and her breath became shallow and weak.

"Ms. Kirkland? Do you understand?"

Mary felt nothing and knew nothing and said nothing and saw nothing. She had not noticed that she had vomited on the floor until after the event. The headmistress pressed a button beneath her desk and Mr. Lewis returned, holding a handkerchief up to his nose as he recognized the smell.

"Mr. Lewis, please escort Ms. Kirkland back to her dormitory. She is to be excused from her kitchen duties for the remainder of the day. She will be expected to spend this free time resting and processing her grief. Please see to it that her meals are brought to her and relocate Ms. Rubenstein to a different room for the night. I'm sure that Ms. Kirkland would rather be left alone and undisturbed."

Mr. Lewis complied with the headmistress's request and gently lifted Mary out of her chair. Her legs seemed to be working incorrectly as he escorted Mary back to Sperare. Mary lay on her bed and did not respond when Mr. Lewis asked her if there was anything he could get for her. Finding his answer in her silence, he gently closed the door to Mary's room and left her in peace.

The rest of the day was an eternity as time refused to enter the room. For all that Mary had suffered and experienced in her stay at St. Philomena's, her old life felt like such a long time ago. She had only been at the school for four days, but in her mind, it had been years. Mary thought of the ravine and her grandmother in her big brown chair, drinking from her plastic cup. She thought of the life she had before St. Philomena's. She felt so young then.

No tears came from Mary that day. She also had no appetite. She was exhausted beyond belief, but no sleep would come to her. It was late in the evening when Ruth came into the room to collect her things while she stayed in a vacant bed for the night. Mary lay on her side facing the wall and did not move when Ruth entered the room.

"Hi," said Ruth.

Mary was still.

"I'm sorry," said Ruth, "that sounds so stupid. 'I'm sorry'. People always say that when someone dies, but it doesn't mean anything, does it?"

Mary was still.

Ruth dug into her backpack and removed Mary's book and compass. She placed it at the foot of Mary's bed and gathered some pajamas and a toothbrush for the night.

"They wanted me to give you those," said Ruth, "is there anything I can do?"

Mary was still, but weakly said no. Ruth lingered in the doorway for a moment until Mr. Lewis arrived to escort her to her temporary accommodation. He looked at the floor and found the tray from Mary's lunch to be untouched.

"Ms. Kirkland," he said, "you really should eat something."

Mary was still.

"I would imagine that bringing you dinner would be a wasted gesture. I will leave your tray from lunch until you feel so inclined as to eat, but I will not be returning with your dinner if you plan on allowing yourself to starve."

Mr. Lewis turned to leave before stopping in the doorway and looking back at Mary over his shoulder.

"Please understand that you have my deepest condolences," he said.

Mary lay in her bed as Mr. Lewis closed the door. The thought of penance and fasting, working, dying, and violence began to swirl inside her mind, but nothing could gain enough traction to keep her focus. There was a sound like that of a mosquito somewhere in the room. It was very small at first and constant as a light, raspy buzz began to fill the air. It was a sound that Mary did not realize she was making. Having run out of breath, Mary drew air into her lungs and screamed silently at the wall as her body shook with hot stinging tears falling down her face.

She took it back. She took it all back. She did not wish her parents dead. She would wash a million dishes and pass a thousand classes to bring them back to life. She wondered if it were possible to take her own life if it meant that they could return in trade. This was a lingering thought that she could not seem to shake, and she did not understand why. She waited for someone to tell her it was all a joke. That her parents had planned to bring her home and this was all some sort of elaborate prank. Behind all her sorrow and grief, behind the anger and pain and hatred that she felt, Mary was afraid. There would be no respite on this night. No consolations and no silver linings were on the horizon. Of all the injustices that Mary had suffered through her life, this was her darkest day.

Mr. Lewis returned to the office of the headmistress and closed the door behind him. The headmistress was going over blueprints for minor renovations that had just been approved by the board of directors. She had ambitions to install new marble steps to the front entrance of the main hall for the following year. This was also a means to an end as the staircase would have to match the portico in an exact pairing. The real prize would be the calacatta viola marble that she had her eye on to compliment the white steps. She remained focused on the blueprints when Mr. Lewis entered the room.

Pressing on a false wall panel, Mr. Lewis opened a small cabinet between two of the bookcases and removed a decanter of bourbon. Pouring two fingers worth in two glasses, he walked towards the desk of the headmistress and handed her one, leaning down to kiss her on the cheek. She took the glass thanklessly and kept her eyes on the plans in front of her. Mr. Lewis sighed as he sat on the red leather armchair and toasted the air silently, taking in a moment of reverence.

"That poor girl," he said, more to himself than anyone else, "do you think she'll be alright?"

"Do you know anyone who is alright?" asked the headmistress.

"I suppose not, no. Does she have any family that we need to contact? Well, do we have the ability to contact any of them?"

"I would imagine that would be a job for the authorities," said the headmistress.

"How did they die?" asked Mr. Lewis.

"Some bear incident, or something," she said, "from what I understand of it, there was a skiing accident and they had both fallen into a cave of hibernating bears."

"Bears?"

"Yes," said the headmistress, "brown bears."

"I'd never known brown bears to be so aggressive as to kill," said Mr. Lewis.

"I suppose this speaks more to the fragile and incompetent nature of the Kirkland's," said the headmistress, "the fact that they understood how to *make* a child is extraordinary. Raising one correctly was clearly too high of an expectation. We've seen what their abilities as parents have accomplished."

"Ms. Kirkland is clearly not meant for success," said Mr. Lewis, "perhaps this time working in the kitchen could be considered training for her future career."

The headmistress made a small noise in agreement. It sounded like she was clearing her throat, but she stopped halfway and took a long drink from her glass of whiskey.

"There's more," said the headmistress, "they were discovered in the cave only after it had been slated for demolition. Not only were they mauled by what would otherwise be passive bears, but the Kirkland's were also blown apart by dynamite."

"Fascinating," said Mr. Lewis, "and what about the bears?"

The headmistress took a sip from her glass and rolled the blueprints up, sliding a rubber band around each end. She looked at Mr. Lewis without an obvious expression, but the corners of her mouth tilted up ever so slightly. Had you never met her before, you would not have noticed. Mr. Lewis recognized the feint almost instantly. The headmistress cleared her throat.

"Well, I don't think they'll press charges."

The unexpected joke landed far too well. The two facilitators laughed heartily in a shared ignobility.

No one at the school knew how their evening truly ended, but there was a gardener who could have sworn that he heard music coming out from one of the second-floor windows of the main hall that night. It was also observed by the faculty that Mr. Lewis and the headmistress were especially chummy with each other for the next few days.

Alright, fine. They had sex. You happy? It was gross and weird, and I don't want to talk about it anymore.

Mary had no way to tell whether she slept at all, but if she had, then the only evidence of this would have been found in her dreams. Whether these were waking nightmares or apparitions of her subconscious, she saw flashing images of her parents and her grandmother whenever she closed her eyes.

When she would drift off to sleep, she was plagued by terrible sights of their death in elaborate fantasies of events. She dreamt that her parents were trapped in a burning building. She saw their skin melting off their faces and smoke rising out of their splintered bones. She dreamt that they were caught in an avalanche and buried beneath the ice, freezing to death. There was a scene in her mind of quicksand and ropes that were just too short to save them. Giant rats and spiders rushed to eat their hands first. Each new death sentence that her dreams produced ended with her parents screaming out her name. Sometimes they screamed for her forgiveness while other times they screamed because they did not know where she was.

The worst nightmares were when she was together with all of them at home, happy. Living there just as though nothing had happened. They were home and Mary had never gone to school, her grandmother had never died, and they were all together watching a movie or old television. She could almost taste the lemon chicken soup. The hum from the television would turn from a comforting sound to that of cruel laughter being filtered through a thick liquid. It was a gurgling laughter that sounded so small before growing to land beside Mary's ear. In the last moments of her dream, she would turn to see the twisted and childlike face of Saint Sebastian looking at her with eyes unblinking from behind a mop of greasy black hair. Then she would wake up.

    She would wake up in her bed and look around the stark reality of her still being at St. Philomena's. The need to call out to her parents in the night was a reflex that she had not experienced since she had been much younger. Knowing that was now impossible brought a deep and heavy weight upon her chest. There would be the last few seconds of confusion as the dream would disintegrate behind her memory and the lingering terrors that she felt were replaced with the abundant indifference of the waking world. Mary was not sure which was worse.

    She woke up alone after the last of her dreams, the room sitting empty and quiet just before dawn. The floor was freezing as she walked to the toilet and nobody else was awake yet. Mary returned to her room and got dressed out of habit, but also because she did not know what else to do. The desire to fall back asleep was a complicated feeling of fear and exhaustion, but it was too early for her to do anything else. At that moment, after so many bad dreams, Mary was unsure if she could take any more surprises.

    Without the capacity to spend any more time in her room, she took her copy of The Wind in the Willows and went outside to sit and read beneath a tree. It was a cold morning with the dampness that accompanies autumn. Opening the book was supposed to be therapeutic and bring some sense of comfort to Mary in her time of need, but she could not make it past the first page.

    She could hear her father's voice reciting the dialogue in each character. He had a habit of deliberate pauses when he found a passage to be particularly funny. The punchline always came with anticipation. Mary had picked up that habit as a reader and there was no other way for her to absorb the story. Her heart began to break even more, and she felt the color drain from her face. Leaning her back against the tree, Mary covered her eyes and wept in the yard.

    Lucy was walking out of Pasce Spiritum wearing jogging gear and shaking her hands to warm them in the morning chill. Her eyes began scanning the yard in the sleep filled wonder of peace before the students would fill the grounds. There was a certain serenity that lay around St. Philomena's, despite itself. She had only just begun to make her way to the track when she saw that Mary was sitting alone on the ground, crying in the autumn dew. Lucy approached Mary with concern for her health and security.

"Mary, what's wrong?" she asked through her jagged morning voice.

Mary embraced Lucy with pleading sobs. Although she tried, Mary could not find the ability to explain how terrible she felt. Lucy wrapped her arms around Mary and held her tightly as they both shivered in the morning. The pain of others caused Lucy to feel pain. This was how it had always been for her and how it would always be. Her sense of self-preservation was a secondary concern in the list of priorities that would shuffle through her life.

"Hey," said Lucy, "come with me. Let's get you warmed up."

She led Mary back to her room in Pasce Spiritum. As an older student, she was permitted to live by herself in a single room of a similarly modest design to Mary's. There was a bed and a wash basin sink beneath a single window, a writing desk instead of another bed, a dresser, a bedside table, and the solemn decoration of a crucifix. Lucy sat Mary on the bed and tried to move her dresser away from the wall as quietly as she could. Behind her dresser was an air vent that she used for her own secret compartment. She opened the iron grate and removed a small electric kettle and a plastic bag with brown powder.

"I'm not supposed to have this," she said, "so don't tell, ok?"

Mary nodded her head in agreement and Lucy held out her hooked pinky. Mary did the same. They shook on it, making their secret official and punishable by death if it were ever to be broken. Lucy filled the kettle with water and poured the brown powder into two small paper cups. Instead of whistling, there was a plastic button that popped up when the water had finished boiling. Lucy poured the water into the paper cups and stirred them with a pen from her desk while Mary sat on the bed and sniffled. Lucy gave a cup to Mary, and she took it quietly in her hands.

"It's not much," said Lucy, "but a little hot chocolate goes a long way with me. Do you want to talk about it?"

Mary slowly told Lucy about her parents and her fear of what lay ahead for her. She did not understand most of what the headmistress had told her, but she knew that nothing would ever be good again. Lucy listened to Mary intently while she sipped her hot chocolate and did her best not to burst into tears. Placing her cup gently on the ground, Lucy took Mary in her arms and held onto her tightly. She wept for Mary's pain the moment her arms wrapped around Lucy's neck.

"It's ok," said Mary, "I'm sorry I made you cry."

Lucy laughed to herself and squeezed Mary tighter.

"Jesus, kid," said Lucy, "you're gonna be alright."

Mary drank the hot chocolate and Lucy drank hers. They took some time to tell each other stories and Lucy did her best to cheer Mary up with some of her best adventures. This worked a little bit as Mary would laugh at the funny parts and get serious when the stories began to get scary. Lucy had to filter some facts from her early days of delinquency to preserve some sense of boundaries, but the overarching message was that there were no guarantees in life. Most importantly, death held no rules and hardly seemed fair.

"I know it's hard," said Lucy, "it may be the hardest thing you'll ever have to deal with. I hope it's the hardest thing that you ever have to deal with. And it never really will go away. The pain, I mean. It will get easier over time because the rest of your life will happen. Things like this, the terrible things, nobody wants them to happen, but they do. The important thing is what we do when they happen. It's ok to feel sad, angry, or nothing. Sometimes I would rather feel nothing. You're going to be ok, Mary. You may think I'm full of it, but you're going to be ok."

Mary looked at the ground and mumbled a little agreement. She found it hard to think that she was going to be ok, but she was too tired to argue.

"Being brave is being scared and doing the damn thing anyway," said Mary.

This took Lucy by surprise as she was not expecting Mary to say something like that.

"That's very wise," said Lucy, "where'd you learn that?"

"My dad," said Mary.

Her tears came back again in force, with a quivering lip and the shame of emotion. Mary dropped her empty cup on the floor and covered her face with her hands while Lucy rubbed her shoulder and tried to think of what to say.

"My mother died when I was fourteen. It feels like such a long time ago, but it wasn't. After she died, I hated the world for a long time. Nobody could convince me that anything would be good. Ever. I did some rotten things and treated people badly, mostly my friends and family. I didn't know how to feel bad, so I let it take the wheel for a little while. I'm not sure what changed. Maybe I did. I hope I did. I'm sorry Mary, I shouldn't talk about myself this much. Are you going to be alright?"

Mary nodded her head. She did feel a little better. She was still terribly sad, but she felt a little less crazy after talking with Lucy. The hot chocolate certainly helped. Lucy gave Mary one last hug before walking her back to Sperare. Mary was grateful for the hot chocolate and made up her mind that Lucy was a very good friend. Wherever the world would take Mary from here, she would never be forgotten.

Mary returned to her room to find that Ruth was back earlier than expected. She was putting her toiletries away and there were twigs and leaves stuck in her hair. She turned to Mary, chuckling to herself, and shaking her head. Small scrapes were on her face and arms.

"I hate the woods," said Ruth, "I hate the woods, I hate this place, and I hate that homo, Lewis. I had to leave that shit ass room they put me in. I was with Burnadette. Do you know her? No, I guess you wouldn't. She snores so loud I didn't sleep at all. I swear, everybody snores around here. I tried to sleep in the hallway but that wasn't happening, so I tried to sleep outside. I got maybe two hours of sleep before I was jumped by a couple of squirrels. Little pricks were mean as Hell. Anyway, how are you?"

Mary burst out laughing at the sight of Ruth. She looked a proper mess, and the absence of humility made it difficult for her to see the humor in her circumstance. All of Ruth's New York diplomacy came out to show itself.

"Aw, blow it out yer ass!" she said.

"I'm sorry," said Mary between giggles, "you look like a bush."

Ruth sat on her bed and started to pick the leaves and twigs from her hair. There was a small patch of thistles knotted in the back of her head which Mary helped to untangle.

"Hey, I talked to my folks," said Ruth, "they were planning on coming up to visit next week and they want to meet you."

"Are they nice?"

"Yeah, they're fine. My dad is kind of a weirdo, but he's funny, and mom is, like, super weird. They're both from Mars, or something. Mr. Lewis hates it when they come to visit."

"Why do they want to meet me?"

"I told them about your parents. They want to help."

Mary was intrigued and terrified. She was developing a growing apprehension towards strangers, and her ability to trust people was dissipating faster than she would like to admit. However, Ruth was different. Mary trusted Ruth.

Mary could not think of any other way to ask for help. There was no one that she felt comfortable speaking to, apart from Ruth or Lucy. Even if Ruth's parents could not be any real help, Mary saw this as a decent distraction from her emotions. It was all too much too fast for Mary to receive any more disruptions. Any stability in life she had expected was left back in the house where she was born. Outside of those wooded boundaries lay a world of constant fluctuation.

Lucy's words were still running through her mind about how there were no rules regarding the events that we experience in our lifetime. With all that had taken place for Mary she felt ambivalent towards what the future could hold. Lucy said that it was ok for Mary to feel nothing, so it was nothing that she allowed herself to feel. There was some comfort in that.

Ruth seemed fuzzy on the details as to how her parents would be able to help Mary, but she assured her that they had the means and capability to do so. At this point, if Ruth's parents decided to kidnap Mary and send her to the moon, then she would not be the least bit surprised. Both girls shrugged and left it at that. They would have to wait and see.

10. Let's Go Mets

The kitchen was blazing hot, and Mary had been at the sink for nearly three hours. Lunch was wrapping up and the final push of dirty trays were coming down the belt to where she stood, rag in hand. Louise had jumped in to help keep Mary from getting backed up, but the giant woman was also struggling to get the pacing right. The cranking and steam shooting clang from machinery sounded like symphonic Hell, but Mary was beginning to enjoy the noise. Every day she wrote a new song.

It had been five days since she had received the news of the death of her parents and there was no conventional way for Mary to feel better. Much of the time she felt nothing at all, which had become a place of rest. When she did allow herself to become emotional, she felt everything all at once. There were a variety of unorthodox methods to temporarily keep her mind occupied, but it was the quiet night that brought the most pain. From this experience, Mary found noise to be a helpful distraction.

"Mon petit chou," exclaimed Louise, "I think we must abandon ship! The Nazi U-Boats are filling our submarine with holes! We are taking on water! We are going to drown!"

"Never!" shouted Mary over the din of kitchen equipment, "fire torpedoes off the starboard side! Release the ballast and surface! Take that, Hitler!"

Mary and Louise made machine gun noises as the Hobart dishwashing machine churned and spat hot steaming water in all directions. Jennifer came to their side waving a little white napkin and holding her finger under her nose like a mustache.

"Monsieur Hitler has surrendered," cried Louise, "we have once again saved the free world! Down with the fascists! Vive la France!"

"Vive la France!" cried Mary.

"Vive my ass!" yelled Therese, "how can you celebrate such foolishness? Look at this mess!"

"My dear sister," said Louise, "the only mess I see is a grown woman with no sense of humor."

Louise snapped a towel at her sister's hand, to which Therese jumped back. She scowled at her twin.

"Please Mary, do not take your education from un cochon ignorant," said Therese, "you will end up in the shit, to be sure."

Louise pressed her nose up with her finger and began oinking loudly as she continued to snap her sister with the towel. Therese threw her hands up in frustration and left the two allies to fight the axis in the Sea of Hobart. Mary and Louise laughed at Therese's frustration.

"I do not know when my sister became so sour, but she has always been that way," said Louise, "it would make more sense if she were a crab or a lobster."

"Where are you from?" asked Mary.

"Mon petit! Surely a young woman as cultured and sophisticated as yourself has heard of the beautiful country of France?"

"I like french fries."

"Dieu, aide-moi avec cette fille. No, petit chou, we are so much more than a fried potato. We are living music! We are the best at everything and the fiercest in battle. We are warriors of love and art. Ah, if you were to see my home then you would refuse to leave. I miss it dearly."

"I'm from Massachusetts," said Mary.

"Ah, yes. The land of the chowder and beans. I have been once to Boston, but it did not feel like anywhere. It was a strange place. Are you from Boston?"

"No," said Mary, "I'm from Amherst. It's very pretty and green. There are a lot of woods around my house…"

Mary trailed off and felt as though she were about to cry again. Talking about home was still too painful. Realizing that it may be impossible for her to return to her house made Mary fight to hold back her tears. Louise pulled Mary into a warm hug as she patted her head.

"Mon petit chou," she said, "it is alright to cry, but you must be strong. We women were born to suffer in this life, and the world will ask much more of you than you could possibly understand. In this moment, even as such a little thing, you carry such weight upon your shoulders. I pray that the world is much kinder to you, but that is never une garantie."

Mary nodded her head into Louise's stomach, accidentally wiping her nose on her apron in the process.

"Ms. Louise," said Mary, "can you come and visit me?"

"Someday," said Louise, "I will come and visit you in your big house and I will bring you lots of delicious food and cakes. And I won't tell Therese. Je donne ma parole d'honneur. She can be a crab in the lake for all that I care."

Louise made her hand like a claw and pinched Mary's cheek. This made Mary laugh and she felt a little better.

"Please come visit me," said Mary, "if I get adopted, I'm going to run away. I don't want to be adopted."

"Where will you go," asked Louise, "are you going to join the circus and grow a beard?"

Louise wiped some suds on Mary's chin, which tickled and made her giggle.

"No," said Mary, "I'm gonna go live in my ravine. I want to build a house and catch frogs all day. Maybe I'll become a detective."

"Ah, sonne comme le paradis," said Louise, "it is settled. I will help you catch frogs and then we will have cake. But we will not have frog cake. Where shall we meet?"

"Six-two-six Apollinaire Road," Mary looked proud as she remembered her home address. She tried to memorize it before she left for the school in case she had to run away.

"Apollinaire?!" said Louise, "are you sure you are not French, mon petit? That is a very important name."

"I think I'm Irish," said Mary.

"Ah, then you truly are born to suffer."

Therese walked quickly from the other side of the kitchen with her arms spread apart in frustration.

"Louise," she shouted, "are you going to help me with the brisket or are you too busy sinking submarines?!"

"Excuse-moi, petit," said Louise, "I have to take my pet crab for a walk."

The two sisters walked away arguing while Mary finished up the dirty trays from lunch. Jennifer sidled up next to Mary and nudged her lightly with her elbow. She did not say anything but gestured for Mary to hold out her hand. Jennifer deposited a small piece of chocolate into Mary's palm and held her finger to her lips, signaling silence. Mary mouthed thank you to which Jennifer simply winked and walked away, whistling some song that Mary thought she recognized, but could not place.

Mary did not mind the kitchen work. It was better than school by a long shot and she liked working with adults better than learning with students her own age. It made her feel important. The work also kept her distracted from her misery, although despair would peek through from time to time in unexpected intervals. Mary would find herself in the middle of a repetitive task when the thought of her parents would cross her mind and the rest of the world would stop. She had been crying less and less each day, but it was especially difficult at night. Sometimes it happened, sometimes it did not. It was still all too fresh. Her days were spent working and doing her best to stay out of the way of the rest of the kitchen crew.

Washing dishes was simple enough but changing out the soap and getting supplies always seemed to trip Mary up. Jennifer and Louise were always very helpful, but Mary felt herself to be a burden on their kindness and would seldom ask for help. When work was over, and when Mary got back to her room, her mind would relax and release all the torment that would have otherwise been squashed by manual labor. It was the quiet hours that Mary feared the most. Because of this, there was never enough work for Mary to do.

She was helping Jennifer take the last of the garbage bags to the dumpsters when she saw Marissa speaking with Therese and Louise a short distance away. They were laughing and smoking cigarettes in a small circle beside a tall white shed where they kept the groundskeeping tools. Mary's eyes slowly scrolled past the three women and landed on the tool shed. She had never really noticed it before, but it felt as though she was jostled from a different kind of dream. There was a sudden metallic flavor in the back of Mary's throat as she started to tremble, despite the heat from the kitchen. The feeling crept up Mary's legs and made them stiffen up as her knees locked in place.

She was beginning to feel dizzy when Jennifer tapped her on the shoulder and brought her back to the task at hand. Mary snapped out of her frozen moment and finished helping Jennifer empty the trash. When she looked back at the shed it was still there, but the feelings that had just dominated her mind were gone. Mary returned to the kitchen, deposited her dirty apron into the laundry chute, and walked back to Sperare for a rest while the prep work for dinner began. Ruth was sitting on her bed as Mary walked in.

"Honey, I'm home," said Mary, "I'm a big important man and I demand respect! Where's my dinner?! Where's my bananers?! I want my bananers!"

She beat her chest like King Kong and made monkey noises across the room. Ruth laughed and put down the textbook she was reading.

"What's next," asked Ruth, "are you gonna mow the lawn?"

"I'm gonna wear sandals and grow a mustache! Then I'm gonna buy a truuuuuuuuck!"

The two girls laughed together as Mr. Lewis entered the room.

"It does my heart well to see you laughing again, Ms. Kirkland," said Mr. Lewis, "no doubt that your newfound career as a dishwasher has left a considerable impression upon you."

The two girls stopped laughing and disregarded Mr. Lewis as a person who no longer required their respect. They were not afraid of him so long as they had each other. Ruth returned to her textbook and Mary simply lay on her bed, flipping open the lid to her grandfather's compass and closing it back and forth.

"Ms. Rubenstein, it would appear as though your...parents have arrived."

Mr. Lewis did his best to sound nonchalant towards Ruth's parents, but the awkward pause and slight curl of his upper lip revealed his true feelings for the Rubenstein family. Ruth chuckled at this and closed her textbook.

"Mr. Lewis," said Ruth, mocking his voice "did they arrive by way of the van or by motorcycle?"

"I believe it is the van today, Ms. Rubenstein."

"That means serious business," said Ruth, "is my dad wearing his helmet?"

"Yes," said Mr. Lewis, "I suppose he is."

"Is my mother wearing her brown jacket with the fringe and the eagle on the back?"

"Yes," said Mr. Lewis, "that she is."

"Hot shit!" said Ruth in celebration.

"King shit!" said Mary.

"Bullshit!"

"Booger shit!"

"Banana shit!"

Mr. Lewis furrowed his brow and was beginning to remark upon the inappropriate language from Mary and Ruth, but the blustering voice of Howard Rubenstein came rolling down the hallway from the front door of Sperare.

"JEEZE LOUISE, WHO'S BEEN RIPPIN FAHTS DOWN HERE?! RUTHIE?! YOU GOT THE SHITS, HON?!"

Ruth's face burned as she buried her head in her pillow.

"DAD! STOP IT!"

"I'M SORRY HON," hollered Mr. Rubenstein, "YOUR MOTHER'S BEEN MAKING ME STOP EVERY TWO MILES. SHE'S GOT 'EM, TOO."

"I DO NOT, YOU JERK!" shouted Mrs. Rubenstein.

The Rubenstein's continued to argue and laugh down the hall until they reached Ruth and Mary's dorm room. Ruth's father was gigantic, maybe the biggest man that Mary had ever seen. He wore a bright yellow t-shirt with the faded words "KENWOOD ORIGINAL TS-990S" in brown print. The fabric barely held together around his large frame. He also wore a leather aviator helmet with goggles. The thin chin straps wiggled around the sides of his face as he moved, making him look even more ridiculous than he otherwise would.

In contrast, Ruth's mother was a thin and sylphlike woman with big dark sunglasses and very big hair. Mary thought she resembled a black dandelion. Mr. Rubenstein slapped Mr. Lewis on the back with the flat of his palm, making him stumble forward and enter a robust coughing fit.

"Hiya, stretch," said Mr. Rubenstein, "grab us a couple'a beers, would ya? Got stuck on eighty-four for four hours and I'm too sober to look at ya."

Mr. Lewis agreed to get Mr. Rubenstein a beer, if only as an excuse to leave the conversation.

"Yo stretch! While you're at it, get a bottle of wine for Lorry here and some cream sodas for the girls! And try not to think about it too hard!"

Mr. Lewis could be seen standing with his back to the Rubenstein's just before the entrance to Sperare. If you were to listen very closely you would be able to hear him say something...untoward. Mr. Rubenstein had to duck his head a little to fit through the door frame, but his presence filled the room as soon as he entered. He scooped Ruth up into the air with his large hairy arms and shook her like a ragdoll as he heartily laughed.

"DAD PUT ME DOWN!" shouted Ruth.

"Fine, fine," said Mr. Rubenstein, "down ya go."

He lowered Ruth back down to the ground. She straightened her uniform and tied her curly hair back into a bun. Mr. Rubenstein leaned back and stretched his arms in such a way that he nearly touched both walls across the room. Mrs. Rubenstein took out a small pad and pen and started writing in a little red book. Mary was curious and a little scared of the Rubenstein family.

"Strike of genius, hon?" asked Mr. Rubenstein.

"Two seconds, dear," said Mrs. Rubenstein.

"She's a famous poet, you know," said Mr. Rubenstein, winking to Mary, "she was invited to speak at a symposium in Switzerland a few years ago."

"It was Norway, dear," said Mrs. Rubenstein, "and it was last year."

"It was?"

Mr. Rubenstein rubbed the stubble that covered his chin as he did his best to consider the reality of time. He finally gave up, shrugged, and said:

"Well, you're still a genius to me."

"Oh, hush," said Mrs. Rubenstein, "just trying to keep the lights on."

Mrs. Rubenstein returned the pad and pencil to her bag and hugged Ruth in her arms. She put her black sunglasses on Ruth's face and they both started dancing and singing an older song from the nineteen-sixties. The jovial moment took a somber turn as Mary recognized an absent feeling that she would never experience again. If it were to be replicated, then it would only exist as a counterfeit that may do more lasting harm than good. Mary looked at the wall until she knew that they had stopped hugging and dancing.

Mr. Rubenstein may have looked ridiculous, but he was not blind. He walked up to Mary and sat on the floor so that the two of them were at eye level. He towered over her like a grizzly with a kitten. Mr. Rubenstein smiled at her warmly and asked if she had ever been to New York City.

"No," said Mary, "is it big?"

Mr. Rubenstein laughed with such unreserved joy that it startled Mary.

"Mary," said Mr. Rubenstein, "it's the biggest thing in the world. Hell, it is the world, depending on who you ask."

"Is it nice?" asked Mary.

"Sometimes it is, sometimes it isn't," said Mr. Rubenstein, "it's what you'd call a living city. Some folks are nice, some folks aren't. Some folks are both at once. Good and bad kind of blur in New York."

Mary thought about her grandmother and said that she understood. Her complicated relationship with her grandmother was a memory that was still painful, but Mary stopped to consider how a city could also be that way. Her thoughts traveled back to her underwater monster city and wondered what kind of monsters lived in New York.

"Say Mary," said Mr. Rubenstein, "how would you like to come stay with us?"

"What?" said Mary.

"Just for a little while to see if you like it. Ruthie told us about your troubles and we're so sorry. We've talked it over and we'd like to adopt you, Mary. We're pulling Ruthie out of the school tomorrow and we'd like you to come with us, if you want to. We thought that this place would be a good school for her, but..."

"But it sucks," said Mrs. Rubenstein

"It sucks," agreed Mr. Rubenstein, "I know you don't know us, and I'm sure you have family that you would rather be with, but we would love to have you stay with us."

Mary thought about their offer and did not know what to say. She felt as though the Rubenstein's were good people, but she was afraid. She had a flashing image of living with Aunt Colleen, and it was enough to make up her mind. Also, the thought of spending any more time at St. Philomena's was enough to do her head in.

"Yes," she said, "I think I would."

"Well don't that just beat the band!" said Mr. Rubenstein, "We'll square away with that gargoyle up in the shit house and then we'll get goin'." Mr. Rubenstein looked around the room and shook his head. "Ruthie, I'm sorry we ever thought this place would be a good idea. Once we get back to Brooklyn, we're gonna buy you Shea Stadium."

"It's Citi Stadium now," said Mrs. Rubenstein.

"Bull. Shit. It has always been Shea Stadium and it will always be Shea Stadium. Oh, Mary. Speaking of which, Yankees or Mets?"

"What do you mean?"

"Oh, Mary," said Mr. Rubenstein, "we're gonna get you fixed up. Let's Go Mets, right honey?"

"Let's Go Mets," replied Mrs. Rubenstein.

Mr. Lewis returned with the drinks for the Rubenstein's and tried to leave as quickly as possible, but Mr. Rubenstein put him in a headlock and made him drink a beer with him. Although Mr. Lewis protested with enthusiasm, he had no choice but to comply.

When the Rubenstein's spoke with St. Philomena's headmistress regarding Mary's guardianship, they had already rehearsed their end of the conversation for most of their drive up to the school. They even practiced some more for a better part of the morning. Much to their surprise, there was no objection from the office of the headmistress. Since the time of her parents' untimely demise, the local authorities had done their due diligence to contact the remaining living members of Mary's extended family. Those they had found were either too busy to raise a child, too selfish to raise a child, or they had no clue who Mary was. Aunt Colleen said that she had never heard of Mary.

The news of Mary's family disregarding her threw Mrs. Rubenstein into such a fit that it nearly sabotaged their plan of adoption. She hollered and screamed about the dirty fucking piece of shit garbage prick shit gobbling two toilet lace curtain shit ass shit fucking mother butt pipe stubby dick blood clot twats. This is a condensed list which was pieced together from what Mary and Ruth could remember when they would revisit the scene later. It developed into their game where they would see who could make the longest list of obscenities. Mr. and Mrs. Rubenstein tried to discourage the game but would often find themselves jumping in to play along.

It was agreed upon by all parties involved that Mary would be permitted into the custody of the Rubenstein family while the adoption paperwork was being processed. She would meet with a social worker and a counselor twice a month until she was eighteen years old, at which point, she would be left to her own recognizance. There would be regularly unscheduled inspections of the Rubenstein home to ensure that they were not homicidal maniacs, satanic cult leaders, hippie dopers, or, worst of all, libertarians. Mary would also be excused from attending the local public school until the start of the next year.

What could possibly go wrong?

Naw, I'm just fucking with you. Mary was fine. Nothing bad ever happened again and there's never really anything worth writing about in New York City. That's it, I guess. No point in dragging out these long goodbyes. I've never been too sentimental anyway, but it was nice seeing you. Ought to do this again soon, blah blah blah...oh. Shit, there are a lot more pages here. Sorry about that. Well, this is embarrassing. I don't even know what's in there, to tell you the truth. I'm not much of a reader. If I had to guess, I would imagine that:

Mary had arrived at the Rubenstein home in the heart of Park Slope. After Mary and Ruth were released from the care of St. Philomena's School, life for Mary became a little more colorful. The Rubenstein's lived on the second floor of a three story walk up; sandwiched above a Portuguese bakery on the first floor and beneath a famous pop singer who-shall-remain-nameless living above them. She was affectionately referred to as "What's-Her-Name" and she kept two dachshunds, both named Frank. Frank I and Frank II. She was hardly an all-night-party style pop singer. What's-her-name would mostly stay at home or go to a quiet restaurant if she was not touring or appearing on some late-night television talk show. There were occasional parties being thrown upstairs, and the Rubenstein's were always invited, but they usually ended at a decent hour. What's-Her-Name was very pleasant and never complained about receiving Rubenstein's' mail by mistake. If she did, then she would politely slide it under their door. The bakery always made cookies for both tenants on Christmas and Easter.

It did take some convincing for Mr. Rubenstein to clear out his home office as Mary would need a bedroom. He had been a ham radio enthusiast for several years and was utilizing the room as a space for his collection of transistor radios. Most of these radios were used as receivers for different channels from around the world. There was one for sports, one for news, one for music, and one for the harmless surveillance of global political dissidents. This surveillance was more from a place of fascination than paranoia.

He called the main transmitter "Big Ned" and would use it to communicate with three people. He had a man in Russia with no name, but an impressive knowledge of American baseball, a fella named Billy in Seattle who talked about UFOs, and a woman in Brazil who had the best recipe for moqueca and other tasty dishes. She was more than happy to share them with Mr. Rubenstein while he helped her improve her English. Unfortunately, Mr. Rubenstein's Portuguese was terrible, and he did not have a mind for languages.

There was a brief conversation with a few hems and haws between Mr. and Mrs. Rubenstein about Mary taking the room for herself, but after a rational and even-tempered discussion pertaining to the unlikelihood of Mary sleeping in the cupboard, he relinquished ownership of the space. Mr. Rubenstein agreed to move his radio room to the abandoned pigeon coop on the roof. There was a better reception up there anyway.

Mary had no possessions aside from her book, her compass, and the suitcase of clothes that had been brought to St. Philomena's. There was a substantial life insurance policy from the death of her parents, but she would not have access to the money until she turned twenty-one years old. Until that time, it was to be kept in a trust fund. When she arrived at the Rubenstein home, she was welcomed by the smell of autumn baking and nutmeg.

The apartment was warm with brown wainscoting lining floral wallpaper from the floor to the ceiling. Portraits of different people hung on the walls in frames of various sizes and the radiator against the wall would occasionally hiss as if it were laughing through its teeth. Mary would later try to time it so she could tell a joke just before the steam escaped, but she never could get the timing right. It was a sizable apartment, and it was confusing to Mary how someone could fit so much space into a building that looked much smaller on the outside. When she asked Mrs. Rubenstein about it, she simply declared it to be magic. Mary asked her no more questions about the apartment. Magic was enough.

Mr. Rubenstein brought Mary into what was soon to be her bedroom. He was brimming with excitement at the prospect of showing his radio collection to someone who had not already seen it hundreds of times. Just as he always had before, Howard tried to tell the jokes he knew about radios and, like every audience, Mary found the jokes to be confusing and could not understand them. Ruth came in to ask Mary if she wanted to watch television, but Mary was curious about the little boxes with all the buttons that were stacked on top of each other. She liked the passive low hum that was being emitted from the collection. Ruth rolled her eyes and told Mary to have fun while she watched television in the living room. Mary tried to remember the last time she had watched television at first, but then the theme song from I Love Lucy came out of the living room and Mary felt the start of a little pit form in her stomach. Mrs. Rubenstein entered the room and gently placed both of her hands on Mary's shoulders.

"Are you hungry, Mary?" she asked, "I'm gonna order a couple of pizzas. We should celebrate! What do you like on yours?"

Mary thought about pizza and I Love Lucy. She thought about driving through the woods and the backseats of cars. She thought about the last thing her parents had said to her and how content they seemed to leave her at St. Philomena's. She thought about how she would never see them again and how much she hated them for it. She thought that all of it was her fault and Mary started to cry. She ran out of the radio room and locked herself in the bathroom, biting the side of her finger between sobs. The Rubenstein's looked at each other with the silent understanding that they had a lot of work to do. Mr. Rubenstein held his wife in his arms and kissed her forehead, lightly rocking her back and forth.

"I know," he said, "I know."

Mr. Rubenstein set to work on removing his equipment from what was now Mary's room. The living room became cluttered with wires, tubes, transistors, antennae, cases, chassis, as well as books about codes, languages, time-zones, mythology, and world cultures. Ruth set to the task of taking broken or discarded parts to make a robot, but her father insisted that every piece was important, and nothing could be spared. The pair would wade through the collection of parts and argue over what was good and what was junk. Mrs. Rubenstein had already become bored with the discussion, so she sat outside the bathroom door while Mary gently cried on the other side.

"We don't have to get pizza," said Mrs. Rubenstein, "is there something else you'd like?"

Mary felt guilty for crying in the Rubenstein home. She felt as though she had become an inconvenience and wondered when they would wise up and chuck her out. She wiped her eyes, blew her nose, and opened the bathroom door.

"I'm sorry for crying," she said, "we can have pizza if you want to."

"Oh, honey," said Mrs. Rubenstein, "I'm sorry it's hard."

Mr. Rubenstein entered the conversation while he held Ruth upside down by her ankles. He was swinging her back and forth as she laughed hysterically, pleading that he put her down.

"So should we have cold mush or broccoli for dinner tonight?" he asked.

"No!" shouted Ruth.

"No mush? No broccoli? Well, how about a couple of smelly old socks filled with beans?"

"No! Put me down!"

Mr. Rubenstein gently put Ruth on the ground and rolled her up in the hallway carpet. The ridiculous event made Mary feel better and start to giggle. Ruth was in stitches. Mrs. Rubenstein was less amused.

"Goddamnit, Howard! That rug is filthy! Get her out of there!"

Mr. Rubenstein unrolled Ruth from the carpet as she laughed and coughed out the dust she had inhaled from the rug. He wiped the dirt from his daughter's face and apologized to Mrs. Rubenstein before returning to his task of clearing the room for Mary.

"He plays too much," said Mrs. Rubenstein, "Mary, Ruth, what would you like for dinner?"

The two girls looked at each other and after a brief huddle decided that the only possible choice would be chicken parmigiana. They were immovable on the decision and pressed this certainty on Mrs. Rubenstein, who wholeheartedly agreed.

"HOWARD!", yelled Mrs. Rubenstein, "CHICKEN PARM!"

"YOU GOT IT!" echoed from somewhere in the apartment.

The sound of crashing metal and some cursing from Mr. Rubenstein followed as one of his big radios had fallen from its shelf, but he soon went to work on the feast.

The table was set, and the sounds of Louis Prima began to reverberate through the apartment. What followed was a flurry of breadcrumbs, flour, wine, long homemade spaghetti noodles and homemade gravy. A light side salad was prepared, and the sound of chicken breast being pounded into cutlets was kept in time to Pennies from Heaven. Mary watched the process with awe. It was different from the chaos that she had known at her old breakfast table. This was chaos that had been made with the love and madness of three people who knew each other well. In the time that she had with her parents, she never felt as though she understood who they were. The Rubenstein's were made of a confidence that Mary had never seen before. It made Mary want to feel more confident. She found them to be insane, but inspirational.

11. I Like Stupid Hats

It was clear that Mary had come from a simpler part of the country, where certain formalities were as foreign to her as if they had come from outer space. Her stay at St. Philomena's had done little to deter her attraction towards a feral life, but it did provide an understanding for how the world would operate in so-called "civilized society". If anything, her scholastic history pushed Mary to doubling down on her desire for an unconventional life. Living with the Rubenstein's allowed a certain middle ground for Mary to retain a good portion of herself while learning how to move in the new environment of a city. The Rubenstein family were not well-to-do snobs, by any stretch of the imagination. They did not know which spoon was for soup and which was for ice cream. Spoon's a spoon. Keep your fork, there's pie. Wash your plate. Leave room for dessert. No, the Rubenstein's were not built to suffer the societal obligations of formal dinner attire or knowing how late is appropriately late when arriving at a party. The Rubenstein's knew how to read people. They could smell a phony from a mile sideways and did their best to find the good in most everyone else. They had been wrong in the past, but you know. Omelets and eggs.

When Howard Rubenstein met Lorry, she was Lorry Keller at the time. He had accidentally attended an open mic poetry night at Roberta's, which was a dive bar he would frequent if the evening required some cerebral lubrication. He was unaware that there was an open mic poetry night. It was not a planned event. He just wanted to drink cheap beer and watch the Mets.

Roberta's was the closest bar to his apartment at the time and one of the only bars in his neighborhood that had yet to be taken over by cocaine-riddled finance brokers. The calculated grime-adjacent atmosphere of the corporate bars attracted certain groups of people who had only heard about the lower classes from watching the news and some shows they had seen on television. In a neighborhood that used to cater to working class families, the stink of urban renewal had risen around the area with hardly anybody noticing. By the time anyone did recognize what was happening, it was too late. The bastards had planted a flag.

Roberta's bar was a study in gray, black, and green with a few rounded tables and thick wooden booths built into the walls. A small stage had been set up in the back where the seating would bottleneck into a small aisle. Howard liked Roberta's because nobody ever really went there. He had never gone with the hope of seeing one of their scheduled events but had once experienced an unexpected punk show when a group of musicians crowded the stage and plugged in their gear unannounced. They were trying to get a rise out of people, but nobody batted an eye. Howard was unimpressed, but he thought it was funny.

On this particular night, however, he was already frustrated by the company surrounding him. Roberta's was more crowded than Howard had realized when he first sat down. A quick scan of the room allowed him to see some neo-beatniks, hippies, suits, punks, nerds, turds, and gooney birds. Howard knew he was in trouble when a young white college kid wearing a dashiki and a Robin Hood hat sporting a long feather walked up to the microphone. Howard wanted to keep watching the Mets, but it was on a commercial. He had already drunk three pints and was feeling grouchy, so he turned his attention to this pipsqueak and thought, *Alright, goof ass. Show me what you got.*

What followed was a slow and drawn-out ooze of poetry that was predictably shallow, ambiguous, and took too long to finish. The young man strung together phrases from popular television commercials while breaking to scream between clumps of words. It was painful to listen to and Howard felt embarrassed for the kid. It reeked of effort. There was nothing the young poet could do to keep Howard from hating him. A young woman sitting next to Howard laughed at the frozen look of contempt on his face.

"He's a genius, you know," she said, "he just got a write up in the Village Voice."

"Hm," said Howard, "if he's such a genius, why is he wearing that stupid hat?"

"I like stupid hats."

"Well, I like the Mets."

Howard turned his back on the local genius who had just begun to cry after a spattering of loose applause. Returning to the baseball game, he noticed that the woman sitting next to him had also turned to watch the television. Although most of her attention was placed on Howard. He felt a hot flush roll beneath his skin.

"Who's winning?" she asked.

"Phillies."

"Oh...do you go for poetry much?"

"No," he said, "not my thing. I just wait until they turn it into a movie."

She laughed and he eyed her with suspicion.

"What's funny?" he asked.

"Nothing," she said, "it's just that that was accidentally poetic."

"See," said Howard, "that's what I mean. You can take anything and say it's a poem. Apparently, it doesn't even have to rhyme anymore. I dunno, the whole thing just feels kind of dumb."

"What do you like to read?" asked Lorry.

"I read the funnies," said Howard, "sometimes Mad Magazine. Grew up on comic books."

"Well, I think poetry is beautiful," she said, "you can get a lot of emotion out of a few simple phrases. Maybe you just haven't heard the right kind of poetry."

"I don't think they make the right kind of poetry for me," said Howard.

"Whatever you say, tough guy."

Howard grunted and returned to the Mets. There was a growing discomfort in his stomach as he was unaccustomed to receiving attention from women. He had dated plenty and had had a few serious relationships in his time, but the experience was still uncommon enough to make him forget his manners. Howard's overly introspective nature tended to make him awkward and inconsiderate. The three pints of beer were certainly not helpful. When he did remember his manners, he would often overcompensate. The virtue of balance was absent from his orchestration. He ordered another beer before looking at his new companion.

"You want somethin'?" he asked.

"Whiskey," she said.

"Whiskey?"

"Whiskey."

"Alright, two whiskeys' then."

The bartender returned with a pint of beer and two shots of whiskey (Catholic whiskey, not Protestant). Another poet had taken the stage and was comparing her menstrual cycle to her most recent string of disappointing lovers. She would be scared if they were late, but never enjoyed their company. They often overstayed their welcome and, for some strange reason beyond her control, her lovers would keep coming back. Lorry laughed at this while Howard continued to feel distracted.

"I'm Howard, by the way."

"Lorelei."

"Lorelei?"

"Call me Lorry."

"Lorry?"

"Yes, Lorry," she said, "what are you, simple or somethin'?"

"I like simple," said Howard, "not my fault you got a funny name."

Lorry aggressively clinked her shot glass against Howard's without spilling a drop. She slammed the drink back in a seamless motion and kept a relaxed expression on her face despite the bitter taste. After a moment of composure, the flavor caught up with her and a tremor fluttered through her body.

"Shit," she said.

The MC called for the next performer to approach the stage and Howard's face sank a bit when he heard them call for Lorry. She turned to him and shrugged while she walked up to the microphone. It was a common occurrence for Howard to say the wrong thing. Sometimes he even took great joy in it. He regularly said that his poor choice of words could be considered an Olympic event. Even so, his criticizing something that was an obvious passion for someone he liked made him feel horrible.

Well, he thought, *we had a good run.*

"Ladies and gentlemen," announced the MC, "I present to you, the rose of Brooklyn! The only star to survive the dawn! Lorelei Keller!"

The audience erupted in applause for the young poet as she modestly bowed her head. She kept her eyes on the floor while a secret smile could be seen creeping around the corners of her mouth. The MC genuflected dramatically and moved his hands through the air to make space for Lorry as she approached the stage. The lights dimmed, allowing for a new atmosphere to spread out from the walls as she gripped the microphone stand. Howard forgot all about the Mets when the cigarette smoke and light around the room drifted across her face. She threw him a quick wink before she began.

The only sound to exist in the world was the voice of Lorelei Keller. The traffic outside went undetected and the tenants who fought upstairs all day and all night called a truce, so it would seem, while Lorelei Keller held the audience in the palm of her hands. She spoke of simplicity in time and how there were no evil angels. She made her arms to be an alligator and sang about pregnant buildings. Howard was struggling to follow a word of it, but somehow, he knew that he liked it and wanted more. Lorry read three poems and was on stage for ten minutes, but the effect on Howard was irreversible. He had fallen in love. Lorry left the stage, and the lights were brought back up to appropriate bar levels. She sat down next to Howard at the bar and asked:

"Who's winning?"

Three months later they were married.

Ruth came along shortly after that. The three of them were very poor for a long time and lived in a one-bedroom apartment in Hoboken, New Jersey. Howard had to work two jobs to Lorry's one while she also worked on her poetry. Their landlady at the time was kind enough to watch Ruth while they were at work, but landlords never really work that much anyway. It was the least she could do considering how much of their income she was already taking in. Things were hard for a long time, but they never went hungry. Howard was thrifty and a very good cook, Lorry was frugal, and Ruth did not eat very much.

Their luck began to change as Lorry was starting to get noticed for her writing. She was quickly becoming an established poet on the rise in the underground circuit of New York City. It seemed every week she would receive invitations to different gallery openings and events around Brooklyn and the Bowery. It did not pay the bills just yet, but her popularity snowballed after she was asked to appear in a feature film and two documentaries about the current evolution of the New York art scene. She was even interviewed by the Village Voice a few times. Her interviewer was considerate enough to leave his feathered cap at home. Once she had appeared in film and print, she got steady work writing lyrics for local up-and-coming pop groups. Their songs began to climb the charts and the money started to roll right in.

Lorry was not especially proud of her impact on the world of pop music, but she was proud of her new ability to provide for her family. Everything came to a head once she signed a five-book contract for three collections of poetry, one novel, and one collection of short stories. The first thing that Lorry did with her new fortune was to buy Howard a leather aviator helmet with goggles. She enclosed a note that read, "I like stupid hats". Lorry Keller-Rubenstein had arrived. If you were to ask her how it happened, she could not begin to understand it herself.

The new financial securities were a strange adjustment for several reasons. Neither Lorry nor Howard had ever seen that much money before, but it also kept coming with no end in sight. After their joint bank accounts had reached a certain platitude, there was a family meeting to discuss moving into the city and finding a bigger apartment. The meeting lasted thirty seconds. Howard quit both of his jobs and felt no amount of pain about it. His friends would chide him and ask how it felt to be a kept man to which he would reply, "It feels good. Really, really good."

As large amounts of money often aid in the security of the unforeseen future, the thoughts of Ruth's potential had now expanded beyond the initial limitations that were set in place by their former poverty. There was nothing wrong with the public school system in New York City, but it was underfunded, understaffed, undersupplied, broken, with plumbing, heat, a/c, and electrical issues as well as malnourishing food, a lingering asbestos removal and rising violence due to a lack of resources and support for the student body. But there is nothing wrong with that. There is nothing wrong with that because most people who attend public schools cannot afford to think there is something wrong with that.

A coalition of parents who fought against the board of education for more funding did exist. They demanded better compensation for staff, safer environments without police involvement, and adequate food for the students. They were constantly being shut down and labeled as obnoxious radicals with too much free time on their hands. They were a Marxist PTA without the involvement of the teachers. Were they to include the teaching staff in their meetings, maybe they would have gotten somewhere. Their greatest downfall was infighting and inconsistent meetings. Any changes that occurred within the group were decided unanimously by committee, but if someone was unavailable or unwilling to vote on a subject, then the motion would be held until such a time that all members could be present. Because of the inconsistent commitment between members of the group, many goals were not accomplished.

Lorry had been a standing member for years before her fame caught up with her. When her financial advancements became known to the group, she was labeled a member of the ruling class and was marked as a bourgeois traitor. Lorry fought to keep her space within the organization, but this developed into a new topic of infighting. After finding her frustrations ascending past the acceptable level of compromise, Lorry said fuck it. The group was so busy fighting amongst each other that the board of education continued to squeeze the students and faculty unabated. Nobody hates the left more than the left. In retrospect, Lorry would later admit that she felt guilty for leaving and should have stayed on to fight the good fight, but this was hindsight. Lorry said fuck it and began to make regular donations to the schools directly, focusing on the programs that helped students eat well.

The choice to have Ruth spend her formative years in the care and custody of St. Philomena's was a point of contention between the Rubenstein's. Howard had apprehensions on the idea of having Ruth go to an isolated Christian institution out of state, her being Jewish and black. The concern that weighed on Howard's mind, as well as Lorry's, was that simply being black and Jewish could be enough reason for others to commit harm.

"I don't like it," said Howard, "I've seen enough horror movies to know that this is how they start."

"Are you about to explain racism to me?" said Lorry, "It's a good school and it'll help her get into an even better one. You don't think she's gonna find racism in New York?"

"I don't like the idea of Ruth being in the middle of nowhere Connecticut surrounded by a bunch of Nazis. Call me crazy!"

"It's not a fucking death camp, it's a boarding school. You know Ruth's been struggling with her classes. I just want to give her more opportunities than we had. She's a tough one, too. I don't think she would put up with any foolishness."

"I went to public school," said Howard, "and so did you! You're a damn genius and I'm...well I'm here, aren't I?!"

Howard stopped talking and sat at the table. He cradled his head in his fists while he grunted and tried to think of more things to say. Howard had a habit of shutting down when his feelings got too big. Lorry stood behind him and began to rub his giant shoulders. They felt as though they could have been made of stone. Stone man with a soft center. Lorry would sometimes forget how much of a softie Howard was.

"Hey," she said, "we can always go get her if it's bad."

Howard grunted again.

"We don't have to decide right now," she said, "let's talk about it some more in the morning."

Howard grunted again and Lorry got close to his ear.

"If you come to bed right now, I'll do that thing that you like."

Howard felt his face flush and his eyes perked up.

"Really?" he asked.

"Come find out for yourself," said Lorry.

And that, ladies and gentlemen, is what they call compromise in the Rubenstein house.

*pause for laugh
*wait for applause
*bow

change the channel

"...present the next installment of Frankie the Fish and his Dancing Pekingese.

change the channel

what else is on...

Sixteen years passed as time only could in New York; quickly and with the callousness of a train filled with lightning rats. It took some time for Mary to acclimate to the pacing and rhythm of the city, but after a few years in the current she had begun to move like a local. Instead of frogs, Mary had pigeons. Instead of bullies, Mary had cops. Instead of ravines, Mary found the party scene and club circuit, with all the flavors they entailed. The Rubenstein's were gold stars all around about indoctrinating Mary into city life, but there were other avenues of experience for which they were underqualified.

With Ruth as a guide and her parents as guardians, Mary's adolescent years were well taken care of. She learned the subway system with the minimal number of expected mistakes. She became familiar with Shea (Citi) Stadium, but although she lived in a Mets house, she never developed a love for baseball. Her scholastic achievements improved from sub-par to hey-not-bad, but she still struggled with numbers and science. She was beginning to flourish in the arts though, and music took the front seat. Her teenage years proved that she thrived in the punk aesthetic and developed a taste for loud, aggressive music. She even joined a few bands. Now well into her late twenties, Mary had established herself as a member of the underground music scene.

One night Mary went to a friend's place for a party. They were not especially good friends, and it was not a particularly exciting party, but the music was good and there was plenty of liquor. Four people were sitting on the floor in a circle passing joints around while an assortment of early arrivals mingled throughout the room. Some folks were already paired up as friends or lovers or something else, but there were also those who just liked to lurk. These folks will generally go to parties by themselves, sometimes uninvited, and just stand in the middle of a room or linger on the wall and watch. Sometimes they watch with a sense of harmless curiosity and sometimes they watch with devious intentions. Sometimes even they could not tell the difference. You can always spot a lurker by how few people talk to them, how little they move, and how generally unremarkable they appear. Lurkers generally live off a steady supply of liquor, coffee, and nicotine. It seems like they never eat. If you do happen to spot a lurker in the wild, keep an eye on them but try not to be so obvious about it. Lurk casually.

Then there's the opposite of the lurker. These examples of social diuretics are always up and around. They spend most of the party checking on other people and making sure that everyone is having a good time, especially if the guests would rather be left alone. Although they might enter a conversation with the expectation of engaging with other people, the topic would often shift to a greedy monopoly of their own importance. They also found joy in introducing two strangers and hoping that they hit it off, just so that they can take credit for it later. These folks live for stimulants. Coke, ecstasy, molly, amphetamines, all of it would amplify their positivity and initiate the quenchless thirst for more of that good feeling, wherever it can come from. It would be foolish to try very hard to find them. They will find you and become your best friend, whether you like it or not.

The sex addicts were the politest of the bunch. Everything came with consent and there were even those who got off on consent alone. They would ask permission for anything and everything and if you were to refuse, they would simply blush and keep it moving. If they did find someone who was willing to partner up, they would disappear for the rest of the night, only to be heard through the walls. If two should happen to find each other, and if they did not already have a jaded history together, then golly, look out. It can set off like a tornado and it would be best to get out of the way. Unless that happens to be your thing.

Some folks took heroin, and they also took naps. You would find them standing in the middle of the room or sitting against the walls with their bodies limp and their eyes open a quarter of what they would normally be. Often present and distant in the moment far away, there was an unpredictable possibility to have an individual on heroin carry a full conversation with you while looking fast asleep. Most of them had a very good sense of humor. Mary always found amazement in the heroin addicts' ability to stand slouched on a fast train without holding onto anything. All other passengers would be jostled around and knocked about by the commute, but the heroin user simply balanced like a surfing monk. She had never seen them fall and they would never miss their stop. It was a mystifying observation.

Like any good party host whose intentions were to ensure a memorable experience, there were a series of available pills on display for consumption without request. If there were also bowls of M&M's or Skittles at the same kind of party, then it would be up to the host to label each appropriately. Of course, there had been a few close calls and instances of foolishness, but most folks had enough sense to know what went into their mouths. It was far from a perfect system, but statistically speaking, the numbers were ok.

Mary dabbled in different things, but she preferred pills. She found comfort in a balance of chemical enhancement and the distortion of reality that they caused. They were small, concealable, and produced no recognizable odors. Cocaine was something that Mary enjoyed, but she was also aware of how much she enjoyed it. She said that it was only on special occasions, but you would be surprised how many special occasions could spring up at any given opportunity. Mary did not consider weed to be drugs. Weed was weed and weed was good. Her favorite moments were the times when she had to stop and ask herself, *Am I high?* If you have to ask yourself, then yes. You are high. Mary liked getting high for two reasons. Firstly, Mary liked to get high because feeling high felt good. Secondly, if she felt high then she could avoid having to feel anything else.

There had been years of experimentation and exposure to different substances and their effects, each with different results. Some settled better than others, but Mary kept to her preferences. She could hang and knew where to get whatever she needed at any given opportunity. The threat of boredom or navel gazing could easily be snuffed out on any given evening. There was a finite value of life that Mary kept for the sake of self-preservation, but there was an unmistakably strong attraction towards self-destruction, if it was on her terms.

Mary took a spot on a window seat next to the makeshift bar in the back of the room. There was a time nearly one hundred years ago when this window seat had been used as a fantastic ornament for pensive observation. The height and solitude of the once quiet apartment had allowed previous tenants the opportunity to visually escape the claustrophobic feeling of the city and watch whatever was happening in the outside world. There was evidence that the window seat had once been adorned with wood carved decoration and soft upholstered cushions for which to lean an elbow on and watch the snowfall or summer rooftop barbecues. Now it was a plank of old wood built into the wall at the base of the window and the carvings had long since been worn down to thin lines. Mary opened a fresh bottle of whiskey and poured herself a generous amount into a glass without ice. She paired the whiskey with a longneck bottle of beer and looked out of the window, down into the silent city streets below.

If this ain't nice, she thought to herself.

"Hello, Ms. Mary," called a voice.

From across the room came the smiling eyes of Joey Boulm. Joey was a lanky thing, all arms and legs with the kind of face you trusted implicitly. He was the first friend that Mary had made when she moved to Brooklyn, but he was Ruth's friend first. Joey had lived across the street from the Rubenstein's his whole life and was a regular guest in their home. Many evenings were spent with Joey coming over after school to do his homework and join the Rubenstein's for dinner. It was never questioned why Joey felt uncomfortable spending time in his own home, but it was understood that Joey preferred the Rubenstein's company. This was not a problem for anyone involved and it was more unusual for Joey to not be around for dinner. Sometimes Lorry would call Joey to make sure he had eaten.

Joey and Mary immediately got along in their youth and soon became best friends. They even tried dating for a while in high school, but it became an incontrovertible truth that Joey was in fact very gay. His coming out was a difficult process as Joey had not yet felt brave enough to admit what he wanted from life. The end of Mary and Joey's romantic relationship only led to their being even closer friends. If anything, it may have saved Joey's life. Now they were truly inseparable.

The teenage years were a difficult time for Joey, as his family were openly displeased at his being gay and he wanted nothing more than to find love and acceptance. Feeling less safe each day, Joey moved out of his parents' apartment at seventeen and stayed with the Rubenstein's for the rest of his high school education. After having been raised to navigate the social demands of a community in which he felt no direct part, embracing his sexuality left Joey feeling afraid as much as he felt free. His own adventures were beginning to take hold and there was a new era on the horizon. His friendship with Mary flourished as they both discovered party drugs around the same time.

    Joey walked through the small group on the living room floor and only accidentally kicked one person. There was a small complaint from the hippie on the rug, but it dissolved into a pathetic mumble of frustration. Joey handed a small box wrapped in yellow paper to Mary, kissed her on the cheek, and wished her a happy birthday.

    "My birthday was three weeks ago," said Mary.

    "I know," said Joey, "but I was out of town on a secret mission. Open it up."

    Mary opened the box to find a five-inch green glass frog with raised blue eyes. It had a pleasant weight and the glass felt cold in her hands. She smiled at Joey and hugged him around the neck.

    "Thank you, Joey!" she said, "it's perfect!"

    "Happy birthday. You want a drink?"

    Mary held up her two drinks and Joey poured himself a tall glass of whiskey. They toasted to each of their good health and Joey downed his drink in a single gulp, causing his face to twist up as the whiskey lingered in his throat.

    "Fuck," he said, "I'm back."

    Mary sipped her whiskey and offered Joey her beer as a chaser. He took it graciously and drank deeply from the bottle. He handed it back to Mary, but she told him to keep it. There was gratitude in Joey's voice before he noticed the fresh tattoo across her knuckles. He took her hands in his and began to examine her life choices.

    "Baby, what did you do," asked Joey, "you have such good hands."

    "Don't be such a nerd," said Mary, "you're not my real dad."

    "Ma'am, if I was your dad, you would be immaculate. What does it say?"

    Mary held her fists together to show "KING SHIT" across her knuckles. Joey rolled his eyes and sucked his teeth.

    "Mary, you're lucky you're so pretty because goddamn."

    "Fuck off," said Mary, "let me know when you're ready to get a tattoo. I know a guy who tattooed Iggy Pop's son."

    "Let me know when I can meet Iggy. Where's your man?"

    "Couldn't make it. He's stuck at work."

    "He works too much," said Joey, "what did y'all do for your birthday?"

    "Nothing," said Mary, "he got stuck at work."

    "Man likes to get stuck. If I was him, I would quit my job and work for you full time. He can't keep doing you like this."

    "It's not his fault. It sucks, but it's whatever."

"How long y'all been together?"

"Just seven months. It's not a big deal or anything."

"*Just* seven months?! Mary, seven months isn't exactly a fling! Now I know I haven't met Danny more than...maybe twice?"

"David", said Mary, "his name is David."

"Fine, 'David'. I haven't met 'David' more than once or twice, but seven months? That's like...ok. Question: How often does he go down on you?"

"That's none of your fucking business," said Mary.

"I rest my case," said Joey, "do yourself a favor. Get an electric toothbrush...or a vacuum cleaner."

"Forget it," said Mary. She had already been ignoring her own suspicions of David's infidelities, so Joey alluding to any of his other shortcomings was far from helpful. Mary had decided a long time ago to carry herself as someone with an openly relaxed view on sexual relationships. She felt that the emotional ownership of another person was immoral and an outdated kind of prison. This is what she told herself.

There was a fair amount of truth to the philosophy, but once the promise of devotion had moved past the realm of a casual relationship and into something more serious, the threat of abandonment would return. Even in Mary's growth and maturity, there were some learned habits and responses that would not allow her to open herself completely to the love of another person. And although it was sometimes difficult to find a partner whose intentions were sincere; anger would only come around when there were secrets involved. It was not the sex that bothered Mary, David was welcome to come and go as he pleased. The dishonesty was what bothered Mary. Seven months is a long time to lie to somebody, especially when you come home smiling.

Joey grunted sarcastically as they sipped their drinks and took in the party. A guest was walking around the room speaking with enthusiasm about a large bottle of specially crafted beer that he had brought with him. He was explaining to people that it was homemade and that he had been cultivating the batch for months. The young man boasted that it was better than anything else being served that night. He had a curled mustache painted on the side of his face, an ironic fashion monocle, and a white rose pinned to his red velvet lapel. He was passing around small paper cups and insisted that everyone got a chance to sample it. For the low, low price of one hundred-fifty dollars, the young brewmaster was willing to make you your very own bottle. Complete with custom, one-of-a-kind, limited-edition artwork illustrated by his girlfriend. He handed Joey and Mary their own little cups and poured small amounts into each. Standing like an expectant chef with sparkling eyes, he watched with anticipation as they drank his beer. It tasted awful, but Mary smiled out of politeness. Joey immediately spit it on the floor and said that it tasted like dog piss. The enthusiast's face dropped, and he left the pair alone with his ego bruised and his night ruined.

"My god, that was bad," said Mary.

"Fucking dog piss," said Joey, drinking from his own beer, "you seen Laura?"

"No," said Mary, "I don't think she's here. Is she coming?"

"Said she was. I'm supposed to pick up from her later."

"Anything new?"

"Naw, just the usual, I think."

"Lemme know if you talk to her. Can you get me some pretty ones?"

"The prettiest. I'll let you know."

A small group of people entered the room and were met with a pleasant reaction from the rest of the party. Joey's eyes locked onto someone in the group and excused himself.

"Listen, I'll see you later," he said, "lose your man and get some strange."

Joey walked across the room and accidentally kicked the same person again without apologizing. He embraced an older man who had arrived with the group and the two kissed deeply as though they had known each other well. There was a fleeting moment of tenderness before they both began to laugh and went into one of the bedrooms, closing the door behind them.

Mary had recognized Joey's boyfriend before they had kissed, but she could never remember his name. Steve or Simon or something. They had met a few times before, but she never had a good feeling about him. He tended to dominate conversations and make people feel smaller than they were. She thought he was a bully, but it was also none of her business who Joey spent his time with. She did find it odd that Joey would be full of such grand advice while maintaining his own toxic relationship. But again, it was none of her business.

Mary returned to her window seat and observed the city below. It was not an unfamiliar scene for Mary as she had spent many nights watching the city from the window of someone else's party. She never could tell how she kept getting invited to these types of things, but her circles ran wide and there was always something going on. Mary would cherry pick different events that seemed unique or ambiguous, but it was often the same scene. There were always drugs. A conversation has no need to be stimulating if you are already stimulated.

Mary took her cue and walked over to the candy bowl that held an assortment of pills and capsules of different shapes and colors. Picking out three yellow ones that she recognized, she popped them into her mouth and washed them back with her whiskey. There could be a serious gamble if you are unsure of what you are grabbing. If this is done carelessly and you miscalculate your limitations, then there is no telling where you may end up. Nine times out of ten you just wake up on the floor of a strange bathroom with vomit and piss on your clothes. There is also the reality where that little extra push over the cliff is all it would take to kill you. Mary had a fair amount of experience, but that did not make her wise.

There had been a few times where Mary had come close to experiencing a lethal error, but thankfully her luck had held up so far. After a few scares, she had begun to learn how to pace herself and find what kind of chemistry played well together.

Someone changed the music from eighties new wave to heavy drum and bass, making the sudden shift abrasive on some of the half-gone partygoers. Nobody complained, but the conversations became louder as the music jumped in volume. The rhythms filled all the awkward silences, taking them away to be forgotten until tomorrow. The music rose severely as more guests seemed to be arriving every five minutes or so. Things were starting to come alive, but it was only midnight. There was still plenty of party left to be had.

Mary was starting to feel good as the rooms filled with the kinds of stories she had already heard dozens of times. Irrelevant gossip, laughter, lousy flirtations, arguments, name dropping, crying, and the sounds of mediocre sex coming from somewhere in the walls layered with the beat coming out of the speakers. It was a party that she could experience and still feel removed from. Mary made passive observations from her window seat perch while her mind started buzzing like the inside of a hornet's nest. She tapped her fingertips together sequentially to the music while counting her teeth with the tip of her tongue. This was a nervous habit that she had developed over the years when she was high, and she usually lost count of her teeth after six.

Switching from whiskey to beer for the sake of keeping hydrated, Mary started to feel a little sick. The air was thick with cigarettes, body heat, sweat, cologne, perfume, and marijuana which swirled around the music and conversation. There was a quick panic which spiked from the base of her skull and ran the full length of her guts. An evacuation of mass quantities was imminent. She heard that voice in the back of her head that said:

Hi, me again. It's been a while, but I just wanted you to know that you're about to vomit quite a bit in... thirty seconds.

"Move!" shouted Mary as she pushed a crowd apart and scaled human mountains to reach the security of someone else's bathroom.

Three people were having sex in the bathtub, but they only slightly protested as Mary proceeded to vomit heavily into the toilet. The pills had been absorbed into her system to where she would remain stoned for the rest of the night, but the combination of whiskey and an empty stomach had knocked a sort of sponge into her brain. The forces working together created a strange focus that kept Mary sitting calmly on the floor while expunging and waiting for the world to stop spinning around her. She thought she heard somebody scream before she fell asleep with her head against the toilet bowl.

    The fluorescent rod above the mirror flickered irregular light that guaranteed nobody would look attractive lying on the bathroom floor. The vomit and piss that Mary was lying in did her no real harm apart from the sour smell and the texture. She woke up with her hair pasted to the side of her head and she had no memory of what day it was. Her head was full of wax, and she was moving underwater while one eye would open just enough to feel pain. The only sounds she could hear were the droning buzz from the light and a combination of snores coming from the other side of the bathroom door. The floor felt cold on her skin and that part was nice, but the growing sensation of consciousness brought other feelings that were less nice. Running her hand down the side of her dress allowed Mary to shrink in disgust with the awareness of what it was that she was lying in. Whether it was her own or someone else's was irrelevant, but Mary would try her best to convince herself that it was all her own.

    Steadying herself with one hand on the lid of the toilet and the other on the side of the sink, Mary did her best to stand up. She made it to her knees before she decided that was good enough for the time being. The water left the tap in a thick flow of cold relief as Mary let the sink fill up and dunked her face for a while. She had nearly fallen back asleep like this, but the sensation of water going up her nose shocked her back to consciousness. She came up from the sink sputtering and coughing while trying to keep her balance and not fall back on the floor. This had proven to fail as her body betrayed her. Mary tilted backwards and landed hard against the wall. With her legs still unsteady she slid down to the floor, letting out a long whoosh of air from her lungs. This was already more activity than Mary could tolerate.

    Fifteen minutes passed until she felt compelled to try and stand up again. The necessity to rinse her dress out in the tub was paramount. Pulling the shower curtain back, Mary found a young man curled up asleep and gently snoring in the tub. He was wearing brown corduroy pants and a light blue shirt with buttons down the front. He was not wearing any shoes.

    "Hey," said Mary.

    He stirred lightly but remained asleep.

    "Come on, man. Get up."

Mary shook his shoulder and the young man inhaled deeply as he turned to see who was shaking him. He then proceeded to cough and curse with the awkward beginnings of a tremendous hangover.

"Can you get up, please?" asked Mary.

"What happened," he said, "where am I?"

"You're in the fucking bathtub so get out."

He muttered an apology, but it took him three tries to jettison his body from the greasy tub. He lay on the floor for a moment until he began to recognize the variety of smells that surrounded him.

"Oh, Jesus," he said, "oh, God!"

Overwhelmed by the simultaneous return of all five of his senses, the young man proceeded to vomit heavily into the toilet. Mary was already peeling her dress from her body, leaving her modesty behind. The young man hung loosely off the side of the toilet, ambivalent to Mary's nakedness as she began to rinse herself off in the shower. The hot water hit Mary like the breath of heaven as she stood naked with her forehead pressed against the shower wall.

"Where am I?" he asked.

"You're at Mike Fisher's place," said Mary.

"My girlfriend…aw, shit. She's gonna kill me. She said she just wanted to pop in for a minute. Probably got pissed and left. What time is it?"

"Don't talk to me."

"Sorry."

He sat on the bathroom floor and did his best not to look at Mary. The steam from the shower brought enough humidity to make smells become flavors that stuck to his tongue. Everything in the room was becoming thicker and his clothes were taking on a new uncomfortable weight. He tried not to look at anything or touch anything as he considered the possibility that no surface was safe.

"I'm gonna go," he said.

Mary ignored him and brought her face against the water falling from the shower head. She liked to let the water rush into her ears and stand with the sound of torrential gales against her inner canal. It had become something of a ritual. She held her dress against the hot water and let the debris fall from the fabric and onto the floor of the tub. There was a good amount of remainder that began to clog the drain, so Mary did her best to grind it down with her heel. It was a weak effort, the kind of idea that you already knew was bad. She gave up almost as soon as she started. Doing as good a job as she could, she flattened the dress out across the shower curtain rod and hoped that it would dry quickly. Realizing that she did not have any clothes, Mary stood in the tub ankle deep in dirty water and tried to call out to the young man from behind the bathroom door.

"Hey!" she shouted.

This was met with a series of groans from other party guests who had been asleep across the different surfaces in the apartment. They had a few choice opinions for what they thought the young man and Mary should do with themselves. Three people were sitting at the kitchen table ripping lines of cocaine off a Yogi Bear plate. They had not fallen asleep and were trying to squeeze that last bit of fun out of a night become morning. Mary's shouting from the bathroom presented no bother to the hyper-stimulated. Their focus and mind crazed effect was all the distraction they needed. Another small bag of cocaine was being emptied on the plate as the young man returned to the bathroom door and asked Mary if she was ok.

"Can you find me some clothes, please," she said.
"What do you need?"
"Fucking...clothes, I don't care."
"What's your size?"
"I. Don't. Care. God, just get me a big t-shirt or something!"
"Ok," he said, "ok, hold on."

There was the sound of shuffling, some more cursing and apologies as the young man scrambled through the loose clothes that lay scattered across the apartment. With the amount of clothing that had been abandoned from the previous night, he thought he had done well. He could have done worse.

"Here," he said from outside the door.

Mary opened the door a crack and looked at him through bloodshot eyes. She narrowed her vision out of general frustration and snatched the clothing from the young man's hands.

"What the fuck is this?" asked Mary.
"You said you didn't care."

The sound of aggravated surrender came from Mary's side of the door along with the sounds of someone trying to dress themselves with a poor sense of balance. Mary opened the bathroom door and walked past the young man without saying anything. Going directly to the kitchen sink, she began drinking straight from the tap in large gulps.

"You're welcome," he said.

Mary had been given a pair of black skinny jeans that were too tight for her and an oversized black T-shirt that read, "BIG PINK" in pink and white letters above a sad looking cartoon panther. There was a rust-colored bandana hanging out of the back pocket of her jeans which Mary used to blow her nose. With the lingering odor of stale cigarettes and the sour smell of alcohol being sweat out of so many different bodies, Mary tried to open the window while the young man did his best to look for coffee. Finding none, he sat on a gauche green paisley ottoman with gold fringe and waited for his head to stop hurting. Looking at things had become painful.

"Have you seen my shoes?" he asked.

"What?"

"They're like, black dress shoes. Size ten with a rounded toe. Oxfords, I think."

"I don't care about your shoes," said Mary, "is there coffee?"

"Not that I could find, no."

"Ugh," said Mary, "why are you still here?"

"Don't worry," he said, "as soon as I find my shoes I'm gone."

The young man stooped down to pick up a pair of black shoes that were tucked halfway beneath the sofa. He pulled them out and did his best to reshape them from having been compressed for so long. Mary watched this process with the slow reaction time that accompanies a hangover. He had already tried one of them on before she interjected.

"Those are my shoes," she said, "do they even fit?"

"They're a little tight," he said.

The front half of his foot barely managed to squeeze into the sneaker, but his heel stuck out like a slipper. He stood up to admire the shoes before removing them and Mary was struck in the chest with a strong wave of Deja Vu. She was trying to place the feeling from memory, or it might have been from a dream, but something about this made her want to cry.

"What's your name?" she asked.

"Don't worry about it," he said, "you're never going to see me again."

"Listen, I'm sorry if I was being a dick. My name's Mary."

"Well, good for you and your father," said the young man, "I wish you nothing but the...there we go."

He reached beneath a sleeping couple that were wrapped around each other and pulled his shoes out from under them. He set Mary's shoes on top of the couch and laced up his own, trying to be as quiet as possible while also working quickly. With one shoe in hand, he cursed under his breath and hobbled his way out of the apartment without a word to Mary. She was still trying to process what had just happened as she leaned against the window seat and watched him leave.

Mary's own phone was still lying on the bar in the back of the room. She turned it on and saw that a slew of messages had been pouring in from the night before. They were all from her boyfriend David. Some of them were fragments of thoughts that ended abruptly followed by apology texts explaining that the previous messages were incomplete and sent by accident. There was a repetitive message saying that she had to call him as soon as she could. Half an hour after that there had been another text asking when she would call, followed by a series of three question marks.

One hour after that message had been received came a long series of paragraphs explaining that he was ending their relationship. David had been seeing someone else for well over a month and he was sorry, no hard feelings, I still love you, want to remain friends, good luck.

Mary put her phone away and looked down to find half of her glass frog broken on the floor.

12. I Can't Do This Anymore

Ruth was waking up in the afternoon after her own party across town from the night before. It was a formal affair that began after the gallery opening which debuted her work as an up-and-coming video artist. Her opening consisted of sequential pieces that centered around the presence of gender and sexual identity among people experiencing homelessness. It was received by most with casual interest in the subject matter. The form and technique were the talking points for the guests as they made their way through the gallery to pause and consider Ruth's message. The opening was positively received, but the review on the second to last page in the next day's Arts & Leisure section of the New York Times would be politely skimmed, at best. Most attendees found the films to be very pretty but thought the subject matter to be too uncomfortable or depressing for anyone to risk discussing their opinions.

The after-party was where the sophistication ended, and the real social attraction began in the form of networking and self-indulgence. In a world where influence is everything and climbing the ladder of success is the core incentive for participation, modesty and altruism often took a back seat unless philanthropy happened to be a person's entire personality. That much generosity could also exist as a different kind of vanity. It was Ruth's party, but she felt more like a catalyst for the event than a host or participant. Many of the party guests skipped her gallery opening and had no idea who she was.

The night unfolded in a ritualistic fashion. There were rules for how to engage in a semi-formal societal setting. Light security ensured that only the right kind of people were allowed admittance to the event, but they were also tasked with gently removing prominent figures who were getting close to embarrassing themselves. Every person of note had their own warning signs of excess that were well known and documented ahead of time. Ruth herself spent a good portion of her evening being mistaken for a member of the catering staff. Whenever she had a drink in her hand, although it was non-alcoholic, an older guest would warn her of the dangers of openly drinking on the job and comment on her choice of attire, asking why she was out of uniform.

If she was not being mistaken for catering, Ruth was asked what mystery man she was with and if he was the artist. Ruth's personal experiences allowed her to recognize these questions to contain multiple meanings. The more she heard, the more she began to make mental notes for her next series of pieces. Those who did know Ruth and recognized her for her work were supportive but said the least. Those who did not know Ruth would gush in a way that was much too kind to be taken with sincerity. There was repetitive language that suggested the rehearsal of a prepared script for those who were too self-absorbed to engage with the work honestly and too cowardly to produce any real criticism. Ruth was trying to have a good time but being new to the formal art scene was proving to be educational.

A few of the party guests would tell Ruth stories about how they personally knew the artist. Ruth would stand and listen to them gush on romantic fantasies and intimate experiences, some even sexual in nature, in which they were favored into the inner workings of their genius. The specific details flourished with exaggerated examples of privilege in which Ruth could foster no memory because they had never happened. She had never met any of these people and would certainly never sleep with any of them. The stories amused her in a strange and surreal way, but she gave no comment. Ruth would simply nod her head and say, "That's fascinating."

She woke up in her bed around one o'clock in the afternoon, having returned home earlier that morning around six. She stretched her arms and legs in the light that barely broke through her thick cotton blackout curtains hanging from her windows. These had been installed in her apartment so as not to find herself disturbed by the sun. Reaching for her phone that was charging on her bedside table, her arm brushed the warm naked body of Julia who lightly stirred with Ruth's touch. Ruth disregarded her phone and wrapped her arm around Julia's chest to pull her closer. She made a small mewing sound and held on to Ruth's arm before turning her head to lightly kiss her on the lips with her eyes still closed.

"Mmmmg'mornin'," said Julia.

"Good morning."

"Good dreams?"

"No dreams."

"Even better," said Julia, "I don't like it when you have good dreams without me. Makes me miss you."

"I make it a point not to enjoy my dreams unless you're in them," said Ruth, "coffee?"

"Yes please," said Julia, "you were snoring again. I think it's getting worse, but I can't tell. How did the party end? I'm sorry I had to leave early."

"It was fine," said Ruth, "bullshit and fine."

"Why bullshit?"

"A whole lot of rich old white people talking about rich old white people and rich white kids talking about rich white kids. There were maybe...three new people that I liked. Laura and Joey B. stopped by, which was nice, but it didn't matter whether I was there or not. A lot of people thought I was one of the waiters."

Julia laughed at this, but Ruth's feelings were still hurt from the party. Recently someone commented on her being an impressive black artist. Ruth wondered if anyone had been complimented for being an impressive white artist. She felt Julia's arms wrapped around her waist as she began to kiss Ruth on her back. It made her tingle all over.

"Well, I think you're a genius," said Julia, "and I would still love you even if all you did was make paperclips. We just gotta figure out how to get money from the rich old white people and then we never have to see them again."

"Any advice on that?" asked Ruth, "you got any insight on getting white people money?"

"Make them feel guilty," said Julia, "we love throwing money at a problem as long as we don't have to be accountable. At least the food was good."

"It was pretty good," said Ruth, "I talked with this older guy who told me all about how he spent a week fucking me in Berlin two summers ago."

Julia looked at Ruth with confusion and she looked slightly hurt. Ruth laughed and started to put her finger up Julia's nose, to which Julia growled and turned away.

"It didn't happen," said Ruth, "he was telling me a story about me, but I'd never met him before. He was fishing for clout."

"Ew," said Julia, "that's just fucking weird."

She pulled herself closer against Ruth's chest and buried her face against her skin. Julia blew a raspberry between Ruth's breasts which made her jump out of bed and laugh.

"What do you want to do today," asked Julia, "I feel like you've been so busy getting this show together that I haven't seen you in years."

"I have one more reception tonight and then I don't have to worry about this again until I have to take it down."

"How much longer do I have you today?"

"I have to leave around four or four-thirty."

Julia pouted about this and leaned over the side of the bed. She wrapped her arms around Ruth's waist, kissed her on the stomach, and looked up at her with her big green eyes.

"Do you have to go?" asked Julia.

"I really don't want to."

"What if we took your Frankenstein cut out and just put some sunglasses on it. We can lean it up against the wall and nobody would know the difference."

Ruth chuckled at this. The Frankenstein cut-out had been a Christmas gift from Mary years ago. It was in a closet behind a collection of coats and miscellaneous items, but she kept it because it made her feel closer to her sister than she did in real life.

"Honestly, no," said Ruth, "nobody would notice."

This made Ruth a little sadder than she was before. She had worked so hard to get to where she was as an artist, but she also felt like a hypocrite because of the financial support she had received from her parents. She would wonder if what she did was good or if she had just utilized her comforts to get noticed by the right people. Were they even the right people to begin with? Did she deserve any of the successes that she had already achieved?

"Go get the coffee," said Julia, "and then let me try and see if I can convince you to stay in bed with me for the next three years."

"I love you," said Ruth.

"I love you, too," said Julia.

Ruth went to the kitchen to make the coffee and turned on the television. No rain today, another subway workers' strike causing delays, seventeen people killed in a mass shooting in a grocery store outside of Oklahoma City, a new panda was born in a zoo somewhere, a body was found in a dumpster behind a Sizzler in New Jersey, and no drastic changes from the day-to-day. Ruth recognized that she felt a numbness to bad news which had developed over the years. It was not that she was unempathetic, she recognized the pain and hurt in other people, but the cynicism of experience meant that very few things surprised her anymore. She brought the coffee back into the bedroom and handed a mug to Julia who was scrolling through her phone.

"Thanks," she said, "did you hear about that dumpster body behind the Sizzler?"

"Yeah, it was on the TV."

"I don't think I've ever been to a Sizzler," said Julia, "We should go. they're gonna get a whole lot of new business out of this."

"You think so?"

"Oh yeah, it's already trending. 'The Sizzler Slasher'. That place is going to be an urban legend spot for a month or two and then forgotten with the rest of old internet. Might pop up again as a nostalgia documentary in ten years, but that'd be it."

"Shit's wild," said Ruth, "all the information in the world at our fingertips and we get off on repetitive porn and conspiracy theories."

"What's the capital of Iran?" asked Julia.

"I don't know," said Ruth.

"Can you explain the mythology and fan theories of that show you like," asked Julia, "Kitty Kitty Bumblebee, or whatever?"

"Well, yeah."

"See," said Julia, "you're just as bad. Come join the rest of us idiots and get back into bed. I want to make you miss me later."

Ruth smirked as she swaggered towards the bed and put a baritone to her voice.

"Hey, baby, didja know I'mma ahtist?"

"God," said Julia, "don't do that! I hate it when you do that."

"Come on, baby," continued Ruth as she grabbed the front of her crotch, "I'm gonna make ya come!"

"Fuck right off with that," said Julia, "I was good to go and then you went all creepy. Forget it. Thanks for the coffee."

Julia cocooned herself with the duvet, covered her head, and turned her back to Ruth.

"Oh, come on," said Ruth in her normal voice, "I'm sorry."

"No creeps allowed in this bed," said Julia.

"Fine," said Ruth, a little deflated, "fine, I'm sorry."

She turned to leave before getting hit in the head with a pen that had been lying on the floor next to the bed. Julia's grinning face was poking out from beneath the duvet, and she playfully bit her bottom lip.

"You are such a pussy," said Julia, "you give up way too easy."

"Oh, you're dead," said Ruth.

And so on, and so forth...

Ruth left her apartment at five o'clock and began to head towards the second reception of her exhibition. She wanted to get there early and help her agent Alex set up for the second opening night. Julia had tried her best to keep Ruth naked and in bed, and to her credit she almost succeeded, but the pride that Ruth had with her work and her need to be recognized as a real artist overpowered her desire to spend another three hours edging closer to orgasm. The decision to leave was a photo finish, to be sure. Ruth did, however, make a promise to Julia that she would be home earlier than she had been the night before while Julia promised to be a little rougher the next time Ruth came to bed. This brought some assemblance of acceptance and anticipation to the time they would spend apart. As soon as Ruth sat down on the train, she received a lewd photograph from Julia on her phone. Ruth spent a large portion of her commute peeking at the picture discreetly and fantasizing about what lay in store for her upon her return.

The gallery had been swept, cleaned, and was relatively empty when Ruth arrived. Her agent Alex stood with their back to the door as they watched one of Ruth's video displays. Ruth stood next to Alex and gently touched their shoulders before Alex turned and greeted her with a big hug.

"Hi," said Alex, "Ruth, this is stunning. Truly, this is incredible. I am so proud of you."

Ruth blushed and looked at the floor. Praise made her uncomfortable, but she strove for validation in a sway of contradictions.

"Last night was phenomenal," said Alex, "we have some good offers, and I've been told that two guys from Museum Ludwig will be coming tonight to see your work. If you can get a residency in Cologne, then all sorts of doors will open for you."

"And you'll do pretty well for yourself off the commissions, I'll bet."

"What," asked Alex, "you don't want your friends to do well?"

"I'm just fucking with you."

The two walked through the exhibition and went over the itinerary for the night's events. The owner of the gallery will welcome the guests at eight o'clock sharp, followed by a statement by Alex as the artist's representative. Ruth would not be expected to speak at all because the artist seldom speaks. Some would argue that the work should speak for itself, but Ruth always thought that was lazy and an easy way to remove the artist from being accountable for their work. If the work could speak for itself, then the artist would serve no real purpose after the fact. This would become another intrusive thought upon Ruth's mind in the early morning hours.

After Alex does their job and represents Ruth in a positive light of brilliance, then a small serving of cocktails and hors d'oeuvres will begin. This will allow the invited guests to experience Ruth's collection of video projects with a nice glass of malbec, or pinot grigio, as well as a delicate arrangement of charcuterie, caviar, and shrimp canape. Ruth will then be permitted to mingle amongst the guests and be mistaken for a waitress or a janitor for the rest of the night. She would love to meet any waiters or janitors that also wore Santorelli with a Botkier bag when they worked, but apparently that was a different kind of uniform. Only after the last guest is ushered out from the gallery can Ruth begin to make her way home to where she will find Julia in bed, just as she had left her, and hopefully in possession of an insatiable sexual appetite.

Thoughts of naked Julia brought Ruth to text her some softcore eroticism. Ruth found an exhilaration to being aroused in public. It had become a kind of game where she would try to reach a tipping point while remaining poised and coherently engaged with those around her. She had just hit send when Alex returned to her side.

"Ruth, come on," they said, "I want you to meet someone."

Ruth followed Alex into a back room where an older man in an expensive suit was watching a video unit that had yet to be mounted to a wall of the gallery. The flickering images showed a video of a naked man who was homeless and washing his penis with a sponge. The scene would split with a woman breastfeeding her child before cutting to a person of Asian heritage staring blankly into the camera. The loop would repeat as soon as he looked like he was about to laugh. Each of the images were shown through a kaleidoscopic array of colors that shifted through secondary tones and blurred distortion. The man turned to Alex and Ruth and smiled passively as they entered the room.

"Ruth, this is Mr. Carter Davis. He's been asking about you all morning."

Mr. Davis extended his hand and Ruth was met with a warm and soft palm, comparable to handling a small loaf of fresh bread. An inoffensive suggestion of European cologne lingered from his wrist.

"Please," he said, "call me Carter."

"A pleasure," said Ruth, "thank you for your interest in my work."

"I was at your opening last night," said Mr. Davis, "I see a lot of potential for growth in what you're doing here. I do have some thoughts if you'll indulge me."

"Oh?"

"What you have here," he said gesturing to the screen on the table, "is bullshit. It's pretty, but it's bullshit."

Ruth's body flushed as she imagined hot nails going into the body of Mr. Carter Davis.

"What do you mean," she asked.

"Have you ever known poverty, Ms. Rubenstein?" he asked.

"Well, yes. When I was young," she said, "before my mother…"

"Before your mother became famous and catered to your every comfort?"

His interjection cut Ruth deeply as she had no argument to deny the reality.

"This may be what poverty looks like, Ms. Rubenstein, but you have no idea what poverty feels like, do you? What it smells like? What it sees in the dark when a gunshot breaks through the bedroom window and into the next room where your children sleep? Have you ever gone to bed hungry? Missed a bill? Wondered where your next meal is going to come from?"

"Now wait just a minute," shouted Alex.

"I do have an interest in your work, Ms. Rubenstein," said Mr. Davis, "but call me when you decide to grow up. Good luck tonight and I hope you have a comfortable evening."

"And what about you," shouted Alex, "'Mr. Board of Trustees'?! Not exactly minimum wage, you asshole!"

"Don't change the subject," said Mr. Davis, "criticize me all you want, but it doesn't make a difference."

Mr. Davis laid a business card on the table in front of the flickering screen. He paused for a moment and asked Alex a question without turning to face them.

"How much is this piece selling for?" he asked.

Alex could feel themselves losing their temper, but they tried to answer his question without shaking.

"Twenty thousand dollars," said Alex.

"Interesting," said Mr. Davis, "I would be curious, Ms. Rubenstein, to know how much each of these...individuals have been compensated for their contribution to your recent success. Do you know how they've been getting on lately?"

Mr. Davis saw himself out. Ruth was numb as the words began to ricochet across her mind. Mr. Davis had confirmed many of Ruth's apprehensions about her work and the walls of confidence that she had built to protect her insecurities began to crumble down around her. Slumping into a chair beside the table, Ruth put a hand against her forehead and stared at the floor.

"I am so sorry," said Alex, "I had no idea that he was going to be such a fucking dick. He's been on the board of trustees at the Met for years. Oh honey, I... I'm so sorry."

Ruth stood from her chair and walked out a fire door, marching down the street with no set destination in mind. She was now convinced that all her work was considered a mockery by everyone who saw it. In her climb towards success and personal fulfillment, despite her concern that the earned attention was all fake, she had never considered the possibility that the masses would reject her. Checking her phone showed that Julia had read her message half an hour ago but had failed to respond. Ruth thought about calling her but found herself instinctually walking into the subterranean bar Bosco's beneath the sidewalk instead.

Bosco's, formerly Roberta's, was now owned by an albino with nystagmus named Reed. Bosco was his dog. Well, Bosco the III, really. Ruth had been to Bosco's a handful of times in a few years but had not developed the kind of relationship where you could be friendly with the owner. She had begun to sneak into Bosco's when she was eighteen but had done so in such a subtle way that nobody seemed to notice. This would become an unfortunate occurrence throughout her adult life, as well. Once Ruth started drinking, it was difficult for her to stop. Because of this, Ruth had been sober for two years.

The bar was peppered with a few people across the room, but it was hardly crowded enough to feel claustrophobic. There was a time when it would be easy to fill Bosco's past capacity, but after the bar had changed hands there were some renovations to allow more seating to increase revenue capacity. A portion of the wall behind the bar was knocked down to make more space for tables and general mobility, but the stage remained out of historic tradition. This was now a place where students from the local jazz consortium could rehearse their material and make a little bit of money. They used to have open mic poetry nights, but they stopped when the crowd became too violent too often. This is what poetry does to people. Keep your children away from poetry if you can help it.

The room had initially been longer than it was wide before the renovations, so the retraction of the bar was helpful in allowing more space for thirsty patrons. A few round tables were added along the wall, but the original booths were kept out of respect for the past. Some of the art remained on the walls from the good old days, but new lighting had been installed beneath the stools and above the large glass mirror that lined the new wall behind the bar. Thankfully these were installed with a dimmer switch.

When Bosco's was Roberta's, there was an almost mythical attraction to romantic fantasy that seemed to be drawn into the place. This was not a terribly unusual trait for a bar to have in New York City, but Roberta's held its own when it came to the stories of the other, more well-known, establishments. One of the popular stories for the bar was when Sonny Rollins got into a fistfight with Enos Slaughter before the Yankees traded him to Kansas City in 1955. There were suspicions that this was the reason why the Yankees traded him to Kansas City, but the reality was that Enos just had a bad year.

There were rumors that James Stewart had punched out John Wayne over a bag of potato chips, Martin Scorsese was found with Sophia Loren smoochin' it up in the mop closet, Eddie Murphy saved a blind man who had suddenly caught fire, and the list went on. Ruth's personal favorite was the story where Frank Sinatra got caught giving Marlon Brando head in one of the stalls of the men's toilet. With the history of fistfights, combustion, and hormonal fumbling that had happened in Roberta's over the years, it was hard to keep track of who was with whom. Ruth was disinterested in the atmosphere or anecdotes that night. Ruth wanted to get drunk. The way she was feeling, it would not take long.

She ordered red wine first out of habit, and when the bartender returned with her glass of cabernet sauvignon, she asked him for a vodka soda as well. When the bartender explained that it was against their policy to serve two drinks to one person at the same time, Ruth nodded and downed the glass of wine in two gulps. She pushed the empty wine glass to the bartender and again asked for her vodka soda. In the span of two hours, Ruth had consumed one glass of cabernet sauvignon, two vodka sodas, one neat whiskey, two beers, and a gin and tonic. After she started to relax, she bummed a cigarette from a fellow bar patron and started her walk back to the gallery. She had not smoked a cigarette since her late teens, but this was more for theatrics than a personal craving. The effect from the alcohol fully hit Ruth when she climbed the steps of Bosco's and was met with the smells of New York City. After that, she was wasted. It was eight-thirty when Ruth returned to the gallery. Standing in front of the chic frosted glass doors, she lit her cigarette and walked inside. Ruth had a plan.

Nobody noticed her at first. The gallery was well attended and there were a fair number of distractions between the social politics and the exhibition itself. Security had become distracted by a rare appearance from What's-Her-Name, who had come to support Ruth but had become the focus of an unwanted pest with too many questions. Ruth blew large plumes of sour smoke in front of her with the hopes of fumigating what she now drunkenly recognized as the cockroaches of the art world. People started to notice Ruth after she pushed a dowager into a table of artisanal toast. The screens on the walls flickered away while all eyes were slowly landing on her. Ruth took the cigarette out of her mouth and extinguished it in somebody's drink.

"Now I know that you all think you're doing *sooooo* well," she slurred across the room, "and I'm sure that most of you are. Because of course you are. But that doesn't excuse you from being the scum of the ffffucking Earth."

Ruth took a drink out from somebody's hand as security began to circle her.

"Have you ever smelt a poor person," she asked to no one in particular, "have you ever shot a child?"

Security was on her quick and she kicked and screamed and bit whatever was in front of her mouth. The scuffle was brief as two large men in suits grabbed Ruth by the arms and legs, ejecting her out the front doors from which she entered. One of them stood guard outside until Ruth left. Giving him the double bird and calling him several choice names that she would later deny for the sake of her own peace of mind, Ruth made her way up the block to the next corner. With no sign of Alex and still no word back from Julia, Ruth hailed a taxi and did her best not to throw up in the back seat. She made it a whole three blocks before the liquor came back up.

Upon returning to her apartment, Ruth found Julia to be gone. This was not entirely unusual as Julia did have her own apartment and was given to evenings of spontaneity, but Ruth did wish that she were there to comfort her. The reality of what she had done was beginning to press upon her inebriation and her mania was falling into a downswing. That untouchable opportunity of her career as an artist which had taken years to achieve had been dismantled in minutes.

So, what, thought Ruth, *poor little rich girl.*

The television was on when she got home. There was an old black and white movie about submarines, so Ruth collapsed on the couch and kicked off her expensive boots that hurt too much to casually wear. There was a passing thought that she should eat something, but she fell asleep as soon as the idea of pizza came into her mind.

Dawn brought the sound of birds on fire, screaming death, and poor hygiene from the tail end of a terrible dream. The room where she had fallen asleep had become the driest place that Ruth had ever known as she opened her eyes and tried to scrape her tongue from the roof of her mouth. There was not enough water in the world to make Ruth feel human again, so she settled for the endless kitchen tap.

She gulped the cold water that fell out of the faucet and ran down her chin onto the front of her dress. Ruth let her wet clothes hang cold against her skin and it brought a comforting weight against her chest. She turned off the faucet and laid her head in her arms as her body went limp against her marble kitchen counters. The surface was cold, which was a nice feeling, but everything else she could feel hurt. Ruth even knew that her hair hurt, in some strange and incomprehensible way.

There was a small white envelope the size of a thank you card left sealed on the kitchen island where she knelt. Ruth dragged it across the marble and found her name scratched in blue ballpoint ink on the front of the envelope. There was a small card inside that read:

Ruth,
I can't do this anymore. I'm sorry
but I've met someone. Just promise me
that, whatever happens, we'll get married
some day. Please don't try to contact me.
-Julia

Tucking the card neatly back into the envelope, Ruth walked to the refrigerator and let the door hang open while she pulled up a chair and sat in the cold light. The thought of eating anything was unappealing and there was nothing that she was looking for. This was an idiosyncrasy that she had developed over the years when she felt overwhelmed. She would sit in front of the open fridge and stare at the bulb while the cold air moved around her. In her current state, the sensation was especially pleasant.

Ruth stared into the refrigerator and thought about Julia in the morning, how she would wrap her whole body around her without even opening her eyes. She thought about Julia laughing at one of her stupid jokes that she had undoubtedly heard countless times before. She thought about Julia dancing. Ruth thought about all of this until tears began to well up behind her eyes. She did not try to fight them as they started falling down her cheeks, but she covered her mouth with her hand as though it would keep the despair from falling out. It was the pain that Ruth needed because if she were in pain then Julia would have to care.

Ruth cried for the better part of the morning. After she had begun to calm down and take stock in Julia's departure, her phone started to buzz in the next room. It was Alex, her agent and confidante.

"Ruth," she said over the receiver, "Ruth, jeez! Where did you go last night?"

"You didn't see me," asked Ruth, "how did you miss me?"

"Oh, you should have been there! There was this psychotic woman who just started screaming at people and fucking the place up. Security bounced her pretty quick, but from what I heard it was some real ugly shit. But hey, whattayagonnado? It's just New York."

Even in her delinquency, Ruth went unnoticed as an existing person. Did nobody recognize her from the night before?

"I'm sorry I missed it," said Ruth.

"Oh, it was right up your alley," said Alex, "hey, are you and Julia up to anything later? I was gonna go see one of those midnight monster movies. They're showing 'Children Shouldn't Play with Dead Things' tonight."

"Julia's gone, Alex."

"What, like she died?"

"I should be so lucky. No, I... I don't mean that. She's gone, Alex. Julia left."

"What do you mean she left?"

"She left a note. She's done. Julia is gone."

"Oh, baby," said Alex, "oh, honey I am sorry. I'll be right over."

Alex had hung up the phone before Ruth could protest, but she wanted to be left alone. Taking the initiative and recognizing the smell of her own hangover, Ruth stripped down and walked into her shower. The steam filled the room in a welcome embrace as Ruth hugged herself beneath the hot water. It fell from the top of her head and ran through her hair, making it cling to her shoulders. Ruth had remembered reading somewhere that people with depression had a habit of lingering in hot showers because it replicated the sensation of human contact. She tried not to think about it too much as memories with Julia continued to painfully flood her mind.

There was a knock at the door as soon as Ruth turned off the shower. It was much too soon for Alex to have arrived at her apartment, so Ruth wrapped a towel around herself and looked through the peephole of her front door. As foolish as it seemed, Ruth held her breath and hoped that it was Julia. It was not. Mary was standing on the other side looking not incredibly unwell, but in decidedly rough shape. Ruth had developed a scale for how well Mary was doing based on what her face looked like. Sometimes her skin would break out and stay pale for days if she was on a bender. If it were pink and clear, then Ruth could relax a little bit. When Mary was on a bender her mood would fluctuate with unpredictable speed. Mary's eyes were clear, but a sense of dread and concern was floating over her expression when Ruth opened the door to let her inside. Ruth asked how Mary was feeling as she entered the apartment and dropped her bag on the kitchen counter. She opened the fridge to rummage for food without saying a word.

"Good'n'you," asked Ruth.

"Hi," said Mary, "sorry I didn't call, but I was in the neighborhood. Figured I'd just swing by. Is this still good?"

Mary held up a loosely wrapped block of cheese. Ruth inspected it and found it to be perfectly fine.

"I have some crackers," said Ruth, "and some jelly if you want some."

"Yes, please," said Mary, "don't mind me. Go finish your shower."

"No, I'm good. What's up with you? You doin' ok?"

Mary chewed on a piece of cheese and allowed her eyes to rest on the envelope on the counter. She reached out her hand to pick up Julia's note, but Ruth managed to snatch it up first and put it in the drawer beside the stove. Mary feigned disinterest but looked as though she were choosing her next words very carefully.

"I'm ok," she said, "but something happened the other night. Something weird."

"Weird for you, or normal person weird?"

Mary swallowed her food and took a breath.

"Remember that kid I told you about?"

"The one that sells acid? I'm all set on that. No, thank you."

"No, the kid I used to see. When I was little."

Ruth took a moment to remember but hardly put all her heart into it. She was not in the mood for nostalgia.

"What, that little weirdo looking for his shoes? What about him?"

"I think I saw him yesterday. He wasn't a kid anymore, but I couldn't shake the feeling that it was him."

"How high were you?"

"Fuck off, I wasn't high. I mean, I *was* high before. I had a hangover, but I wasn't high. Not anymore."

"Listen Mary," said Ruth, "it's really not a good time for me right now so would you mind if we just pretend to have a normal relationship?"

"Come on Ruth, I'm serious! Something really weird is going on."

"Isn't that the problem, though? Don't you always have something weird going on? You're always in trouble or depressed or fucked up with something. I'm not your therapist and I'm not your mom. I have my own problems that I have to deal with, and I don't have time for your crazy shit!"

The weight of Ruth's statement began to settle around the room. Ruth could see that she had hurt Mary and felt conflicted as to whether she should apologize or double down on the sentiment. Finding herself at an impasse, she chose to make some toast in silence. Mary grabbed her bag and headed for the door without saying a word.

Ruth stood in her kitchen as the smell of toast began to emanate from the little oven that she had plugged in on top of the microwave. She took Julia's note out from the drawer beside the stove and read it four more times before putting it back in the envelope and holding it in both of her hands. She took it out again to read it but felt so heartbroken by the printed words that she slowly sank to the floor as the timer for the toast began to ring.

13. You're Gonna Be Ok

Joey was feeling quite proud of himself after having kept both obligations with the Rubenstein girls. He had managed to deliver Mary's birthday present and support Ruth in her gallery opening all in the same week. It was common for Joey to be out and about in the city with different destinations on an evening of debauchery, but he loved any opportunity that came around in which he could spend time with Ruth and Mary. He even managed to squeeze in some surprise sex at the gallery, which was always a bonus.

Joey had maintained a loving relationship between Mary and Ruth throughout the years, but the three of them seldom did anything as a trio anymore. Mary and Ruth had been drifting further and further apart over time and would often use Joey as a messenger instead of speaking to each other directly. Joey was okay with being a go-between, but he did miss the idea of the three of them enjoying each other's company as a group.

The morning found him making his way down N 5th street, and he had just left Cooperman's Bakery when his phone began to ring. Laura's name flashed across the screen and Joey smiled to himself with the hope for good news. He cradled the receiver between his chin and shoulder as he tried to adjust the boxes of coffee and bags of bagels in his hands. When the call connected, Laura was speaking to someone else mid-sentence.

"...always works for me. I can't even...Joey? Hey! What's going on, babe?"

"Oh, you know," said Joey, "got some coffee and bagels. Bringing them back to Sam for his work...thing. What, uh, what's up with you?"

"I'm just calling to say that I love you, and I miss you, and that there's some new deliveries that I need you to make."

"Oh," said Joey, "anything new and exciting?"

"It's always new and exciting, darling. Close to fantastic, from what I've been told. When can you get here?"

Joey put his bags of bagels on a bench and checked the time on his phone.

"I can be there by three or three-thirty."

"Ok, babe. Just bring the usual and I'll set you up. You're colossal."

Laura hung up, leaving Joey to balance his phone with the coffee and bags. He had been sent by his partner Sam to pick up a large order for a private work breakfast that they would be hosting from their apartment. Another of Sam's coworkers had initially been designated to host their breakfast meeting but had to leave his apartment after a pipe burst from the upstairs neighbor's bathroom. A large portion of the apartment flooded, and they were relocated to temporary housing at a Best Rest Motel in Ho-Ho-Kus, New Jersey. It was then suggested that the meeting take place in Chanson le Salon in Tribeca, but Sam insisted on hosting in their home.

He offered their apartment as a more reasonable option for an intimate work setting without distractions. This was an excuse to flex his vanity through hospitality while simultaneously showing off his collection of sculptures and limited-edition art prints. Their apartment walls were strategically designed with what Sam called a "guiding eye" to help draw the guest to a room specifically utilized to display Sam's own artwork. Joey loved Sam, but not as much as Sam loved Sam.

Joey and Sam had met in a bathhouse in Alphabet City after a series of delinquent misunderstandings managed to trap them both; hiding in a claustrophobic storage room that had been built for the shape of a single, average-sized person. There was a moment of shock and surprise when they discovered that they were not alone in the darkness, but that surprise became the invitation to a charming conversation. They chuckled about how it was so odd that they had managed to hide in the same room and how peculiar it was that they were both so hard. These situations have a way of working themselves out, but it never hurts to have a friend there to help.

After they finished understanding each other's circumcisions, they left the bathhouse in search of food and drink. Sam suggested Joey join him at his favorite after-hours Chinese restaurant, of which Joey held no singular objection. After a very relaxed and bountiful meal, Joey went home with Sam to his apartment for a brief showing of Sam's collection of sculptures. It was a very brief showing before they managed to press some new enthusiasm until the early morning hours. That was five years ago, but all the days in that time were not always pleasant.

Sam and Joey had never believed in marriage or monogamy, but that did not mean that Sam was incapable of jealousy. It became clear to Joey that Sam had a penchant for heavy drinking whenever Joey would be on a date with someone else. Joey would often return home to find Sam alone, drunk in the living room and listening to sad Vic Damone records. On the good nights Sam would be happy for Joey to have returned home, but on some occasions, he would be moody and inconsolable. Sometimes he would become violent. Sam never went on dates, despite their shared agreement, but Joey always kept Sam informed on who he was seeing and whether they were going to be sexually active. They were getting tested regularly and always kept full transparency between each other. Except when they did not.

Joey had been frustrated with their relationship for quite some time. When Sam proposed that they should move in together after two years of dating, it felt like the right thing to do. Joey was enthusiastic and he loved Sam very much. Shortly after he moved in, he noticed the wild mood swings that Sam would exhibit over what could otherwise be dismissed as minor inconveniences. Sam would sulk after he would do or say something hurtful towards Joey, but he also had a habit of remembering each slight that Joey had committed. Sam's memory was photographic when it was in his favor, but foggy if it were to work against him. With all of this, Joey still loved him.

The small gathering of Sam's coworkers was meant to brainstorm a new advertising model for their brand. They were charter members of an internet startup, and the goal was to craft the hypothesis for the business. There had already been some interest from potential investors to review their presentation, but they still needed to land on what it was that their brand would do. They had no product, no marketing strategy, and no target audience, but they did have a name: Corodasoft Enterprises. Joey returned to the apartment with bags of bagels and two boxes of hot coffee. The meeting was already underway and there was feigned applause as Joey put the breakfast food on the kitchen counter.

"Hi guys," said Joey, "sorry it took so long."

"Let me help you," said Sam.

He stood close next to Joey and whispered with his back to the group.

"Are you trying to embarrass me," he asked, "what took you so long? Were you *making* the bagels?"

Joey was frustrated with Sam but kept his tone low and flat.

"I had to take two buses to get there. We hit traffic. I'm sorry."

"Well, don't be sorry just pour the coffee."

Sam slapped Joey's ass as he returned to the group, but this only amplified the small glowing anger that was growing in Joey's stomach.

"Sorry for the hold-up, gang," said Sam, "I just hope Joey saved some bagels for us."

The group laughed at this while Joey's hands began to shake. It was at this time that he realized that the bakery had packed the bagels without any butter or cream cheese. There was also no milk, cream, or sugar packed with the coffee. There were plenty of napkins, though. Joey turned to face the group and delivered the bad news.

"Uh, sorry guys. It looks like they forgot to pack any cream cheese or milk and sugar. I can run back out to the store and pick some up real quick."

"You didn't check," asked Sam, "you didn't look in the bag before you left?"

"I was in a rush," said Joey, "I'm sorry, I was trying to get back."

"You're fucking useless, you know that?"

Sam walked back to the kitchenette while his group remained silent. The suggestion of potential confrontation was making them uncomfortable. They stared at the floor in anticipation for a blowout fight. Sam reached into his wallet and forcibly stuffed two twenty-dollar bills in Joey's front shirt pocket while he hissed in his ear.

"Go to the store," said Sam, "and get some fucking creamer."

Joey went into his room without saying anything and threw some clothes in a bag. He packed a wad of cash that he had been saving for the past three years, a toothbrush, his phone charger, and a paperback copy of Paradise Lost. Walking back through the apartment, he found Sam attempting to entertain his coworkers as they ate dry bagels and drank black coffee. When he saw Joey with his backpack, Sam rushed to the door and tried to intercept him.

"Where are you goin', babe?" asked Sam.

Joey let his flat stare linger for a beat too long before he answered Sam's question.

"Goin' to get some fucking creamer."

Sam's coworkers began to pipe up with special requests now that it seemed to be an option.

"Can you get me some oat milk instead?"

"Oh, and non-dairy hazelnut creamer? The one with the pig on the bottle?"

"If you find any soy veggie cream cheese substitute, that would be really cool of you."

"Can you grab me an apple muffin?"

Joey lingered at the door and stared into Sam's eyes while more requests kept coming. They were standing so close to each other that Joey could smell the faint tooth decay that lingered out of Sam's open mouth. Without looking back to the group, and while remaining locked in Sam's gaze of anger, Joey agreed to the special orders as he closed the door behind him, thankful that there were witnesses present in case Sam felt compelled to do something stupid. He made it two blocks down the street before his phone began to buzz wildly with rapid texts from Sam. Joey did his best to ignore them and turned his phone off. He would need more money than what he had saved, so he headed to Laura's for the new shipment of drugs. He was already debating whether he was going to sell them or steal them.

There was a violinist playing on the subway platform while Joey waited for the next train that would take him over to Laura's neighborhood. Up until this point he was too angry to allow himself the time to process the decision he had just made to leave Sam and the apartment for good. Now that he had left, he was still unsure if it was something that he wanted to do. This was not an entirely impulsive choice on his part.

Joey had been saving money for just such an emergency and he had been planning on leaving eventually. It had not occurred to him that it could happen so quickly and without warning. Joey gripped the strap of his backpack with his hand and stared at the tracks that ran beneath the platform. The violinist was playing a rendition of a popular radio song that drew a few people's interest, but none of their money. He was playing well, but with the noise from the trains and the general murmur of foot traffic, much of his playing was lost to anyone but himself. Still, he played on.

Joey reached into the side pocket of his backpack and pulled out a small white tube with a plastic flip-top lid. There were a few of these tubes hidden behind a second inside zipper. He popped it open in a quick motion and retrieved two white capsules, taking them immediately and without water. He leaned his head back and focused on getting the pills down. They would guarantee a slight distortion in his auditory and visual perception while allowing his pulse to drop just below resting. Other side effects include joy, serenity, and distraction from the inner workings of the human heart. His mind wandered in such intense thought that he had barely noticed when the train he needed had stopped right in front of him and opened its doors.

The train ride itself was smooth apart from the gnawing anxiety of what Sam's messages would say. Joey had a pretty good idea of what the gist would be. After allowing the drugs to work their way into his central nervous system, Joey was beginning to feel more comfortable about reading Sam's messages. He turned his phone back on and it shook violently as it received every message that had been sent in the time that it had been turned off. When the phone stopped vibrating, it showed that there were forty-seven unread texts from Sam, two from Mary, two from Laura, and three notifications from his dating app for men who were near his location and looking for casual sex. Considering that he was on his way to Laura's apartment now, he decided to read her messages first.

Laura: (1:45) Hey babe, just wanted to let you know that my friend Pete is here and he wants to meet you! He's the friend from college I told you about that used to write for the sex column. 8===D I told him about you and that you were coming and he got real nervous. Hope Sam is being less of a dick these days.

Laura: (2:18) OK, Mr. Cool! No need to respond or anything! Just come in through the garden door when you get here. Pete can't wait to meet you ;)

Beautiful, thought Joey, *sorry, Pete. Not today.*

Joey was in no mood for company, and sex was nowhere near his range of priorities. He wanted to talk to Laura, get higher, pick up, and push so he could start making more money and look for a new place. He thought about asking Laura if he could crash with her for a day or two, but he always felt uncomfortable asking favors from other people. Being in someone else's debt was never a place that Joey wanted to be. His reluctance to ask for help would often lead to more unhealthy consequences. There was the possibility that he would be able to get at least one night's sleep with this Pete person but relying on friends was hard enough. Strangers seldom carried a feeling of security. Sexy danger, sure, but never security.

I'll just play it by ear, he thought.

He was about to move on to Mary's messages, but a woman quickly boarded the train and began shouting down the aisle of the car.

"Woooooo," she shouted, "somebody's pussy STINKS!"

The woman began to scrutinize each passenger. Her long arms and legs spread out in strange angles as she maneuvered down the aisle of the train car. A large pair of black sunglasses covered most of her face while a dollop of white hair lay neatly coiffed on top of her head.

"Somebody's gotta get to the GYN!" she shouted, "is there a doctor in the house?! Haw haw haw haw!"

The commuters remained unresponsive to the woman's suggestions, but there were those who were foolish enough to make eye contact with her as she made her way through the train. An older woman with a cane was watching the display and shaking her head from her seat. The two women began to stare each other down as the train continued rolling on the bumpy tracks.

"Oh," said the woman, "I'm sorry, your highness. I suppose you think you're something else. You think you're better than me? I'll bet it's you. Yeah, I know you all right. You're the one stinkin' up this train."

The older woman with the cane said nothing but continued to stare down her accuser.

"So, you think you're the queeeeeen? Are you the queeeeeeeeen?! All high and mighty. I ride this train every god.damn.day and every day somebody's pussy fucking stinks. Well, fuck you and fuck this train and fuck your rotten pussy!"

In a quick motion that went nearly unnoticed, the older woman flicked her wrist up and drove her cane right between the legs of the screaming woman. There was an audible smacking sound as the cane connected with the woman's how's-it-goin' and she crumpled to her knees on the floor. The train pulled into the next station and the woman with the cane quietly rose from her seat. She departed onto the platform and continued with her otherwise uneventful day. Her opponent lay on the floor of the train shouting for someone to help her. As is with most cases in New York City, nobody did.

After the event had withered away, Joey returned to his phone to see what Mary had sent him. He had to read the messages a few times because it was difficult to make sense of her writing. Also, his eyes were beginning to wander. Joey was distracted and trying to figure out if the train had suddenly grown carpet or if it were just especially textured this time in the afternoon. The thought of reaching down and seeing how it felt was already moving his body to the floor when the train suddenly jerked and nearly threw Joey from his seat. Righting himself allowed his perspective to shift focus and he returned to Mary's messages. They read as though Mary had been experiencing a manic episode.

> **Mary:**(1:37) Joey, something happened at that party
> I need to talk to you
> Boy in the bathtub
> If you're busy, it's cool
> I just don't know what to do

> **Mary:**(1:39) Never mind
> It's cool
> We're cool
> Everything is cool
> Thanks for everything

Joey tried to decipher the message within the message. Something was not being said that she needed to tell him. This was an inconvenient time to begin to worry about Mary, but she said it's cool. Everything is cool. He tried to remind himself to remember to call her back later. Under most circumstances this would be an easy thing to do, but now Joey was feeling distracted by everything around him. The train pulled into the station that Joey was waiting for, but he nearly missed it in his haze. He managed to squeeze through the doors just as they were closing, and he fell flat onto the platform. Dusting himself off and checking his pockets for all his belongings, he made his way up to the street and onto the world above ground.

It was a quick walk from the station to Laura's apartment and Joey was starting to level out. Feeling good. He decided not to look at Sam's messages and that he did not care whether Sam was angry. Based on their personal history and Sam's irregular affection, Joey had very little faith in Sam feeling worried. Instead of obsessing over Sam's authority, Joey walked down the sidewalk and tried to focus on the world of life.

A robin sitting on a wrought iron fence watched him as he passed and never broke eye contact. The bird proceeded to shit down the iron posts as it stared at Joey with indifference. What should the robin care for a shit? Joey found this to be an inspirational display of perspective and would try to keep that in mind if he needed it later. The rest of the world around him continued to move with its own variety of needs and purposes.

The back garden door to Laura's apartment was unbolted and slightly open as Joey pushed his way into the basement. He was greeted by Mr. Biscuit the cat, of whom he was quite fond. Biscuit was old and half blind. He would hug the wall when he walked, using the side with his bad eye to give himself a better sense of direction around the apartment. Biscuit yowled at Joey in greeting and purred as he pressed his head against the leg of Joey's pants. Biscuit always seemed to perk up whenever Joey came to see Laura and Joey loved him very much. On a better day he would have remembered to bring treats. He made a promise to bring double next time.

Two voices were coming from the kitchen down the narrow hall from the garden door. There were a series of empty cardboard boxes lined against the wall which made navigating the space through the hallway a little difficult. Biscuit took the lead and guided Joey through the clutter with his one good eye. Vinyl records were hanging on the walls with push-pins holding up their centers. Names like Bobby Darrin and Dolly Parton zigzagged up and down along the walls of peeling paint and stains from years of unknown sources. Laura, and whom Joey presumed to be Pete, were standing in the kitchen laughing and cooking. It was obvious that they had quickly pivoted their conversation when Joey entered the room. Pete was smiling and leaning against the kitchen counter while Laura stood over a boiling pot, stirring it with a wooden spoon.

"Hi-hi," said Joey, "and how are all you beautiful people?"

He embraced Laura and they exchanged polite kisses while Peter said nothing and gave Joey the up-and-down.

"Hello, Joseph," said Laura, "this is Peter. Peter, this is Joseph."

Laura used full first name when she wanted to impress someone. The formality was a trait of Laura's that Joey thought to be silly. Pete nodded subtly as he continued to eyeball Joey from head to toe and back again. Joey nodded politely and put his bag down in a chair while Mr. Biscuit hugged the wall, yowling for food. The kitchen was hot as Laura had the oven and the stovetop running at the same time. It was not an uncomfortable temperature, but it was enough to make Joey feel lethargic and more tired than he already did. The combination of the drugs and the heat made him yawn and want to lie down. Joey sat at the table and rubbed his eyes with his fingertips until his vision blurred.

"You want some soup," asked Laura, "I've got some bread in the oven, too."

"Naw," said Joey, "I'm good, thanks. Smells good, though."

Pete sat down next to Joey and tried to start a conversation about his experiences in New York. He said he was from a state that Joey had only heard about but had no interest in visiting. Specific information was forgotten as soon as it was received. Joey was not interested in trying to pay attention. He would occasionally nod and agree with a statement that Pete made about the train or the scene or the general cost of living. It had already been a busy day for Joey, and he was still tired from the previous night's escapades.

There was nothing in reality, or in any state of consciousness, that could raise any interest or desire to pursue an entanglement with Pete. Joey hung on to the conversation out of politeness and exhaustion. Once he got the product from Laura, he would linger for another fifteen or twenty minutes before making an excuse to leave. Joey felt uncomfortable asking Laura for a place to crash now that Pete was in the mix. There were other places he could go so he decided to save the favor as a last resort. Laura grabbed her coat and hat before she started to walk out the back garden door.

"I have to step out for a minute," she said, "Joseph, be a darling and feed Biscuit. And Peter, you keep an eye on Joseph. I won't be long, so you can leave the pot to simmer. I already turned the oven off. You two need anything while I'm out?"

Joey and Pete both declined Laura's offer, but she said that she would return with a little something for the two of them. Laura left through the back hallway and out of the garden door, closing it behind her with an audible lock of the deadbolt. Joey and Pete sat awkwardly at the table trying to decide who should say something first. Joey, who would have been much happier with just Mr. Biscuit for company, got up to feed the cat in an effort to buy himself some time and avoid a conversation with Pete. Feeding Biscuit would not take any time at all, but he would do his best to draw out the process and keep Pete bored. Unfortunately, it worked a little too quickly.

"Well, I'm bored," said Pete, "tell me about yourself."

"Ohhhh, I'm not very exciting," said Joey, "just your normally maladjusted sexual deviant. Dysfunctional family, neurotic, etc. etc. Typical New Yorker, born and bred."

"I think you have more to offer than that," Pete stood next to Joey and placed his hand on his shoulder, "I find you very exciting."

Joey shifted his weight and moved out of reach from Pete's hand. Pete chuckled and put his hands in his pockets, shaking his head.

"I get it," said Pete, "Laura told me about your situation. I don't want to rush you, but I think you should know that I'm interested."

"Thanks, Pete. Don't get me wrong, I'm flattered, it's just not a good day for me."

Joey was spooning a can of wet food in a bowl for Biscuit when the cat walked into the room making an unfamiliar noise. The orange tabby wobbled into the kitchen cabinet with both of his eyes closed, shaking lightly before his legs suddenly went out from under him. His body went stiff, and he proceeded to have a seizure on the floor. Biscuit's good eye shot wide open as he continued making a terrible sound. Joey jumped into action to save the cat while Pete remained unbothered.

"It couldn't be *that* bad," said Pete, "I mean, I think I could make you feel pretty good. Help take your mind off things. Maybe we can teach each other a thing or two sometime."

Joey disregarded Pete's advances. He was trying to remember what to do if a person was having a seizure. Joey had a cousin who was epileptic and had once witnessed an episode like this, but he had never been directly involved in the care required. He gently placed both hands on either side of Biscuit's body to hold him still without applying pressure. The drugs blurred everything around him while the rush of adrenaline felt confusing.

"I can wait if you want to talk to Sam first," said Pete, "but it'd be a shame to waste a good opportunity. Laura said Sam can be kinda difficult. Heh. It might be more fun if we have to sneak around."

"Shut up and help me!" shouted Joey.

"It's just a cat," said Pete, "it'll be fine in a minute. You go outside and you'll find five of those fucking things. Honestly, things so old it's probably going to die soon anyway."

Joey pulled a t-shirt out of his bag and scooped up Biscuit's trembling body, wrapping it around him in a bundle. Holding the cat close to his chest, he grabbed his backpack and made for the back garden door. Pete continued to say something to him, but he did not hear a word of it. All he could focus on was the weak body of Mr. Biscuit gently shaking in his arms.

"It's ok, buddy," said Joey, "you're gonna be ok."

Joey jogged down the street and flagged down a taxi. The driver stopped but refused the fare when he saw the cat in Joey's arms.

"No pets," he said, "no pets in my cab."

"Come on, man! I gotta get to a vet!"

"So? What do I care? Take the bus. No pets in my cab."

Joey cursed at the cab driver while the taxi took off down the road. Rage and fear were the only sensations that he could understand as he took out his phone and searched where to find the closest emergency vet. He found one to be further than he would have liked, it would mean taking the subway to get there. Joey gently rocked Biscuit in his arms and did his best to remain calm until he found the nearest subway entrance. He jumped on the train that pulled into the station as soon as he got to the platform, managing to find a seat that was unoccupied. It was the first bit of good luck that Joey had received all day.

Biscuit was purring at a fast and erratic pace which was not an expression of ease or comfort. He lay trembling and mewed weakly while Joey continued to talk to him. Biscuit's giant pupil locked with Joey's panicked eyes in a plea for help, and Joey felt the aggravated urgency that comes with a slow train. His altered state was less than helpful in this time.

"I'm sorry, buddy," said Joey, "I'm so, so sorry. Hang on, buddy. You're gonna be ok."

The train rolled along down the tracks before the screeching brakes threw sparks up the side of the car. The lights flickered twice before going out completely as the train lost power. Sitting underground in the darkness, a series of groans came from the other passengers while Joey began cursing everything he knew in his mind. There was no voice over the intercom to explain the delay as the train was stopped dead in the tunnel. Joey kept talking to Biscuit, but his words of consolation were just as much for himself as they were for his injured friend. A voice in the dark told Joey to shut the fuck up, but he ignored them and kept talking to Mr. Biscuit.

The thought of leaving the train and running the length of track to the next station came to mind when the sound of doors at the ends of the car began opening and slamming. This idea was crushed when the passengers began to shout in alarm as a group of burglars began rolling everyone they could under the cover of darkness. Women were screaming about their purses and men's wallets were forfeit as the sounds of violence and impact were coming from different angles. Fists on meat could be heard in sickening thuds. Joey felt someone rip Biscuit out of his arms as a hard punch landed on the side of his face. He could not see who it was in the darkness, but the sound of Biscuit's panicked mewing faded as he was carried into the next car.

Joey did his best to stand up and pursue the kidnappers, but the punch, the adrenaline, and the strength of the drugs had made him disoriented. Gripping for any support in the darkness, he made his way to the end of the car towards the direction he thought the thieves had run. When he opened the door between the cars, he found only his t-shirt hanging from the chain railing. He screamed for Biscuit but found no reply apart from the power returning and the train continuing down the tracks. The impulse to jump from the car entered his mind for a moment before his shaken imbalance and fear gripped the rest of his senses. Grabbing the shirt from the railing, Joey returned to his train car to find someone else had taken his seat. He stood against the door, held the shirt up to his face and tried not to cry. He was unsuccessful.

The next stop on the train was as good as any other at this point. Joey had to leave the train, along with several other passengers that had been traumatized by the assault. This was an unfamiliar station, and he was not sure where he was, but he was ambivalent about the specific location. All that he knew was that Biscuit was gone.

The crowded platform moved around him while his fellow commuters pushed him with their shoulders as they passed. Someone told him to get out of the way, but he stood still like a lamppost in the middle of the thoroughfare. A commuter walking past him scoffed and complained about the junkies in this town as he proceeded to describe what Joey was wearing and how he needed a bath.

The stairs leading up to the street were filled with the different stories of other people. The crowd murmur bubbled around the station with different kinds of music playing loudly from different people's speakers. Some folks were laughing with their friends and some folks just talked to themselves. One old man was screaming at a poster advertising aspirin. The world continued moving, never stopping, and never thinking to give two figs about a sick and missing cat. The world did not give two figs about Joey, either. Or at least that was how he felt. Someone must have taken all the figs.

There was a liquor store on the corner in front of the subway exit and Joey had entered the shop without thinking about it. He walked straight to the counter, ordered his usual half pint of whiskey served in plastic, and proceeded to drink on the curb just a few blocks down the street. He took a long pull from the bottle and refused to acknowledge the phone that had been ringing back-to-back in his jeans pocket. If there was ever a time when Joey wanted to hurt someone, this was the closest he had come in a long while. The traffic moved slowly before him while Joey Boulm attempted to remove his feelings and ignore the throbbing pain on the side of his face. He was nearly successful until an orange tabby began to turn figure eights between his legs. Joey instinctively reached down to pet the animal before bursting into tears and dropping his plastic bottle of whiskey onto the street.

The evening had begun its descent over the city by the time Joey made it back to Laura's apartment. It would have been easy for him to take the train back, but the dread that he felt about talking to Laura made the long walk all the more appealing. He was drunk but felt it necessary to explain to Laura in person what had happened to her cat. Explaining it to her over the phone felt cheap and he still needed to pick up the drugs she wanted him to sell. He needed the money and peace of mind.

A strong pressure headache was forming in his temples as he got closer to Laura's apartment. Joey was exhausted when he tried to open Laura's back garden door, but it had been locked and bolted from the inside. The sound of voices on the other side made him feel sick in anticipation of the difficult conversation that he was about to have. Now the prospect of staying with Laura was definitely off the table. Even if it were an option, he was scared to stay in the apartment after losing Biscuit. This was not as much for the fear of Laura's anger, but the knowing that Mr. Biscuit's absence would be impossible to ignore. Joey knew that if he were to stay at Laura's then he would not be able to sleep.

The events of the day had left Joey feeling especially worn down and broken. He blamed himself for the disappearance of Mr. Biscuit and was preparing himself for Laura's wrath. They were close enough as could be expected for a supply and demand relationship, but Biscuit was family. Feeling lost and afraid, he knocked on Laura's garden door. She answered with Mr. Biscuit in her arms, he was flicking his tail and purring loudly.

"There you are," said Laura, "what happened to you? Pete said you got all fucked up and left with Biscuit. I gotta say I was a little nervous when he came back without you."

Joey's heart leapt into his throat as the smiling eye of Biscuit focused on his face. His playful meow told Joey that everything was going to be ok. Laura put Biscuit on the ground and ushered Joey inside while the cat led the way, hugging the wall as he went.

"He was filthy when he got back," said Laura, "where'd you lose him, anyway?"

"It's a long story," said Joey, "I thought he was dead."

"Aw, poor thing," said Laura, petting Joey's head, "you must have been freaking out!"

"I've been drinking."

"No shit."

"Is Pete here?"

"No, he had to go. He did leave you his phone number though if you want it."

"No, thank you. He's a big ol' piece of shit. Biscuit started having a seizure, but the entire time I was trying to help Biscuit, Pete was trying to fucking flirt."

"Sounds like Pete. Biscuit has seizures sometimes, but he would have been fine. It's no big deal. Really, Joey, you're so high strung."

"Well, what the fuck was I supposed to do," said Joey, "'oh, never mind the cat. He has seizures all the time. How many fingers can I stick in your asshole?'. Why'd you set me up with someone like that?"

"I dunno," said Laura, "I thought you guys would hit it off."

"Why, because we're gay?"

"No! Come on, Joey, look, you know me better than that."

"You put me in a dangerous situation with a creep! There was a medical emergency that I was unprepared for, and this dude was a total weirdo! What about this guy screamed, 'Oh, this is the man for Joey'?"

"He was an easy lay! I thought you could use a booster!"

"Fuck you, Laura."

"Fuck me? Fuck you, Joey! I try to get you laid, you steal my cat, lose my cat, and then come back in here all wasted and offended? Get over yourself."

Laura reached into a canvas bag and pulled out three bundles. One was filled with a large brick of compressed marijuana while the other two were a variety of different drugs that had been sectioned off and portioned into their individual classes. She laid them out on the kitchen table while Biscuit rubbed against Joey's leg and Joey put a wad of cash into Laura's hand.

"Here's to start," he said, "I'll bring you the rest when it sells."

"Good," said Laura, "bring me an apology too, while you're at it."

Joey said nothing more to Laura but knelt to give Biscuit a final hug. He wanted to tell the cat that he was not planning on coming back. The money he had been saving for three years would stretch out farther if he could get out of the city. The drugs he was planning on stealing would float him even more. If he were to come back, he would be prepared to find violence waiting for him. Biscuit rubbed his face into Joey's hand and let his fingertips press against the sides of his mouth.

The night outside was unremarkable when Joey left Laura's apartment. New York's otherwise alluring seduction can become somewhat muted to the residents who live there long enough to fall into routine. Having been born in the city, Joey was in a perpetual state of feeling underwhelmed. Today was the first time in a long time that the fear and unpredictable nature of city living had managed to make its way into his life. With his bag stuffed with drugs, he made his way through the streets, still feeling fuzzy. It could have been the lingering effects of the liquor and drugs or just the exhaustion from the day. It was most likely all three, but he was too tired to think about it for long. Everything was giving him a headache. He tried calling Mary but received no answer. He felt wrong leaving a voicemail, so instead he just texted her a message that read, "Call me" and left it at that. Looking through his dating app he had found at least four people who would be willing to provide shelter. This is a rare occasion in and of itself because it was unusual to find someone who was willing to host. He started a conversation with an older man who seemed the most harmless and bland while ignoring another incoming call from Sam.

14. Didja See It?

Mary left Ruth's apartment building and walked towards the subway. Ruth's words had hurt Mary in a severe way because Ruth knew how to hurt Mary. Lashing out like that was a tactic that had developed during their teenage years but had lost none of its potency with age. It had been a long time since they had managed to enjoy a casual conversation.

The transition from late summer to early autumn was ambiguous as the temperatures maintained the high seventies with a promise of the coming night's chill. Mary's stride was fiercely New York in a purposeful march that implied a serious destination that was nobody else's business. If you attempted to stop her and ask where she was going, there would be no hesitation in her pace. She walked with her shoulders out and head held high.

Today's destination was a court mandated therapy session with a counselor appointed by a judge. This had come about when she had a brief misunderstanding with the NYPD as to what constituted grand theft auto and aggravated assault. Three months prior had found Mary in her usual party scene with a handful of unfamiliar faces in an unfamiliar Manhattan loft.

There were a few friends of which she shared a more casual acquaintance, but she was still having a good time. As the evening wore on into the late-night celebration there was an influx of young men from Columbia University all arriving at the same time. This was unexpected and not entirely ideal as the group began to gleefully take up intrusive space in a previously shared setting of fun and goodwill. They scrambled to catch up to the inebriation of the other guests by becoming as drunk as humanly possible in a short amount of time. The Columbia students then proceeded to single out young women who were by themselves or others who looked as though they were experiencing discomfort by their raucous behavior. The young men saw these reactions as a challenging invitation of conquest. They descended upon their prey with aggressive swagger and insipid banter, making sure that everyone knew the importance of their station. Mary was approached by a young man with the kind of style that required consistent maintenance and the confidence that exclusively accompanies mediocrity. He smelt like a magazine and looked like an asshole.

"Hey babe," he said, "you here alone?"

Mary was silent and continued to look out the window. He stood there with the anticipation of a successful seduction but was met with a wall that Mary had built years ago. He repeated his question and was met with the same absence of reaction. When Mary tried to walk past the young man, he pivoted his body and stood in her way.

"I can tell you're not like the other girls here," he said, "everybody here's so...I don't know, basic. You know what I mean?"

Mary turned in a different direction in an attempt to escape the conversation, but he stood in her way again and started to speak in a more aggressive tone.

"Whoa, where you goin', babe? You know, you look familiar. Have we met before?"

"Please get out of my way," said Mary.

"Come on now, don't be like that. It's a party, right? Just gimme a smile. Don't you know who I am? I think you might have heard of me."

Mary looked up at him and remained as expressionless as she could manage without showing her anger. She could feel her fingers reflexively tighten around the neck of her beer bottle while craving the kind of violence that would make an army general blush.

Normally Mary would try to carry herself as a chaotic optimist in her reactions to the world. After having tried nihilism for a period of time, she felt that if nothing truly mattered then she may as well do the good thing. This was a philosophy that she would try to keep in practice, but her frustration with the world would occasionally cause spontaneous and impulsive behavior. On this occasion, she was not exactly feeling very Zen.

"I know you," she said, "you're the serial rapist and hate crime enthusiast who thinks that aids jokes are funny. You've never *had* to work but what you *have* done is try to convince women that you've got some kind of magic dick, which probably is a full-time job in and of itself. You're only in school for the parties and the prestige. You have a job waiting for you at your daddy's business once you either graduate or get expelled, whichever comes first. You've got the whole world waiting for special little you in a neat little suit. Your favorite movie is probably Fight Club. Please get out of my way."

"What's with you," he said, as he grabbed her arm, "you some kind of dyke or somethin'?"

Mary's eyes burned holes into the young man while her face continued to remain expressionless. Without breaking eye contact, she poured the rest of her beer down the front of his pants. He yelped and jumped back, spouting out bigoted rhetoric about his presumptions around Mary's sexual proclivities. He continued to criticize how she looked when she smashed her empty beer bottle over his head, giving him a nasty gash across the side of his face. His hands shot up instinctively to cover the wound and Mary punched him in the stomach as hard as she could. With her spiked adrenaline and newly sprained wrist, she fished the car keys out from his pocket and left the party. The crowd parted a clear path for her exit without hesitation.

Once Mary stepped outside, she allowed herself to feel the fear and anxiety that was otherwise suppressed upstairs. Her hands were shaking when she found a Maserati that reacted to the key fob she had stolen. Mary had never been in a Maserati, much less driven one, so she did not want to waste an opportunity for a new experience. She ran every red light driving to Little Odessa and parked on the beach just in time for high tide. The car was recovered the next morning and the damage from the salt water was so severe that no amount of body or engine work could bring it back. It had to be scrapped. Acts of Poseidon were not covered under the insurance policy.

In lieu of time served, and out of consideration for the young man's reputation at Columbia University, his family opted to settle on a year's probation with mandatory community service and psychiatric counseling for Mary. If the case went to trial, then the young man's behavioral history would be under such an illuminating scrutiny that it could potentially derail his social trajectory. The family wanted as little attention brought to Mary's assault as possible. Heaven forbid there be an unnecessary obstacle that could leave a mark of condemnation upon his suspiciously immaculate record.

Her therapist's office was not too far from Ruth's apartment, but Mary would have to take the train and change lines once. As long as nothing happened, she should get to her appointment on time. With her hands deep in her jacket pockets and her hair bouncing with each step, Mary's stride slowed to a stop as she approached the doors to the next subway station. They were locked shut in the early afternoon. She stood and stared at the doors as if they could be opened by sheer force of will, but there was no hope of that. She tugged on the chain lock twice before cursing under her breath and walking to the next closest station entrance.

There are sections of Delancey Street that receive less attention than some other parts of the main thoroughfare. With the length of road so massive it would not be so unusual to find a corner here and there that remained uninspected. When Howard told Mary that New York was a living city, it became a term that was forever embedded in her mind. It became an abbreviation for what kind of life feels the most entitled to express itself. There are shining spires and soft satin perfumes that float on cold snow falling out through the night. The smooth rounded angles of pride that were founded and cared for over hundreds of years collect faces and names like the inner rings of a tree. There are portions of the city where the darkness never reaches. Where the bright protective light caresses each of those in perilous need of salvation. There are people made from years of love, work, and sacrifice that grow into better versions of the ones who first guided them, in the hopes of guiding others in their own lives.

There are also people who do what they must do to survive and provide, even if it means causing the death of another person. There live those driven mad by the pain of being alive. The single thread that keeps someone alive, whatever the reason, is often the only driving force in a person's need for survival. It can be a very thin thread on any given day. The living city of birth and rebirth. Redemption and damnation. Sex and death. &.

Mary was walking past an abandoned storefront on Delancey St. when two men emerged from around the corner. She was startled but tried not to show it. Years of similar situations allowed her to quickly adjust her trajectory and side-step the two men as they slowly turned and leered at her.

"Where you goin?" said the taller of the two, "stuck up bitch."

Mary did not turn around. Her pace remained consistent as she felt around her pocket for the knife she kept in a secret compartment.

"You better keep walkin'," he shouted, "fuckin' bitch!"

Mary kept walking. The threat of being followed was aching in the back of her skull, like a small animal gnawing on her neck. Fear was a very real thing to Mary, and she was never one to ignore the signs. Part of her was screaming to run while the other half of her brain refused to endanger herself any further by showing fear. If she were to run, then they would most likely give chase. Mary kept walking. After she felt there was a good distance between them, she ventured a glance over her shoulder to find that there was nobody following her. The muscles in her shoulders relaxed a little bit and she was reminded that breathing was an in-and-out effort. Mary let out a long-held breath and kept walking.

This was not the first dangerous encounter that Mary had experienced living in New York. This sort of thing happened so frequently throughout the city that it had become expected anytime she left the house. The earliest example that she could remember distinctly was when she was thirteen years old. She was riding the subway with Lorry on the way to a doctor's appointment when she noticed that an old man was staring at her on the train. She watched him as he stared but did not notice how his hand was moving beneath his long coat. Lorry Keller-Rubenstein noticed. She hollered and grabbed hold of the old man's collar, making sure that his nose would break in such a way as to remain asymmetrical for the rest of his days. No one stopped Lorry or Mary when they got off at the next stop. They had a long talk with Howard and Ruth when they got home that night. This had become behavior that Mary would eventually come to expect but never fully grow accustomed to. It scared her each time, but she refused to show her abusers that fear. Unfortunately, it would come into her life in different ways almost every day.

It took Mary about fifteen minutes before she found the next subway station to be locked as well. She considered the timeframe of calling for a taxi but as soon as the thought crossed Mary's mind, the city bus that was heading in the same direction pulled to a stop where she stood. Blessed with such luck, she found herself a seat near the back behind the wheel well and settled in for the commute. She only made it five blocks before the bus came to a complete stop. The doors opened as the bus driver suggested that the passengers depart if they were in a hurry.

Mary remained seated and looked out the window to see if she could identify the cause of the delay. What she saw was a marching band, dressed in powder blue, white, and gold, positioned in the middle of the street with a fanfare of bystanders, students, and faculty from Columbia University. With an upcoming football game against Cornell, their historic rivals, the Columbia marching band had selected this street, day, and time to begin their rally march through the city. There were street vendors and acrobats, clowns, a caged lion in a blue sweater that looked both scared and bored, and the usual pack of onlookers that love a parade. The bus would be immobilized for the foreseeable future until the street was cleared.

Unable to turn down the smaller side streets that splintered out from either side, the bus driver removed his hat, leaned back, and calculated the overtime and hazard pay that the day would provide him. He had recently been thinking about buying a pool table and the prospect was looking better by the minute.

Having the bus prove useless forced Mary to abandon ship and begin rehearsing the conversation she would have to have with her therapist. There was a kind of three strike system when it came to an unexpected absence of an appointment, but Mary had never been late or absent, so her anxiety was relatively low. She had never been a big fan of marching bands either, but a new hatred was brewing in her heart. This was not a terribly hard sell for her, considering her previous experiences with Columbia University. Walking past the crowd Mary saw a young man with a fresh scar running down the side of his cheek. They locked eyes for a moment before Mary gave him the finger and spit on the ground.

Ringing the office of her therapist provided an odd coincidence as the doctor had taken a sick day and had forgotten to contact Mary ahead of time to reschedule her appointment. Mary feigned offense and said it was decidedly unprofessional to leave a poor unfortunate like herself out to dry without so much as a warning. The receptionist was blasé in the exchange and hung up the phone in the middle of their goodbye. Therapy would have been the perfect opportunity for Mary to discuss her recent encounter with a forgotten memory, but there was also some relief in her not having to talk about it and risk being institutionalized.

In the moments of unexpected fortune, when events seem to take a suspicious turn for the better, a small celebration is justifiable. The day was new, and it allowed a certain exhaustion to develop alongside relief. Like over winding a watch and then letting it go, the energy that had been stored within Mary's anxieties had suddenly drained from her body when she realized that she had nothing to do. What a sudden and unexpectedly beautiful day.

But this new lack of obligation did not entirely distract Mary from her recent bout of strangeness. The absence of distraction would permit her obsessive nature to spiral out immaterial suspicions and theories that would have no calculable result outside of paranoid delusion. Was there a difference between coincidence and fate? Does the weight of one's actions determine the central path of their life, or is it inconsequential in the universal spectrum of consciousness? Does what you do matter? What matters? Does anyone? Mary needed a drink.

She lit a cigarette and called up Joey Boulm to see if he was free.

"Mary! Hi," he said, "are you ok? Where are you?"

"Stuck behind a shit ass marching band," said Mary, "I'm about to beat someone to death with a tuba. Is it a felony if you beat someone to death with a tuba, or is it a mis-d-minor?"

"Ok, I'm going to hang up now."

"No! No, Joey, I'm sorry. I need...I need to talk to somebody. Something...happened."

"Yeah, I was gonna say. You alright? I got your messages. Sorry I didn't get back to you. Last night was wild. Got a little out of control. Now that you mention it, I could go for a drink."

Mary heard Joey say something to someone else in the room. There was a small argument before Joey returned to the call.

"Where are you?" asked Mary, "is that Sam?"

"No, I'm staying with a friend," said Joey, "things kind of...things got bad."

"Are you ok?"

"Not really, no," said Joey, "but I'll be fine."

Neither of them spoke into the phone as a static tension of city noises began to crackle over the line.

"Ok," said Joey, "deep breaths. You ever been to Bosco's? Cute little place. There's a bar dog."

"They got a bar dog?"

"They got a bar dog."

"Ok," said Mary, "When are you free?"

"Just lemme get dressed and I can be there in forty minutes. Plus, or minus."

"Alright," Mary said through a sigh, "I'll see you soon."

"Bye, baby."

The day, presumably, was saved.

Mary made it to Bosco's in about half an hour. A train line heading towards the bar was open, on time, and mostly empty. Naturally, as soon as she casually traveled towards an incidental location, there were no obstacles. Mary entered Bosco's and took a seat in a booth towards the far end of the room. There were two old men sitting at the bar and a large dog snoring heavily on the stage while drinks were being served by an albino. The two men at the bar looked stuck in time as the smoke from their cigarettes curled around the hair that was growing out from their ears. One of the older men was talking with the bartender about baseball as his companion stared open mouthed at the ceiling. His milky glossed eyes would dart from different points while in low tones he would say to the others, "Didja see it?". His question went unanswered while his friend gently rubbed his back. The albino, whom you have undoubtedly guessed was Reed, affable barman, remained engaged with the conversation and continued to take inventory of his multicolored liquor bottles that lined the mirrored wall behind the bar. The color palette of bottles looked so calculated that it could have been mistaken for a facade or backsplash, but as each vessel was lifted and wiped for dust, alcohol would slosh and slide up from inside of the glass. Mary looked to the wall of the booth and ran her finger over an old pair of letters deeply scratched into the wood. They were carved inside a crooked heart and the initials read "FS♥MB".

"Hello, Miss," said Reed, as he stood above Mary.

He was taller than he had appeared from behind the bar. His movements suggested an individual with such grace and fluidity that he could move without being heard unless he wanted to be heard. Mary was too distracted to notice Reed coming toward the table and it was a little intimidating to suddenly have him standing so close. The room appeared to dim around his body with the halo of a saint around the top of his head. Mary rubbed her eyes until the effect could dissipate, but it only made it worse. After she made a few attempts to rub her eyes, all that she could see was an incandescent glow around a shadowy figure.

"May I see some I.D.," he asked.

Mary fished through her bag and retrieved her driver's license. It had been years since she had driven, apart from the Maserati incident. Even so, Mary always managed to keep her license in order and never let it expire. Reed looked from the license to her face and back again before returning the card to Mary.

"Ok," said Reed, "What can I get you?"

"Can I get a cider, please," said Mary, "I'm waiting for a friend. He should be here soon."

Reed looked around the empty bar before replying.

"I'll do my best to reserve him a seat."

Reed left to get Mary her drink. She looked at her phone to text Joey that she had arrived, but there were three texts from Ruth that caught her attention. The first was a long block text of an apology mixed with manic guilt and shifting blame that was difficult to read. The second message felt more condensed and began to touch upon Ruth's breakup with Julia, of which Mary had not been aware and was now beginning to feel guilty for having been angry. The third text simply read, "I'm sorry."

Mary began to respond to Ruth when Joey walked into the bar. She stood and hugged Joey tightly in her arms while he held onto her and squeezed her as though it had been months since they had seen each other. He ordered a beer from Reed before letting go of Mary. The two friends sat in the seasoned booth of the dark and empty bar while the elderly man continued to look at the ceiling and tug on the sleeve of his friend.

"Hi, Joey," said Mary, "thanks for coming out."

"Oh, don't thank me," he said, "I came out years ago."

"Shut up," said Mary.

She reached her hand across the table and gave Joey's fingers a gentle squeeze. They felt cold and stiff, like he was trying not to make a fist. Joey reluctantly placed his backpack between himself and the wall while he leaned his shoulder against it.

"What's up with you," asked Mary, "your hands are freezing."

Joey laughed nervously and wiped his mouth before sticking both hands under his armpits.

"Fine, yeah. I'm fine," he said, "just cold is all. Is it cold in here?"

"No, not at all. What's going on?"

"I may have fucked up," said Joey, "I may have fucked up bad."

Joey told Mary about Sam and Laura, about the harrowing adventures of Mr. Biscuit and the failed advances of Pete. He told Mary that he had stolen a sizable amount of drugs from Laura while being in a state of crisis, but now that he felt that he had calmed down a bit, he was reluctant to bring them back. Mary tried to listen to what Joey was saying, but her mind was too occupied by her own cluttered thoughts. She heard what he was saying, and she understood most of it, but there was a large portion of her mind that was blocking the reception of new information. Her attention returned to the words stolen drugs.

"What do you have?" asked Mary.

"There's about three pounds of good weed, a lot of cocaine, lots of pills, two pounds of mushrooms, and two vials of blotter acid."

"What kind of pills?"

Reed returned to their booth with the drinks. Neither Mary nor Joey said thank you as the drinks were delivered. They straightened their backs and became quiet as Reed hesitated for just a moment over the table. He returned to the bar and continued to entertain the old men with stories of the Yankees World Series win over the Mets in the year two thousand. Mary watched the man who was staring at the ceiling while Joey continued talking about Sam. After a few minutes, Joey stopped talking to see if Mary would notice.

"I'm sorry, am I boring you?" asked Joey.

"No, man. I'm sorry."

"Well, come on. Didn't you have some big crisis or something? I just depressed myself so hearing about your problems will make me feel better."

Joey finished his beer and gestured to Reed for another round. Reed complied with a fresh beer and Joey drank half of it before Reed made it back behind the bar. Mary was starting to feel too warm and uncomfortable. Her throat had gone dry, even with the cider.

"I don't know where to start," said Mary, "well, David left me?"

"Is that a question?"

"I don't know," said Mary, "he texted me."

"Over text?"

"Yeah."

"He broke up with you over text?"

"Yeah."

"You know why he did that?"

"Why?"

"Because he's fucking dumb."

"Shut up! He's not dumb. I wish he was dumb."

"If he can't see how great you are, then he's dumb. And he breaks up with you over text after seven months? Chicken shit. What the fuck is his problem, anyway?"

Mary sipped her drink and stared at a blank spot on the table. Joey, in recognition of his insensitivity to her situation, took her hand in his and squeezed it.

"I'm sorry," he said, "looks like we're both just a couple of jerks, huh? Christ, there's nothing more boring than a broken heart."

Mary wiped her face with her free hand. Her vision was still blurry and there was a slight headache forming behind her eyes. She sipped on her drink, but it was starting to make her feel worse.

"I could have him secretly killed," said Joey, "or strip him naked, stuff him with peanut butter, and mail him to the zoo."

Mary smiled and said, "No, thank you."

"Good, that was my plan for this weekend anyway," said Joey, "they're having a special kink night at Central Park Zoo that's peanut butter themed."

This would normally get a laugh out of Mary, but she gave a polite chuckle like she was working in an office instead of having drinks with her best friend. Joey's concern was growing as he noticed how pale Mary had become.

"What else is going on," asked Joey, "I get the feeling that this is more than just a David thing."

"It won't make any sense," said Mary, "but I have to tell you something."

Joey looked at Mary with sincerity as he recognized the gravity in her voice. Thoughts of new party gossip and controversy were quickly dismissed as Mary divulged her childhood story about the boy and her grandmother. She told him about the woods where she grew up and the strangeness that surrounded the place. She talked about the shed and her parents and the school that she attended. It all came flooding back to her memory as she began to dig back into the past.

Many of her words became automatic translations of flashing images that were all but nearly forgotten until the moment she thought to speak about them. Joey was quiet and let Mary talk until she finished her story with the events of running into the boy again at the party from the other night. Joey clenched and unclenched his jaw in his seat while Mary continued to feel nauseous.

"Do you think I'm crazy?" asked Mary.

"No," said Joey, "no, I don't think you are crazy. Delusional, maybe, but not crazy."

"And I don't know how to explain it," she said, "but the whole thing gave me such a weird feeling...it felt like I had left my body. Like I had gone somewhere else, and I still haven't come back yet. Do you know what I mean? Does that make sense?"

"DMT," said Joey, "or maybe ketamine."

"Come on, Joey, I'm serious."

"You know what I think? I think you got a little too fucked up at the party. You had a rough night, and you have a lot of bad old family shit to unpack. You saw some guy in a bathtub, and it freaked you out. Now I'm not a doctor, but am I wrong?"

The length between his words and Mary's silence began to grow and spread across the room. There had been a low frequency hum that ran as an undercurrent of background noise since they had sat down but was beginning to grow with intensity. It was the kind of sound that would hardly be noticed unless someone had pointed it out. It could have been an old refrigerator somewhere or the distant sound of the subway. Whatever it was had just been noticed by Mary as her vision continued to blur. The old man at the bar, with his mouth still open and his eyes still searching the ceiling, swallowed hard as he dared not to look away from his investigation. Reed continued to mark his inventory while Bosco began to kick in his sleep.

"Didja see it?"

A long black length of shadow shot several arms down from the ceiling without warning and gripped Mary by the neck. Shadow took form as thick grease and malignance. The grim face of an angry child resembling Saint Sebastian followed the opposite ends of the long, steaming arms, displaying the image of youth's rage and vengeance. It screeched and screamed horrible breath down onto Mary who was immobilized by the phantom's grip.

Bosco jumped up like a dog gone mad and proceeded to howl from fear while shitting across the stage floor. He tried to run away but could not gain any traction as he continued to slip and yelp in panic. Joey fell out of the booth, catching himself on an exposed nail that sliced a long stretch of his pant leg. Blood began to pour down through the gash almost immediately while he attempted to grip his leg and close the wound.

The two old men were knocked down from their stools while Reed reached for the pistol he kept underneath the bar. Despite his nystagmus he was a crack shot and marksman, but the ammunition he unloaded upon the shadowy form had no effect. Round after round was shot from the handgun as the bullets passed through the darkness only to hit the wall. Reed quickly considered alternative options while the arms that reached down from the ceiling seemed to multiply into the hundreds.

The low rumble that had gone nearly unnoticed was now amplified to a deafening metal-on-metal scraping sound that filled every space in the room. Everyone covered their ears to the noise that had now been pushed past the point of human tolerance. The effort of Bosco's howling carried such an intensity that it sounded like his lungs were about to burst.

Mary was lifted out from the booth and into the air as the length of ceiling shadow gripped her neck with ferocious intensity. The spectral and frozen scowl of unrepentant cruelty lay behind a slick mop of thick and sloppy black hair that dripped across the floor, leaving an awful stink and stain burning holes in the wood. Unable to scream or get a word to leave her mouth, Mary could do nothing more than close her eyes to the smoke and try to claw at the immaterial form surrounding her. She felt herself begin to lose consciousness as sleep overtook her, but she fell from the air and landed hard upon the table before she could succumb to its lasting effects. In a stroke of desperate and accidental genius, Reed turned on every light in the bar, eliminating all shadows. Once the light spread across the room and pushed the darkness out of sight, the phantom was gone, and everything became still.

Nobody moved at first. Mary lay on the table coughing and clutching her throat while she brought large gulps of air into her lungs. Joey lay on the floor, panicked and bleeding. Reed stood with his hand still on the light switches as he scanned the ceiling for any sign of evil that might be lingering above them. Bosco began to whine and look ashamed of the indignity that he left spread across the small stage. One of the older men was trying to revive his friend who had suffered a heart attack during the event.

"Mike," he said, "oh, god, Mike, no…"

The old man gently lifted Mike's head from the floor, though his eyes were unresponsive. He pulled his friend close to his chest and began to quietly weep, stuttering apologies and talking in broken sentences. Mike had become an inconsequential casualty in an unnecessary conflict, but that did not define his worth as a person. His funeral would later be sparsely attended, but those who would attend could not imagine a world without him.

Joey lay on the floor hyperventilating and waiting for his heart to slow down. He held his hand against the wound in his leg and began packing it with bar napkins as best he could. The thin paper ripped and stuck to his skin in clumps of red as the blood continued to seep through the cheap tissue. Joey tried to push himself up to his knees as he felt his body flush and the need to vomit rising from his insides. Mary was nearly catatonic with her eyes wild and staring up to the ceiling. Her finger lay across her lips as she began to bite along the side of it. The sound of weakly broken moans was shaking out of her lungs. Having made it to his feet with some difficulty, Joey grabbed Mary by the shoulders and pulled her up into a sitting position.

"Mary," he cried, "Mary! Are you ok? What the fuck was that?"

Mary said nothing but wrapped her arms around Joey's neck and sobbed deeply into his shoulder. Joey embraced her and the two friends sat frozen in place while Reed continued to scan the ceiling. Mike's lifeless body lay in his best friend's arms as it slowly began to grow cold.

Processing the aftermath of an unexpected event can take time. Sometimes what we experience can have lasting echoes of effects that may not immediately manifest into our consciousness. Small parts of acknowledgement and understanding may peek out as we feel comfortable enough to do so, but larger parts of an internal wound can take years to open. In that time, however long it takes, certain behaviors and perceptions of the world may become distorted. The way back, the memory, can shift over time as well. The human mind will protect itself if it feels as though it is under attack. This can also include removing certain memories or covering up parts that are too painful to recall. With lost time or re-written memory, the accurate details of a traumatic event may cause unpredictable panic, fear, and anger in the individual reliving the moment. Mary had forgotten a lot over the years, whether intentionally or accidentally, but somehow, she was not altogether surprised when the ceiling reached down and tried to kill her. It almost felt like coming home.

Locking the door and pulling the blinds allowed Reed to begin his analysis without the possible interruption of unexpected guests. He gently put his hand on the shoulder of the old man who was cradling Mike's body. Guiding him up from the floor and into a nearby chair, the old man removed his overcoat and laid it across his friend to allow him the earned dignity of having died. He sniffled and wiped his nose on his hand before Reed gave him a glass of straight whiskey. He also poured one for himself. The room was quiet apart from the shivering sound of people trying not to cry. Reed approached Mary and Joey who were still in each other's embrace.

"What did you bring into my bar?" asked Reed.

Mary was unable to answer his question through the fear and sobs that were still choking her.

"Can you take a fucking step back, please," asked Joey, "back the fuck up!"

"That thing seemed awfully interested in you," said Reed, "maybe not, but I don't know. Anything like this ever happened before?"

"If you don't back up right now…"

Joey turned to face Reed who raised his hands to prevent any further conflict, walking backwards to the center of the room. Clearing his throat, he called for Bosco to come to his side, which the dog immediately complied. He consoled the frightened animal before addressing the group.

"Before I call the police," he said, "I think we should all be on the same page. Now we have one man dead."

"Mike," said the old man, "his name is Mike…was Mike."

"Mike is dead," Reed continued, "these two are hurt, and there are fresh bullet holes in the wall. Now I don't have cameras in the bar. Don't believe in 'em and I would like to have as little of a police presence here as possible. Ever. So, here's what happened: Someone came in to rob the bar. The fucker grabbed her by the neck as a hostage. Big boy here tried to play hero, knocking him down and getting his leg cut. I pulled out my gun and missed. He ran for it. Mike had a heart attack in the middle of the action. Are we clear?"

Everyone nodded their heads in agreement without saying a word. There were glances and expressions of fear and sorrow between all of them while Bosco continued to clean himself. Reed reached for the phone behind the bar and called the police.

After the police arrived and the story was told, corroborated, expanded upon, and corroborated once more, they wrote everything down for their evening reports and said that they would follow up soon. When the group was asked for a description of the assailant, nobody on the scene could recall what the individual looked like. Attributing the lack of description to the effects of shock, the police shook their heads and concluded their investigation. Another dead-end crime in New York.

Mike's body had been removed by the coroner and would be taken to the nearest morgue for an autopsy and storage until the family could secure funerary arrangements. His friend left the bar without saying anything more than a weak goodnight. Reed was kind enough to give Joey basic first aid and an extra pair of pants that he had from the lost and found in the back room. Joey was not thrilled at the prospect of wearing someone else's used pants that had been sitting in a damp cardboard box for lord knows how long, but his jeans were covered in blood and had nearly disintegrated. The donated pants were hardly a perfect fit, but after everything that happened, Joey did not care.

Before saying goodnight, Reed made Mary and Joey promise to never return to the bar. There were no hard feelings, but Reed was superstitious and did not believe in coincidence. Mary and Joey had no objection and departed in peace. Left with a layer of Bosco's shit across the stage, Reed poured himself a tall glass of wine and closed the bar for the remainder of the evening. He kept the lights on all night.

....

"Mary?" Joey was waving his hand in front of Mary's face. "Mary, you good?"

Mary was lying on the floor and staring up at the ceiling. Her eyes felt thick with a pain behind each socket as she blinked twice and gagged slightly. Bosco's looked as though it had been untouched from the scene that Mary had just experienced. Reed and one of the old men were standing above her with Joey and Bosco the dog was sleeping peacefully on the stage. The look of concern on their faces was genuine, but the older man soon returned to his friend and his drink.

"What happened?" asked Mary.

"You went all blank and started talking to yourself," said Joey, "You were telling me about that guy at the party and your eyes went all glassy and you fell over. You stopped breathing for like a minute straight and it looked like you were choking. I think you had a seizure."

"Did I?" asked Mary. "What happened to the...wait. What happened?"

Joey took a deep breath and collapsed back into the booth.

"Why does everything I love have seizures?"

What had happened was still lingering as a feeling of overwhelming panic. It had not yet become a memory. The event was fragmented, only coming through as exaggerated flashes of misunderstanding, but was real enough to convince Mary that she was still under attack. Reed walked over to their booth and crossed his arms as he scrutinized Mary.

"Are you on anything right now?" asked Reed.

"No," said Mary, "no, we're straight."

"You should tell me if you are," said Reed, "do I have to call an ambulance?"

"No, I..." Mary trailed off and stood up. She walked to one of the older men at the bar and placed her hand on his shoulder. He was looking up at the ceiling.

"Didja see it?" he asked without looking at her.

"I did," said Mary, "I think I did."

"You'll see it again," he said, "it comes and goes, but you'll see it again."

The other man at the bar interjected into their conversation.

"I'm sorry about my friend," he said, "Mike gets confused. See's things."

"Right," said Mary, "right, yeah."

15. The Glitter Ghost Fun Factory

    Light poured in through the early morning hours of the Rubenstein's apartment. Howard had barely slept for worry of his adopted daughter Mary, whom he never thought of as adopted, despite what the law said. Howard and Lorry loved Mary from their first introduction, and they considered such titles as nothing more than flimsy bureaucracy. Mary would always be Mary to them. She was their beloved daughter and rogue dreamer. They raised both Ruth and Mary under the same roof, with the same food, and the same rules:

Be kind.
Be brave.
Be careful.

    These were the three major foundations of parenting on which the Rubenstein's had built their house. Kindness firstly, above all else, because kindness can easily become overlooked and is one of the strongest weapons against evil. Bravery because it is difficult to be alive and sometimes it is even more difficult to stay alive. It is brave to persevere over the adversity of events that you will encounter in your life, but it is also brave to know when to ask for help, and how. Being careful did not mean cowardice, but planning. If you cannot be good, be careful. It was illuminating for both Howard and Lorry to watch the two girls grow up in the same environment and yet react so very differently to how they were raised.

    Ruth had the indoctrination of having been a Rubenstein from birth. She always knew how to be a Rubenstein. Mary had some difficulties fitting in with their family because the habits and learned behavior from her previous life were cemented into her wiring. Where Ruth would engage a problem with the confidence of a specialist, Mary would often spend most of her time thinking about the problem instead of approaching it head on. Ruth was brave, Mary was careful, but they were both kind, to a point. Being so close in age and experiencing their teenage years simultaneously did lead to a series of unfortunate incidents, but those are the good times.

Ruth and Mary had both taken similar roads up until their late teens. Mary had found the warm invitation to chemical intervention a welcoming divergence from her feelings, which had become the driving catalyst in her choices. Ruth played around with drugs for a little while but ultimately it would become Mary's preferred vessel for internal communication and psychic divination. Ruth instead became obsessively interested in the electronic world of visual art. This became her church. The growing differences between Ruth and Mary's interests brought a rift into their relationship. Mary had a feeling of both abandonment from Ruth and the understanding that she was simultaneously pushing her away. This was an unspoken fear between them both until they ultimately drifted apart. They never talked about it.

Soon after that, Mary began to distance herself from Howard and Lorry as well. Mary loved them dearly with her whole heart. She was grateful for everything that they had done for her, but she was also afraid of them. She was afraid to disappoint them and to have them think less of her. If they were to abandon Mary because of her deviancies, then she would never be able to recover from their rejection. It was impossible for Mary to trust them because that meant they would have to trust in her. This was too big of a responsibility for Mary to approach with sincerity.

The love that she felt for Howard and Lorry had become twisted by fear and resentment. The fear of rejection was based on the assumption that her behavior would upset them enough to leave her, just like everyone else in her life. It was a vulnerability that she had been trying to close off for a fair amount of time now. In Mary's eyes, if she let someone get too close then they would know how to hurt her.

The life insurance policies left for Mary by her parents were a large enough sum to secure her immediate independence from the Rubenstein's. At least until she could figure out what it was that she wanted to do with her life. Now even a large sum of money can be decimated over a weekend in New York City. With a growing chemical dependency in one of the most expensive cities in the world, Mary had to adapt quickly and make some sustainable choices.

She had joined up with a communal living situation where twelve or so people of no specific identity shared a residency in a dilapidated building in the deep Bronx. It would not be unusual for a new roommate to appear suddenly in the middle of the night while you were asleep. You may be gently awakened, or rudely at times, to the sound of someone shuffling a mattress into the room where you are trying to sleep or dropping their bags with a heavy sigh. If in the morning no one was in the room with you after all, it would be hard to differentiate between reality, a dream, how high you were the night before, or some combination of the three. But there was always food and they never seemed to run out of toilet paper. The cluster of tenants referred to themselves as the Glitter Ghost Fun Factory and some members even started their own bands.

Mary had some musical talent, more than most of the other residents. Because she found that everybody seemed to want to play the guitar, she played bass. There were artists of all makes and models in the GGFF. Poets and writers abounded but were only moderately annoying. They mostly drank too much and talked amongst each other about their favorite subject, which was nothing. The painters were temperamental but filled with so much self-loathing that they mostly kept to themselves, which they also hated. There were two sculptors who were the most kind and understanding of the group, but because of their amiability were often exploited into carrying the responsibilities of others. The actors were the worst. Never spend time with actors. If they could sing and act? Put them on a boat and blow the fucker up.

Mary's time was not often spent at the GGFF, if she could help it. She mostly utilized the space as a place to sleep and a hideaway for her accumulated treasures. There was a locked room in the back of the apartment that was too small for more than one person to sleep in, so Mary received a guarantee that no one else would be using the room if she was willing to pay a little more rent. Without the certainty as to whether Mary would need the room for any given night, it was agreed upon that the space would be reserved exclusively for her if she needed it.

There was a small twin mattress on an iron frame tucked into the corner of the room and if you opened the door too quickly it would smack the bed. Mary found this out the first night there when she came home drunk and nearly broke a portion of the door. Apart from the bed, there was a short chest of drawers with a flat top where Mary stacked her books and smaller trinkets. Mary had grown fond of forgotten things and was becoming a little bit of a hoarder, but with a room that small it was hard not to. There was a space that was kept clear of anything else and held her two most treasured possessions.

Her grandfather's compass hung from a string looped over a nail sticking out from the wall and a tattered copy of The Wind in the Willows lay upon a footstool beneath it. Mary still lacked the courage to read the book and it had been years since she had opened it. There was a fear of rekindling dormant memories that were, in her mind, best left in the past. It had become less painful as the years had gone by, but after a time she could not remember what her father's voice sounded like. She was unable to decide which felt worse, so she just put the book down altogether. She could not bring her heart to sell it or throw it away.

Mary's band was called Butt Soda, and they had a strict no practice/no songwriting policy. Their formula was based on spontaneous performances that could never be premeditated or repeated. At the start, the band would set up and play outside wherever they could find an electrical outlet. This proved to be more expensive than they had anticipated due to the citations they each received for noise violations of a city ordinance. This was also difficult because it was impossible to run away from the police while carrying a drum kit. After two of their members were arrested for disturbing the peace and assault on a police officer, the band began to develop a small cult following.

When Butt Soda received a few invitations to perform in proper venues, they decided that it might be worth trying to play inside where the likelihood of being arrested would be of a smaller percentage. They were then all arrested after their first indoor show when their drummer at the time had taken too many stimulants and proceeded to cut himself while masturbating from behind the kit. There was so much blood that they had to close the bar for one week and deep clean the premises. After their first indoor performance, they were an underground sensation.

These would have been good enough reasons for Howard Rubenstein to worry about his daughter Mary, but they were all old incidents and unknown to him. Mary felt it was in her parents' best interest to remain uninformed of her activities. In Mary's consistent distancing from her adoptive family, there were long breaks from communication that could stretch for indeterminate amounts of time.

They had all been experiencing one of Mary's disappearances, but Howard felt as though something else was wrong. The feeling was difficult to name, but it was overpowering and impossible to ignore. He knew that something unstable was moving within their universe and without a direct target in which to aim his anxieties, his thoughts often turned to Mary. Howard was also a hypochondriac so when these feelings did surface, he would try to recognize this and calm himself with his radios. Without any other explanation, this time felt different. No amount of radio conversations would distract him long enough to forget his feelings.

When Mary was little, and grew to trust the Rubenstein's over time, she had divulged a certain number of edited truths from her childhood. Edited memories were what she preferred; bits of reminiscence cut up like paper and folded to resemble something wholly other. Snowflake memories. The kind that look smaller than they are until you unfold them and see all the holes. The shed had become a simple scary basement, and the boy became a fellow classmate that annoyed her. Mary's grandmother was a kind old woman with dementia while her parents were just…busy. Howard and Lorry knew well enough to read between the lines about many of the experiences that Mary had chosen to share with them. The Rubenstein's felt uncomfortable holding Mary to a duplicitous suspicion, but there was the reality that Mary's past was her own and it was not their place to cross that boundary.

Howard was looking out from the bedroom window as the sun brought golden shadows to fill the space in the room. He would slowly try to weave his fingertips between the specks of dust that he could see but could never feel or touch. His giant hand would move through the air and the immaterial specks would spin and dart away from him. This was his favorite time of the day. Lorry was still asleep, letting out half words and syllables while she dreamt of uncommon things. Howard always did his best not to wake her up, but on that morning, he intentionally nudged her with his arm until she darted her head back at him with alarmed annoyance.

"Wuzzat," she said, "w'happen?"

"I don't know what to do," said Howard, "I don't know what to do."

Lorry turned to wrap her arms around Howard's massive frame. His body had a light red spread of fuzz that seemed to cover every surface. He mostly slept naked due to the amount of body heat that he would produce during the night. Lorry never minded this as she was always cold. She would sleep in her underwear and a loose tank-top that always managed to slip one of her breasts out of place. She adjusted her top and buried her face into Howard's side. She loved the way he smelled in the morning.

"What do you want to do?" she asked.

"I want Mary to come home. I want to tell her that it's ok and that we love her. I want to keep her safe. I can't do that, can I?"

"No one can keep anyone safe forever," said Lorry, "we can try, but she has to live her life. Best we can do is be ready to be there when she needs us."

Howard said nothing but stared back out the window. He rubbed Lorry's back to which she grunted in approval, turning to allow him better access to her early morning body. He would then run his fingernails against her skin until she stopped making noises and fell back asleep. These were the good mornings. Warm mornings where there was no rush or reason to jump out of bed and half-heartedly go to a half-hearted place. Not a single thing that they had to do that morning was as important as making breakfast and enjoying how they felt pressed against each other. The rest of the city moved on without them. The bakery downstairs had already sold most of their finest goods.

It was hard for Howard to accept the feeling of powerlessness when someone that he loved needed help. What was even more difficult for Howard was the lesson that he would often do his best to ignore. Sometimes removing yourself from a situation can be more helpful than being present. It was hard for Howard not to take that personally. He saw it as an abject failure on his part if he was unhelpful, but there was a subconscious arrogance in the need to be involved. It is from arrogance that you cannot trust others to know what it is that they need. Howard struggled with where he had control over his life and when he had to let things go. With the best of intentions, Howard lay in the bed and continued to let his fingers float through the air.

Hours later, after Howard and Lorry decided to wake up and eventually get out of bed, and after a surprise bout of intense morning sex, the kind where nobody cares about who has yet to brush their teeth, Lorry was making pancakes. Howard was taking a shower and listening to the radio talk about the Mets and how much realistic optimism should exist for their being in the World Series. So far it was looking pretty good, but then again it was the Mets. Lorry had just taken the freshly made pancakes and put them in the oven to keep warm when the doorbell rang.

Ruth entered with hesitation. As much as she was looking forward to breakfast with her parents, she really had wanted to cancel. Guilt kept her present as she had already canceled plans with them twice in the last month. The other deciding factor was that now with Julia gone, Ruth came to realize how few friends she had. She was caught in the push and pull of feeling lonely and wanting to be left alone. Ruth gave her mother a hug and a kiss before sitting at the table while Lorry poured the coffee. Howard came out from the bathroom wrapped in what would have been an adequate towel for a normal sized person but was comically small on him. Not wanting his daughter to see him naked, he hustled his way to the bedroom when he saw Ruth in the kitchen. Lorry removed the pancakes and made three plates beside a thick slab of butter, blueberry jam, real maple syrup, synthetic syrup, caramelized apples, and a mixed berry compote. Eggs and bacon were on deck.

"Thanks, mom," said Ruth, "maybe just the coffee for now."

"You're not eating?" asked Lorry, "what's wrong? OH! How was your big gallery opening? Your father and I wanted to go, but we were both so sick we only left the bed to use the bathroom. He hardly ate anything the whole time, the big dummy. But tell me, how was the show?"

"Fine," said Ruth, "talked with this guy Carter Davis. He's on the board of trustees at the Met."

"OoOoOoOo," said Lorry, "That's exciting! What did he say? What did you talk about?"

"Nothing important. Mostly economics."

"It's all money with them," said Lorry, "no passion. No soul."

"How was your show?" asked Howard. He entered the kitchen and immediately made a plate of five pancakes, three eggs, and seven strips of bacon. After setting the plate on the table, Howard poured himself a glass of water, orange juice, and coffee with lots of milk and lots of sugar.

"It was fine," said Ruth.

"She talked to some hot shot from the Met," said Lorry.

"No kiddin'," said Howard with a mouthful of food, "you gonna get famous, you think?"

"Fame isn't everything," said Lorry.

"Right, right," Howard remarked as he scanned the furnished apartment that was bought and paid for.

Ruth sipped her coffee and did her best not to dread the following question that was routinely unavoidable. The combination of sorrow and fear made it difficult to swallow her coffee.

"How's Julia," asked Lorry, "she still sleeping or just too busy for breakfast?"

"Julia left, mom. She, ah, she left me."

Lorry got up and gave Ruth a hug. She experienced a strong impulse to push her mother away, but Ruth let the embrace fill her with a quiet anger that she would later make space to acknowledge. There was no reason why contact with her mother had made her angry because she was already angry. The physical touch only amplified her negative emotions. She was just about to push Lorry away when she let go. Howard looked at his daughter, shook his head, and returned to his plate. The kitchen table was where Ruth decided to lend her focus. If she looked at anything else, then she knew that she would start to cry. If she were to start, then she may not be able to stop. Instead, Ruth simply cleared her throat and sipped her coffee.

"I came home from the opening and found this note," said Ruth, "'I've met someone, promise you'll marry me, please don't contact me,' that kind of thing. I tried to call her a few times, but she hasn't answered. I don't know. I just don't understand why she left."

Ruth began to tear up but stifled it with a cough and folded her hands on the table. Howard continued to eat until Lorry rested her hand on his and shot him a quick look that read "stop". Howard placed his fork on his napkin and rested his hands flat on the table. He watched the warm mixed berry compote drip off the side of his pancakes.

"Ruth," said Lorry, "whatever Julia is going through, it's probably a good idea to let her go. I'm sorry, baby. Who knows? Maybe she'll reach out sooner or later. Maybe not at all. You never can tell, and that's the worst part of it. She may call you sometime, but you can't count on it. Never count on it. Grieve, by all means! Grieve however you need to, but something is obviously wrong, and she didn't know how to communicate that to you. She said she's seeing someone, so you have to leave it at that. Now I'm not defending her choice to leave but torturing yourself isn't going to get her back."

Ruth sat in silence as she slowly stirred her spoon in her coffee. She knew that her mother was right, but she would not allow herself to acknowledge it. If anything, she hated her for making sense. Ruth wanted to come home and find Julia sitting on the couch or lying in bed reading comics. To find Julia back in her apartment doing anything at all would be enough to have Ruth want for nothing more. She held onto a pathetic hope that it had to be some kind of joke. The kind that ended with so many kisses. The thought of wanting an apology never crossed her mind.

Lorry rose from the table and put a stack of three pancakes, eggs, and bacon on a plate with lots of butter. She put the plate in front of Ruth and said, "Eat."

The Rubenstein's enjoyed a quiet breakfast while Ruth contemplated suicide.

After breakfast, the three Rubenstein's climbed the back stairs that led to the roof. There was a small half patio set up from abandoned furniture that had been collected over the years and a large, round glass table that was set in a steel frame. Howard and Lorry sat in their favorite chairs while Ruth walked to the edge and looked down into the street. Apart from a few scattered cars that were parked along the side, the street was relatively empty. Ruth nudged a small stone off the roof with the toe of her boot.

"Honey," said Lorry, "remember when you and Mary used to play up here and we would get so mad?"

"You would get mad," said Howard, "I let them up here half the time."

"And thank you so very much for that," quipped Lorry, "anyway, we never worried about your judgment or your being too reckless. We were just worried. I want you to know how proud I am for how you've grown up."

"Hey, me too!" said Howard.

"And Howard, too."

Ruth turned from the edge of the roof and sat down beside her parents. Her chair was a green plastic frog with worn out eyes poking up from the back rest. She scooted the chair forward across the black tar roof and rested her hands on the table that had been warmed by the late morning sun.

"Am I a fraud?" asked Ruth.

Lorry and Howard were surprised by the question. They had never seen a ripple of insecurity from Ruth before. She had carried herself with such drive and certainty that the question was almost ridiculous.

"Why do you think you're a fraud?" asked Howard.

"You guys have given me so much," said Ruth, "I'm grateful for everything, really, I am. I just feel like I haven't earned it. I don't know what poverty feels like. I don't know what it feels like to go without. Does that make me a bad person?"

Lorry and Howard looked at each other. Had they done harm in providing so much for their children? A parent that desires a better life for their child can easily overcompensate for their needs. There is also the uncertainty as to whether they are administering an appropriate amount of discipline. Perhaps a mistake that they had made was in the absence of specific guidance when a problem would occur in both Ruth and Mary's childhood. The Rubenstein's would give advice and give space for the girls to talk through any conflict, but had that been enough? Had they accidentally spoiled their children?

"What you do," said Lorry, "makes you. Nobody is good or bad. Well, some people are bad, but everyone has the capacity to be good."

"Except for Ronald Reagan," said Howard.

"Except him."

"And both Bushes."

"Fine, yes, but…"

"Clinton is a piece of shit, too."

"Fine! Yes! We've never had a good president! We get it!"

"I'm just saying," Howard began to pick beneath his fingernails.

"My point, Ruth, is that no. You're not a bad person. Bad people don't think that they're bad people. You do such good things, beautiful things. Honey, I'm your mother. I would tell you if you were full of shit."

Ruth found some consolation in this, but it was still difficult for her to believe that she was living without flaunting her privilege. This was only one of the many worries that Ruth had knocking around in her mind. She changed the subject to shift their attention.

"Mary stopped by the other day," she said, "she looked ok, for Mary. Just tired."

"How is she?" asked Howard.

"She's going through it," said Ruth.

"Is she still living with all those kids in the Bronx?" asked Lorry.

"I don't know," said Ruth, "I think so. You guys remember that little boy she used to talk about? The one she knew when she was little?"

"Maybe," said Howard. "Back home for her, yeah?"

"Yeah, that weird neighborhood kid," said Lorry, "he was pretending to have amnesia or something. Kept losing his shoes?"

"Oh, yeah," said Howard, "what about him?"

"She said she saw him at a party the other night."

"No kiddin'?" said Lorry, "how's he doin'? What's he doin' in New York?"

Ruth proceeded to come clean in the truth about the boy's interactions with Mary and what Mary believed were supernatural experiences. She brought her parents up to speed on Mary's childhood fears and her abusive grandmother. The explanation may have taken all of four minutes, but Ruth began to second guess her own judgment after each word that left her mouth. The balance between Mary's privacy and her safety was starting to tilt. Ruth felt as though her betrayal of Mary's trust outweighed her necessary boundaries. Once Ruth finished wrapping up the details, Howard leaned back in his chair and rubbed his forehead.

"Ok," he said, "so she had an imaginary friend growing up. She thinks he's back and grown up now. What do we do? Is it a bad thing?"

"This could get bad," said Ruth, "Mary wasn't making much sense, and I may or may not have been a little mean. I had just found Julia's note and I was feeling shitty." Ruth put her hand in her pocket and let her finger rub against the edges of the envelope. "I think she may be cracking up."

"Should we call her?" asked Howard, more to Lorry than Ruth.

"I tried calling her this morning," said Lorry, "I try to call her every weekend."

"When was the last time you talked?" asked Ruth.

"It's been over a month," said Lorry.

Howard sighed heavily as he stood up from his chair. He walked towards the door leading back to the apartment without saying anything to Lorry or Ruth.

"Where do you think you're going?" asked Lorry.

"I'm going down to the Bronx to get our daughter back."

Howard knew exactly where Mary had been staying. In the previous year, before he had recognized that his interventions into Mary's life were causing more harm than good, he had followed Mary to see where it was that she was staying. He stayed out of sight while Mary walked home to her small room in the Glitter Ghost Fun Factory. Once he saw where she had gone, he memorized the street number and recognized the only floor that seemed to have electricity. He felt guilty for having followed her that night, but he rationalized it as gathering information for the worst-case scenario, should it ever occur.

Returning to the address provided no new information for Howard as the street and building looked unchanged from his last visit. It was still daylight when he arrived, but there was no obvious activity through the windows of the building. After walking around the tenement in search of the best point of access, he shouldered his way through the front door.

It was unlocked, but not the preferred entrance for the residence of the GGFF. Its pathway was cluttered with debris from the past few years. Trash was chucked and piled high against the entrance. Stepping over a broken baby carriage and some plastic bags filled with used take-out containers, Howard disturbed two cats that had been asleep beneath the pile. They both shrieked and howled as they ran down the hall while Howard himself had been so startled that he jumped nearly a foot in the air. Once his heart stopped pounding in his chest, he walked up the stairwell that led to what he presumed to be the GGFF floor, although he did not know its name.

He stepped cautiously on each stair so as not to announce his presence and find the threat of a call to the police. There was a possibility that having police in the building would do more harm for everyone involved, so there was some small security in the assumption that nobody wanted them there. Even with each intentional step, the stairs were old and creaked beneath Howard's weight. The carpet that had once been clean and neatly tacked was now so moldy and compacted that removing it would likely bring some of the wood up with it. There was a sponge-like quality to the steps instead of the desired sensation of padding. Even through his boots, Howard knew that the steps were always damp.

The second floor of the building was quiet but had the muffled cries of children and television sets coming out through the walls. Howard began to walk with a normal gate at this point. No sense in sneaking around an occupied floor. He rounded the banister and was beginning his climb to the third floor when a commotion began above his head. The sounds of an argument could be heard between two or three people and it was only escalating as Howard proceeded up the stairs.

"You've never cared about me," came a woman's voice, "never! All you care about are your stupid fucking stories and your stupid fucking songs!"

"How can you say that" this must have been the boyfriend, thought Howard, "who's been paying your rent for the past five months?! Who's been helping you stay sober?! Me, that's who!"

"Fuck you," she said, "you think I've been sober?! You've been so busy with your bullshit that you haven't even noticed me! Well, here's a surprise, asshole! I've been high this whole time and I've been fucking your brother! He's a better fuck than you've ever been."

"I'm sorry, Bob," this must have been the brother, thought Howard, "I never wanted to hurt you. It was supposed to be a one-time thing. I didn't want to hurt you."

"I sure as hell did," she said, "so take your faggy little poems and your stupid little songs and get the fuck out!"

There was the sound of a scuffle now as the two brothers began to wrestle on the floor. The young woman shouted something about a knife, so Howard jumped up the last three steps and grabbed both men, lifting them off the ground by their collars with his giant hands. The two brothers froze in fear at the sight of Howard and the young woman began to shriek as she begged him to put them down.

"Stop it," she said, "we're actors! We're just rehearsing a scene! Put them down, please!"

"Please don't kill us," said one of the young men, "we haven't got any money!"

The other young man had accidentally pissed himself from the shock. He covered his face with his hands and tried not to cry as the damp odor began to fill the hall. To be honest, the smell made little difference to the state of the hallway.

Howard kept the two boys elevated as he was still confused and did not really know what to do. He was frustrated enough to want to shake them, but he was also mindful enough not to get pissed on. He put them on the ground and took a step back with his open hands above his waist, showing that he was unarmed.

"I'm sorry," he said, "I'm sorry I didn't know."

The three actors became elated at this seal of authenticity and began to hug and congratulate each other. Even old piss pants cheered up a bit. Howard began to rub the bridge of his nose with his thumb and forefinger, closing his eyes in aggravation.

Actors, he thought to himself.

"Excuse me," he said, "is there a Mary Rubenstein that lives here?"

"Who?" said the young woman.

"Mary Rubenstein," said Howard, then raising his hand, palm down, "about this tall, blonde hair, but sometimes it's green or blue?"

"That's like, five people I know," said the young man who had not pissed himself.

"What's her thing?" asked the young woman.

"Whaddya mean?" asked Howard.

"You know, her *thing*. Like, what does she do?"

"Oh," Howard thought on this for a minute, "she plays in a band, I think?"

"Oh, Mary from Butt Soda," said the young woman.

"What?"

"Mary from Butt Soda. Oh man, they're great. Very Avant Garde."

"Yeah," said Howard, "they really do it for me. Where is she?"

"I haven't seen her," said the young man. Again, not the one covered in piss.

"Mind if I come in?"

"You a cop?" chimed the suddenly emboldened young man covered in his own piss.

Howard shot him an eye that said, *Please. Give me a reason*.

The three actors refused to allow Howard entry as they could not find a way to prove that he was related to Mary or that he knew anything about her. On the one hand, Howard found this to be an admirable quality that spoke highly of their ethics and loyalty. They protected each other. Although it certainly was an inconvenience now. After taking into consideration the personal politics of the actors' unlikelihood of calling the police, and the presumption that he could throw each of them down the stairs with ease, Howard simply walked through them as though they were a short field of wheat. They offered light protest but then resolved themselves to their fates while they scurried into their rooms.

Howard walked through the apartment as though it were boobytrapped. He stopped to look at show flyers that had been pinned to the walls and the scattering of art that was spread throughout the apartment. In the single bay sink sat a bong filled with black water surrounded by an assortment of dirty plates, bowls, and cutlery. They were soaking in warm beer. An open gallon of milk sat on the counter beside an unwrapped roll of paper with something that could have been meat. These were next to five or six open tins of cat food, some of which were still half full. The smells in the room had eyebrows.

Howard exited the small kitchen through a door that led into a large open space with long tapestries hanging from hooks attached to what could have once been track lighting. They ran from side to side in an angle too awkward to have been intended for curtains. The long sheets of fabric made sharp walls that cut the room in different sections used to cover people who wanted some assemblance of privacy. Howard carefully entered the space, making sure not to disturb anyone. A variety of new smells made the kitchen seem less offensive. Body odor was prevalent. This was combined with an undertone mix of incense, perfumed oils, cigarettes, and the obvious presence of animals.

Some pockets of the room were empty, while other spaces had people reading or scrolling through their phones. Some people slept. A boy that could not have been older than twelve lay between a dog and a space heater while a cigarette smoldered between his fingers. He looked at Howard and asked if he had any food. Howard said nothing but turned his back and walked down another hall.

The hallway had two long bath towels that were being utilized as rugs on the hardwood floor. Neither was long enough to reach the full length of the hall, but their purpose seemed more practical than ornamental. The crooked angles that were crumpled on the edges made Howard think that the towels may have been left to cover some kind of spill. When he shifted a corner of the towel with his boot, a fleet of cockroaches scattered in different directions. He jumped in reflex and managed to stomp two before the rest disappeared between the baseboards and the molding. Howard looked down the hall and found a small door at the end with a purple "M" painted on it. When knocking provided no response, he opened the door with caution and prepared himself for more unpleasantness.

The room was small, about the size of a large walk-in closet, and it had a single twin bed along one wall from the door to the back. The door could only open halfway as it thumped against the mattress that had been flipped off the bed. Howard could barely fit past the door, and once he was in the room, he could only stand in one place and shuffle his feet to turn around. His neck was crooked from the height of the ceiling.

There had been signs of a struggle as parts of a small table lay broken and splintered on the ground with what looked like dried blood on the floor and the walls. Some books had been ripped and thrown around the room. Howard picked up a dog-eared copy of the Selected Poems of Lorelei Keller-Rubenstein from the floor and opened it carefully. The pages were all marked and tagged with small notes that Mary had made. She scribbled out some parts and replaced them with her own lines while other passages had notes of approval and validation. Some stanzas and pages were simply marked "Love". Howard carefully returned the book to the top of the dresser as though it were made of crystal.

After finding Mary's copy of the Wind in the Willows ripped in half his mind traveled to a dark place. He knew how much Mary loved that book. She carried it with her everywhere when they had first taken Mary in, but whenever Howard offered to read it to her, she always refused. Once she had explained that her father used to read it to her, Howard understood and left it alone. Seeing it discarded and tattered on the floor scared him more than anything else.

It had been over a month since Mary had answered their calls and even before that she was not the best at communication. Howard thought about going to the police, but then reconsidered. Mary would be lost in the system as another missing person in a city made from millions of missing people. The police would be of no help. Howard rubbed his tired eyes and decided to return to Brooklyn with no good news for Ruth or Lorry. Turning to leave the room, Howard saw a note on the floor that he had overlooked. It was a small piece of light blue lined paper with red ink that had taken a purplish hue after it had dried. The note read:

Goin home.
Back in a few days.
Don't touch my shit.
-M

Howard turned the note over in his hand a few times thinking that there would be something else written on the paper. He looked for some kind of clue to decipher what Mary could have meant. If she said she was going home, then she would have made it back to their apartment in Brooklyn by now. A flash of light crossed the center of Howard's brain and although he was self-admittedly a little slow on the uptake, the hypothesis hit him in his guts. Mary had left the city.

16. Thank You, Loose Lips

Mary and Joey left Bosco's soon after Mary's episode. Reed had pressed Mary to go to the hospital, but she refused any medical attention. She promised not to hold Reed or Bosco's accountable if anything were to happen to her after they left. With her head still fuzzy, and with Joey becoming increasingly concerned, they walked to the nearest liquor store and bought a bottle of cheap whiskey. Mary was dodging the stretches of shadow left from the buildings and trees in the afternoon sun, making sure to avoid any contact with them. She gave no explanation to Joey after he asked her what she was doing, but she tried to walk a little more carefully without looking like a crazy person. After finding a suitable park bench with no overhanging branches, the two friends cracked into the bottle that was unashamedly obvious inside of its brown paper bag. After a few sips passed back and forth, Joey Boulm spoke.
"What was that back at the bar?" he asked.
"I don't know."
"You ever have something like that happen before?"
"I don't know," said Mary, "maybe when I was little. I don't really remember."
"What was the last thing you remember?"
"It was like a dream," she said, "but it was so real. There were these hands that came down from the ceiling and started choking me. I remember the old man at the bar died, and you got hurt, and the dog was shitting everywhere."
"You saw all that?"
"Bartender was shooting at the thing but missed the whole time."
"Do you want to go to the hospital?" asked Joey.
"No," said Mary, "I don't know. I don't know."
With choked breaths and profanities, Mary began to cry and lightly punch the side of her head. If there were some far away reason as to why her life was beginning to collapse, then there might be an action to knock the reason out. Unable to think of a better solution, Mary continued to lightly punch her head. Joey pulled Mary against his side and cradled her head in his hands. He loved Mary and hated seeing her like this, but Joey

did not have the tools to appropriately handle a mental breakdown. He took a large pull from the bottle and made a face when the whiskey hit his throat. They were both drunk and were each beginning to feel a little sick. He pulled out a small bag of pills from his jacket pocket and handed two to Mary after taking three himself.

"Thanks," she said.

They sat in silence for a while longer and watched the people come and go past their bench. Mary wondered about their lives, as she would in times when the need for distraction came around. She thought of where they lived and where they came from. She considered who they loved and who no longer loved them. The stories of every person entered her mind and brought new dimensions across each face that passed. Her eyes were scanning the park before they rested on an older man with a dog who was sitting on a bench opposite theirs. He was just a little way up the path, but he had a clear view of Mary and Joey, whom he observed with an expressionless face. His dog lay on the path beside the bench with the slow rising of its chest to be the only indication of life. Mary stared back at the man for a little while until she felt it suspicious and asked Joey if they could move on.

"Joey," she said, "do you know that guy?"

Joey did his best to look without being obvious, but he could not recognize the older man. It is common to run into someone you know in New York. Lots of people stuck to their neighborhoods and hardly ventured out past a ten-block radius. Even if he had known who this man was, Joey was not in the mood for socializing.

"I don't think I know him," said Joey.

"Can we leave?"

"Yeah, let's go."

Drunk and uncomfortable, Mary and Joey continued to walk through the afternoon. Neither of them spoke but were both caught in deep thought over their lives. The growing developments in Mary's behavior was a concern for Joey. His own problems were swirling around his mind, but with Mary's current condition, he felt as though her crisis took precedence. Her anxiety made him anxious, but he knew that he could not leave her to face this alone. Mary was about to say something when her phone began to ring. There was a bad connection and static as the line cut in and out. The voice on the other end of the call was coming from a man that sounded as though he were speaking from the bottom of a well.

"May I speak to Ms. Mary Kirkland?" said the voice.

"Speaking, yeah. I mean it's Rubenstein now, but yeah. Same Mary."

There was a loud pop and more static from the line.

"Ms. Kirkland, I regret to izzzzzzzzzz ungphzzzzat your aunt Colleen Coggeshall has passed. You hazzzzzzzzzzzzolences."

"Oh," said Mary, "who is this?"

"My name is qrzzzzzzzzpresent the law officzzzzzzzzzand Howe. I am thzzzzzzzzestate and there has been a nuzzzzzzzzzzzzeft to your care."

"I'm sorry, could you repeat that? I don't have a good connection here."

"We need you to sign some paperwork tozzzzzzzzzzzzz your inheritance. Now the house on Apollinaire Road and the land zzzzzzzzzzzzto you, but there are othezzzzzzzzzzestate that must be discussed. When can you be available?"

It was difficult to discern what the person on the other line meant, but from what she could piece together, Mary had inherited her childhood home. She did not know what to say. Mary looked at Joey who made a confused expression as he had not been able to hear the full conversation. The voice on the other end of the phone repeated the question as the static continued to build and buzz in Mary's ear.

"What's the address of the house, please?" she said.

"The house zzzzzzzzzztwo-six Apollinaire Road," came the voice, "it iszzzzzzzzzzpulated in the will that zzzzzzzzzheritance."

"Give me a date and I'll make myself available," she said into the phone.

There was a sound that could have been confused with coughing coming from the other end of the line.

"Would you be available to zzzzzzzzzzzzdays?"

"I'm sorry, could you repeat that please?"

"Can you make it here in two days?"

"The day after tomorrow?"

"If possible, yes."

"Yeah, I can do that."

"Splendid. I'll send you an email with the detailszzzzzzzzeeting you."

Mary hung up the phone and stared at the number that was flashing as PRIVATE on the screen. She felt nothing for the death of her aunt. She had no recollection of the last time that she thought of Aunt Colleen, but there was a sensation of dread that accompanied the thought of her owning the house where she had been raised. The last time that Mary had seen Aunt Colleen was at her grandmother's funeral. She had never tried to contact Mary in all this time, and that was fine. Mary would have avoided her anyway. It would make sense that Aunt Colleen would have taken the house after Mary's parents had died. She had always made suggestions to Mary's mother and father about potential renovations.

"Stop that," said Joey.

"What?"

"Stop biting your finger."

Mary had not noticed that she had been gnawing on the side of her finger again. The skin was beginning to become raw, and it stung in the open air. There was a chance that Mary was experiencing the early stages of an affliction called autosarcophagy, according to one of her former therapists. Once Mary had done some research on the condition, she thought it was stupid and the furthest possibility from her reality. This did provide her with a new term for an otherwise unknown compulsion, but this was held as a mere morbid fascination. Looking down at her finger made Mary feel confused and concerned. She had thought to have gotten past the habit over the years, but it had somehow managed to return.

"Does Sam still have a car?" asked Mary.

"Shit, I'm not going back to that apartment."

"We need a car."

"What for?"

"My aunt died and left me a house. I have to go back home and meet with a lawyer. Sign some paperwork."

"Back home," said Joey, "I always thought you grew from some kind of fungus."

"I'm serious, Joey. I don't know what this means, but I think it may have something to do with all this weird shit. Will you come with me?"

Joey scratched the side of his face and looked around for a reason to decline Mary's offer. The concern that Joey felt for Mary was enough to keep him by her side, but there was a strong feeling that this behavior was out of his depth of understanding. Finding nothing to justify his staying behind, Joey made the choice to keep an eye on Mary. It would do him well to get out of the city and away from Laura and Sam.

"Is there gonna be more of that weird shit?" he asked.

"Maybe," said Mary, "I don't know. Probably?"

"Shit," said Joey, "what the hell. Adventure. Come on, I know where we can get a car. I was thinking about getting out of the city anyway."

Joey led Mary to the subway that would take them into Queens. Joey had a cousin that worked for a guy who sold cars behind an ice cream parlor. If his cousin was working, then it might be possible to borrow a car for a short period of time. Or at least until the owner noticed it was missing.

The train ran with a few delays that seemed to draw out additional aggravations from commuters; ones that were already feeling hostile. Mary tried to stare at the floor as two men got into an argument with someone over a misplaced accusation. One of the two men was convinced that a young man had attempted to steal his wallet from the back pocket of his jeans. The youth rebuked the accusation, and the two men began to speak in violence. Some of the other passengers on the train recorded the conflict on their phones and tried to instigate them to do something more than just talk. Joey was drunk-plus and felt the lingering traumatic event from his last ride on the train. When the accuser took out his phone to call the police, Joey came in swinging. He caught the man in the jaw with a right hook and the fella went down and stayed down. It was a one in a million shot that Joey could never replicate again if he tried. The commotion caused the other passengers to get more riled up as the train pulled into the next station. Joey grabbed Mary's hand and they left the car, leaving behind the howling mass of people who were either elated or terrified by the violence. This was not the stop that Joey had intended to get off from but given the circumstances it would have to do.

The Brooklyn neighborhood was unfamiliar to Mary and Joey as they had not yet arrived in Queens. They stumbled down the roads directionless until they felt better than they had on the train. Mary stopped to vomit as the drugs and liquor had mixed with her adrenaline in a disagreeable way.

The excitement from the train had left an entirely overwhelming sensation after a full day of entirely overwhelming situations. It was merely a passing phase as Mary leaned her head on her hands and vomited against the brick wall of a tenement building. She did her best to ignore the jeers and complaints that were coming from the folks that lived there, as they were clearly upset that Mary had been sick. She made a passive wave of her hand that signaled both an apology and a request to be left alone. After a few minutes, she felt better, and they continued on their way as evening crept in.

"This is stupid," said Mary, "we have to go back to my place."

"What, in the Bronx?"

"Yeah, I have to lay down somewhere. Have to pack a bag."

"Hold on, I'll get a cab."

Joey stepped onto the street as a taxi had already been moving towards them. With a wave of his arm, the cab stopped and the two fell into the backseat. With a little luck, it would be bringing them to a territory with which they would feel more familiar. Mary closed her eyes as the taxi gently rocked her to sleep.

She dreamt of the ravine. She was a child again and the frogs had grown to the size of compact cars. Their eyes flashed like headlights in the darkness and although she felt warm, she could see that the water stood frozen in place. She had a jar in her hand and was trying to get the giant frogs into the small glass container. There was a stuttering of motion as she pressed the small opening against their shining skin. The frustration had mounted to where she had started to cry in the dream while the river itself seemed to mock her failures. She woke up with a start as the taxi driver stopped the car suddenly and laid on the horn. Mary wiped her eyes and looked at Joey who felt equally exhausted with his shoulder slumped against the door, staring at nothing out of the window. The taxi driver continued to scream out to another car in Portuguese as he rolled on down the street. Try as she might, Mary could not fall back asleep.

The taxi pulled up to the Glitter Ghost Fun Factory and Joey carefully opened a compartment in his backpack that held the cash he had been saving for three years. With the added paranoia of stolen drugs, he pulled a twenty and a ten out of the bag and handed them to the driver. Mary stepped out of the cab with Joey while the driver screamed something at them. Without having comprehension of the Portuguese language, Mary simply said thank you as she walked away from the taxi. The cabbie had no desire to reciprocate her parting words but sped down the street in search of his next fare. The night was young.

The residents of the GGFF were animated in preparation for a gathering of immense proportions. The house had a rotating schedule for event coordination and this night had fallen on the shoulders of a young man named Birdie. Birdie played drums in Butt Soda, a replacement after their last drummer had died from drinking rubber cement on a dare.

Birdie had a deep connection to the underground party scene of the Bronx. He was far from being a name, but he kept in the loop of events and would be seen from time-to-time at different locations. Tonight, he had taken it upon himself to host his first event. It was to be intimate, not set to be a big affair, but it was his own and there was a lot to do in preparation. When Mary and Joey entered the house, they climbed up the staircase and ignored three actors who were rehearsing a hackneyed bit that annoyed Mary for reasons that she did not care to understand. Once inside and through the kitchen, they found Birdie on a ladder hanging tapestries down from the track lighting which cut across the high ceilings. There were several of these long sheets zigzagging through the room, each making a different section for partygoers to enjoy. He said something to Mary that she missed, but she would have ignored him even if she had heard what was said. Mary needed to lie down.

Mary entered her room with Joey close behind. They closed the door and lay on the bed together with Mary curled up as the little spoon under Joey's warm and careful arms. They both let out a long, heavy sigh as the formerly absent feeling of security floated over them and finally settled on their bodies.

"You want to sleep, or you want to stay awake?" asked Joey.

"I want to sleep," said Mary, "just for a little while. I just need to lay down for a bit."

"Ok, Ms. Mary. You want the light on or off?"

"On, please."

Joey kissed Mary on the back of her head as the two friends lay in the small embryonic room. The rest of the house moved around them in a flurry of activity outside of the door. The slow sound of some unknown band came muffled through the walls in a cascade of soft breakbeats and synthesizers while the lights in Mary's room stayed on. They both began to softly snore.

The party had been in full effect for a few hours when Mary's door flew open, and two women wearing dayglo jumpsuits launched into the room with a flurry of fists and profanities. They landed heavy blows upon each other as they fell upon Mary and Joey, knocking Joey off the bed and hitting Mary multiple times in the confusion. The frenzy, now with Mary included, rolled off the bed and landed squarely on top of Joey who was hit hard as the melee intensified. Once the mattress flipped on top of them, pinning each of them down, the kicks and punches became especially localized. Party guests crowded the door shouting encouragement as the violence had now become self-contained within the small room. There was no space for the fighters to gain any real advantage, but the proximity made it even more likely that the kicks and punches would land.

Someone ripped the mattress off them and the two women in jumpsuits sprang up to standing while Mary and Joey were left on the floor. Joey immediately guarded his head with his arms while the two women continued to beat the living daylights out of each other. Mary's books went flying off the dresser and the small end table in the corner became demolished as one of the women fell backwards on top of it. Two people jumped into the room and grabbed the fighters, pulling them away from each other. The four of them left the room in a huff as the crowd parted to let them pass. Someone slammed the door behind them leaving Joey and Mary alone and on the floor. The party continued on the other side of the door and the sound of laughter rose above the music.

What had lasted a little more than a minute had done its damage to both Mary and Joey as well as the room. Joey braced himself with a hand on the bed frame as he slowly stood up from the floor. He offered a hand to Mary, who had made it back to sitting up, the two friends assessed the damage to the room and each other. They had both been struck in the face and were bleeding from their noses. Joey would have a nice shiner in a few minutes and Mary had a split lip.

"I hate it here," said Mary. She was only half joking as her love of the GGFF had been dwindling for some time now. If there were to ever be a catalyst for her to leave, this would be close enough for motivation.

Joey laughed and winced in pain as he ran his hand over the large bump forming on the back of his head. Neither of them had felt much of what had happened in the moment, but the sensations were coming around in delayed reaction. Mary kept her hands on her forehead as she scanned the small room. The two friends started picking up the pieces of furniture without saying anything. Mary found half of her copy of The Wind in the Willows on the floor, decimated. Pages were strewn across the room and the binding was torn beyond repair. Mary looked at half of a page showing an illustration of Toad Hall in all its splendor before she threw the book against the wall and sat on the floor with her head in her hands. Small drops of blood began leaving her nose and mixing with her tears that were spotting on the hardwood floor.

"Hey Mary," said Joey, "you still need that car?"

Joey held up a set of keys that had fallen out from the pocket of one of the women who had been brawling in the room. It was a car key without a starter fob, but it hung on a keychain that read Loose Lips inside a bejeweled red mouth. Mary smiled at their fortune and began to pack a bag. In a moment of sudden panic, she began digging through some debris that had fallen in a corner of the room. Lifting more broken furniture and ripped comic books showed that her grandfather's compass, which had fallen off its hook in the fight, was intact and still functioning. She held it against her heart and nearly prayed.

"I have some money saved up," said Joey, "and we've got enough drugs to sell along the way. If this car checks out, we should be good to go."

"I still have most of my parent's life insurance. We'll be fine."

"How much did they leave you?"

"I got it seven or eight years ago and it was two hundred-fifty thousand dollars. I think I have about one hundred twenty-five thousand left, or something like that."

"Goddammit, Mary," said Joey, "shit, we could have bought a bunch of cars with that."

"Don't have to," said Mary, "thank you, Loose Lips."

Mary scrawled a note on a blue piece of paper and taped it to the door before they left.

Night had swept across the Bronx in the navy-blue haze that bordered the circles of light around the working streetlights. Mary now had a new apprehension of dark places due to the Bosco's incident, causing her to move a little quicker in the night than she would have before. Whether or not the assault had been real, because to Mary it had felt very real, her eyes continued to scan the different angles and shadows that stretched from either side of the street. Any movement that she could perceive in the darkness felt like a preliminary ripple of Hell. With their senses on high alert, Mary and Joey walked down the street and were beginning to realize how difficult it would be to find someone else's car without a starter. The only identifiable marker on the key was a familiar looking "H", marking the brand. Mary and Joey had never known anything about cars.

With no other information to go by, their plan of escape had become daunting. They were walking down a side street nearly three blocks from the building when Joey made an alarming noise. Mary was relieved as she was expecting another terrible event to occur, but instead found Joey standing beside the ugliest car that she had ever seen. He was smiling and pointing to a rusted black Honda Civic with the words Loose Lips airbrushed along the side in a viridian script with gold trim. Mary put the key in the door and the car unlocked. She took the passenger seat and Joey Boulm took the wheel.

"I thought gay guys couldn't drive," said Mary.

"That's a myth," said Joey, "we can drive, we're just bad at it. Do you want to drive?"

"Fuck no," said Mary, "I can barely keep my eyes open."

Joey opened another plastic tube from his backpack and offered it to Mary.

"You want a pick-me-up?" asked Joey, as he popped two pills into his mouth.

"No, man," said Mary, "if I don't get some sleep I might die."

"Suit yourself. I'll wake you up once we get some distance from New York."

Mary settled into her seat and was just about to doze off when Joey asked her a question. She kept her eyes closed but tried her best to pay attention.

"Mary?"

"Yeah?"

"Where are we going?"

"We're going to Amherst."

"Where the fuck is Amherst?"

"Massachusetts."

"That's home?"

"Mm-hm," said Mary, "feels like a lifetime ago. I don't know what home feels like now."

"Home for you must be something special," said Joey, "was that the place with all that witch stuff?"

"That was Salem," said Mary.

"Great," said Joey.

"But there's haunted shit all over Massachusetts."

"Great..."

Mary laughed politely in reflex as Joey turned the key to the ignition and the sounds of Seal came through blown speakers. They were never going to survive unless they were a little crazy.

They had been driving for over two hours and had already entered Connecticut when Mary woke up in the dimly lit parking lot of a motel. Joey was talking to someone inside at the registration desk. There was a missed call from her mother and two unread text messages from Ruth, but Mary did not want to be thinking about them yet. The time was four forty-seven in the morning and Mary was starving. Yellow fluorescent light hummed dully above a row of three vending machines, not more than twenty feet from their car. She tried to wave down Joey, but he was shamelessly flirting with the older man who had gotten stuck working the overnight shift. Mary abandoned her signals and walked over to where she could potentially grab a bag of candy and a soda.

The selections were meager, but name brand options were available. The machine itself was old and only accepted exact coin change in a dented slot. There was no space to accept folding bills and no card reader to expedite the purchase. The prices were contemporary in the way that the machine was still asking for two dollars and fifty cents for a candy bar, but Mary thought that was stupid because who carries that much change anymore? Who carried change at all anymore?

Mary dug through her bag searching for any hard currency but could not find enough to buy a stamp. The best she could do was a nickel and two pennies, which themselves were a mystery as to how they had gotten in her bag. Mary kicked the machine without enthusiasm and waited for something to happen. When nothing did, she leaned her back against the wall and scanned the nearly vacant parking lot as five am crept in.

The wind carried the last gasps of summer humidity across Mary's face with a smell of fresh tar and grease that had collected on the pavement. She remembered a similar smell from the roof of the Rubenstein apartment when the summer sun would be at its peak and begin to melt the tar. Mr. Rubenstein would try to shade his radios under tarps, but those had created a kind of green house where mushrooms would grow from the different metal boxes. Mary had eaten one of those mushrooms when she was little, and she got so sick that she had to be taken to the hospital. She had not thought about that in years.

A pair of headlights pulled into the parking lot and slowed to a crawl. The car crept along the empty spaces and made its way to where Mary was standing, slowing to a stop. The passenger window rolled down and there was a short little balding man in an ill-fitted green tweed suit behind the wheel. He looked at Mary through his thick glasses and with his small, puckered mouth. The whole package made him resemble an owl. Mary found the man to be a little too familiar, but decidedly unplaceable. After a few moments of uncomfortable silence and heavy breathing from his part, the little man spoke.

"Are you working?" he asked.

"I don't work here," said Mary, "my friend is inside trying to get a room."

"How long?"

"What?"

"How long does he have you?"

His breathing got quicker as the slightest layer of perspiration began to form on his forehead.

"I don't mind waiting," he said.

His hand could not be seen but there was a repetitive motion to his arm that suggested self-indulgence.

"Fuck you," said Mary, "fuck you and your greasy-ass dick!"

Mary kicked the passenger door of his car with the flat of her boot, leaving a sizable dent. The old man made a face as though unholy spirits were leaving his body, and he shook behind the steering wheel.

With mouth gaped in ecstasy and his eyes rolled back into his head, the little man proceeded to ejaculate inside of his green tweed pants. The laughter that proceeded to dribble out of his mouth would stay with Mary much longer than she would like. Joey exited the office when he heard Mary yelling and ran full speed at the car. He was about to rip the little man out from the driver seat when he hit the gas and took off laughing, all the while his middle finger hung high out from his window. Joey and Mary stood watching as the taillights drifted up the ramp leading back to the highway and faded into the night.

"Are you alright?" asked Joey.

"I'm fine," Mary said flatly, "did you get a room?"

"Yeah, it's just a single bed, but that's all they had left."

"It's fine. Do you have any change?"

Mary gestured at the machine to which Joey shook his head no. There was a diner behind the motel that had opened for breakfast, so they decided to clean themselves up after eating. Joey opened the door to the room, and they were greeted by the damp smell of mildew camouflaged by the artificial smell of air fresheners. There were little green and blue cardboard pine trees dangling from the ends of the furniture that stood scattered all around.

The room was a good size, but none of the furniture matched and it all looked like it had been collected from a depressing swap meet. The bathroom, however, looked deceptively clean. Mary wondered what it would look like beneath an ultraviolet light when she saw that the towels had a few pubic hairs woven into the fibers. The bar soap in the sink and in the tub were both the same size and brand, both having been unwrapped from their packaging and recently used. Nothing happened when Joey flushed the toilet the first time. He flushed it again but holding the trip handle down for a few seconds provided the weak sound of progress towards the idea of a proper flush. He traded glances with Mary as they both came to a mutual understanding that they would only be there for a short time. They would have a mediocre breakfast, rinse themselves off, sleep for a few hours, and then be back on the road.

The diner was just opening when they walked through the door. The long tubes of light hanging from the ceiling looked sickly encased by stained frosted visors. The plastic shields that may have once been an opaque white were now a crusted yellow from years of absorbing aerosol, grease, and cigarette smoke. They were greeted by a little old man with such a curve to the top of his spine that it made him exert a strong effort if he wanted to straighten his back. He looked up at Mary and Joey and involuntarily made a face at their state. The old man had seen a lot of transients come through the diner, but he never could abandon his own prejudices. He nodded to himself in confirmation once they were close enough for him to smell. With an annoyed gesture he led them to a table in the back of the otherwise empty room.

"Good morning," he said, through a thick Greek accent, "my name is Xenos. Coffee?"

"Yes, please," said Joey.

"No, thanks," said Mary, "just water."

"Okie dokie," he said with a little wave as he turned around and waddled behind the bar.

It was becoming clear that he was the only staff working the diner so their time there might be longer than previously anticipated. Mary started fumbling with a sugar packet while Joey looked out the window. Xenos returned with the water, but no coffee.

"Percolator is broken. I have instant coffee if you want it."

"Fine," said Joey, "thanks."

"This is my own coffee," said Xenos, "I don't serve it to customers."

"Thank you, really."

"It's just that the percolator is broken, yeah? I don't usually do this sort of thing."

"I really appreciate it," said Joey, "sincerely."

"So instant coffee is ok?"

Joey closed his eyes and took a deep breath.

"Xenos, may I please have some of your delicious instant coffee?"

"Ok," said Xenos as he walked away, "ok. Instant coffee for the gay man."

Mary started to laugh in a pained way.

"What the hell is this place," asked Joey, "who's responsible for this?"

"Imagine if this was your last meal," said Mary, "what if Xenos was the last person you talked to?"

"I'd kill myself."

"So, no problem then."

Joey laughed and covered his face with his hands. Xenos returned with a paper cup of unstirred instant coffee for Joey who accepted it politely. The water was lukewarm.

"No clean coffee mugs," said Xenos, "paper is better."

Joey looked behind Xenos to see a row of clean porcelain coffee mugs hanging over the bar, but he was too tired to say anything about it. Several things were beginning to become clear. Xenos took a pad of paper from his pocket and a pencil from behind his ear. He looked at Mary and Joey without saying anything as he impatiently waited for their order. It took them a few moments to understand what he was doing. Joey picked up the menu and began to order when Xenos interrupted him.

"No," he said, "the real lady first."

Mary was approaching the level of annoyance where apathy starts to take over as a form of self-preservation. Xenos could have been singing for all that she cared. Mary looked through the menu and ordered pancakes with eggs and hash browns.

"Very good," said Xenos, "very good."

He began to walk away before Joey reminded him that he wanted some food as well.

"Right, yes," said Xenos, "what do you want?"

"Can I have an egg sandwich please? With bacon and cheddar cheese."

"No more egg," said Xenos, "she ordered the last of it."

"'No more egg'?" said Joey, "we're the first customers and you're out of eggs?"

"You can have my eggs," said Mary.

Xenos forced a smile to Mary, but it quickly faded as he turned his attention back to Joey.

"No bacon, either" said Xenos.

"Fine," said Joey, "just a cheese sandwich then."

Xenos walked back to the kitchen talking to himself in Greek. Joey slid down his chair beneath the table and groaned, missing the all-night noodle and dumpling place that was next to his and Sam's apartment.

"I hate it here," he said, "how much you wanna bet that he spits in my food?"

"That might make it better, actually."

"God, don't be gross," said Joey, returning to his seat, "what is wrong with Connecticut?"

"I actually lived here for a while," said Mary, "I wouldn't recommend it."

Xenos returned a few minutes later with a plate piled high. The food looked damp, brown, and gray. There was little to be had in the means of desire, but it was food, and they were adjusting to a life of disappointment. Xenos put the plate in front of Mary with three small paper cups: two with syrup and one with ketchup. Shuffling back to the kitchen, he returned with a small egg sandwich for Joey.

"I found more eggs," said Xenos, "eat."

Joey lifted the kaiser bun from the top of the sandwich. There was a sorrowful weight drawing his eyes to stare into the idea of what Xenos considered to be eggs. They sat limp and yellow gray as though they were hatched from a pigeon. After staring at his sandwich for thirty seconds, Joey dumped some ketchup on the eggs, dropped the bun back on, and devoured the thing in a few bites.

"How's the sandwich?" asked Mary.

"He forgot the cheese," said Joey, "no bacon. Bread is stale. All I could taste was ketchup and I'm fine with that."

"You want some of mine?" Mary offered her plate to Joey who inspected the food and then graciously declined. Mary picked around her food and shuffled it on her plate, periodically pouring more syrup on one side and then ketchup on the other.

"So, what are we doing?" asked Joey, "what happens in Amherst?"

"Well, I have to go to some attorney's office and sign some paperwork. After that, we go back to the house I was born in and try not to get murdered by ghosts, or some shit. I ever tell you I was born in a bathtub?"

"No," said Joey, "how very European. Did it give you any superpowers?"

"Yeah," said Mary, "I can smell an asshole from a mile away."

This got a laugh from Joey.

"That must make dating interesting."

"I think I'm done with that," said Mary, "maybe I'll go nun."

"Oh, please," said Joey, "you'd burn up as soon as you stepped foot in there. What do they call it, nun factory? House of nuns? Nun station? Where do the nuns live?"

"I don't know," said Mary, "I'm so fucking tired."

Joey's phone buzzed rapidly as a new group of texts began to come in from Sam. Joey had left Sam's messages unread since they had left New York, and the count was climbing past the triple digits. He turned off his phone and put his head in his hands.

"Joey, I'm sorry. I've been so wrapped up in my bullshit that I haven't even checked in with you. You ok?"

"No," said Joey, "but I'm sure I will be."

"Is there something I can do to help right now?"

Joey smiled at Mary's offer and shook his head.

"Honestly, Mary, dealing with your wacked out bullshit makes me feel normal. Like, I'm not thrilled that you're going through something, but I'm glad I can be here to help. Shit, am I even helping at this point?"

Mary threw her arms around Joey and kissed him on the cheek.

"Baby, you're everything," she said, "seriously though, I can't imagine what you're going through right now. Have you talked to Sam at all?"

"No, but he's tried to talk to me. I have something like two-hundred texts and a few voicemails."

"Jesus," said Mary, "how did you stay in that relationship so long?"

"I don't know," said Joey, "I think I kind of got stuck in that weird idea that he'd get better. Like, if I stuck it out then there'd be a chance he'd see that he was hurting me and change. I guess it's an education for next time."

"No," said Mary, "there won't be a next time because the next guy you fall in love with is going to take such good care of you that you won't even remember who Sam is. He's an asshole and you haven't done anything wrong. You deserve love."

It was difficult for Joey to make space for himself to be heard. Having grown up in a hostile and abusive environment had taken his understanding of love down unexpected avenues. Joey started to tear up on this, so he gracefully switched the focus back to Mary.

"So, are these the kind of ghosts that like to fuck, or what?"

"Shit," said Mary, "I can't even remember the last time I had sex."

"Really?"

"Yeah, David wasn't exactly a generous lover. I used to go down on him for a long time, like, every time we had sex. It always felt very one sided."

"People like that should be launched into space."

"Yeah…"

Joey smiled to himself and wondered whether should ask his next question.

"Did he ever ask, 'didja cum'?"

"Oh my god, nearly every time."

"I'll never understand that," said Joey, "'Hey babe, didja cum?' Does it look like I did?! Get down there and get back to work!"

"It's like some weird trophy, right," said Mary, "like having sex with you isn't generous enough, now I'm going to give you that? If you can't tell when I'm cumming then you don't deserve to know."

"That's one of the many reasons why I love dick," said Joey, "not a lot of mystery there. They're simple, hot, and kind of cute. Like a fun little mole rat."

Mary continued to swirl the ketchup around her disappointing eggs while her mind reflected on memories with David. Joey noticed the dip in her mood and returned to the topic at hand.

"So, what's the house like?" he asked, "is it Addams Family, or what?"

"I remember it being really big," said Mary, "I don't know what it's like now, but I remember parts of it were scary. There was this big upstairs room, like a tower. Used to spend a lot of time up there, but it got…weird. A lot of my grandfather's paintings were up there. Got too creepy."

"Damn," said Joey, "so you haven't been back to this house in, what? Ten years?"

"Sixteen, give or take. Maybe more."

"Are you nervous?"

Mary sipped her water and took a bite of pancakes as she shook her head. She would not allow herself to look Joey in the eyes.

"Shit, I'm nervous," said Joey, "you seem awfully calm about all this."

"Believe it or not, I don't find it all that unusual."

Joey watched Mary as she continued to eat her pancakes. There was something different about her that he had never noticed until this moment. Maybe it was something that had been with Mary all along, hiding in plain sight. The quiet way in which she carried herself began to feel heavier to Joey as they shared the same space without distraction.

"What happened there?" he asked, "back home, I mean."

Mary stared at the table as she quietly chewed her food. She tried to find the right way to explain what she herself had never fully understood. The best she could do was to shake her head and say, "I don't know."

The breakfast sat in such a way as to bring the need for sleep. Mary and Joey were already tired and burnt out from the past week, and the last twenty-four hours had been the push over the cliff. If given the opportunity, a live bed of nails would be paradise enough.

It was a short walk back to the room they had rented, but the task of returning to the motel was a force. Mary had a habit of walking like a penguin when she was tired. She waddled all the way back to the room as Joey trailed behind. The door to the room was stuck this time and it only opened after Joey managed to shoulder it twice. Somehow it all looked worse in the daylight, so Mary shut the curtains and turned on the bedside lamps. Only one of them worked. In the dim shaded glow of a sixty-watt bulb, Mary turned on the rabbit-ear television to find Planet of the Apes coming through bad reception. Charlton Heston was being hosed down in his cage and his teeth never looked whiter.

"I'm gonna shower," said Joey, "you need the facilities?"

"Yeah, lemme pee," said Mary.

Mary closed the door and looked at her reflection in the mirror. There is something magical about the lighting in a motel bathroom. Whatever angle you show the mirror, everyone looks like Lon Chaney Sr. Even looking at the face of the person standing next to you is something different from what you see in their reflection.

Mary was thinking about this when she noticed something move behind the shower curtain. She turned slowly over her shoulder, uncertain as to whether she had seen something or if she was just that tired. Time stopped and refused to move until she could see something ripple the fabric again. With the only sound slowly dripping out of the faucet, Mary slowly moved to turn the curtain with every synapse in her brain telling her that it was a bad idea. Never one to take her own advice, Mary gently lifted the curtain to the side and waited for something to launch itself and attack. When nothing did, she attributed the illusion to her exhaustion and general sense of dread about returning home.

Although she had told Joey that she felt a casual indifference towards her childhood, it was a lie. Home was a place that she had been running away from mentally as well as physically for so long that the idea of going back truly frightened her. It was difficult to always name it when the feelings came about, but there were moments when she would get so lost that her thoughts became locked to the house. Although years of chemical dependency had done their best work to cloud the memory of her childhood, the worst of it would surface in her dreams.

Mary left the bathroom for Joey to shower, and she laid down on the bed. There was little to no give in the mattress. She was too tired to care, and she could have fallen asleep anywhere at that point. Staring at the motel ceiling provided an array of mysterious stains left by previous guests. One of the smears across the ceiling was beginning to resemble a circus tent and Mary thought about the last time she had been to the circus. She had gone once with Lorry, Howard, and Ruth to Coney Island when she had first been adopted. She remembered having a good time. The clowns scared her a bit, but aside from that it was fun. Mary thought about calling the Rubenstein's and just letting them know she was ok, but she was unprepared to answer the questions that they may ask. Still, she wanted to hear a warm and familiar voice.

Charlton Heston and Roddy McDowall were on the television having a heated discussion about the societal rights of man when a scream rang out from the bathroom. Then came a volley of screams as Joey began to fight off an unknown assailant. The sound of crashing and inhuman screeching filled the air as Mary jumped into action to help her friend. She opened the bathroom door to find an owl coming straight for her face. Having only a moment to duck out of the way, she felt its wings and body bounce off the top of her head before she fell to the floor and took cover. The owl flapped around the room in a panic, screeching in terror of its own entrapment. Joey had curled up in the bathtub and covered himself with the curtain that he had accidentally ripped off the rod while Mary crawled on her stomach to the door leading outside. The owl beat its wings and continued to shriek as it crashed against the walls and into the lamps. Once Mary had gotten the door open, the bird took its cue from her incentive and flew out into the early morning. Mary lay on the floor while the voice of Charlton Heston pressed his indignation against the world.

"MARY!" screamed Joey.

Mary ran to the bathroom to find that Joey was lying in the tub, wrapped up in the shower curtain. A large bruise was forming on his forehead to match his black eye and blood had begun to pool in the plastic creases of the shower curtain. There was a deep cut down his left side and it bled a dark crimson. He lay naked on the floor, wrapped in the plastic curtain that covered his trembling body.

"What the fuck was that?!" screamed Joey.

"I think that was an owl," said Mary, "are you hurt? How bad is it?"

"I don't want to look," said Joey, "I don't want to look at it!"

Mary turned Joey to his side and found a small river of blood coming out from the gash.

"It looks pretty deep. We may need to go to a hospital."

"Fuck," cried Joey, "I can't do this."

"It's ok, I can drive?"

"No, Mary, I can't do this! I'm out! I quit!"

"What?! Joey, no, I need you!"

"You need a shrink and an exorcist! I'm not gonna die getting attacked by birds and fucking goblins. I'm sorry Mary, but I'm out."

"What am I supposed to do?!"

"I don't care," said Joey, "I'm catching the next bus back to New York. I can sell drugs for Laura and be happy about it. She doesn't know I bailed yet. Maybe Sam will take me back. Shit, I can't do this, Mary! This is some twilight zone bullshit."

"Joey," Mary cried, "Joey I can't do this alone!"

"Mary, I love you, and I'm gonna pray for you, but this is too much."

Mary helped Joey get to his feet and they assessed his wounds in the bathroom mirror. The gash on Joey's side was not as deep as Mary had initially believed and the bruise was more superficial than anything else. Joey cleaned the wound with motel soap and water. He wrapped a dry towel around his waist while Mary did her best to convince Joey to stay.

"Joey, please don't go. I don't know what to do!"

"Keep the car," said Joey, "we passed a bus station so I'm heading that way."

"Let me give you a ride then."

"No, thank you. I don't want some wolf to come out of the air vent or some kind of demon laying eggs in my brain or whatever else you've got chasing you."

"Can I give you some money?"

"Shit," said Joey, "for all you know that might be where this all came from. I'm all set."

Joey got dressed and left the motel room. Mary stood in the doorway and watched her only real friend disappear into the morning light. She cursed at him, saying vile and personal things that she would later regret, slamming the motel door after finding that there was nothing she could say to make him stay. It bounced against the uneven frame and Mary had to slam it twice more before it closed completely. She stood in the middle of the room and bit the side of her finger before laying on the bed.

In the moment of futility, when a person recognizes what little control they actually have over almost every situation that they find themselves in, there can be a great calm that fills in the absence of security. It's a sensation that can be closely compared to seeing a trash compactor at work. The moment expands to allow all your hopes, expectations, and comforts to fall together into a bin, only to be compressed beyond recognition and left as a disfigured cube of its former self. All arms and eyes. Everything you had struggled for and dreamt of could fit uncomfortably in your front jacket pocket.

Xenos smiled and waved to Joey as he watched him walk through the parking lot. Joey ignored him and when he passed Xenos, the old man made a series of off-color European hand gestures.

Mary lay in the bed as Charlton Heston and Linda Harrison rode on horseback through the Forbidden Zone. Alone again, as she had often always felt whenever something terrible had happened, Mary thought terrible things and closed her eyes. She fell asleep almost instantly, and she did not dream of owls.

17. Welcome Home

    Amherst is nestled in the Pioneer Valley of western Massachusetts, beside the Holyoke Mountain range. The population at the time of the census taken in the year two-thousand ten was upwards around thirty-seven-thousand, eight-hundred nineteen people. Taking into consideration that the population census of New York City in the year two-thousand ten was eight-million, eight-hundred four-thousand, one-hundred ninety, that would allow the population of Amherst to remain nearly undetectable within the New York City subway system for an indeterminable amount of time. There may even be room for all of Rhode Island, as well. Mary found herself to have the opposite problem whereas an individual she stuck out in Amherst like the sore thumb of a gorilla. On fire. In a shopping mall. Speaking Esperanto. Mary was on day three of wearing the same clothes and without access to the proper facilities required for hygienic rejuvenation, she stank. Stunk? Stank, I think. She smelled bad. Smelt?
    Never mind.
    The shower in the motel was out of commission after Joey was attacked by the owl, and finding an alternative would require too much energy. Mary had only been asleep for a few hours when an exterminator knocked on her door to the room, telling her that it was scheduled to be fumigated and she had to leave. This came as no surprise to Mary, almost expected at this point, so she slept for a little while longer in the car before she continued her journey.
    Amherst was a college town with its own share of strange folk and passive locals, but theirs was a more performative display of individuality among the people. Each oddity or expressive display was calculated and crafted to the specific parameters of the presenter. There were no natural quirks that ventured further than the possibility of a speech impediment or an undiagnosed mental health issue. Those who were truly off the beaten path were seldom ever seen and that was by their own design. Mary arrived in Amherst strung out, exhausted, desperate, and feeling maniacally impulsive. She looked like Hell. Mary parked Loose Lips down

an alley side street away from the public and sat in the driver's seat a while after pulling the keys from the ignition. She had a bad headache.

Autumn had begun in Massachusetts and there were people milling about to watch the leaves change color and take in the pleasant calm of the western portion of the state. Businesses kept signs outside of each little shop along the main street advertising the best local fare offered to those visiting from out of town. Maple candy and seasonal soups were popular items as well as flavored finishing salts and books on local folklore and history. Show flyers were stapled to telephone poles and tacked to bulletin boards for local bands supporting touring acts, neither of which anyone had ever heard of. A tour guide in colonial dress was leading a small group around the square while the patron's snapped cameras at what would be considered ordinary to anyone who lived there. Wherever you are, you can always spot a tourist. Mary was not sure what she looked like, but she knew what she felt like.

The address for the attorney's office was sent to Mary in an email along with instructions and the required paperwork she would need to claim her inheritance. She had her birth certificate, social security card, and driver's license, but they were each weathered from time and disorganization.

She stored all her paperwork in a gallon sized plastic bag. The years of wear and bad storage had torn the seal at the top. The bag was usually rolled up as a tube and taped along the sides to keep the papers from falling out. In doing so, many of the documents had become worn and ripped along their edges. Mary stuffed the plastic bag into her satchel along with a small flick knife the size of her thumb, a sweater, two joints in her half-pack of cigarettes, and a small pill bottle filled with capsules of different shapes and sizes. She took two small blue pills and washed them back with an opened lukewarm beer she found beneath the passenger's seat. It tasted foul and she belched out a smell that would be concerning to any medical professional. Checking her reflection, she took a brush out of her bag, gave herself a once over, and stepped out of Loose Lips and onto the street.

Memory is a funny thing. Much of what we can remember is questionable at best, once you consider the fact that memory is subjective. Not to say that we all run around making things up, but there is a fair amount of misremembering that we each experience throughout our lives. How often do you find yourself in an argument with a friend over events that happened so many years ago? Who was there, who was not, what was or was not said, etc., etc. The fact of the matter is that we craft many of our own memories to maintain what we want to remember. It's more comfortable that way. There is a fair amount of recollection that is based on irrefutable facts, but the part that we play in each memory is often sculpted to suit our incentives. If you want to be a hero, you create a version of yourself that unquestionably did the right thing. If you hate yourself beyond recognition, you will sometimes manufacture details that prove, beyond the shadow of a doubt, that you are the scum of the earth. If someone has been wounded, or made to feel wounded, then grudges and revenge can be put into place, even if they only exist as exaggerated fantasy. If you had been left behind by someone whom you deeply loved, then you can convince yourself that the love may still be there without ever questioning if it had ever existed at all. You can spend years away from an otherwise insignificant event in your life and still feel an echo of the same emotions in the moment that the thought re-enters your mind. Memory is a funny thing, and Mary was beginning to recognize different parts of the town square and different parts of her life.

There were sections of Mary's history that she had intentionally removed, but some memories, often considered to be altogether irrelevant, flooded back to her as soon as she stepped out of the car. The simplicity of the insignificant is a subtle anchor that can link different memories together.

When Mary saw a root poking up through the sidewalk beside what used to be a movie theater, it brought her back to when she was little. She had been running down the sidewalk after seeing a movie, which she also remembered. Her foot had caught on the root, tripped, and skinned both of her knees as she skidded off the cement. Her mother had carried her back to the car and cleaned her cuts with some cotton and alcohol that she bought from the pharmacy. Mary remembered the sting of the alcohol against her scrapes and the ice cream she got later. The memory came all at once and ended just as quickly. In all its insignificance, it still made her feel sad. Mary checked the email on her phone for the address of the attorney's office before any other memories had a chance to creep in.

The dry air of the radiator hit Mary in the face when she walked into the law offices of Albertson & Howe. She shivered with the temperature shift and became more comfortable coming in from the chill. The reception area was of a modest size with the kind of slate gray and pale blue motif that guarantees no imagination whatsoever to whomever had given the final say on the design. Mary was beginning to feel nervous as she approached one of the two receptionists that sat behind a handsome wooden desk.

"Good morning," said the receptionist, "can I help you?"

"Hi, yeah, my name is Mary Ruben...sorry, Mary Kirkland. I received a call about collecting an inheritance?"

The receptionist opened a large ledger and cross-referenced it with the computer screen. Her head leaned back to allow better access to her bifocals while her face scrunched into a central point as she typed. A focused expression gave the impression that her skull would collapse and suck the rest of her features into the chasm it created. Mary tried not to think about that as her eyes wandered around the room.

"Kirkland...Kirkland.... Kirk.... land! There you are," she said, "We wouldn't be able to see you today without an appointment. They're booked solid with clients and meetings for the rest of the afternoon. We might have something tomorrow morning, I think."

She typed away on the keyboard. Her eyes darted back and forth between words and symbols that she had become familiar with over the past twelve years of employment with Albertson & Howe. The receptionist heard music between her keystrokes and kept a rhythmic orchestra in her mind when she worked. Incidentally, she had spent the past three years writing a musical about a receptionist that worked in a law firm. The working title was "Madam Subpoena", and she would play the lead, of course. All she needed was the ending, the music, and an erotic love interest resembling Kurt Russell. Nineteen eighty-six Kurt Russell, specifically. Finishing her search for the next day's schedule, she emphasized the final three strokes on her keyboard.

"Could you come back tomorrow at nine-fifteen?" she asked.

"In the morning?"

"Yes," said the receptionist, "our office closes at five, and we do our best to keep regular business hours, Ms. Kirkland."

Mary fiddled with her hands and fought the urge to nibble on the side of her finger. She decided to pinch it instead, although the result was unsatisfactory.

"Is there a hotel nearby where I can book a room?"

"Oh, I'm afraid whatever we have will be booked solid for the rest of the week. Lots of folks come in to watch the leaves change and this is the best week to see it. We're also starting the Fisher Festival today, so that's gonna draw a lot of traffic. You may be able to find a motel off the highway or further out from town, but even then, it might be tricky."

"It's fine," said Mary, "I'll figure something out."

"I'm sure you will," said the receptionist, "if I could make a suggestion?"

"Sure."

"It might be a good idea to have a bath before your meeting tomorrow. Now I don't mean to offend, but you are a little...distracting at the moment."

Mary gave the receptionist a passive thumbs up and turned to leave the foyer. The fresh outdoor air hit Mary in the chest and her body stiffened up as a quick gust of wind seemed to run right through her. She lifted her arm to smell herself discreetly, and it was true, she smelled terrible. Smelt?

Dammit.

A commotion was gathering up and down the sidewalk as an official looking man on the city hall steps approached a microphone to address a crowd. Mary lingered on the steps across the street from the podium to listen for a moment, although her interests were minimal, at best. A giant man, both in height and width, raised his hands to signal attention while the microphone produced the sound of light feedback.

"Ladies and gentlemen," he said, "it is my pleasure to welcome you to the start of the fifty-third annual Fisher Festival!"

The audience erupted in cheers and applause at the commencement of such an ostentatious event. Mary had no memory of a fisher festival when she was growing up, but then again this did not seem like the kind of activity that her parents would have enjoyed. The large man held his hands up in acknowledgement of the enthusiasm of the crowd from behind the microphone.

"Now as we all know, the fisher is a complicated animal filled with all the feral beauty of nature in its majesty. And not unlike our own lives, the life of each fisher is filled with events that make them who they are, every fisher has a story to tell. You could say that, maybe, there's a little fisher in each of us."

The giant man made a face like a weasel and held his hands up to his chin as though they were paws. This drew out laughter and nods of affirmation from the crowd. Mary took her sunglasses out of her pocket and wiped the lenses before putting them on. The sun was brighter than she would have liked and the enthusiasm from the crowd was making her headache worse. Mary lit a cigarette behind a mother and infant while the giant man continued his speech.

"Now let's all have some fun this weekend," he said, "but remember, do not approach a fisher cat under any circumstances if you see one in the wild. We all love the little rascals, but they are still wild animals. You wouldn't go sneaking up on Dicky Halford if he's been at the bar all day, would you?"

This brought more laughter from the crowd and someone, presumably Dicky Halford, yelled, "It's true!". The woman with the infant turned to Mary with a general look of disgust for her cigarette smoke while Mary just smiled and waved at the baby. The orator shook his head at the well-known antics of Dicky Halford and held up his large hands to silence his audience.

"You know we love you, Dicky," he said, "so instead of catching a fisher, try to *catch* the good food, the good weather, and the good people while you're in town. And try to look for an appreciation in the fisher's tenacity and gumption. For when God made the fisher, he said it was good. And who better to represent our high school mascot, eh?! Go Fisher Cats!"

More applause and cheers spread gleefully from the crowd while Mary tried to find a kindred spirit who could join her in not fully understanding what was happening. The woman in front of her had already walked off, and all she could find were blue balloons and hand towels spun around in the air; some with the faces of a cartoon weasel on the front.

"So, remember when you're out and about today, keep an eye out for the noble fisher. And try to stop by Mrs. Maulbecky's bakery for her 'Pekan' Pie special. I heard a 'tail' that she's already running low as we speak! And be sure to say hello to the Sisters of String at Loom & Doom for their double bi-weekly overstock sale. Have fun everybody and be safe! Go Fisher Cats!"

A stereo speaker played him off the podium to the tune of Macarena as the crowd began to disperse, leaving Mary wondering what a fisher was as she stood on the steps of the law firm of Albertson & Howe. After deciding that she could not find the energy to care, Mary walked down a side street away from the people and sat beneath the shade of a red maple tree. She had a need to catch her breath, and she had found new anxiety in waiting until tomorrow for the meeting. Not having anything to do until the next morning, Mary was faced with a new sense of tension. She had been on the move for so long now and with such intensity that the thought of having a moment of levity was frightening her. Her eyes bounced from person to person who passed her by, all wearing novelty shirts that read "Kiss My Ass, I'm On Vacation", "Will Trade Girlfriend For Beer", or some other iteration of contempt towards anyone foolish enough to threaten their good time.

Mary performed some quick searching on her phone to look for available hotel rooms, but the closest vacancy was almost one hundred miles away in a place called The Buttonhole Inn. It sounded neither helpful nor appealing. With no set direction in mind, Mary started walking down the street in search of food and, with any luck, a place to sleep. Finding shelter would be a problem better faced after a hot meal and a drink. Mary was on Kellogg Avenue when she began to remember something.

Kellogg Avenue, thought Mary, *Kellogg Avenue...what was on Kellogg...oh my god.*

Mary nearly sprinted down Kellogg Avenue in the direction of Captain Nemo's Pizza. An old feeling was recognized as soon as Mary took the turn onto the street, but she could not remember the last time she had thought about Captain Nemo's.

Please be the same, she thought, *pleasepleaseplease.*

Captain Nemo's was gone. The building was there, now with a tattered red fabric awning hanging over the door, but the restaurant that had given Mary the most joy was gone. "Best Pizza In Town Or I'll Eat My Hat!" was the painted sign left chipped and peeling off of the restaurant window. A sign to lease the building was leaning against the glass from inside. It looked like nobody had moved it in years. The diving suit was nowhere to be found, and a collection of crumbling leaves rested inside the doorway. Mary walked up to the front door and cupped her hands around her eyes to help see inside. The counter was the same, and the powerless soda fridge was dark and empty in a corner of the room. The menu board hanging on the wall just read, "Thank You For All The Wonderful Years." Mary drew a small heart in the dust on the window with her finger.

Fuckers, thought Mary, *motherfuckers*.

Mary was not angry at Nemo. She would always love him and value the kindness that he had shown to her. She was angry that the town seemed to move on. It was becoming unlikely that Mary would find anything remaining from her childhood in Amherst. The house may be the only thing left, but it was the last thing she wanted. Mary was wondering whether Nemo was alive or dead when she walked back to the town square and saw a confusing restaurant sign.

It was one-thirty in the afternoon when Mary entered Lucky Spumoni's, a gastropub that looked suspiciously clean and advertised authentic Irish/Italian cuisine. With the defeat of Captain Nemo's and the tired reaction to a town grown increasingly unfamiliar, Mary saw the crossed Irish and Italian flags above the door as more of a warning than an invitation. She took a seat at the bar and hung her bag on a hook by her knees.

The restaurant was busy with tourists and locals sharing a space that had previously been occupied by the bar regulars. Those who felt some kind of ownership over the place saw the presence of tourists as an invasion and an affront to everything they held sacred. Having nothing else to complain about, and few other places for them to drink comfortably, the regulars took it all too personally. The collection of disorganized bric-a-brac and fake mafia wanted posters on the walls brought a confused and disorienting atmosphere that was providing Mary with a new sense of fascination towards an experience she had never considered: getting plastered in a novelty restaurant. She made a mental note that she might have to revisit this place in the future. In the meantime, however, there was drinking to be done.

A bartender with impeccable hair and a calculated five o'clock shadow nodded to Mary as he approached her. He gave her his best crooked smile as he leaned one elbow on his side of the bar. His eyes carried the whimsey of a natural liar.

"Mornin'," he said, "oh wow, never mind. 'Good afternoon'. Ha-haaa, waddya know? It's almost two. Anywho, how's it goin'?"

"Fine, yeah," said Mary, "Miller Lite, please."

"Sure, sure, not a problem. Can I see some I.D.?"

Mary fished through her satchel and pulled out her plastic bag filing cabinet. She unrolled her parcel on the bar while the bartender chuckled to himself at the display. He started to make a joke before he stopped himself and watched Mary continue to rifle through her paperwork. After the second failed attempt at humor, he simply rubbed his chin and waited for Mary to provide her identification. Mary removed her license and handed it to the bartender who took it cheerfully.

"New York, eh?" he said with a face, "better watch out for those Red Sox fans, am I right?"

"I don't like baseball," said Mary.

"Come over to watch the leaves change, then? Or are you here for the Fisher Festival?"

"No, I won a house on the Price is Right. I gotta go fist fight Drew Carey for the keys."

"Oh," said the bartender, "...congratulations."

He handed Mary a full pint of beer which she drained in three gulps. She pushed the empty glass back to the bartender and knocked on the bar twice, signaling for another round. The bartender refilled the glass and asked Mary if she wanted to see a food menu. She agreed more from a sense of humor than from a place of hunger. The menu was a long, double-sided lamination with a leprechaun jumping into a golden pot full of spaghetti. The menu carried a variety of unappealing amalgamations. Mary skimmed the menu and came across such miscarriages as corned beef meatballs in a cabbage gravy over ziti, shepherd's pie lasagna, black pudding bolognese, and something in green crust called a Saint Patrick Stromboli. Mary ordered a cheeseburger with fries from the kids' menu.

"We can't serve you from the kid's menu," said the bartender, "sorry, it's a rule."

"What's the difference?" asked Mary.

"Well, I don't know," said the bartender, "it's a rule, see? You're not a kid, so you can't order from the kid's menu."

"Alright," said Mary, "then I'll take another beer."

Finishing her third beer, Mary stood up from her stool and dropped a few crumpled bills on the bar before grabbing her bag and heading for the door. The bartender collected the money while shaking his head, not realizing that Mary had left him a thirty-dollar tip on a three-beer tab. He would only come to realize this at the end of the night when Mary's crumpled bills would stand out from the rest. Whether or not Mary had intentionally left him the large tip held no consequence for her sensibilities. She always over-tipped wait staff and bartenders regardless of how their service was. This bartender was a prime example of a person whose obnoxious behavior was crafted from a lifetime of feeling fundamentally lonely, but that personality flaw did not disqualify him from working and sustaining a life. Mary still wanted to hit him with a small car, but he could not say that she had left him a lousy tip.

The beers had brought along a pleasant little buzz that helped to distract Mary from the cold air outside. Still, she wrapped herself up in her sweater and lit a joint as she made her way back to Loose Lips. The smoke burned in her throat with the comfort of familiarity as she fought back the urge to cough. She held her breath until she felt dizzy and let a long plume of smoke fall out from her nose and mouth. It was one of the few times where she could convince herself that she felt no pain.

Different groups of people were dispersed amongst their purposes and destinations while Mary considered her options. She could sleep in her car, although it would be too cold to get any real sleep. There was still the question of bathing, as well. She could find a relatively harmless person who may be interested in paying for overnight company. She'd never really done that before, and it was more of a passing thought. This was a risky option as she was sure that the men in Amherst were not much different than the men in New York City. They may have been quieter, but that felt more devious. The idea was filed as a last resort.

There was the possibility for shelter in the bus station rotunda. The terminal had benches inside, vending machines, and a bathroom where she could scrub up a bit. She was leaning towards the bus station idea when she saw a couple walking towards her. They both stopped and looked as though they may have recognized her. It was a man and a woman that stood like dull bookends in a sad library. She thought that they could have been looking past her, possibly looking for one of those fisher cats, but they were staring directly at Mary and were becoming much more enthusiastic. Mary rested her hand on the knife in her bag and waited for them to approach her.

"Mary?" said the woman, "Mary Kirkland?!"

"Hi," said Mary, "yeah, hi."

"Oh, my gawd," squealed the woman, "Mary, look at you! It's me, Elizabeth! Lizzy Brandt! Well, Lizzy Spinoza, now."

She looked up at her husband who dully showed the slightest expression of a smile. He flicked his hand up briefly which Mary interpreted as a greeting.

"You remember Addison," said Elizabeth, "oh wow, look at you!"

"Yeah," said Mary, suddenly self-conscious, "look at me."

"You are so punk rock," said Elizabeth, holding up both hands in the metal horn signal. Mary tried to smile, but her face would not follow instructions.

"What are you doing here," asked Elizabeth, "Where are you living now?"

Elizabeth and Addison looked like the kind of people that you would see in a catalog advertising boutique camping gear. Addison had outgrown his awkward adolescent looks, to be sure, but there would always be lingering traces of the odd little boy who struggled with self-confidence. He had a good face and a hefty slouch. Elizabeth had grown into the kind of person who dumps relationship pictures on social media so that everybody can know how happy she is. Mary imagined Addison's expressionless face; never changing in the flip-book style presentation of so many Christmas cards. They probably had a golden retriever named Buster and infrequent, unimaginative sex. Mary had a quick thought of Buster fucking Addison's expressionless face, but then shook it out and asked herself, *What's wrong with me?*

"I'm here on business, actually," said Mary, "My aunt Colleen died, and she left me the house. I have to meet with a lawyer tomorrow and sign the paperwork."

"Oh, I am so sorry to hear that," said Elizabeth, "we were all so sad when your parents passed on. They were such good people, too. How come you didn't come to the funeral?"

"Oh," said Mary, "I didn't…no one ever told me."

"You didn't know there was a funeral?!" said Elizabeth.

"No, I…"

Mary felt the onset of a panic attack before Elizabeth changed the subject.

"Are you moving here?" asked Elizabeth, "are we going to be neighbors?!"

Mary wanted to run.

"Well, I'm in New York now, so I couldn't just stay. I have a lot of work there that I have to wrap up. Lotta cleanup that I have to do."

A breeze wafted Mary's smells towards the couple, causing Elizabeth to curl up her nose and hold her sleeve against her face. She turned to Addison, seemingly un-bothered by any of his five senses, and whispered something to him. Addison shrugged and lightly nodded in agreement.

"Ok, bitch," said Elizabeth, with a smirk, "where are you staying?"

Mary wanted to say that she had a room somewhere, but Elizabeth spoke quickly, never giving her a chance to think of a good lie.

"You're staying with us!" yelled Elizabeth, "That's where you're staying!"

"Oh, no," said Mary, "I couldn't impose."

"I'm not hearing it," said Elizabeth, "we have a guest room and everything! Come with us and we'll...get you cleaned up."

Mary became resigned to her fate as she followed Elizabeth and Addison back to their Volvo. Elizabeth drove, because Elizabeth always drove, and despite the chill of early autumn air, she immediately rolled all the windows down so as not to be subjected to the variety of smells that were emanating from Mary. They drove away from the city center and down a winding wooded road that snaked through the burgeoning trees. The thickness of the woods brought Mary back to an emotional state that she had forgotten about over so many years. Her mind brought back a cavalcade of memories tied to play and long games, lost tombs and missing teeth. She looked out the window and for a split-second thought that she saw monsters running along the side of the road. She had been too distracted to even notice that Elizabeth had been talking to her.

"...promotion last year, so he's only a few years away from being junior manager at the store. After that, he can really set his career into motion. It may not be glamorous, but somebody's gotta do it."

Elizabeth ruffled Addison's hair and he chuckled before silently moving it all back into place.

"What about you?" asked Elizabeth, "what are you doing in New York?"

"Oh, um. I'm in a band. I play around the city and, you know, book shows and stuff."

"Très glamour," said Elizabeth, "living that lifestyle Bohème?"

"Not really," said Mary, "I'm doing ok."

"You know, I can't remember the last time I saw you."

Elizabeth let the moment hang in the air as Mary began to understand where she was going with her thoughts. Mary felt her stomach knot up in anticipation of an unexpected argument. She was in no mood to reminisce.

"I remember being friends for so long," said Elizabeth, "we'd ride the bus together and I'd let you copy my math homework."

"No," said Mary, "you would copy *my* math homework."

"Like I would ever do that," scoffed Elizabeth, "you were so bad at it. I had to basically walk you through the assignments. Honestly, Mary, how did you graduate, anyway?"

"It was just different in New York."

"That's right," said Elizabeth, "I forgot that you were sent away to that special school for retarded kids. Jesus freaks, right?"

"Yeah, right."

"Well, that explains it, then. I'm so happy that you managed to find a program that could help you understand things better. Anyway,"

Elizabeth looked back with a wide, toothy smile, "It's so good to see you, Mary."

They continued in silence with an occasional snort coming from Addison as he was in a perpetual state of clearing his throat. Elizabeth would pat his shoulder and say, "That's enough, dear," but he would only stop for a minute or two before starting up again. Mary considered the charity of homicide. They pulled into a driveway in front of a single-story ranch house painted powder blue with a white trim border. Elizabeth got out of the car and walked to the passenger's side to open Addison's door.

She laughed and said, "I keep forgetting the child-locks are on. I don't know why, but I never remember to unset them."

A glance from Addison let Mary know that Elizabeth intentionally kept the child-locks on. Addison was beginning to be shown in a new sympathetic light in Mary's eyes, but this sympathy was quickly becoming contempt for such a pathetic display of humanity. If you were to dote after anyone on Earth, why would you choose Lizzy Brandt? Mary shrugged it off and recognized it as another of life's great mysteries. What a shitty, shitty mystery.

Mary entered the home of Elizabeth and Addison Spinoza to be greeted not by a golden retriever named Buster, but a doberman pinscher named King. She somehow found this to be more offensive. King immediately struck Mary's crotch with his nose and snorted mucus all over the leg of her jeans. Elizabeth and Addison were too slow to notice, so Mary quickly wiped her leg on the arm of the couch.

The home inside was itself bland and unremarkable. There was matching furniture that was positioned as though they were on display for sale. Their formations were deliberately posed while everything in the room had the cream on beige palette of the incredibly uninspired. Store bought paintings of coastal lighthouses hung in perfect symmetry while the words **It Is What It Is** were stenciled across a wall in a papyrus script. Mary began to reconsider moving past the idea of sleeping at the bus station so quickly.

"Welcome," said Elizabeth, her arms open, "welcome to our sanctuary."

She made a motion to hug Mary before she remembered the smell and took a step back.

"You'll probably want to freshen up," she said, "let me show you where the bathroom is. I'll get you a towel and some soap."

Two boys came sprinting through the house, each with a fistful of mud from outside. They began to punch each other, causing a slapping sound as their wet fists spread the dirt across the walls and floors. Elizabeth then abandoned her hospitality and threw herself into a complete fit of maternal embarrassment.

"Boys," she said, "Tucker! Dawson! What is wrong with you?! Stop it now!"

The two boys ignored their mother and proceeded to hover around Mary, dancing and reaching out to her with their muddy hands.

"Boys! I'm sorry, Mary. Boys! We have company!"

Addison watched with mild interest as their two sons kept teasing Mary with the threat of contact. In a motion too subtle for observation, Mary reached down and gave a hard pinch to the skin behind Tucker's arm. The boy immediately jumped back and began to cry.

"Oh, Tucker," said Elizabeth, "you're so emotional! I swear he's never like this."

Mary simply nodded and shrugged.

"Hey man," she said, "it's just kids."

Elizabeth led Mary to the room she would be staying in while Addison took care of their sons. The room was even more bland than the other parts of the house, but Mary had no intentions of staying there long enough to care. She dropped her bag on the bed and followed Elizabeth to the bathroom where she was given exact instructions on how to use the shower while Elizabeth reiterated how good it was to see her again. Mary smiled politely and thanked Elizabeth for her hospitality, all the while hoping for a subtle house fire. Nothing crazy, just enough to ruin their lives. Elizabeth left the bathroom for Mary to clean herself in peace while she searched for her children and her child-like husband.

Now this was a room of opulence. Mary was beginning to recognize where the attention to detail had been prioritized in the house. She stripped her clothes off and left them on the floor in a corner of the room as she began her inspection of the Spinoza's most intimate space. It was a genuinely gorgeous bathroom, and three times the size of her room at the GGFF. Mary was impressed but she would never allow them the satisfaction of the compliment. She did, however, begin to rummage through the taller storage cubes that had been presumably shelved away from the prying hands of Tucker and Dawson.

There were no specific items that Mary was hoping to find, but she thought there had to be something to explain all this need for compensation. In the back of a shelf, behind a cube filled with old magazines, Mary found a half-filled pack of stale cigarettes, a lighter, and a used pregnancy test that showed positive. The pregnancy test looked new. After a decidedly predictable expedition, Mary turned the combination of knobs to take a shower. It took her a few tries, but she got there.

The water came out from the shower head with munificent force as Mary stood naked outside of the tub. Steam quickly filled the room and fogged up the mirror before she had time to close the shower curtain, but it was a luxurious transition into fresh heat. There are very few ways in any given language to appropriately explain the sensation of stepping into a good shower. Mary's head became drenched in the kind of pleasantness that feels like how a good cake tastes. She stood for a full minute not doing anything but allowing the water to pour over her face and breasts while she lightly hugged herself. Turning her head from right to left allowed Mary the opportunity to fill her inner ear canals with warm water so she could achieve the sound that she loved so much. She allowed herself the treat of turning her head more than she normally would, savoring every sound.

Looking down, she could already see some dirt and grime circling the drain, so she decided to get to work. There was a new and pristine loofa set aside for Mary along with unopened aromatic soaps and lotions that boasted exotic ingredients from foreign lands. Each item was responsibly sourced, of course. Soon Mary's skin was glistening beneath the hot running water as more gray suds washed down the drain. She considered staying in the shower a little bit longer, but instinctively turned the water off and stood motionless while soap and water dripped down her body. Something was wrong.

"Hey Lizzy," called Mary, wrapping a towel around herself, "Lizz?"

There was no response to Mary's call as the rest of the house remained silent. Had the Spinoza's decided to step out for a bit while Mary was in the shower, there was no way for her to have noticed. Mary looked out the small bathroom window that opened out to the backyard, but no one was there. She could see a small flowering dogwood tree standing in the yard beside a white shed that looked weathered and in need of a fresh coat of paint. The familiar taste of a lingering metallic flavor settled in the back of her throat as her hands began to shake.

She tried to look away, but her eyes would not move from the scene outside. If there were a wind that blew across the yard and into the rows of bordering pines lining the property, then there was no way of telling as there was no sound or movement outside. All was still and upsetting. The surge of new adrenaline mixed with the residual humidity from her shower caused Mary to feel light-headed as she gripped the sink for support. Her vision fell into a tunnel and darkness lined her peripherals. The floor appeared to fall away as she collapsed upon it.

Mary fell for ages at first, onto the floor and then inside of it. She could feel her body compressed to a proportion that suggested she would never escape from the second dimension and would only exist on this plane of perspective. Her face then flattened to a spreadable paste that expanded through the cracks in reality and found its way into a cup of coffee being drunk by Theodore Roosevelt. Before the brim of the mug could brush against his mustache, President Roosevelt's hair grew out thick and black as he let out the howl of a wolf that shook the pince-nez off the bridge of his nose. The sound traveled across the void and carried what was left of Mary with it. She understood a celestial purpose that had been so far confused by the presence of humanity in the universe. She knew everything in an instant, but the information was lost just as quickly as it was received. The only link to the memory was the word "alligator".

Like a friend in hiding, how the joy fell through her and brought speed to her expulsion as she flew through the particles in the air. President Roosevelt had disappeared and was then replaced with the giant mechanical owl which once had stood upon the grandfather clock in Mary's home. The hour and minute hands moved once more as two mice in love spinning carelessly this way and that in chase. Neither had regard for the rules of time. The whole experience brought a certain dread onto Mary. Her legs, which were non-existent up to this point, began to hurt. Her body had returned to an organic human shape except that her torso had remained flattened and stretched out across the endless grid of a green and black computer drafting screen. *I am the y axis*, she thought to herself. Without context and with no point of reference, Mary knew this to be true...

"ALLIGATOR," screamed Mary as Addison held her head in his hands. Elizabeth's mascara was mixing with her tears which were running down her cheeks from fear. Mary was lying on her back, wrapped in a towel, and cradled by Addison while Elizabeth knelt over her in a panic. Mary had just been revived back to consciousness and there were a few moments where she did not know where she was. One of the mirrors had been smashed and shards of glass had scattered across the white tile floor. Each piece caught the light as though they were deep sea pearls.

Mary blinked twice before settling back to the reality that had briefly eluded her. She was more upset by seeing Elizabeth blubbering over her than by what she had just experienced. There was an incomplete memory of the dream, but she did not know why she was on the floor. She knew that she was uncomfortable, but the pain was too small and in too many places for her to focus on a single source. Her attempt to stand was met with instability and small cuts from the shards of glass, so she turned her body away from Addison's all too eager hands.

"What happened," asked Mary, "fuck, my head."

She ran her hand through her hair and winced as a portion of it tangled around her finger, sticky with blood.

"Let's get you to the hospital," said Elizabeth, "come on, Mary."

"No, I'm fine. I just need to clean up."

"Mary, we are taking you to the hospital. Addison, grab her arms and lift."

Addison attempted to cup Mary's breasts with his hands as he gripped her for support. Mary shot an elbow into Addison's ribs, and he let her go.

"I'm fine," said Mary, "I'm not going to a goddamn hospital. I just need to lay down."

The popping sound of broken glass trailed behind her as Mary made her way to the guest room. Elizabeth was trotting behind her with crisp white towels on each arm, trying to keep Mary's blood from staining the carpet. She placed two towels on Mary's pillow before she could lay her head down.

"Do you need any medicine," asked Elizabeth, "I didn't know you had a condition! You're not going to die or anything, are you?"

Mary smiled to herself at Elizabeth's ineptitude.

"Yes," said Mary, "I need my medicine. There's an unmarked pill bottle in my bag. Could you get it for me?"

Elizabeth's hands were shaking as she dug through Mary's bag. She pulled out two unmarked pill bottles and showed them to Mary, who feigned confusion as to which one to take.

"You shouldn't tease her," came a small voice, "she's only trying to help."

Mary looked to her left and in a corner of the room, sitting in a chair, was a young boy wearing corduroy trousers and a blue shirt with buttons down the front. He was wearing her old childhood shoes. Mary threw both pill bottles at the boy who remained still and unblinking.

"Get out!" screamed Mary, "Get out of here!"

Elizabeth jumped and scurried out of the room, apologizing all the way. It felt as though Mary could not take in any air as she sputtered and coughed trying to steady her breathing. The little boy picked up the two bottles and returned them to Mary who was now cowering in the bed and pushing herself backwards against the headboard.

"Have I ever hurt you?" asked the boy.

"No," whimpered Mary, "I don't think so."

"Then why would I hurt you now?"

"I don't know," said Mary, "I don't know, I don't know."

He handed Mary the pill bottles and smiled as he took a step backwards.

"Welcome home," he said, "it really hasn't been the same since you left."

Mary opened one of the bottles and swallowed two blue capsules without any water. She gagged only for a moment before the pills made their way down her throat and into her system. She tried to expedite the effects by taking a third. Mary closed her eyes and attempted to perform some breathing exercises she had learned in counseling.

"Did you find me?" asked the boy.

"Maybe," said Mary, "I think I did, yeah."

"Where was I?"

"In a bathtub," said Mary, "it was at a party…in New York."

"No," said the boy, "I've never been to New York."

"Who are you?"

The boy's expression dropped in a subtle display of a passing thought best left unsaid.

"I'm not the only one," he started again, "before we…"

The boy's face went still, but only for a moment before he coughed, wiped his face, and groaned in aggravation.

"I promised not to tell," he said, "how was your birthday?"

"What?" asked Mary.

"Your birthday was recent, wasn't it?"

"You're a month too late."

"Damn," said the boy, "I used to be good at this."

"You know what," said Mary, "I don't care. I don't fucking care. You can be whoever you want to be or whatever. No, thank you, I don't care anymore."

"That's not really up to you," he said, "sometimes you don't get to choose who or what you care about."

"Enough with this bullshit you weird little fuck!"

The boy looked genuinely hurt, but he nodded and walked to Mary's side. She looked insane with the blood matted hair stiff on its side and her eyes bulging out of her skull. The boy reached out to touch Mary's hand.

"I'm not supposed to do this," he said, "but just this once…"

His finger grazed the top of Mary's hand. There was barely any noticeable contact and the only proof that they had connected at all came from the sensation of fire running through Mary's veins. Mary saw light that burned holes in the sky.

She was walking through the woods once again as a child, but she knew that she was somebody else. The sounds and smells of another summer day surrounded her, and she felt uncomfortably hungry in the shade of the trees. She removed her shoes to feel the dirt and grass beneath her feet; all in her search for a deeper connection to the world.

Someone was walking by her side, but the figure felt both foreign and familiar, as though the memory refused to be placed. It walked beside Mary without any descriptive form while she asked about going back home for lunch. Mary's companion promised in a deep and muffled voice that they would be home soon. In her grouchy and sour discord, Mary threw her shoes into the river with a defiant tantrum. The feeling of hands smacking against her face hit like flashes of light. Each strike brought a new spring of violence to her vision and her face grew hot with rage and fear. Mary began to apologize to her companion and was met with loud language, none of which could be understood. A final blow brought Mary to her knees as she continued to fall through the forest floor. Her skin became coated in a clear plastic that sealed as a vacuum around her now adult body. The growing sensation of velocity rattled through her mind.

Deafening. When that word comes up you think of loud noises. The reality is that there is no noise. It is not a gradual process that causes deafness. It is an instant. Sound does not exist anymore, not in the way we are familiar with it. At that point sound transcends auditory comprehension and it becomes strictly physical. The vibrations grow to be so enormous that the sounds themselves are too large to hear. I would imagine the feeling of being thrown into the center of a star without temperature and being shaken so violently that you disintegrate from the inside out. This is the closest that Mary would come to describing that sensation.

Mary was back in bed in the Spinoza's guest room. The boy was gone, but she had already begun to forget what had happened. There was something important that she was supposed to remember, but there were only fragmented images crossing her mind. A portion of memory lingered, and it created an emotion that Mary was having difficulty explaining in words. Although to be fair, trying to explain an emotion at all is damn near impossible, even on a good day.

A color hung in Mary's mind where words could not generate. Red sat in the center of an oblong shape that spread beneath where she lay. It was as though she had remembered a dream from long ago that had since been forgotten. An overwhelming sorrow spread lightly throughout Mary's body, and she found some comfort in the weight that it brought. The capsules she had taken were winding up to their full effect now and an intense wave of synthetic calm washed over her turbulent mind. The red center of the oblong turned gray as Mary closed her eyes and fell into a dreamless sleep.

18. I Need To Know You

Howard was thinking. He was sitting in the living room chair, picking at the skin around his fingernails, and he was thinking. No one else was home at the Rubenstein apartment, but Howard was fine with that. He wanted to have some time by himself to think. There was the delicate balance of conflict between his wanting to respect Mary's privacy and his desire to intervene as a concerned parent.

When Ruth had come to breakfast and told Howard and Lorry about Mary's recent bout of mania, Lorry had asked Ruth if she would be able to help reel Mary in. Although her concern for her sister was present and sincere, Ruth was too tired to devote that much emotional energy to Mary's well-being. Her parents did not fault her for it outright, but they were disappointed. This led to a bigger discussion concerning the appropriate course of action to caring for Mary while also avoiding the bad habit of excusing harmful behavior. Accountability was another foundation to the Rubenstein home. If Mary needed help, then they would help her. What they could not do was allow her the refusal to accept accountability for her actions. This had led to other altercations in the past, but those were themselves educational opportunities for the Rubenstein's. It allowed them the experience to develop the appropriate tools to approach future conversations. The conversations were still difficult, but it was a work in progress.

Howard was thinking about Mary's first birthday that she had with them after her adoption. It was her first birthday without her parents, and without her family. Howard wanted to go all out and prepare an abundant party to make Mary feel as though she were a real Rubenstein. Lorry, being the more pragmatic of the two, thought it might be better to have a party that would put less pressure on Mary. Howard bucked a little, as he often believed in grand displays of affection, but ultimately, he agreed, and an intimate gathering was planned. They had done their best to put a simple party together, but even with the balloons and the cake, Mary was distant and detached. She did her best to remain present and grateful, but she would experience waves of dismissal and felt like sulking on the day. When Lorry started playing the piano Mary began to perk up. She played a sad, slow song that sounded like long walks in the autumn after disappointing news. There were no lyrics to the tune, but the music spoke on its own. The sentiment drifted clearly through each hanging note. Mary sat captivated by the song and would later request it frequently when she was feeling down. When she got older Mary had found a vinyl pressing of the original artist's recording and listened to it repeatedly over the course of a week. After that she would keep it handy for when the world felt too big.

Howard rose from his chair and walked to the stereo where they had their record collection stored beneath the turntable. He began to thumb through some of their old albums, each record carrying flashcard memories of his youth, old girlfriends, his early days with Lorry when they were poor. Even when they had nothing, they had music. It was always there, and it had kept them sane. The record with Mary's song on it was nearly worn out from the number of times that she had played it, but there was only a limited amount of background noise when Howard put it on the turntable. Still kneeling in front of their record collection, he started to hum along and continued to reminisce about Mary's early life in their home. There were other songs on the album, but he only wanted to hear the one.

Flipping through the other records, Howard paused for a moment on a copy of Rumors by Fleetwood Mac. He would always tease Lorry about it when they first started dating, but he secretly loved the album. It was an extension of Lorry and there was no way to separate her from the record. There was a passing thought of what life would be like if Lorry were to die before him and he quickly stuffed the record back onto the shelf. He continued to dig through the records until he found a neutral album, one that he could enjoy without becoming sentimental. He loaded the record on the turntable and sat back in the chair while the upbeat sounds of Tom Petty began to fill the room.

The sound of Lorry returning home shook Howard out of his trance, and he cleared his throat as he stood up from his chair. He lowered the volume on the turntable while Lorry started humming along.

"Hey big fella," she said, "oooh, I love this album. It always reminds me of you. You ok? You look tired."

"Yeah," said Howard, "just having a think."

"That bad, huh?"

"I just don't know what to do. Have you talked to Ruth today? She didn't answer when I called."

"We were supposed to get lunch, but she said that she had a last-minute meeting with Alex."

Lorry brought two large grocery bags into the kitchen and put them on the counter. She was starting to put a can of beans in the cupboard when Howard walked up behind her and put his arms around her waist. He nuzzled his face into the back of her neck and produced a heavy sigh. Lorry felt her skin become electric whenever Howard did this, but he only embraced her like this when he was feeling overwhelmed. She loved how he always felt warm and how his arms would pull her against him gently. Howard was very aware of his size, and she felt it imperative to encourage him to be comfortable with vulnerability.

"I love you," she said.

"I love you, too."

They stood like that in the kitchen for a few minutes before Howard let out a long breath, kissed the top of Lorry's head, and helped her put away the groceries. It was quick work and Lorry had already started dinner before Howard could finish storing the last of the dry goods. Lorry put on an apron that said **This Guy Rubs His Own Meat** and watched as her husband lingered in front of the open refrigerator.

"Use your words," she said, "please don't shut down on me."

"I'm scared." said Howard, "I know that this isn't new. Mary has a habit of disappearing. I don't know why, but this feels different. Maybe I'm just tired."

"What feels different this time?"

"I can't explain it," Howard sat across from Lorry and folded his arms on the table, "I had a dream the other night. Maybe two days ago, but it was so vivid. I dreamt that Mary was being ripped apart by dogs and I couldn't do anything. I just watched it happen and I remember crying in my sleep and screaming and trying to scare the dogs away, but they didn't even stop to look at me. It was such a real feeling that I woke up terrified."

Lorry walked around the table and sat in Howard's lap, putting her arms around his shoulders. She squeezed him and kissed him three times before burying her face in his chest. Howard loved it when she did that.

"I don't understand it," he said, "but it's different this time."

"What do you want to do?" asked Lorry.

Howard was quiet and his eyes stayed on the table as Lorry started rubbing his back. He spoke honestly while shaking his head.

"I want to go get her," he said, "I want to go get her and I want to bring her back home."

"What if she doesn't want to come back?"

"I'll figure it out."

"*We'll* figure it out."

Howard looked down at Lorry in his lap and she kissed him on the nose.

"If you want to go get her," she said, "then let's go get her. But we're gonna need a plan."

"Right," said Howard, "we don't even know where she went. She said she was going home, but we don't know where that is."

"It's in Massachusetts, isn't it?"

"Is it?"

"I think so," said Lorry, "I have her paperwork in the lockbox beneath the dresser. I'll get it."

Lorry returned a few minutes later with a fireproof lock box where the Rubenstein's kept their important paperwork. The birth certificates, diplomas, contracts, mortgage papers, and personal documentation were kept in a vaguely organized catalog system. It was a little cluttered, but everything was there. Lorry began to dig through the papers to find that Mary's adoption forms only mentioned the town of Amherst without specifying an address. It was a start, at least.

"So, we go to Amherst," said Lorry, "then what? Start knocking on doors?"

"We go to St. Philomena's," said Howard, "the address may be in their files."

"You're brilliant, love."

"No, I'm scared. I'm scared and angry and I don't know what I'm going to say if we find her."

"*When* we find her," said Lorry, "come on. We can practice on the road."

"Should we get Ruth?"

"No," said Lorry, "no, we'll call her, but I think she's dealing with her own shit right now. If we all show up Mary might feel like she's under attack."

"Right," Howard took his leather helmet off of the wall and tugged it down on his head, "we taking the bike or the van?"

"Let's take the van," said Lorry, "starting to get a little too chilly for the bike. Besides, we can park off the highway and have sexy time in the woods."

Howard chuckled and blushed at the idea.

"You're a freak, you know that?" said Howard.

Lorry tried to put her arms around Howard, but he was too wide for her hands to touch.

"I'm your freak," said Lorry, "let's go get Mary."

Ruth was in fact dealing with her own shit. Even with her attempted self-sabotage, her opening was a success. The two gentlemen from the Museum Ludwig in Cologne were very impressed by Ruth's work and had communicated a desire to sit with Alex and Ruth to negotiate residency at their museum. There was a lunch meeting set at the Algonquin hotel and Ruth was arriving earlier than she had anticipated. This was a new habit for Ruth as she had previously maintained the eccentricities of a scatterbrained artist. She was serious about her work, but punctuality had never been a priority.

Ruth had been to the Algonquin on two previous occasions. The first was out of necessity when she had been lost on a bender of drinking all day and she needed to use the bathroom. It was a game that she and her friends would play when they would get drunk together and see how many hotel bathrooms they could use in one day. On that occasion, Ruth had lost her friends in the shuffle of the Christmas shoppers and had entered the Algonquin by accident.

She had known of the hotel and its notoriety in the city's history but had walked past it so many times that she had never realized where it was. Having a recently modified sense of balance from a series of strong gin and tonics, Ruth took her time and sauntered through the lobby trying to look inconspicuous. The problem with trying to look natural is that you never do. Trying to look natural makes almost everyone look like a crazy person. Ruth was no exception as within five minutes of her polite wobbling through the lobby, a short and thick man in a suit cheerily approached her.

"Checking in, miss," he asked.

"No," slurred Ruth, "no, I'm jussht looking for a huzzbind. You got those here?"

"I can't speak to that, miss, but I do know you could do worse than here at the Algonquin," he reached out a thick pink hand with hairy knuckles, "my name's Martin. I'm the head of security."

"You gonnaresst me, Martin," said Ruth, "how...(hic)...how old are you?"

"I'm sorry miss, but if you're not a guest of the hotel or dining in the restaurant, then I'm going to have to ask you to leave."

"Oh, but I am dining here," said Ruth, "you don't think I'm dining here? I'm dying to dine here. I dine here...frequently. I may just die here."

Ruth laughed at this and tried to calm herself before she broke into the kind of giggling fit that led to tears.

"May I walk you to your table," asked Martin.

"Yes," said Ruth, suddenly becoming poised, "yes I believe you should."

Ruth took the arm of Martin, who stood a foot and a half shorter than she was. She leaned a good portion of her weight upon him for support. For his lack of stature, Martin was deceptively sturdy.

He presented Ruth with a level of patience that she herself would admit to having not deserved, but Martin was funny like that. He brought Ruth to a table that sat beside a family of four (father, son, mother, daughter) and she bowed to Martin and kissed his hand. He politely shook his head while chuckling to himself and wiping his hand on the sleeve of his jacket. Ruth waited until Martin was out of sight before trying to make a run for the bathroom, but she also wanted to look at the menu while she waited. This was a habit formed over time where Ruth had to read a menu if it was in front of her. If she was walking past a restaurant that had a menu posted outside, then she had to stop and read it. She could never be sure if there were any items that would be worth returning for.

Before Martin had completely disappeared, a server approached Ruth's table and asked if there was something that she would like to order. Feeling caught on the spot, and now really needing to pee, Ruth just said the first thing that came to mind.

"Uhhhh chicken fingers, please."

"I'm sorry, miss, but we don't serve chicken fingers on the menu. We have bone-in wings, but no fingers."

"Ah, I see," said Ruth, "oh, well never mind. Good lord, what's that?!"

The waiter turned to look where Ruth had pointed but in her exaggerated attempt at escape had managed to trip after catching her foot on the leg of the chair. Her body splayed out like a starfish as Ruth flopped on the neighboring family's table, taking it down with her. A freshly served plate of fried calamari flew up in the children's faces, spraying their eyes with vinegar from the sweet shishito peppers. A fork flew up and stabbed the mother's upper lip and the father caught a side of the table in his mouth, causing him to bite off a portion of his tongue.

The room filled with the noises of a family attacked by one of the most prestigious lunches in the district. Ruth, in an unusual display of agility, had rolled out from the culinary melee and began to crawl away from the scene. The server had become overwhelmed in helping the family while a choir of wails emanated from their battered mouths and faces. Sliding out of a side door brought Ruth into an alley that connected to W44th St. Turning her collar up and driving her hands into her pockets, Ruth shuffled off into the bustling crowd in search of a different toilet.

The second time Ruth had been at the Algonquin hotel was the following year around a different Christmas. The decorations adorning the hotel entrance and lobby were tastefully minimalistic and carried the spirit of the holiday with dignified admiration. Just as the shy party guest may fascinate your eye beyond any other gimcrack on display, the hotel trimmings were just as attractive and delicate in repose. Ruth was sober so far on this occasion and had stopped in the hotel to have dinner with a blind date. Her childhood companion Joey Boulm had set her up with a friend of his that he thought Ruth might like. She had initially protested because she had wanted to focus her time on her art and felt emotionally unprepared for the commitment that comes with dating. After some light teasing from Joey, she finally agreed to meet his friend. Her name was Julia.

Ruth was late, which was unsurprising since she was often always late. She entered the Algonquin hotel with a mixture of anxieties. She was excited about the prospect of a new romantic adventure, but she was also aware of her previous visit and was curious to see if anyone would remember her. She entered the restaurant holding her breath.

"Good evening, miss," said a young hostess from behind a sleek black podium, "have you made a reservation for tonight?"

"Yes, I have. It should be for two at eight-thirty under Ruth Rubenstein. I'm sorry I'm a bit late."

"Not a problem, miss. In fact, your guest has only just arrived. Right this way, please."

The young woman led Ruth through the busy restaurant, past the tables and conversations that blended together. A variety of colognes and perfumes intermingled and created an atmosphere in which the din could thematically curl around the mix of fragrances. Ruth was beginning to feel a little claustrophobic until she saw Julia sitting by herself at their reserved table.

The first thing Ruth noticed was Julia's hair, loud and golden as wild curls, each length perfect in their asymmetry. It framed a rounded face with the kind of mouth that looked as though it had been made to smile. And when she did, her full lips parted seductively to show a brief example of an endearing snaggletooth. The kind of subtle imperfection that beautifully tied it all together. For the first time in her life, Ruth felt truly intimidated. She choked on her hello as she sat down at the table.

"Hello, yourself," said Julia, "this place is faaaaancy."

Ruth nodded in the affirmative and her eyes darted around the room to focus on anything other than Julia. She was not ready for this kind of immediate attraction. Ruth was beginning to panic. The sweat had already started.

"Have you been here before?" asked Julia.

"Yeah, once," said Ruth, looking at a happy family of four dining a few tables away.

"Oh...well, it's nice to meet you."

"I'm Ruth."

Julia started to laugh at Ruth's romantic fumblings, but she did not want to be mean about it. Ruth felt her entire body flush and regretted ever having said anything at all.

"I hope so," said Julia, "if Ruth does show up and he's some big biker dude, then we may have to make a run for it."

Ruth barked out an awkward laugh and aggressively sipped her water, trying her best to hide the portion that missed her mouth entirely. She began to scan the menu, having forgotten how to speak or read.

"Ok, 'supposed' Ruth," said Julia, "what's good here?"

"Oh…well, everything. Absolutely everything."

The server approached the table and bowed politely to Ruth and Julia, he offered to begin their meal with drinks to which Julia stated, in a serious tone, that she would like to order one of everything.

"I am sorry, Miss," said the server, "although I admire your enthusiasm, it is against our policy to provide that much alcohol in a single serving. Would you consider ordering one drink at a time before moving on to the next?"

"Not the drinks," said Julia, "I meant the food. We'll take one of everything."

The server and Ruth exchanged glances and shared a light chuckle at the presumed joke, but Julia's face remained serious. The server cleared his throat and tried to maintain his professionalism.

"Everything, Miss?"

"I'm sorry, young man," said Julia, "but I don't find this the least bit amusing. I have a hyperactive thyroid condition, not that it is any of your business, and I require to eat twice my mass in the course of a few hours, or my heart will burst, and I will die. Now I know for a fact that you would not want to be responsible for my death and the lasting trauma that it would cause my fiancé, either. Not a mere two weeks before our wedding day."

Julia gestured to Ruth who did her best to read the menu and keep her hands from shaking. The sweat was really coming now.

"I am terribly sorry," said the server, "I will alert the kitchen immediately. Please consider your first round of drinks to be gratis."

"I suppose it will have to do," said Julia, "please do not speak to us for the remainder of our meal."

The server opened his mouth to say something, but then thought better of it. He nodded and quickly walked back to the kitchen in the kind of trot that makes a person look silly. Ruth waited for Julia to explain herself, but as soon as the server was out of sight, Julia covered her mouth to hide a silent laughing fit.

"What the hell are you doing?" asked Ruth.

"I haven't got any money," said Julia, "do you?"

"What's wrong with you?!"

"You should see your face!"

A different server returned with two glasses of champagne. He said they were compliments of the Algonquin, to which Julia dropped her expression to stone and silently mouthed thank you without making eye contact. Ruth thanked the server and took her glass without looking away from Julia.

"You're insane," said Ruth.

"And you are fascinating."

Ruth had never been called fascinating before. She knew that she had a good face and a decent personality. She was proud of her legs and her hair. The otherwise undisturbed attribute of the metaphysical compliment had suddenly stirred something new within Ruth's heart. Julia held her glass out to Ruth's who reflexively clinked her rim to Julia's.

"Here's lookin' up your address," said Julia.

"Hi," said Ruth, "Jesus, what's wrong with me?"

Julia giggled and bit her bottom lip as she rose from her seat. She sidled up next to Ruth and made her scootch over to make space for the two of them to be closer. Julia was practically sitting in Ruth's lap at this point, forcing Ruth to lean her shoulder against the window. With her heart beating in her eyes and the powers of speech ripped from her mouth, Ruth started to feel dizzy. The jasmine and bergamot perfume that Julia was wearing had diminished any of the other aromas that were hanging in the Algonquin Round Table. The temperature of Ruth's body burst as Julia's breast grazed her right arm. Ruth caught her breath as she had forgotten to exhale when Julia leaned closely and whispered into her ear.

"Hey," said Julia, "do you want to know a secret?"

The sensations going through Ruth's body should have been illegal. She nodded lightly as a shiver ran her over.

"I set this up to meet you," whispered Julia, "I've wanted to meet you since forever ago. Would you believe that?"

Julia nipped Ruth's earlobe and purred in her ear.

"I was with Joey B., you know Joey, but we were at a party, and...I *saw* you there. And I knew that I had to know you. I just didn't have the nerve to ask you."

"I fuh...find that very hard ta...to believe," said Ruth, shakily, "I don't think you're short on nerves."

"What, this," Julia leaned back and gestured to the restaurant, "I don't care about this. This is all performance. All of it. We are living art. Pure theater. Just look at this set! No, you're...I need to know you."

The Round Table of the Algonquin Hotel was in full display before them, and Ruth drank in the setting for Julia's theatrical mania. It was cinematic in its grandeur and everyone dining that evening looked like the kind of film extras who you could see in black and white. A line of servers began to exit the kitchen carrying a series of large chrome trays, each loaded with an example of every menu item. Julia snapped back into character and returned to her seat across from Ruth, making sure to look as snobbish as possible. An empty table was cleared and moved beside theirs to provide enough space for the food. Ruth's eyes grew wide at the display while Julia returned to a stoic and disinterested expression. Their initial server was replaced by an older gentleman who asked Julia if the presentation met their expectations. Julia turned her nose up slightly as she scanned the buffet from beneath her eyelid.

"I suppose this is fine," she said, "thank you."

The serving staff bowed and left them to enjoy their meal.

It was received as a delicate feast, where Julia remained poised and performed as a duchess would. Ruth sat confused as she nibbled the food with an unshakable feeling of guilt and paranoia. She was just beginning to enjoy herself when a short thick man in a suit approached the table.

"Merry Christmas, ladies," he said, "I hope that everything is to your liking."

Julia was about to say something when Ruth kicked her under the table. Ruth looked away from him and said everything was fine.

"Well, my name is Martin. I'm the head of security and I'm going to have to ask you to leave. Now I would appreciate it if you would come to speak with me in the back office, please. I would hate to disturb the other guests and rob them of a fine evening's meal."

"Sir," said Julia, "I will allow you the misfortune of embarrassing yourself once before me, but I warn you, I am a diplomat for the United States government on leave from my duties in Japan. Any slight against our persons will be met with extreme prejudice to the fullest extent of the law."

Martin smiled and said something in Japanese. Julia tried to keep her composure, but it was clear that she was in over her head. He addressed Ruth, who sheepishly turned to him.

"My apologies," he said, "it would appear as though we still don't serve chicken fingers on the menu. Now please, come with me."

Julia grabbed a large pork chop and smacked Martin across the face while Ruth picked up a bowl of quinoa and slammed it down on top of his head. The two women beat Martin senseless with scallops, salads, and a marinated miso striped bass that would have paired nicely with a 1996 Pavillon Blanc du Château Margaux. Unfortunately, the bar had recently sold its last bottle to an Albanian machine-parts conglomerate in town on business. If you were to ask him about it, he would say that he was underwhelmed by the wine.

Ruth and Julia made a dash for the exit, knocking over a bellman who was carrying a vase that was donated to the hotel by an actual diplomat from Japan. The bellman tumbled across the floor and the vase broke into several pieces against the front desk. Julia stopped to take a picture with her phone while Ruth kept running. The photo would later be sent to their friends and family as a Christmas card the following year.

Once Ruth and Julia had managed to escape from Martin and the security staff of the Algonquin hotel, they took a taxi to a dumpling house in Chinatown. After that, they were inseparable.

That was the last time that Ruth had set foot in the Algonquin hotel. The pork chop assault, as it was later called, had been four years prior and Ruth felt as though enough time may have passed to allow her some anonymity. And who's to say whether Martin would still be head of security, anyway? Everything would be fine. Besides, this was a new Ruth. An established Ruth. She was an artist and artists are expected to be controversial, right? But the weight that rested heavily on her mind was not the possible repercussions of her past delinquencies, nor was it the meeting with the Museum Ludwig. No. What was pressing through Ruth's thoughts was the glaring absence of Julia.

She entered the lobby of the Algonquin hotel and paused as she played through the initial steps of their first date and shared assault. It was too early for Christmas decorations, but she projected the thought of holiday themes across the room while a melancholy feeling drifted across her mind. The sensation settled in the moment and made it clear that a part of Ruth had gone missing. She shook her head and decided to wait at the bar until her party arrived.

The bar was busy, but not packed. Alex had reserved a table for the meeting at nine o'clock, but it was only eight-thirty, and their table was otherwise occupied. After much apologizing from the hostess, Ruth assured them that it would be fine and that she would be happy to wait at the bar. After a moment of reflection, she ordered a glass of champagne and toasted the air.

There were several people in the restaurant, most dining together in pairs or in groups of three or four, but a single diner sat by themselves at a table near the window. Ruth tried her best not to stare at them, but the more she watched the more she realized that the person dining by themselves was waiting for someone else to arrive. There was no singular tell as to whether this was true or not, but the patron's body language, facial expressions, and the frequency of which they checked on their phone gave the impression that they were sitting with anticipation. Ruth had been staring at the person for too long before they looked up and made eye contact for a split second. Ruth reflexively straightened her back and pretended to scan the bottles of liquor behind the bar. When the bartender noticed Ruth reading the bottles, he came around and asked her if she wanted anything else. She politely declined and slightly turned her head to see if the lone diner was still looking at her, but they were gone.

On another day the incidental moment should have left no singular impression upon Ruth's mood, but with her mind still obsessing over Julia's absence, Ruth took out her phone and started drafting an email:

Hi.

It's me.

I don't know what to do. I hate this and I hate this feeling and I hate you almost as much as I love you. And I do love you, Julia. I love you so much that it's disgusting. I wish you would call me and come over. I don't even want to fuck. I just want your time. I want to see you look at me again. I want to look at you again.

I'm doing ok, I think. I'm sitting at the Algonquin, if you could believe that. Alex is bringing these two hot shot bigwigs from Germany that want to show some of my work. We'll see what happens, but I'll say this much. I was in rare form for that last opening reception. Honestly, I think you would have loved it. Got so drunk that I got bounced by security from my own opening and they still didn't know who I was.

Wakka wakka.

Why did you leave? I'm sorry, I know you said not to contact you, but this hurts so fucking much, Julia. I don't know what to do and you're all I can think about. I'm probably going to delete this. Why did I write that? Maybe I'm not ok.

-R

Ruth stared at the email and read it three or four times before saving it into her drafts and putting her phone away. Glancing at the lone diner's table she saw that a young man and woman had taken their seats. They looked very much in love. Taking her phone out from her bag she opened her draft emails, found the one addressed to Julia, lingered over the message for ten seconds, and hit send.

Twenty minutes later Ruth was still nursing her first drink, although the fizz had all but run out of the champagne and the temperature had turned wrong. The restaurant was in motion with the night hoppers and the business associates enjoying a late supper or an early drink, depending on how the evening was shaping out to be. Ruth heard Alex calling out to her as they entered the restaurant.

She turned to see Alex escorting two older gentlemen, presumably the representatives from the Museum Ludwig. Ruth left her glass of champagne at the bar and joined the three at their reserved table with appropriate introductions and customary small talk to help everyone settle into themselves. The criticisms of transportation and social observations gave the conversation enough levity to allow a relatable buffer to form for the group. If they could agree on the common inadequacies of travel, then there was at the very least a foundation of understanding. Two rounds of drinks and the first course of appetizers were served before the night's focus approached the idea of business.

The two men from Cologne were Mathias Meyer and Tomas Jager, both curators and co-chairs in the fundraising commission of the Museum Ludwig. Mathias and Tomas were thin men that moved with calculation and presented themselves as impeccably clean. There were enough distinctions in their features to help differentiate between them, but Tomas also maintained a certain delicacy in his speech while Mathias sounded more enthusiastic. He also kept an elegant and immaculate mustache that had been manicured to perfectly cover his upper lip. Alex had been gushing to them both over Ruth's most recent gallery opening and the two men were very interested in getting to know the artist in a real way.

"Ms. Rubenstein," said Tomas, "we are delighted that you have agreed to meet with us. After we witnessed your opening, we knew that we simply had to meet you in person."

"Oh, yes," said Mathias, "Tomas and I are in total agreement. You are an inspiration."

"That's very kind of you to say," said Ruth, "but I have to admit that I've been thinking about moving my work in a different direction."

"Don't you dare," said Mathias, "I would hate to think that you have gotten cold feet after being ejected from your reception. It really was a spectacular event."

Ruth blushed with embarrassment and felt the need to explain herself. Mathias continued before she could speak.

"We, Tomas and I, have been involved in curating many different styles and variations of performance art. It has become something of a specialty of ours."

"It's true," said Tomas, "we have seen many different presentations come through Museum Ludwig. We can say with the utmost confidence that we felt privileged to see the raw passion in your eviction."

Alex and Ruth were confused. The two hosts looked at each other and assumed there might have been a language barrier. Ruth saw things moving in a way that she had not initially anticipated. She was slowly realizing that this had nothing to do with her video work.

"I'm sorry, Tomas," asked Alex, "what do you mean, exactly?"

"To have a gallery opening become an engaging art piece is the work of a genius," said Tomas, "we have seen it attempted before, yes. Countless times, to be sure, but the artist rejecting themselves? Now that is an enlightened presentation."

"Now this is where my partner and I land in disagreement," said Mathias, "I had perceived the piece as the art *itself* rejecting the artist. For whom better to deny the existence of its creator than that which had been created?"

"Wrong, as usual," said Tomas, "you must excuse my friend. He was raised to have overly romantic ideations."

"And you have clearly become an accountant!" said Mathias.

The two men laughed heartily, cheered each other's glasses, and then turned to cheer Alex and Ruth.

"We must have you exhibit in Cologne. It would be an honor," said Mathias.

"Absolutely," said Tomas, "please allow us the privilege to eject you from our museum."

Ruth did not know what to say. She had accidentally stumbled into greatness or had at least tripped on its threshold. Alex, never one to ignore an unexpected opportunity, quickly scribbled a number on a cocktail napkin, folded it, and handed it to Mathias. He opened the napkin and remained expressionless while he showed it to Tomas. The two men muttered to each other in German for a few moments before nodding as Mathias slipped the napkin into the inside pocket of his jacket.

"Agreed," said Mathias.

"We will make the arrangements," said Tomas.

The two men from Cologne ordered two bottles of champagne to be brought to the table. All hands were shaken, and cheeks were kissed as the agreement was reached.

"What did you write on that napkin?" whispered Ruth.

"Don't worry about it," said Alex, "let's just say that with my ten percent I can buy a house in Montauk."

"Well," said Ruth, "alright then."

The champagne had arrived and all at the table were merry. Even Ruth was beginning to warm up to the idea of becoming a performance artist. Her mind was opening to the potential applications of combining her video work with an additional live performance. It was something that had often crossed her mind, but she had never settled on the thought long enough to bring it into fruition. With all that was unfolding before her, she would have to reconsider her approach to her work. Ruth had been lost in thought when a hand rested firmly on her shoulder. She turned to find Martin, head of security, red-faced and boiling over, glaring at her through gritted teeth. He spoke in a low and steady tone.

"You are leaving," he said, "right now."

Panic began to course through Ruth's body as her fantasies abandoned her and reality tightened its grip upon her shoulder. Tomas looked at Alex and laughed awkwardly, asking if this was some kind of joke. Mathias' eyes immediately lit up and he began to applaud, driven into the spirit of the event.

"Oh, this is too much," he said, "I was not prepared for another performance so quickly!"

"Ahhhh," said Tomas, "and you were acting so coy Ms. Rubenstein! Wunderbar, meisterin! Wunderbar!"

Martin practically lifted Ruth out from her chair as he began to escort her out of the restaurant. She protested loudly from a fresh surge of adrenaline, kicking, and screaming against Martin and the rest of the world. Martin carried her through the lobby of the hotel and pushed her so firmly out of the front doors that her body lifted off the ground before landing on the sidewalk.

"If I so much as see you in Manhattan again," shouted Martin, "I am going to have you arrested and burned at the stake!"

Ruth lay on the curb and tried her best to catch her breath. A small crowd had gathered in the lobby as word began to spread that Ruth was a famous performance artist. The restaurant patrons flooded out onto the sidewalk to get an autograph or picture taken with Ruth as she wiped the debris and cigarette butts off her best dress. Someone put their arm around her for a photograph and placed his hand directly on a smear of dog shit that had stuck to her hip. After the picture was taken, he held his hand up with pride as he excitedly explained to passersby that it had come off her dress. Out of breath, confused, and bruised, Ruth Rubenstein had arrived.

19. I Love A Good Nightmare

St. Philomena's had closed in twenty-seventeen after a flood of baleful accusations against the staff were brought to the public's attention. Several arrests were made and millions of dollars' worth of legal compensation were distributed to the families of the students who fell victim to the abuses. The consequences fell primarily on the shoulders of Mr. Lewis and the Headmistress as they were the directors of administration and the caretakers of the school. Mr. Lewis was sentenced to twenty years in a state penitentiary on charges of child abuse, child endangerment, willful negligence, conspiracy to perform abuse on a minor, assault, embezzlement, and other nasty things that collectively stupefied a grand jury to the point of consternation. He lasted five days in federal prison before he was stabbed to death by his cellmate over a disagreement regarding a bag of peanut butter cups. The headmistress, unwilling to admit to any wrongdoing perpetrated by herself or the faculty, hanged herself in her office before the police could arrest her. She used her finest rope.
 The property and land were acquired by a German financial firm in a bidding war against a Japanese industrial group in twenty-fifteen. During this conquest, thirteen assassination attempts were committed against each groups' president and a series of violent attacks were committed against the two firms' properties. Seven different hotels and factories owned by both companies were burned to the ground. There was also the destruction of a small village in France owned by the Japanese firm which had been purchased as a strategic shipping port. A fire had begun in one of the oil tankers docked in the harbor and had spread throughout a large portion of the residential areas around the seaport. There was no proper evidence to designate blame, but four hundred people were killed in the village. All these events were perceived as unfortunate industrial accidents and both presidents made sizable donations to the other's relief funds. There are rules in the world of finance.
 The dormitories and buildings surrounding the grounds of St. Philomena's were demolished and replaced with a large concrete foundation that covered a total of twenty acres. The additional fifty acres

of woodland which surrounded the newly laid foundation was cleared and cut down to make space for a small municipal airport, two competing grocery stores, some bars, restaurants, shops, a movie theater above a bowling alley, a building designated for pre-K through high school, and four apartment buildings to house the factory workers. In the spirit of industrial drive and confidence the foundation was soon supporting the Yankee Doodle Noodle Company: a subsidiary of the Happy Frog Television Studio, Channel 88. The factory would go on to create such products as Cat-O-Racks, prescription sunglasses for cats, Little Ms./Mr. Muzzle, a child noise suppressant and tranquilizer for ages four to fifteen, Watts-A-Matta-You Italian lightbulb koozies for Italian light bulbs and, of course, Yankee Doodle Noodles, their top-seller. Now in arctic mint flavor.

Many of these products were shipped to the factory piecemeal after having been partially assembled and separately packaged at different factories overseas. This form of production was established to adjust labor expenses and derive materials at cost instead of providing each involved worker an adequate living wage. If the workers were making more money, then they would be able to leave the small industrial town and find prospective happiness somewhere else. The powers at be could not allow that to ever surface as a possibility, so they maintained a barely livable wage that was guaranteed to be spent back into the predetermined entertainment provided by the company. The workers would find comfort and solace in spending their money at the restaurants, movie theater, shops, and bowling alley. These were supplied by the company in a way to placate any residual sense of stagnation that accompanied an employee's hourly wages. It also put the money back into the pockets of the German property owners.

The American factory workers would inspect the products and test for durability as well as quality while a different section would assemble the components received in each shipment. Any items that were seen to be unfit or inadequate for retail sales would be burned in the giant furnace and an investigation would be held to determine whether a machine was responsible for the discrepancy or if it was the result of an employee's shoddy craftsmanship. This furnace was the size of two school buses if they were to be placed side-by-side. Should any worker be found taking the inadequate product home with them, then that worker would be suspended for a week without pay and have the lost revenue for the item deducted from their following paycheck. Workers were seldom fired because it was difficult to find people willing to work under these conditions.

Plumes of black smoke were always pouring from the towering chimneys of the Yankee Doodle Noodle Company: a subsidiary of the

Happy Frog Television Studio, Chanel 88. Howard and Lorry were very confused as they stepped out of their van and onto the visitor's parking lot.

"What the fuck is this?!" asked Lorry.

The Rubenstein's watched as a tour bus loaded with passengers left the parking lot and drove towards the factory. The words Yankee Doodle Noodle were scrawled across the side of the bus in the tasteful script of the American Constitution. The smiling face of George Washington, wearing sunglasses and a toothy grin, his hair made from thin spaghetti, was throwing dabs on the side of the bus.

"Oh, I've had these before," said Howard, "they gave me diarrhea."

"Fantastic."

"Do you think we should catch the next tour?"

"I'd rather have diarrhea," said Lorry.

"Are we sure this is the right place?" asked Howard.

"I think so," said Lorry, "I mean I can't tell, but this was where the guy at the gas station said it was."

"Typical. Can we go to just one gas station where we don't end up in a post-apocalyptic noodle factory?"

"No dear," said Lorry, "apparently we cannot."

"Whelp," said Howard, "I'm out of ideas."

Howard and Lorry opened the back doors of the van and sat down. Lorry's legs dangled freely while Howard's feet were planted firmly on the ground. They both watched the fleet of employees, each dressed in blue coveralls with white hardhats, changing shifts in two lines, passing each other in opposite directions. Their movements were so mechanized that it was difficult to tell where one line ended and where the other began.

"Do you think they're happy?" asked Lorry.

"I mean, what's happy mean," Howard replied, "do I think they like their job? Maybe. I don't think anybody grows up wanting to work in a factory. Sometimes you don't have a choice."

"Accessibility," said Lorry.

"How's that now?"

"Accessibility versus opportunity," said Lorry, "I was reading an article that talked about the difference between opportunity and accessibility. Like how everybody has the opportunity to be an astronaut but it's not accessible to most people."

"Or how anybody can be a doctor if they have the means to become one."

"Exactly," said Lorry, "talking about opportunity as the answer to personal achievement is disqualifying to those who don't have access to those resources."

"So, say that I want to be a racecar driver," said Howard, "but I don't have access to a racecar."

"Or the means to get one."

"I could steal one."

"But then you'd go to jail."

"I can be a racecar driver and still go to jail."

"Anyway," said Lorry, "sometimes you have to take what you can get. What's accessible to you. That doesn't make you any less of a person, but there's a stigma around the idea of unskilled labor."

"Unskilled labor," scoffed Howard, "people that use that term should work in a fast-food restaurant for a week. Putting up with all that shit, on your feet all day getting yelled at by people who don't even look you in the eye and then claim that you're paid too much? That's unskilled? Showing up every day to the same kind of abuse because your family can't afford you losing your job? That's unskilled?"

"I never understood the argument about folks getting another job if they don't like it," said Lorry, "I mean, sure that's a good idea, but the crap job is still gonna exist for someone else to suffer through."

They sat watching the workers move in and out of the factory. It was a cold day, but not terrible. The sky was spread cloud gray and covered any potential blue that could sneak in from the afternoon. Looking up they could not see the sun.

"I ever tell you about the time I worked in that fancy restaurant?" asked Howard.

"Maybe," said Lorry, "you do like to retell stories."

"Well, if it's going to bore you then forget it."

"I'm just teasing," said Lorry, "tell me a story, papa."

Howard smirked and nudged Lorry lightly with his elbow.

"I've had so many jobs that I can't keep track of them all. This one always stood out for me, though. I'll never forget this job. Man, it was bad. I was twenty-two and I was working at this high-brow place. Very fancy. Expensive. My buddy was working as a bartender and when I told him I was hard up for work he got me in as a server, at first. After the interview management felt they wanted me to start as a food runner just so they could get an idea of how I moved. Maybe they could tell it wasn't going to be a good fit from the start, I dunno. I was big and clumsy and not really cut out for...fancy stuff. Anyway, it was just all around bad. Part of my training was them putting three glasses of white wine in front of me and making me guess what kind of wine each one was."

"How are you supposed to know that?" asked Lorry.

"Exactly," said Howard, "I think they were just trying to make fun of me. I didn't get any of them right, and they just said that I wasn't ready to be a server. I mean, even when I tried to joke around with some of the guys it would never land. Everybody was so uptight. I never got comfortable in the job and the people were just awful. Never seen somebody spend forty dollars on a cheeseburger and fries."

"Was the cheeseburger magical?"

"It was good, but it wasn't forty dollars good. I hated that place. I didn't last a month."

"Did you quit?"

"Oh, no I was fired. This was one of those places where every plate has one of those chrome toppers on it. We were supposed to leave the lids on until everyone at the table was served. That way we can lift the lids altogether and give them an 'Ahhh' moment. It was stupid. Anyway, I was bringing a plate of ravioli to a table and the plate was so hot. I kept trying to move it around under my hand because my fingers were getting burned, but when I tried to readjust it, I accidentally sent it flying across the room."

"No, you didn't!"

"It was something else, I'll tell ya. The whole thing splattered against the wall, red sauce all over this woman, babies crying, a real needle-across-the-record moment. I laughed because I was nervous, but I knew that was it. Two days later after a shift they gave me the boot."

Lorry put her head against Howard's chest and rubbed his back.

"I'm sorry that happened," she said.

"Fuck 'em," said Howard, "no love lost there. What's the worst job you've ever had?"

Lorry had to think about this. She knew Howard had a longer and stranger work history than she did, and she wanted to think of a comparable story that could stand up to Howard's bizarre experiences. After a few moments in thought, Lorry began to laugh and covered her face in her hands.

"Are you laughing or crying?" asked Howard.

"Laughing," said Lorry, "oh, man I forgot about this. So. I was working at this copy place, copies, laminations, digital transfers, right? It was mostly whackos coming off the street trying to make the cheapest copies of their manifestos. You know the type. Birds aren't real, the moon isn't real, lizard people, the whole thing. The funny thing about it is that most of those conspiracy theories usually just lead to antisemitism. Which I know is your favorite."

"We have been known to control the weather," said Howard, "have you heard about our secret space lasers?"

Lorry told Howard to shut up and jostled him to the side.

"So, like I was saying, it was either that, cheap businessmen trying to get reports printed up, or like, big family jobs. This woman came in for a special job where she wanted all these photographs scanned and copied to a DVD. Her husband had just died, and she needed the DVD for his wake. Kind of a family album type of thing. So, she comes in with these four kids and they're all just so sad. I was processing the order and I, uh, miscalculated the cost for the job."

"What, you overcharge her or something?"

"No, I *under*charged her. I told her the whole job would cost around seventy-five dollars, but when she came back to pick up the DVD two days later, she was charged four hundred and seventy-five dollars. She was so pissed that they gave her the job for free. I was off that day, so I got a call from my manager. He was so angry. Called me an idiot. Said I was useless. Man, I'd forgotten all about that. I went into work the next day and was fired after being there for ten minutes."

"Why do they always make you come in to fire you?" asked Howard.

"Seriously," said Lorry, "he could have told me over the phone. Save me the bus fare. Stupid ass."

Lorry scratched Howards back and he took her little hand in his own. He kissed the top of her head and pulled her in tightly for a squeeze.

"I love you," said Lorry.

"Love you, too," said Howard, "I'm glad neither of us work at those places anymore."

The workers had entered and exited the factory as the shift whistle blew across the parking lot, signaling to all tardy employees that their lack of punctuality could be met with disciplinary action. Actions that would carry consequences for them and their families. You would be hard pressed to find a smile working at the Yankee Doodle Noodle Company: a subsidiary of the Happy Frog Television Studio, Chanel 88.

"Come on," said Howard, "let's grab some food at one of these weird spots."

The restaurant was called Captain Lou's Caboose, with a cartoon illustration of a fat man wearing the clothes of a train conductor. His posterior was comically large and animatronic as it wiggled from side-to-side. The interior looked fresh and new with a renovated spin on a retro diner aesthetic. Chrome stools with red vinyl seats lined a long white bar top that faced a bevy of waitresses in matching powder blue uniform dresses that ended just above the knee.

They moved in synchronization as the waitresses would shout an order into the kitchen window, hand them a slip, pour drinks and grab utensils with placemats, and return to each table to check on their patrons. It was a full restaurant with families and children running between the tables while their parents did their best to corral them out of embarrassment. Everyone seemed to know each other while apologizing about each other's children.

A young woman entered the restaurant closely behind the Rubenstein's and hurriedly walked towards a door marked EMPLOYEES ONLY. She was wearing the same blue coveralls from the factory and was already unbuttoning as she pushed through the swinging door. Howard and Lorry took a booth in the far corner so as not to be directly in the center of the maelstrom. A child from across the room shrieked in torment as they had been apprehended by their presumed parent.

"Wow," said Howard, "just wow."

"You want to go somewhere else?"

"No, not a chance. This is a nightmare."

"You're so weird," said Lorry.

"I can't help it," said Howard, "I love a good nightmare."

A waitress rushed past their table and dropped off two menus without saying anything. She moved on to the next table with a full tray of drinks balanced perfectly on her flattened left hand. Her next table was a group of four young men who took it upon themselves to verbally harass the waitress while she delivered each of their drinks. The waitress had been smiling at the table, and even managed to squeeze in a joke at her own expense. She left the group with a stone face as she quickly moved on to her next table.

"Wow," said Howard.

The menu was filled with cartoonish names for traditional diner options. A Ruben was called "Hobo's Delight", spaghetti and meatballs were called "Track and Wheel", and a "traditional Cajun gumbo" was called the "Firebox". Lorry questioned the authenticity of traditional Cajun gumbo in Connecticut, but she dismissed the suspicion as irrelevant.

The same factory woman who entered Lou's Caboose after the Rubenstein's was now standing at their table wearing the powder blue waitress uniform. She looked a little frazzled but smiled all the same as she offered them coffee.

"Yes please," said Howard.

"Yes, thank you," said Lorry.

"Do you want the Oil Can or the Goodnight Irene?" she said, without looking up from her pad.

"The what now?" asked Lorry.

The waitress closed her eyes in embarrassment at her own job and said, "Decaf or regular?"

"Regular, please," said Lorry.

"Yeah, same," said Howard.

She was gone from the table, pad in hand, and stopped at three other tables before returning behind the counter and assembling four sets worth of drink orders. In the style of a perpetual motion device, she began a new loop that brought her back out from behind the bar and onto the floor, stopping at each of her tables to deliver their orders. When she returned to the Rubenstein's table, she materialized a pen from the mysterious bundle of hair on the back of her head and showed them the smile she had been rehearsing for years.

"Hi," she said, "are you all set to order, or do you need another minute?"

"Oh, maybe just another,"

She was gone before Howard could finish his sentence. They watched her smile float across the room with the determination of a prize fighter.

"Unskilled labor, amiright?" said Lorry.

"I couldn't do this," said Howard, "Hell, I tried. Couple of times."

"If I order the ravioli, will you bring it out for me?"

Howard blew a raspberry at Lorry and threw a sugar packet at her.

The Rubenstein's looked over the menu and tried to find two meals that required the least amount of effort from the staff. They both settled on pancakes, adequately titled the "Short Stack Smokestack" with eggs and bacon. The waitress had already returned by the time that they had made their decision. Howard and Lorry both said pancakes at the same time, and the waitress kept moving without stopping at the table.

"She's good," said Howard.

"She's incredible," said Lorry.

Above the activity that buzzed around the restaurant, an argument in French, presumably laden with profanities, burst out from the kitchen doors as two identical women of age and size continued to shout at each other while parading through the restaurant.

"Tu es stupide comme un vache!" said the one.

"Well at least I do not resemble une vache!" said the other.

"Oh, it is perfectly sensible to be insulted by une mésange stupide. Surtout quand le lait dans ses seins a tourné!"

This last remark must have been a doozy because the two French women began pounding on each other furiously in the middle of the restaurant. Children screamed as their parents scrambled to move them as far away from the fight as possible. Mothers covered their children's ears (although the language was French and without subtitles. They should have covered their eyes instead).

The men in the restaurant tried to interject in their own passive way, but none of them physically engaged in the scuffle. It was more performative where enough people could see their effort. They were not really trying at all. Howard had started to stand up and intervene in the fight, but Lorry grabbed his hand and shook her head at him. He hesitated for a moment before he sat in their booth and watched the fleet of waitresses jump on the two women to pull them apart from each other.

They were separated and held at a distance until they both began to calm down. Their own waitress was holding the arms of one of the women when the other one spoke.

"Super, maintenant nous allons aussi perdre ce travail!"

"Dès que ces salopes maigres me lâcheront, je vais te casser le nez!"

"I would love to see you try," said the woman, "I am going home. If you do decide to return, then you can expect me to be asleep by five-thirty. If you are to wake me for any reason, then I will cut off your ears and glue them to a donkey! However, I would not want to insult the donkey. We are going to lose this job just as we did at St. Philomena's. I have suffered from your antics for far too long."

The woman stormed out from the restaurant as the waitresses began to release the other. The woman who had been left behind stood stunned in the middle of the room as the sounds of frightened children and frustrated parents moved away from her. She sat down in a chair next to the Rubenstein's booth and leaned against their table as she shook with adrenaline and anger. Lorry looked at Howard with concern as he awkwardly patted the poor woman on her shoulder. It was meant to bring comfort but was unsuccessful.

"I do not know what to do," she said, "if we lose this job then we are truly abandoned. God will have abandoned us."

At that moment, another woman entered the restaurant floor from the door of a back office. She did not stop to assess the damage and she did not speak to anyone else in the dining area. The woman walked with a commanding presence towards the Rubenstein's table. She stopped and looked down, speaking in a low voice to the shaking woman sitting in the chair.

"Get the fuck out of my restaurant," she said, before turning around to go back into her office. The swinging kitchen door flapped with authority.

The French woman began to wail as she was escorted out of the building by two plaza cops. The waitresses each took to their sections and apologized to their customers as the accusations and complaints began to grow from each table. Many meals would be compensated for the disruption. Howard and Lorry's waitress came to the table to apologize but was met with understanding from the Rubenstein's.

"Who were they?" asked Lorry.

"Therese and Louise," said the waitress, "twin sisters. They've worked here since this place opened a few years ago. They used to work here back when it was a school, but damn if it isn't a shame. They been fighting a lot and got three warnings about it already. I hope they're gonna be ok."

"Excuse us," said Howard.

The Rubenstein's dropped some money on the table and left the restaurant to find the French woman in the parking lot. She was sitting against the trunk of her car and staring off at the factory while her lip quivered in self-pity. She blew her nose into a tissue as the Rubenstein's approached her.

"Excuse me," said Howard, "are you ok?"

The woman said nothing but waved them away while keeping her back to them.

"We don't mean to bother you," said Howard, "but could we ask you some questions about St. Philomena's?"

The woman began to cry louder now. If it was not from pure frustration, then it was a culmination of everything else that had happened to her over the past few years. She blew her nose again and turned to face the Rubenstein's.

"Leave me alone," she said, "I have already told you that I never knew what was going on at that school! Do you think I would have allowed all that to happen if I had known?! Oh, leave me alone, please!"

She struggled to fit her keys in the car door, but her hand was shaking so violently that they dropped onto the pavement. She left them lying on the ground and folded her arms on the top of her car. Howard backed away as he began to realize that he was only making the situation unnecessarily hostile. Lorry gently stood next to the woman and asked her for her name.

"Louise," she said, "Louise Souci. You are not from the newspaper?"

"No," said Lorry, "no, we're looking for someone. Our adopted daughter went to the school. She's...disappeared and we think that she may have gone to the house where she grew up. We were hoping to find out if the school had the address."

Louise scoffed at this.

"That school," she said, "my sister Therese and I, we worked at that school for twenty years. And for what? Pour quelle raison?! We loved those girls. All of them. They were like our own children..."

Louise began to gently weep and covered her mouth with the back of her hand. Lorry impulsively wrapped her arms around the large woman whom she embraced with genuine compassion. She looked at Howard who was staring at the ground with his arms crossed. She knew that he had always hated that school. Having never heard of any predatory repugnance on behalf of the students before, she could see his face changing three shades of red as he thought back to any times when he might have missed something having happened to Ruth or Mary.

"Did any of the information get archived," asked Lorry, "were there any digital records?"

"They destroyed all of the records after the trouble," she said, "it would be difficult to find any information of the kind."

"Would those records have been made available to the city hall or the town clerk?" asked Lorry.

"C'est possible," said Louise, "I would imagine that the school would have reported a list of their students to the town in case of an emergency, but the office would be closed until tomorrow."

"Do you remember a kid named Mary Kirkland, by any chance," asked Howard, "she was younger. Probably around ten or eleven years old at the time."

Louise paused at the name.

"Kirkland," she said, "Mary Kirkland?"

"Did you know her," asked Howard.

Louise's face shifted between elation and concern at the recollection of Mary and the thought that she might be in danger.

"Mon petit chou!" exclaimed Louise, "and her parents had died. Oh, and you kept her safe all these years. Bless you for that."

"Sorry, I'm Lorry. This is Howard. We had another daughter in the school so when we took her out, we took Mary with us."

"After all this time," said Louise, "oh, what is she like now? Is she pretty? Oh! Is she kind?"

"How did you know Mary?" asked Lorry.

"The headmistress of the school was a terrible woman," said Louise, "a monster. Mary had difficulty adapting to the school. She would get into trouble. The headmistress starved Mary and forced her to work with us in the kitchen. My sister and I did our best to help her, but she was such a dark child. She was beautiful when she was happy, but she had suffered so much that it had made her terribly sad. She would go to very dark places of the heart. It would always be a challenge to bring her back. I had hoped that she would have found some peace by now."

"Do you know where she lived before the school," asked Howard, "did she ever tell you where she came from?"

Louise thought about this. She knew there was a time when a promise had been made. In all her gathered sincerity, Louise had intended on keeping that promise when the time was right. In the sixteen years from when she had met Mary the thought of surprising her with cake in her home would often return to her memory. Sometimes, on very bad days, Louise would smile to herself and wonder whether Mary ever made it back to her ravine. She thought of young Mary in the woods with her frogs. Mary's house, in Louise's imagination, would be shaped in such an odd way. She was not sure why she had assigned Mary an unorthodox house, but it seemed to suit her. Louise saw a long driveway that cut through the woods and led to the house at...

"Six-two-six Apollinaire Road," said Louise, standing surprised with herself that she remembered, "in Amherst, I think. Yes. Six-two-six Apollinaire Road. I am sure of it."

"Really," asked Howard, "are you sure? How can you remember something like that?"

"Because I loved that little girl," said Louise, "she was like my own daughter, and I would have done anything for her. I cannot permit myself to forget love."

Lorry wrapped her arms around Louise and kissed her on the cheek.

"Thank you," she said, "how can we ever repay you for this?"

"If you find her...when you do find her, tell Mary that I am sorry," said Louise, "I am sorry to be so late, but I am on my way."

Howard and Lorry thanked Louise again and apologized about her losing her job.

"Oh, it is already a memory," said Louise, "and a bad one at that. Therese and I will find other work. We are not ready to die just yet."

More hugs and kisses were distributed with care as the Rubenstein's bid Louise farewell. The French woman wrote down Mary's home address on a slip of paper and the Rubenstein's returned to their van, eager to get back on the road. Louise pulled up alongside them in her small car and shouted from the window.

"Il n'y a rien de plus fort que le pouvoir de l'amour! Même la mort doit reconnaître sa force!"

"You got it," shouted Howard.

"What did she say?" asked Lorry.

"No idea. You want to grab those pancakes now?"

"Hell no," said Lorry, "let's get the hell out of here."

"You think the address she gave us is good?"

"It's a point in the right direction, anyway."

"Tallyho," said Howard.

Their van rolled on into the gray afternoon towards a destination without certainty. There was no guarantee of what they would find at the address Louise provided, but it was the best shot that they had regarding Mary's whereabouts. Howard drove away from the complex, happy to leave it behind and thankful that he could. Lorry started playing with Howard's hair as he drove, which he did not like too much but also did not mind. As night descended upon their journey, the headlights came on and the radio was turned up.

Slow ride.

Take it easy.

20. You Wanna Meet My Folks?

The law office of Albertson & Howe was freezing as the boiler had gone out the previous night and was in the process of being repaired. Mary, having successfully managed another shower without incident, and dressed in her most conservative clothes, entered the law firm with disappointment as the office was colder than it was outside.

She wore what she called her "interview clothes" as they were the most appropriate for job interviews, funerals, weddings, and any other occasion where you must look better than you feel. It was a simple black pullover sweater over a white button-down dress shirt. The shirt collar and sleeves were exposed at the neck and wrists to allow a contrast against the thin black fabric. This was accompanied by a black pair of chinos and black low-heeled pumps. The ensemble helped to accentuate her freshly styled short crop of bright yellow hair. The color was called "electric lemon".

Mary had needed a trim even before she had arrived in Amherst. Luckily Elizabeth had some shears in the bathroom which were utilized for a fresh undercut. Feeling better than she had in days, Mary sat in the office, tapping her fingers on her knees, and waiting to face her future. She kept her coat on, but she could still see her breath when she exhaled. The time was nine forty-five and Mary had been waiting for a little more than half an hour to be seen. There were a few other clients waiting, but none of them seemed to mind the cold. They were locals.

Despite their passive insistence that Mary stay longer, Elizabeth and Addison were genuinely keen on seeing Mary leave. They were pleased to have the self-gratification of using their hospitality to feel superior to Mary, but her tenacity had proven to be more overwhelming than they had anticipated. They pleaded with Mary to stay and hoped that she would refuse, to which Mary herself took a few minutes to torture them with indecisive consideration.

After she had her fun, she shook her head and thanked them for letting her stay for the night. This brought an end to the politics of their societal obligation, at least until there was a convenient opportunity for Mary to repay them for their kindness. Mary had no intention of ever allowing that to become a possibility. If a time did come when Elizabeth and Addison were in need, she could think of a few sadistic fantasies in which to show her gratitude. Mary played with these scenarios as she waited in the cold law office of Albertson & Howe.

A frail man in a stained sports jacket stood up from behind a desk and called out Mary's name. She calmly rose from her chair but was all too ready for the opportunity to finish the navigation of probate. Mary thought that the old man looked to be a prime candidate for authoritative bureaucracy and that meant the day would be long and arduous. She introduced herself and was escorted into a hallway that led to an attorney's office.

They walked past large portraits of lawyers long dead, all of them older, balding white men wearing glasses and ties. None of them were smiling, but it may have been more disconcerting if they were. The old man brought Mary to a dark wooden door where he knocked twice before opening. The thought of so many framed and smiling faces in a place of law carried an uncomfortable undertone that Mary could not shake. The serious expressions meant serious business and that could only exist without emotion. This was what Mary had wanted but done quickly.

They entered the room to find a simple desk and bookcase with two pairs of taxidermied birds on the wall. Two electric space heaters were running high beside the desk, and they did help raise the temperature slightly, but Mary decided not to remove her coat. Two men in gray suits and wool knit caps entered from a side door and took their seats at a desk on the opposite side of the room. They opened their suitcases and brought out a few folders and documents, laying them across the table. The taller of the two removed his mittens and reached out his hand to Mary to greet her politely. The other attorney wearing fingerless gloves began taking notes on a yellow legal pad of paper.

"Ms. Rubenstein," he said, "thank you for coming on such short notice. I'm sorry for your loss and I hope that this hasn't terribly inconvenienced you."

"Thank you," said Mary, "my aunt and I weren't that close, but thank you."

"Did you know your mother used to work here?" asked the attorney.

"No," said Mary, "no, um…I was not aware of that."

"She was great," he said, "wonderful woman. She definitely stood out. Now, we just have some paperwork to sign, and you'll be all finished here. I'm sure you'd like to go to the house and begin your assessments."

"Can I move into the house?" asked Mary.

"It's your house," said the lawyer, "you can do whatever you'd like with it."

He opened a briefcase and placed the last will and testament of Colleen Coggeshall on the table. The bundle of papers was smaller than Mary had expected, so she was already feeling more at ease. The less time she had to spend in the attorney's office, the better. Her knee was bouncing up and down while she sat and waited for them to begin.

"This won't be very complicated," said the attorney, "since you're named as the sole beneficiary, it does simplify the process. Now, do you have any questions before we begin?"

"No," said Mary.

"Alright. Feel free to stop me if anything feels unclear."

Mary nodded with understanding as the attorney continued to explain what she had inherited from her deceased aunt. The other attorney continued to scribble on his notepad, occasionally taking a moment to adjust his wool hat.

"Along with the house," said the attorney, "you will receive a portion of the surrounding land, equivalent to twelve acres with a property line that extends into the woodland. That will be staked off to designate where your property ends. You have the legal right and ownership to any and all physical items within the home, to be done with as you wish. You will receive an inheritance of thirty-five thousand, two-hundred fifty dollars and a nineteen eighty-six Chevrolet Celebrity. It still runs, as far as I know."

Mary nodded her head throughout the meeting, but only as a gesture to show that she understood what the attorney was saying and that they could move the process along. Her intentions were not measured by the assurance that there would be financial security in the inheritance. Mary recognized this meeting as a means to an end. One that could hopefully begin to explain the only mystery that has ever mattered in her life. Now with the boy's return, there was little else that Mary could focus on.

Where some would argue that the search for love or God would be the ultimate answer, neither of these mattered to Mary. She had sworn off both love and God for personal reasons and had become drawn into the world of the inexplicable. If there was a logical answer to Mary's episodes, then she would find it in the house. She hoped that she would, anyway.

The question of how many of Mary's memories had been real or fabricated was repeating on a loop in her mind. With the acquisition of her childhood home, there was a link that could hopefully create the necessary space to allow her to ask these questions in earnest. With any luck, she may find some peace with the answers.

The attorney involuntarily made a face when Mary produced her plastic bag filled with all her paperwork, but everything they required was present. After a few signatures and some copies of receipts in triplicate, Mary owned her family home. All parties in attendance shook hands and

Mary was halfway out the door when the attorney told her one more thing.

"If you'd like to pay your respects," he said, "your aunt is buried in the family plot beside your parents. They're in the little cemetery up the way past the library."

Mary stopped in the doorway and a nauseous sensation of dread began to coil deep within her stomach. There was a reflexive idea that she should say something like "thank you" or ask for more details, but instead she just cleared her throat and left. The two attorneys blew into their hands and cursed the maintenance man who was already two hours late.

There had been countless childhood nights that stretched into months where Mary had fantasized about visiting her parents' graves. In all the time she had spent forgetting what she could, there was a nearly instantaneous spring backwards to the fresh feeling of loss. Now that she had an opportunity to see them, really see them, she was unsure if she could.

Mary was a homeowner, a detective, an addict, and quite frightened. Walking away from the law office and towards the library made Mary feel like she was an orphan all over again. It would never matter what age she was; she would always feel like an orphan. Having been left on her own to face the perilous levels of her history, Mary felt more alone than she ever had before.

The stone path beside the library led down a small park beside a church. Families were enjoying an extended section of the Fisher Festival with a live band playing classic rock and roll and food trucks parked along the road. The smells of fried dough and cooked sausages were everywhere while a song by Creedence Clearwater Revival was declaring that a bad moon was indeed on the rise. Mary kept her eyes on the ground as she walked with her paperwork tucked beneath her arm. She passed the park and walked behind the walls of the church towards the modest presentation of a local cemetery.

It was a quiet place. Small whispers of grass and autumn leaves twitched on the ground as the wind carried light and low between the headstones. The band could still be heard playing off in the distance, but Mary's focus landed on the rows that stretched out before her. Some of the graves were very old and much of their markings had eroded over time. Moss and lichen crept around the sides and corners of the older headstones while those graves with newer markers each looked tame and manicured. Mary felt solemn as she walked slowly through the rows of people long since dead or recently passed. Her eyes were scanning the dead with hope, and fear, that she could find her parents' graves. The placements of each tombstone seemed to be in no clear arrangement, but it was not long before Mary found four graves along the back of the cemetery wall:

Colleen Coggeshall. Marcus Kirkland. Loretta Kirkland. Francis Jane Kirkland.

The music stopped and a small applause could be heard coming from around the front of the church. Mary sat on her knees and started to pull single blades of grass out of the ground, thinking of nothing. All the time spent; all the years collected where Mary had rehearsed speeches for this moment were gone. The scenarios where she would turn around and find both of her parents standing behind her, alive and well, had become disregarded as the fantasies of a sad and lost child.

Sitting in front of their graves brought no feelings of peace or satisfaction into Mary's heart. She could hear her father's voice again, reading to her in the evenings and talking about adventures on the river. She thought of his ineptitude with practical things. She could see her mother's face, framed in concentration, and distracted from play while working hard to maintain the stability of their family. She pressed her fingers on the spot where her grandmother's brass buttons had hurt her cheek all those years ago. Mary had not noticed that she was crying until she realized she had stopped breathing.

"Fuck you," said Mary, "fuck you. Fuck you. Fuck you! You fucking! Left! Me!"

Mary lay flat on the grass and buried her face in the dirt. She screamed into the ground as though her parents could hear her and sobbed deeply in the bitter reunion. There was no one else around to witness her breakdown, but even if there were an audience watching her spectacle, Mary would have remained unaware. Her rage became grief and regret in a matter of seconds.

"I'm sorry," she wept, "I'm sorry I wasn't better. I didn't want to go away..." Her breath caught heavy in her throat. It came out in bursts and short gasps. "Why did you make me go away?"

"Mary?"

A small voice from behind startled her back from her despair. Mary lifted her face from the ground and gripped the earth in her hands as her rage toward the boy had become monumental. She swore that if he was not already dead, then she would kill him. Mary turned her head expecting to see the little boy that had been haunting her entire life but instead saw the sad eyes of Joey Boulm staring back at her. He smiled weakly with his hands in his pockets and his shoulders slumped.

"Hi Mary," he said, "I am so sorry."

Mary said nothing as she leapt from the ground and wrapped her arms around Joey. She squeezed with all her might, and he winced as she pressed against the freshly dressed wound on his side. He bore the pain as best he could. The tears falling from her face became absorbed by Joey's jacket and she wiped her nose on his collar.

"You wanna meet my folks?" she said, half laughing through the tears.

Mary and Joey sat on the grass while Mary brought him up to speed on her dead family. She talked about some warm memories that she had not thought about in a long time while Joey quietly picked at the blades of grass that grew around the stones. After a few minutes, Mary got quiet and wiped more tears from her eyes. When Joey wrapped his arm around her and pulled her in, she let loose with the quiet sobbing of an exhausted individual.

"I know," said Joey, "I got you."

"Where did you go," asked Mary.

"I made it halfway back to New York but then I felt like an asshole. Hopped a different bus back and hitchhiked the rest of the way. I only got into town about ten minutes ago. Do you know how hard it is to change clean bandages in a Greyhound bathroom?"

"Thanks for coming back."

"I'm just happy I found you."

"Can we get some food," asked Mary, "I'd like to get some food."

"Whatever you want," said Joey, "as long as it's not a Greek Diner."

"What if Zoro, or whatever his name was, is working when we get there?"

"I'll kill you."

This got a laugh out of Mary and Joey felt good to have come back. The two friends left the cemetery arm in arm as Joey caught Mary up on his harrowing adventure from the road. She was thrilled that Joey had returned, and it made whatever came next feel more manageable. They passed an old man walking through the park, who turned and stopped as though he recognized a memory that he could not place. Once Mary and Joey had turned the corner of the little church, he rubbed his hand over his bald head and cursed as the band started playing Sweet Caroline.

Lucky Spumoni's had cleared out some by the time that Mary and Joey sat down at their table. The same bartender was flirting with two older women while doing his best Tom Cruise impersonation (you'd think he'd be doing Cocktail, but it was Jerry Maguire, of all things). Mary settled into the booth as though she had been to the restaurant countless times while Joey read through the menu in horror. The server was a tall freakazoid with a straw-hair-bowl-cut. He looked as though he were pushing fifty but shooting for twenty-five. He made an exaggerated entrance to their table and asked if he could get them anything to drink. Joey said he wanted one of everything.

"Excuse me?" asked the waiter.

"Never mind," said Joey, "just a Jack and coke, please."

"And for you, miss?" the waiter stood in anticipation as he swept the hair out of his eyes.

"Shirly Temple for me, please," said Mary, "extra cherries."

He left their table to get their drinks while Joey looked on through the menu with scorn.

"Why," he said, "why can't we go to a normal place? Why do you hate me, Mary?"

Mary punched Joey on the shoulder hard and asked him why he ran away.

"I know!" said Joey, "I'm sorry! I got scared! My naked life was in danger by a fucking owl, and not in the fun way. I promise not to leave, though. Never again. I'm with you till the end on this one."

"You better be!"

"Scout's honor."

Joey turned the menu over from side to side, hoping to make some sense of what it was he was reading. He was trying to manifest other options for people who understood how to enjoy good food. There was a hope that had faded from his heart when he found the picture of a bowl of spaghetti on the menu. In the time of a mouse's sneeze, Joey accepted defeat when he saw the green tomato sauce and the name of the dish. Regarding the sneezing mouse, Joey almost made the same sound.

"What the fuck is shamrock spaghetti?" he asked.

"I will give you one hundred dollars if you get it," said Mary.

"I hate you."

The waiter returned with their drink orders: a Shirly Temple for Mary, and a glass of coke for Joey with a shot of whiskey on the side. When the waiter asked if they were ready to order food, Joey just waved the waiter away without looking at him. Joey held each of his drinks in his hands and stared at Mary with his mouth open in disbelief.

"I fucking," said Joey, "hate you."

"Serves you right," said Mary.

"Yeah, maybe."

Joey took three big gulps through his soda straw before dumping the whiskey into his drink. Once the alcohol had landed in the glass, he finished the rest of it in three more gulps. Mary started laughing as she ate a bright red cherry off the end of a red plastic sword. She offered Joey a sip of her Shirley Temple, which he accepted with a smile.

It had been decided that neither of them would be ordering food from the restaurant, but they took their time at the table all the same. If the waiter came back to take their order, they would pretend to skim the menu and make small noises to themselves only to say that they were still thinking but would like another drink. After the third visit to their table, the waiter stopped coming around. Mary and Joey were on their fourth round of drinks, with Mary having already switched from Shirly Temples to vodka sodas, and were both beginning to feel a good buzz settling in.

"Was it weird," asked Joey, "seeing your parents, I mean."

"I really wasn't ready for that," said Mary, "I'd spent such a long time thinking about it, fantasizing about what it would be like. When I saw their graves, it didn't feel real. Not until it became very real. Too real."

"Was that the first time you were over there?"

"Yeah," said Mary, "nobody told me about the funeral when I was a kid. I didn't think there was anything left to bury."

"So," said Joey, "when you die,"

"*If* I die," said Mary.

"Excuse me. *If* you die, and there's no body to bury, what do you want in your coffin?"

"Hmm. I dunno. Probably my compass. What about you?"

"Ok. So. I've thought about this."

"I'll bet."

"Shut up. So, I want a copy of Giovanni's Room by James Baldwin, a half pint...no, full pint bottle of Dumb Rummy's bourbon, enough weed to sink a small boat, and a cheesesteak from Vernon's on 4th street."

"Shit," said Mary, "that sounds so good right now."

"Better than the shit they serve here," said Joey, "you ever read Giovanni's Room?"

"No, is it good?"

"Ugh, so good."

Mary and Joey continued to talk and drink while the haircut waiter became more and more frustrated. After their fifth round of drinks, Mary began to gently laugh to herself.

"What's so funny?" asked Joey.

What had started as a light chuckle had begun to evolve into a laughing fit. Mary's laughter was only escalating, and her face went bright pink with her words jumbling together. Trying to form a sentence was an effort in futility. She kept making an "owwwa" sound with her arms flapping weakly. Finally, she managed to say two words.

"An owl?!" she said, breaking into more hysterics.

"Oh, no," said Joey, "that's not funny. I am traumatized!"

"Whoooooo," said Mary, pretending to bite Joey's neck.

"That's it," he said, "I'm leaving."

"Nope," said Mary, "*we're* leaving."

The waiter returned to check on them, but Mary put four twenty-dollar bills on the table and ran out the door. Joey slid out from the vinyl booth and shook the waiter's hand, dramatically thanking him for everything as he chased after Mary. She was already in the car with the engine on when Joey walked out of the restaurant.

He jogged to the passenger side door and threw his backpack in the back seat while Mary asked him for some cocaine. Joey protested slightly in opening the drugs that they were supposed to sell, but alcohol, desire, and distress had them both looking for an escape from their feelings. Joey dipped his house key in a small bag of cocaine and they each took two bumps. Mary shook her head violently and slammed down on the horn as she screamed as hard as she could from sheer pleasure.

The noise accidentally scared an older couple who had been walking through the parking lot and carrying some balloons they had just bought from a vendor. They were not fast enough to catch the strings before the blue and white helium balloons drifted up into the sky. Mary and Joey had not seen this, but I wanted to share their tragedy as it would be unfair to let such a disaster go unnoticed. You're welcome.

"Joey," said Mary, "I take back almost all the bad things I've said about you."

"So," said Joey, rubbing his nose and sniffling, "what now? Find another motel with kangaroos, or something?"

"Nope," said Mary, holding up the deed, "you're coming to look at my haunted-ass house."

The reunited friends drove Loose Lips down the back roads of Amherst which would lead to Mary's childhood home. Mary was behind the wheel and cruising at a steady seventy-five miles an hour down the winding tar roads that cut through the thickening woods. Her heart was in her throat as the combination of drugs and scenery began to take on a more familiar shape. She tried not to grind her teeth, but her jaw was feeling stiff as she bounced the tip of her tongue against her top row of molars.

"How old were you when you left?" asked Joey.

"Eleven, I think," said Mary.

"And you haven't been back since?"

"Nope."

"Are you ok?"

"Well, I have the theme song to Reading Rainbow stuck in my head and it's making me incredibly depressed, so no. Probably not ok."

Mary shook her head while she looked out the window; scanning the forest for monsters who might be chasing after the car. After fifteen minutes of back roads, they pulled up to the driveway that led to Mary's inheritance. It was a mile from the main road to the house, but Mary stopped the car halfway. She got out without saying anything to Joey and walked up to a set of trees that were a few yards from the road.

Mary knelt in the ground and dug her fingers into the dirt, pulling out large clumps and rubbing them between her hands. She closed her eyes and held her hands up to her face, breathing deeply in the comfort of an old familiar smell. Her body felt so much then.

"What are you doing?" yelled Joey from the car.

"Nothing," said Mary, "just trying to remember something."

She rose from the ground and wiped the dirt from her knees, turning back to the car. Joey was in the passenger's seat fixing himself another bump of cocaine, but the young boy was also staring at her from the back seat. Mary refused to acknowledge the boy but got behind the wheel and took another bump from Joey. She looked in the rearview mirror to see the small neutral face she had known all her life.

"Are you feeling ok," asked the boy, "are you sure you're ready for this?"

"Shut up, pipsqueak," said Mary.

"What'd I say?" asked Joey.

"I wasn't talking to you," said Mary.

"Ok," said Joey, "just let me know if you're gonna...do something."

The driveway led through an opening in the tree line that surrounded a large piece of land with an unusual house in the middle of the clearing. Her childhood home carried with it the air of a devious challenge, daring those foolish enough to come inside. Mary's mouth had gone dry as the car came to a stop. She cleared her throat as she cut the engine.

"Is it weird to be back?" asked the boy.

"Feels like I never left," said Mary.

"Is it weird to be back?" asked Joey.

"Weirder by the minute," said Mary.

They left the car and Mary started walking around the house. Memories flooded her, and she heard the familiar voices from distant snapshot moments. She thought of old parties and birthdays, holidays, and snow. There was a long line of bird's nests that had fallen from the roof and lay in a row along the side of the house. Some birds had resigned themselves to their fate of ground dwelling while others had clearly fled from the disappointment. The lawn was overgrown and unkept with many spiders climbing between the blades of grass. A few cardinals chirped and flitted from tree to tree.

She turned to Joey with a blank expression in her eyes. The resonance from Mary's return, which at one point in time had been waiting in anticipation of reaction, stood out front and center. Mary's survival was now pinned on the overwhelming acceptance of her surroundings as a place that simply existed. Her emotional attachment to memory was already beginning to cloud her judgment. The cocaine was not helping much, either.

"I never thought I'd come back," she said, "it's exactly the same, but it looks smaller."

"So, apart from ghouls, do we have to worry about bears or hillbillies or something?" asked Joey.

"I don't think we have to worry about them," said Mary, "they're the next street over."

"Heh. Well, I'm still gonna worry. I've seen this movie before, and the best friend doesn't do so hot. I'll never feel safe around owls again. No, I'd have better luck in L.A., and that's saying something."

"Joey," said Mary, "thanks for coming back."

Joey lightly punched Mary in the shoulder and pulled her in tightly, kissing her forehead. She fished out the key to the front door and they entered Mary's childhood home.

The entrance led them towards the moments that Mary had experienced in her youth. She immediately recognized the smell of the house and knew where everything used to be. The row of coat hooks at the door looked the same and there was the chart of her developing height penciled onto one of the door frames. The last line read Mary - Age 10.

Mary became confused and annoyed as they continued into the house and found most of what she had known in the kitchen had been rearranged by her aunt. Parts of the house had fallen into disrepair by the neglect of Aunt Colleen, but a few rooms were kept clean and manicured with new furnishings. There were some hiding places that Mary knew were left untouched, but some of the house's initial design had been adjusted to her aunt's personal taste.

What had once been a kitchen of white linoleum and beige countertops had been converted to a flat avocado and mustard color palette; with the kitsch rounded appliances that sported the vintage look of the nineteen fifties. The Kit-Cat clock and picture of Betty Boop on a motorcycle tied it all together. Looking up showed that a sizable stain from water damage had disintegrated a portion of the ceiling. Gray water from plaster and mold was dripping from a broken pipe down onto the rim of the kitchen sink. Mary ran her hand over the edge of the sink and disappeared in thought.

....

"Where'd you go just now?" asked Joey.

"What do you mean?" asked Mary.

"You were saying something I didn't understand and then you kept apologizing."

"I didn't say anything."

"You've been standing there talking to yourself with the faucet running for at least a minute. I tried to snap you out of it, but you just kept going. I thought you might be having another seizure."

Mary had not noticed that the faucet was running, but she quickly turned it off and walked into the next room.

The open space that would have led into the living room had been replaced by a new wall painted black with a red door in the middle. The framework around the door was ornately carved wood with paisley swirls, roses, and golden faces expressing different emotions. The decoration traveled the entire length of the doorframe with the theater masks of comedy and tragedy above it.

"What the fuck is this?" asked Mary, "this is too weird."

"I take it this wasn't here before?" asked Joey.

"No, this was the living room. What the fuck..."

The door was locked, but none of the keys seemed to fit. Mary would have to go back to the attorney's office and see if there was a key that had been missing from the lot. Joey lit up a joint and handed it to Mary who felt guilty smoking pot in what she still considered to be her parent's house, but this anxiety was quelled as she remembered that it would upset Aunt Colleen to no end. Mary inhaled deeply and released a long plume of smoke that lingered in the hallway. Joey stood at the foot of the stairs leading up to the second floor and looked towards the unknown.

"What's up there?" he asked.

"Everything else," said Mary, "My room. My folks room. The tower."

"You want me to come with you?"

"Yes, please."

"Do I have to come with you?"

"Yes, please."

Mary and Joey approached the stairs carefully and with great hesitation. The emptiness of the house was beginning to wear down on Mary's nerves while Joey had already been a ball of anxiety. The drugs were making them both especially paranoid, but their apprehensions would have remained even under the influence of sobriety. There had been a revelation growing between them that there were no rules anymore, and anything that could happen would happen. With their imaginations approaching the darkest scenarios, they climbed the stairs on a hair's breadth of confidence.

The sudden return to her childhood home had Mary reeling between feelings of sentimentality and fear. There was love retained within these walls, but she could not help feeling that they were being watched. Joey held on to Mary's hand, but it was just as much for his own benefit.

They first entered Mary's room, or what had once been Mary's room. She flicked the light switch on the wall, but nothing happened. It became clear that Mary's aunt had converted her childhood bedroom into an exercise room and office. There was a treadmill and stationary bicycle that had both collected a fair amount of dust from the years of neglect.

They had been tucked away in one corner of the room as well as a table with an older desktop computer and several piles of papers in different folders marked IMPORTANT. A poster of a frazzled cartoon woman yelling "Acck!" on a treadmill chasing a piece of chocolate cake hung on the wall.

There were photographs that had been framed, some mounted on the walls while others sat on a desk, with pictures of Aunt Colleen in different vacation destinations like Greece and Jamaica. Bleached white domes against blue ocean waters stood behind Aunt Colleen in her sunhat and tropical swimsuit, her arms around a bronzed young man with dark curly hair. He looked politely bored. Another photograph showed Aunt Colleen dancing wildly to a steel drum band with all the musicians looking at each other in confusion. You could almost hear them saying, "Is this lady for real?" Mary closed the door without entering and turned towards the room where her grandmother had slept.

The door to her grandmother's room was heavy and it took both Mary and Joey pushing with their shoulders to open it. A piece of the ceiling had fallen in front of the door, making it difficult to create enough space for them to enter. The debris dragged and scraped across the floor as their efforts slowly made progress. After a few hard shoves, the door opened enough for Joey and Mary to squeeze into the room. Mary tried the light switch on the wall, but again, nothing happened.

She found the room to be relatively unchanged, apart from the natural erosion of neglect. The bed she had known was the same, right down to the flat mattress that had long lost its bounce. The closets had a fair amount of her grandmother's clothes left behind and it was clear that the room had not been cleaned out after her death. Joey picked up a small container of body powder from the top of a short dresser and opened it, allowing the fragrance to fill the air. It was a scent that Mary had not experienced in over a decade but became instantly recognizable. She coughed into her hand to suppress the dust that was thick enough to wear.

"What's in that little room?" asked Joey.

"What little room?" asked Mary.

Joey pointed to a small door that was built into the wall. It was no bigger than three feet high. There was no doorknob, but instead there were three small latches with padlocks.

"That's weird," said Mary, "I don't think I've ever seen this before?"

Joey pushed on the door without success. The latches were secured, and the locks were strong.

"Do you have the keys?" he asked.

Mary dug through her bag and retrieved the keys that had been individually labeled for the house. None of them had been fitted for the padlocks and there was no sign as to where they might be.

"I think some keys are missing," said Mary, "I'll check with the lawyers and see what they say." Mary counted down the number of locks with her fingertip. There were only three, but she was having a hard time counting. Her focus was beginning to slip. "So, we need these, and one for that weird middle door downstairs."

"Do you think this is where the ghost boy lives?" asked Joey.

"That's not funny," said Mary.

"I mean..."

Mary looked at the door and lifted her finger to her mouth. Joey gently pressed her arm back down to her side and asked her if she wanted to kick the door open.

"Listen, the last thing we need is racoons and skunks getting in here."

"You're telling me you're not the least bit curious?"

"I'll get in there eventually," said Mary, "it's probably nothing. I mean, it doesn't smell like someone died in here. Hundred bucks says it's just photo albums and a bowling ball, or something."

Joey wiggled his fingers towards Mary in a haunted gesture while she shot him a look of annoyance. He simply shrugged and pulled out a drawer from a nearby dresser, gasping in sudden alarm.

"What is it?" asked Mary.

"Turbans," said Joey, "these turbans are fantastic! Can I have some?"

He held out a small collection of terry cloth turbans that her grandmother would sometimes wear around the house. Even with her gruff exterior, she would balance out her femininity with small accessories from time to time. Mary waved Joey on with permission, and he began to select his favorites from the drawer.

"Help me lift this up," said Mary.

They each took a side of the fallen ceiling. It began to crumble in their grip and after they managed to move the broken part of the ceiling away, they found a dead bird lying on the ground beneath the waterlogged debris. From the looks of it, the bird had been dead for a long time.

"Oh dear," said Joey, wearing a jade terry cloth turban, "that's not a great sign."

"It's fine," said Mary, "everything's fine. Just a normal everyday thing. This is just what happens to curious chickadees."

Joey contemplated geometry and physics for how the bird could have gotten into the room, but he became bored and continued to look around. Marry gently kicked the little bird with her foot and swept it under the bed.

"I really want to get in there," said Joey, looking at the little door, "old people have such weird stuff."

"I think it's full of junk," said Mary, "my grandmother was a sick woman. She was sick for a while, I guess. Maybe she, like, thought she was hiding treasure or something."

A sudden memory rang through Mary's mind and her mouth dropped in shock.

"Waaaaaaait a minute," she said, "Wait a minute! I have seen this before!"

Mary laughed maniacally while Joey waited for an explanation.

"I remember now," she said, "when I was little, I tried to get in there once to play submarine. My grandmother found me and beat the shit out of me!"

"She hit you?" asked Joey.

"I mean, it wasn't a big deal or anything. She used to hit all of us."

"That's kind of a big deal, Mary."

"Naw, it's fine. I probably had it coming. Man, I can't remember the last time I'd thought of that."

"Well," said Joey, "I could see why you'd forget."

Joey removed his turban and dropped it on the bed. They both stood in front of the little door, staring at it and expecting something to happen.

"What if it's like...noses and skulls or the bones of dead children or something?" said Joey.

"So not the bones of living children?"

"Ugh, I'm not sure which is worse."

"It could be anything," said Mary, "I'm gonna call those lawyers before their office closes. From what I've been told they like to keep regular business hours."

Mary called the offices of Albertson and Howe and spoke to the receptionist she had met the day she had arrived. Mary asked to speak to someone about the keys and was then transferred to three different offices before she spoke to someone that would be able to help her. The voice on the other end of the phone sounded young, but under the pressures of occupational performance. He said he would make an inquiry about the missing keys and that he could drop off any extra copies that they find. Mary thanked him for his punctuality, and he said that he could be at the house within an hour's time.

"He's gonna look into it," said Mary.

They left her grandmother's room and returned to the hall that extended the length of the second-floor landing. Mary stopped to look at the door to her parents' room but made no effort to approach it. After she stood still for a few moments, she turned to the stairs and descended back to the first floor with Joey close behind.

"What's up that way?" asked Joey, pointing to a door at the other end of the second-floor landing.

"That's the tower," said Mary, "I don't want to go up there yet."

Joey made no attempt to push Mary further on the subject, but instead returned to the general nature of things.

"How long are we going to be here?" asked Joey.

"I don't know," said Mary, "couple of days, I think. I have to figure some shit out."

"Well, if that is the case then we need to make a run for supplies. Can we go back into town and hit some shops?"

"Yeah. I want to see something first. Real quick."

Mary left the house and started walking through the backyard. Her legs were moving with casual momentum while her heart was beating out from her chest. The tree line and woods were still in the afternoon chill that had landed in the clearing. It was likely to bring an early morning frost tomorrow, the first frost of the year, which would then slowly melt in the rays of the sun and leave the grass slick and wet for the rest of the day. The beginning of boot and sweater weather.

Mary walked towards the flowering dogwood tree that she had dreamt of for so long and she laid her hand upon a spot where she had ripped off a branch all those years ago. A smaller branch had begun to grow in its place. Had it been spring, then blossoms would have begun to appear. Mary caressed the small branch between her fingers and kissed it before continuing into the woods. With the sacred understanding of countless millennia, the forest embraced her once again.

"I'll be by the car," yelled Joey, "good luck with the devil, or whatever! Tell him I said hi!"

Mary did not hear him as she continued to her ravine. She knew the path and could have walked it blindfolded, but she now saw it with an older pair of eyes. The world grew sharp around her in the dense shadow season of autumn. A sensation began to register within her chest that she was not expecting, but it felt warm. There was a small furnace burning within her and she had a growing impulse to sprint into the woods, never to return. Mary felt feral and impulsive until she came to the crest of an incline.

Her mind was blank as she approached the ravine that she had sought out so often as a sanctuary. The water was moving and running downstream as it should in the split between two points of a hill. The ground was hard in spots, undoubtedly altered by the coming winter and the lack of attention from travelers. Even the frogs were beginning to hibernate. Mary sat down on a familiar rock for a moment when the voice of the little boy came from beside her.

"Are you still afraid?" he asked.

"No," said Mary, "well, a little, yeah. I'm mostly just…sad."

"That's ok," said the boy, "I used to get sad too. I miss it sometimes, but not as often as I'd like."

The pair sat together as the wind was picking up and the bare swaying branches were creaking in their own conversations. Mary had the flicker of a memory and stuck her fingers in the cold water, letting it run through and around the V they made. The sound of a whip-poor-will floated through the air.

There was so much that had remained unchanged, just as it had been long before Mary had been born. Mary had changed, certainly in most respects, but there was something reawakening inside her that had been asleep for a very long time. The feeling made her want to fly. It was warm and not entirely unpleasant, but its presence reignited a certain sorrow that Mary had known to exist all her life. The thought of drugs passed through her mind and how badly she wanted more. She decided to walk back to the car and ask Joey for another dip into the supply.

Mary heard voices growing as she approached the house. They sounded casual and kept the tone of a small-talk conversation in that way where you do not know how to engage with someone personally, but you feel as though you need to say something. They were talking about birds when Mary broke through the tree line and walked through her backyard.

Joey was talking to someone in the driveway wearing a light gray suit with an accordion folder tucked under his arm. This must have been the person she had spoken to over the phone regarding the missing keys, but as she approached the two men she began to feel as though she recognized him. It was not until she saw his face that she felt certain that they had met before. When Mary came closer to where they were standing, the man in the suit shook his head and began to laugh.

"Uh, hi," he said, "nice to see you again."

"Have we met?" asked Mary.

"New York," he said, "you found me in the bathtub. I was a dick. You were a dick. Remember? Good times."

Mary's stomach dropped and she felt her face flush. It was the young man she had seen at the party. She had had so many questions that day which were left unanswered, but they had escaped her. She extended her hand in an infantile gesture for peace.

"Hi," she said.

He introduced himself as James Burgess; a name to which Mary had no immediate connection. He shook her hand gently and said his intentions were not to make things uncomfortable. He genuinely thought it was a funny coincidence, but Mary felt embarrassed all the same. James held up a small plastic bag that had been previously sealed with a special adhesive tape.

"Sorry for the mix-up," he said, "these should be the rest of the keys."

Mary looked through the bag but could not find any keys small enough to fit the padlocks that she had found in her grandmother's room. There were keys of different shapes and sizes, but none were the same.

"Are these all of them?" she asked.

"Should be," said James, "this was everything we had on file."

"Thanks."

Joey cleared his throat and interjected in the growing silence.

"I'm gonna go...take a shit," he said, "but you two have a good time catching up."

He left Mary and James to themselves and entered the house. The two stood awkwardly as the evening brought a chill.

"Would you like to come inside?" asked Mary.

"Thanks," said James, "not for too long, but yeah."

Mary and James went inside and walked into the kitchen to make some coffee. She found just enough left in the back of a cupboard to make a small pot and reminded herself to buy more when they went into town. There was no sugar or milk, but James said that he did not mind. The two stood in an awkward silence before Mary decided to initiate small talk.

"What were you doing in New York?" asked Mary.

"My girlfriend...ex-girlfriend, had a friend there," said James, "We were party hopping when we hit that place, but I must have been way gone by then. I honestly don't remember too much. Did you used to live here?"

"Long time ago," said Mary, "My great-grandfather built the house. I lived here with my parents, but they died when I was young, so I was adopted by a family in New York. My aunt just died, so I got the house. Now I just have to figure out what to do with it."

"We had met once before." said James, "before New York, I mean. Although you may not remember it. I didn't notice until I saw your name here. Didn't know who you were in New York."

"Really," said Mary, "when was that?"

"Must have been fifth grade, I think," said James, "Remember the Mummy's Tomb? You threatened to hit me with a stick."

"I really don't remember that," said Mary, "I remember the Mummy's Tomb, but that...ohhhhh. Right. Yes. Sorry."

"Well, I don't hold a grudge. And I don't mean to dig up the past too much...you get it? Mummy? Dig up the...never mind. Forget it."

"Sorry," said Mary, "my memory isn't great."

"Don't worry about it," said James, "what's a little childhood trauma between friends."

A more awkward silence filled the room as Mary and James had run out of things to say. Mary became quiet as she did not want to explain her mysteries to James. She regretted asking him inside, but she felt it was the right thing to do. Now she wanted nothing more than for him to leave so she can take more drugs. Her fingers fidgeted on the countertop with arrhythmic patterns. James was looking through the cupboards in search of a coffee mug but stopped himself as he became self-conscious in his possibly feeling too comfortable in someone else's home.

"I'm sorry," he said, "where are your mugs?"

"Oh, I don't know," said Mary, "I don't know where anything is anymore."

James continued his search until he found a collection of dusty novelty mugs from different places in the world. He found a mug with a pair of roosters on it wearing sombreros and firing pistols in the air. The word "Cancun" ran down the handle in a yellow and brown lasso script. He rinsed it out and set it aside.

"So how long have you lived around here?" asked Mary.

"Most of my life, yeah," said James, "we moved here when I was around ten or eleven with my folks and my brother, around the time we met. Moved to Minnesota for college but came back here three years ago."

"Your folks still around here?"

"My folks are, but we don't have the best relationship. My brother died and it kind of broke up the family. Messed us all up. Probably one of the reasons why I headed that far out for school. They've been sick, so I moved back to help take care of them."

"I'm sorry."

"It's cool. We've been getting along better. Still bad sometimes, but better."

"I know the feeling," said Mary.

She said that she did, but she did not. Not really.

Any sort of strain put upon the relationship between Mary and the Rubenstein's was built from her strong need to remain distant from her family. Despite their kindness, she had often felt like an uncomfortable guest and a burden in their home. This was not true, but searching for reason in the unreasonable was an impossible task that led to complicated feelings. What should have been received as supportive love was misinterpreted as a personal affront to her vulnerabilities. In a lasting battle for self-preservation, Mary did her best to keep her walls up and strong. She understood the following results to be the natural course of things.

"I really should go," said James, "I have to get back to the firm."

"'The firm'", said Mary, "sounds so official."

"Firm, office, whatever. Anyway, if there's anything else you need, please let us know."

"Thanks," said Mary, "sorry again about…you know."

"Don't worry about it," said James, "good luck with everything."

Mary saw James out and watched him leave down the driveway back to the road leading to town. Joey returned to the kitchen and started to pour the coffee into the Cancun mug.

"So *James*, huh?" asked Joey.

"Shut up," said Mary.

"What? I didn't say anything."

"Mind your business."

"'Oh James'", teased Joey, "'I'm so sorry! Please forgive me! Ohhhh nooooo! Don't you dare...*punish* me!'"

"You're such a dick," said Mary, "he's not even that cute."

"Then how come you're biting your finger?"

Mary quickly pulled her hand down and wiped it on her pants.

"Didn't you say you wanted to go into town?" said Mary.

"I do, I do," said Joey, "but first I think we should go through these."

He dumped a series of pill bottles on the table.

"Seems as though Aunt Colleen was heavily medicated."

"Huh," said Mary, "I suppose the responsible thing would be to drop these off at a pharmacy."

"Or..."

"Or..."

Several tinted containers of different sizes were lined up alphabetically by label. The width and height for each bottle resembled soundwaves moving on a frequency that would pass undetected to ordinary people. To Mary and Joey however, there was a secret song and rhythm to each capsule.

These would make you hyper, while these would make you sleep. If you mix these ones here with alcohol, then you may forget how to breathe. These ones were fine if you needed them, but if you did not require the prescription for health reasons then they would keep you up for three days while you thought about collecting other people's hair. There were even some prescriptions that neither of them had ever heard of. There was a cornucopia of potential outcomes. Even with the combined knowledge of Joey Boulm and Mary Rubenstein, the possibilities were endless.

Having become lost in their curiosities, the pair of psychotropic explorers opted for a "light touch" instead of diving full steam ahead. Mary took two Parichlocal Xirmatide while Joey helped himself to a single dose of Purfomoxolytenal. These were considered safe to mix with alcohol in low doses so two novelty mugs were found, rinsed, and used to drink the whiskey that Mary had brought along with her. It was a bottle that started out full, as most bottles do, but it had not taken long to have a large amount of liquor become consumed over the past few days. Still, there was plenty left for a good time.

Feeling a little loose and foolish, Mary and Joey took a more curious approach to the other drugs that had been left behind by poor old dead Aunt Colleen. After an hour of chemical alchemy and whiskey filter, Joey suggested they try some of the new keys on the locked doors that they had found.

"Where's the bag," asked Joey, as he refilled his mug.

"I don't know," said Mary, dreamily "maybe it's up there somewhere."

Mary lay on the ground, scanning the ceiling and tracing the air with her fingers. The trails left behind from the sides of her hands seemed to glow in refracted light from a temple of mystery. Soon Mary forgot all about the bag of new keys.

Joey thought Mary to be lost as he looked around the room for a new fascination. His initial anxieties about the house were beginning to lose their edge as the liquor and drugs became engaged with his faculties. Joey was walking through the hallway when he dragged his foot across the bag of spare keys that were lying on the floor in plain sight. The plastic bag had torn along the bottom and a few keys spread out across the hardwood floors. Joey had a passing thought about how nice the hardwood floors were, but when he knelt to pick up the keys, he lost his balance and fell onto his side against the wall. A framed picture of Aunt Colleen hugging a scared looking Alice Cooper fell from the wall and struck Joey in the head; leaving the lingering taste of heat and shock that comes with a sharp and fresh pain. He rubbed the spot on his head where the frame had struck him and thought about his father.

The key in Joey's hand was short, no longer than the first knuckle on his right ring finger. There were only two teeth pointed down and the rounded handle had a faux ruby on either side. Looking around the hallway for a potential clue as to what this key would open, his eye landed upon the large red door centered on the black wall leading into the living room. The key turned the lock with a click, and a creak of the door. That was all it took to allow Joey access to one of the undiscovered portions of a once familiar home.

"Mary!" he shouted, "Mary, get over here!"

Mary came out of her fuzz with the shock that provides a brief sobriety in times of alarm. She rolled off the floor and stumbled on all fours towards the voice of Joey Boulm. He was standing on the other side of the door in front of a large area that had once been Mary's family living room.

The space had been redecorated by Aunt Colleen into a BDSM dungeon. Mary and Joey stood in the doorway looking down a short set of steps that lay beneath a plush red carpet stretching from wall to wall. The room itself had been rounded out on either side while keeping flat walls connecting the two crescent ends, making a strange oval shape. The flat walls each had a collection of toys, devices, costumes, and gear that would guarantee to satiate any carnal appetite, depending on one's tastes. The center of the room held a massive, padded X with straps for the wrists, ankles, arms, and legs. Next to it was a short box with a lid and a circular hole cut out of the top. Even at their most sober, Mary and Joey would have reacted much in the same way.

The two friends squealed with joy as they took an inventory of every piece of debauchery that could be found in the room. There was a small war of flying dildos that they launched at each other like mortars, and they took turns going through costume changes and seeing what potential, if any, there was to be having an orgy in the future. After a brief paddle fight, the two collapsed on the soft carpet steps trying to catch their breath. Joey had changed into a wrestling singlet while Mary wore a leather mask with zippers on the eyes and mouth.

"Yo, Aunt Colleen was a freak," said Joey, "this shit is wild."
"This is fucked up," said Mary, "God, I almost hate this."
"Please don't change a thing in this room."
"I could sell tickets."
"Oh my god," said Joey, "are you gonna be a dominatrix now?"
"Why, baby? You lookin' for a good time?"

The two friends laughed and left the room unlocked. They were uncertain of its capacity in their lives but curious about its potential. Mary and Joey returned to the kitchen where she poured out more whiskey while Joey took two capsules of Bupolazedene. He dry-swallowed the pills and shook his head from side to side until he became dizzy and fell over. This made Mary nervous until Joey began to laugh from the floor and held his hand out for more whiskey.

21. CASH ONLY

Winsted, Connecticut, can be a very lush and green place, but some parts are also very dusty, dry, and brown. It is both a lush and dusty place with median property values and low expectations. Stay on the road long enough and you will mostly see older car models from the eighties and nineties. They keep things in motion while the city itself remains floating in time. A fair number of residents have lost or are in the process of losing their driver's licenses due to an inordinate number of citations for driving under the influence. The influence of what? That depends on what you have.

Many of the locals have been known to walk on the shoulder of the roads because the sidewalks that do exist lead into bushes or ditches. Some sidewalks just stop altogether. There are twelve different churches of varying sects of Christianity as well as a Kingdom Hall of Jehovah's Witnesses and a synagogue, although you would be hard pressed to find a large community there that keep the Jewish faith.

There are nine pizzerias, twenty bars, eight antique/thrift stores, a community college, and a variety of old factory buildings that have been left unutilized and in disrepair for well over fifty years. The best usage of these buildings has become places to practice graffiti art, skateboarding, and the American pastime of underage drinking. There's also a Dairy Queen.

As of the twenty-ten census, the population of Winsted was seven-thousand, seven-hundred twelve persons. The town was founded in seventeen-fifty at the junction where the Mad River and the Still River meet. The Mad River had been named as such because it is known to flow in the opposite direction than most rivers would. Since before the seventeen-hundreds, the Still River had been considered a dead river due to the local Danbury farm community utilizing the area as a dumping ground for waste and toxic debris. There was no opportunity for real ecology or life to exist throughout the seventeen-hundreds, or even after.

In the eighteen-sixties, the textile and hatting industries were inadvertently poisoning the river with the addition of mercury nitrate. The mercury was a residual trace from a chemical used to remove animal fur from pelts in the process of making felt. The runoff from these factories, and the history of pollution from the farming communities that existed upstream, had left the Still River uninhabitable. This was the way until a court ruling in the year eighteen ninety-five mandated Danbury to take responsibility for the state of the river. There were minimal efforts made by the city until the year nineteen seventy-two when the Clean Water Act was passed, and the federal government became involved.

In the nineteen-fifties a flood ripped Winsted in half. One side of the main street was cut down and split, leaving a long ditch that ran like a scar through a large part of the town. Having many jobs and homes lost, and many factories destroyed, the people of Winsted still blame the flood for their troubles to this very day. Howard and Lorry managed to split the rear axle of their van half a mile from the town.

The Rubenstein's had been traveling north on route eight through Connecticut on their way to Amherst, Massachusetts, when there was a pop/bing/clang/crunch sound beneath their van. All those sounds happened to occur simultaneously so you could imagine their surprise when it came without warning, but these things seldom arrive with a countdown. They were at the tail end of the highway which would cut through Winsted and lead up into Massachusetts when the axle split, forcing Howard to muscle the steering wheel just to get the van onto the shoulder of the road.

The wind had been picking up from over the hills which surrounded the area and rushed down the slopes into the valley where Howard and Lorry had landed. It was becoming a bitter cold where the sky is so blue that it hurts your eyes. Without the insulation of snow to absorb the drop in temperature, Howard and Lorry remained in the car with the heat going and the radio on while they waited for a tow-truck. Forty minutes later, the flashing yellow lights came rolling right along.

It was a tight fit in the front cab once the driver got the van on the hook, but it was a short trip to the garage where the repairs could be made. Lorry and Howard took some extra layers from their suitcases and stepped into the garage office. It smelt like rubber and diesel, which are not entirely unpleasant smells.

Three men were milling about in plainclothes, simple jeans and thermals beneath t-shirts. An old coffee can that was half filled with sand and a quarter full of cigarette butts propped the back door open. The mechanics were friendly and accommodating, if not a little scruffy, but Howard and Lorry could tell that they were good people. They liked them very much. The manager was a skinny middle-aged man with a bristly mustache and a New York Yankees baseball cap. He had been going over the van a few times for half an hour and had returned to the office to give the Rubenstein's an assessment.

"Now I don't have to tell you that your axle is gone," he said, "there's no saving that. Gonna have to replace it. But there's another issue with your battery and the cooling system. Now the battery I can swap out now, no problem, but the clamps and hoses are shot, and I don't have the parts here for your make and model. There's an auto store in the next town over that may have them, but we're closing in twenty minutes. I'd say go pick up the parts and come back tomorrow and we can get that goin'."

"How long would it take to get a new axle?" asked Lorry.

"At least three days," said the mechanic, "but it's Friday so it might be longer."

"Is there a motel or something we can stay at?" asked Howard.

"There're a couple of places, yeah," said the mechanic, "kinda tricky to get to without a car."

"Can we get a taxi or a car service?" asked Howard.

The mechanic chuckled at this.

"Not gonna find a taxi 'round here. Nobody really drives for a service, either. Lemme make a call, I might be able to set somethin' up."

"Thanks," said Howard, "hey, let's go Mets, right?"

Howard extended his closed fist for a comradery bump from the mechanic, but it was only met with a raised eyebrow and a small reciprocating tap.

"Right," said the mechanic, "sure."

Howard gave the mechanic his number and thanked him for his help. With nothing more to be done but to sit and wait for parts and repairs, Howard and Lorry left the shop and decided to find something to eat.

They were walking down a hill lined with old colonial houses that had been converted into sectional units for different families to share. A colorful banner attached to the side of what had once been a clock factory was advertising studio apartments. The building's brick facade promised a rustic industrial atmosphere and cozy river views. Scattered sidewalks broke off and re-emerged as though they were dipping underground and resurfacing through the patches of grass and brown dirt that lined either side of the street. Howard and Lorry opted to walk on the shoulder of the road as the streets were not busy, and it seemed wide enough to be safe. They walked down the hill until it brought them to the main drag that held most of the commercial businesses.

The right-hand side of the street was lined with three-and four-story buildings that held small shops and restaurants on the ground floor while the higher floors advertised office space for lease and more apartments for rent. Some of the shops looked as though they had been closed for a long time while Help Wanted signs still clung crooked in the windows. Many storefronts were filled with antiques and furniture collected from different places over the years. Many broken dolls were placed in the windows staring out into the street.

Counter to the line of buildings that were on the right-hand side of the road, the left side of the main street was cut through by a ravine and overgrowth that extended from the ground up to trees that stood ten feet high. It was a quiet day, and the roads were empty apart from a scattering of pedestrians walking around.

"Not a bad little place," said Howard, "maybe a little sad, but the people seem friendly enough."

"It's kind of spooky," said Lorry, "feels like everyone's left town."

They walked past a sandwich board advertising a large cheese pizza and a pitcher of beer for fifteen dollars, which suited them just fine. They nodded in agreement and entered the restaurant while the cold dust in the street whipped into the wind.

The classic pizzeria setup was in full display with the familiar trappings of authenticity. Red vinyl benches lined the brown walls while stained glass lamps hung like chandeliers over tan tables. A soda fridge hummed in the corner beside a glass dessert cabinet showing full cakes, pastries, and other assorted small confections. Three Brazilian men were arguing and joking behind the counter while the Greek owner smoked cigarettes beside the open back door. It was clear that his children were working as servers and the smell of heat and fresh bread was wafting out from the wide standing ovens. Howard and Lorry sat themselves in a booth and settled into comfort while a jukebox played an old Billy Joel song.

"This is nice," said Lorry, "it reminds me of a place we had in my old neighborhood."

"Me, too," said Howard, "it's even got the punks."

Howard motioned with his head and Lorry turned to see a group of four young punks in the corner drinking coffee with their feet resting on skateboards. They had the uniform down and a variety of technicolored hairstyles that bore the markings of poisonous tree frogs. They looked like they were having a good time. There were some guitar cases behind their booth which made Howard smile.

"I think they're musicians," he said.

"Do you think they're any good?" asked Lorry.

"God, no. Not at all."

"Perfect.'"

A young server came to their table with a big smile and her hair in a ponytail. She greeted the Rubenstein's amicably as she dropped off some menus while Howard and Lorry began to debate how old she was.

"She can't be older than thirteen," said Lorry.

"I was twelve when I started working," said Howard, "I was a dishwasher in a place like this. It's what you do."

Howard's phone began to buzz with a local number on the screen. It was the mechanic and he had managed to convince his cousin to give them a lift to where they needed to go. Howard explained that they were just sitting down for lunch and asked if his cousin would mind waiting.

"Where you at?" asked the mechanic.

"We're at...what's this place called? Big Jim's Pizza and Subs," said Howard.

"Makes sense. I'll ask him to swing by. He'll be waiting outside for you."

Howard thanked the mechanic and told Lorry the good news.

"Nice folks around here," she said as she looked over the menu.

They decided to keep it simple with a large cheese pizza and a pitcher of Pabst. The waitress received their order cheerfully and bounced back to the POS terminal to place it. Billy Joel ended, and Lou Reed came on with an invitation for the listeners to take a walk on the wild side.

"Feels like I'm back in college," said Lorry.

"I'll take your word for it," said Howard.

"You ever think about going back to school?"

Howard shook his head and chuckled a bit.

"For what," he said, "just to be the crusty old man with a bunch of bright young faces? No, thank you. I wouldn't even know what to study."

"You could just pick up a class or two," said Lorry, "doesn't have to be a big thing."

"Naw, I'm good. I have you, Ruth, and Mary and that's all I need in my life. Just give me my radios on the roof and I'll be happy as anything."

The conversation dwindled as their thoughts returned to Mary. They agreed to talk about it on the drive to Amherst, but it had yet to come up. Howard and Lorry were both dreading the conversation. Now with the crisis in the forefront of their minds, they were left with nothing to talk about until the pizza arrived. Lorry reached across the table and squeezed Howard's hand. Howard squeezed back as they smiled at each other's love. The moment was broken by raised voices at the door. The owner was confronting a short, bearded man in a red flannel coat who was trying to get into the restaurant.

"No!" said the owner, "No, you get out! I'll call the police!"

"I got business inside!" said the man, "I'm supposed to, HEY! get your hands offa me!"

The two men came to blows as they took the fight to the street. Dust rose from the sidewalk as they rolled across the ground, trying to gain leverage. A few punches landed from both men, but a fair amount just caught the air. Like most scuffles, it was over almost as soon as it had begun. Howard had managed to make it outside with the intention of breaking it up, but it had already ended. The restaurant owner was standing over the man who lay on his back. They were both breathing heavily while the owner called the police. As soon as the owner of the restaurant managed to get through to the police, the man on the ground rolled onto his heels and sprang up, running down the street. He was much faster than he looked. The owner continued to yell obscenities at the assailant while he spoke with police on the phone.

"This motherfucker," he said, "comes in drunk, starts a fight. I'll fuck him up, I see him again."

The owner spit some blood on the sidewalk before returning to his call.

"Yes, hello," he said, "I was just attacked by Tommy Mamaluke. Five-foot five, hundred and fifty pounds, hair as brown as his asshole. Yes. Yeah, that's him. He's goin' down Main St. Check Billy Ray's or the Whole Donut. No, I'm not trying to be funny!"

He hung up the phone and shook his head at Howard.

"Every time that motherfucker comes in here, we get trouble. I can't fucking believe it, man. Stupid. I'm trying to run a restaurant and he comes in high all the time, drunk. Scaring kids and shit. This is supposed to be a family place."

"Is he kind of the local drunk?" asked Howard.

The owner laughed at this.

"Man, everybody here is the local drunk. I'm drunk right now, but I'm not an asshole."

Howard looked up the street where the man had escaped and made a small and curious noise to himself. Both men returned inside to find a fresh pizza with a cold pitcher of beer waiting at the table. The owner patted Howard on the shoulder.

"Hey man, listen," he said, "I'm sorry about that. I'll get this pitcher. Please enjoy, alright?"

"Thank you," said Lorry.

She had already eaten half of a slice of pizza before Howard had sat down at the table. He shook his head and poured himself a tall beer in a faded glass. The punks remained unbothered by the workings of the outside world.

"Everything cool?" asked Lorry.

"Just the local flavor," said Howard, "how's the pizza?"

Lorry closed her eyes with a mouthful of pizza and gave a thumbs up as she wiggled in her seat with approval. Howard meant to sip on his beer but unintentionally drained half of the glass without thinking. His phone began to ring with the mechanic's number again.

"My cousin Tommy come through there?" asked the mechanic.

"Oh," said Howard, "ah. He may have. I think he might get arrested. There was a fight."

The mechanic sighed heavily into the receiver.

"I told him to call me so I could let you know. He knows he's not allowed to go to Big Jim's, but I should have known better. Sorry about that."

"It's...fine, yeah. No problem."

"I'll call you back."

The mechanic hung up the phone and Howard shook his head as he lifted a slice of pizza from his plate.

"What's up?" asked Lorry.

"That little fella that got tossed," said Howard, "that was our ride."

"Seriously?" said Lorry, "that's wild. What do you want to do?"

"I dunno, the guy from the shop said he was gonna call me back."

"Okie dokie," said Lorry, "eat'cha pizza."

The Rubenstein's enjoyed the rest of their meal in peace while the jukebox played Purple Rain and all the punks sang along. The mechanic did return the call to the Rubenstein's and said that they could find his cousin Tommy at Billy Ray's, a local bar. When Howard asked the mechanic for Tommy's number, the mechanic said that it would be tricky as Tommy did not have a proper phone.

"It's more like a walkie-talkie", he said, "he's not allowed to have a cell phone, legally."

"Ask him if there's someone else that could give us a ride," said Lorry.

Howard asked the question, but his face remained expressionless.

"Tommy's a good guy," said the mechanic, "he's good behind the wheel."

Finding no alternative sources for transportation, and after asking three different people off the street, the Rubenstein's started to walk the short distance between Big Jim's and Billy Ray's.

Howard and Lorry were at a crosswalk as a church was leading a funeral procession of mourners and rented limousines through the main street. They watched the cars slowly parade down the road and off to one of the seventeen cemeteries that peppered the Litchfield township. Not knowing who was being buried or where, they felt nothing more than curiosity as the stretch of black cars caught reflections from the sun. The wind had settled down and it felt like the air was warming up a bit. It was still coat weather, but less aggressive and biting. Once the motorcade had cleared the intersection, the road became quiet again.

The Dairy Queen was closed for the season, but even with the windows boarded up, older faded pictures of ice cream and slush drinks covered the front of the building. Sun bleached photographs showed images of syrup shaved ice and sundae parfaits next to the smiling mouths of a family without fear. A family where the only fear is running out of ice cream. Lorry took out her little notepad and jotted something down.

Just a block away from the Dairy Queen, the Rubenstein's crossed a little bridge that would take them over a portion of the Mad River and into the parking lot of Billy Ray's. There was a square of sidewalk with the word WEBSTER spray painted diagonally in blue. The script was sloppy and punctuated by a used condom with a knot tied on the end and a crumpled pack of cheap cigarettes. The sidewalk broke into a square of dirt where cement used to be but had since been removed for unknown reasons. Lorry took out her little notepad and jotted something down. On the other side of the bridge, a bright green and yellow banner declared that Billy Ray's was indeed a real place and the Rubenstein's entered through the heavy red door.

A sudden blast of voices broke out from the room as the bar was filled near to capacity. No one looked at the door as the Rubenstein's entered, but a quick scan of the room had proven that finding Tommy Mamaluke would be more difficult than they had anticipated. The jukebox was high volume blasting Who Let the Dogs Out by the Baha Men and everyone seemed to be having a very good time.

It was a good size room of green with black trim in an L shape with a scattering of square tables. Four men were shooting pool and laughing at a joke while others were mingling about and drinking from table to table. Howard and Lorry made their way to the bar and flagged down a large woman wearing a tight black t-shirt with a rhinestone jolly roger on the front. She shouted something indiscernible which they understood to be a greeting, but it was difficult to hear anything over the crowd. They had to shout everything to be heard, and even so, that did not guarantee comprehension.

"HOW YA DOIN'," said the bartender, "WHAT'LL YA HAVE?!"
"WE'RE LOOKING FOR TOMMY MAMALUKE!" said Howard.
"WHAT?!"
"TOMMY! TOMMY MAMALUKE?!"
"COMIN' RIGHT UP!"

The bartender scurried down the other end of the bar and began to make some drinks while Howard and Lorry looked around the room and tried to spot their assigned guardian. It was difficult to discern the faces of each person in the bar. All the men were short with beards and stubby hands that worked for a living. They all had the kind of creases that formed in the face from long years of physical labor, nicotine, and drink. Having failed to get a good look at Tommy Mamaluke at the restaurant, Howard and Lorry were lost. The bartender returned with two full pint glasses and two shots of brown liquor. She smiled at them as she dropped each shot into the two glasses of beer, overflowing them and spilling over the rims of each glass.

"BOILERMAKER!" she said, "KEEPIN' IT OLD SCHOOL!"

Howard and Lorry were not sure what to do, so they handed the bartender their credit card, which she promptly refused.

"CASH ONLY!" she said, pointing at a sign above the bar as validation. A small confederate flag hung next to it, which the Rubenstein's thought odd considering their proximity to the Mason-Dixon line. Lorry grunted and turned away from the bar in the hopes that if she could not see the little flag then it would just go away. Howard ran his hands through his pants pocket and produced a twenty-dollar bill. He handed it to the bartender who smiled and thanked them very much. She did not return with change.

The Rubenstein's took their drinks and silently communicated through a series of facial expressions and eye contact that they may as well make the most of it. They clinked glasses and each took a sip. It was not the best drink they had ever had.

Two teenagers in a booth were being bounced out of the bar after it had been discovered that they were underage. There was a brief scuffle, but nothing to really amount to anything. The Rubenstein's took advantage of the vacancy and slid into the empty booth along the wall. Once they had settled in and resigned themselves to their drinks, they scanned the room for the man they were supposed to find.

The bar moved like a fantastic machine, having each person act as an integral part of a mechanism locked in a purpose. It may have been a purpose without reason, but that in and of itself was a purpose all the same. After they had finished their drinks and started to loosen up a bit, the place seemed to be relatively harmless. Lorry found a food menu on a neighboring table and showed it to Howard.

"Do we dare?" she asked.

"No," said Howard, "we do not."

The two began to laugh as Howard got up to get another beer.

"You want anything?" he asked.

"Whiskey."

"Whiskey?"

"Whiskey."

They smiled at each other, and Howard went to order the drinks. Howard returned with a beer and two small whiskeys which he and Lorry both clinked before knocking them back. They were interrupted when a little man in a red flannel coat and black watch cap stumbled over to their table. He looked to be in rough shape when he sat next to Howard and there was no life behind his eyes. The breath he emitted stank heavily of liquor and gingivitis. He wheezed as he introduced himself.

"I'm Tommy," he said, "you the Jews? Huh. Never seen a black Jew before."

"I'm sorry, what?" asked Lorry.

"My cousin said I was supposed to pick up a couple of Jews and bring 'em to a motel or somethin'? You them or what?"

Howard was already feeling a little tipsy and was not sure how to approach this situation without violence. He calmed down a bit when he felt Lorry squeeze his arm beneath the table.

"No, sorry," said Howard, "don't know what you mean there."

"Oh," said Tommy, "oh, sorry. Never mind."

He waved them off, mumbling something about fifty dollars, and stumbled back to a pool table where he quickly tripped and fell.

"Can we go?" asked Lorry.

"Yep," said Howard, "let's get the fuck out of here."

The Rubenstein's left Billy Ray's as the sun was going down. It was only four in the afternoon but with the winter months rapidly approaching, the sun would not last all day. They walked back over the bridge with their hands in their pockets and considered their options. The cold winds had started again.

"Ok. We can't sleep in the van," said Lorry, "and we can't sleep outside."

"Maybe we could hitchhike?" asked Howard.

"No, I don't like our odds. What with the Nazis and all."

"True, true."

Howard and Lorry walked back past the Dairy Queen and down Main St. onto the village green. It was a small stretch of park with a fountain and a bandstand in the center. Rows of trees stood along cement paths and the whole green acted as a median that connected two streets that ran on the opposite sides. There were lights strung up in the trees that gave an incandescent haze to the mist that was settling in the early autumn evening. It was genuinely beautiful and felt out of place from the rest of the town. As they entered the green, they could hear someone lightly strumming away on a guitar from up the path.

There was a young man wearing corduroy pants and a blue button-down shirt sitting alone in the bandstand. He looked to be in his mid to late twenties with a generally calming air about him. He was playing something slow and sad while he quietly sang to himself, stopping occasionally to smoke a cigarette and jot something down in a notebook. He stopped playing when he saw the Rubenstein's approaching and extinguished his cigarette on the cement floor of the bandstand. He did not stand, but he waved to them in welcome as they began to climb the small stairs that led up to the stage.

"Evenin'," he said, "how's it goin'?"

"Hi, ah, sorry to bother you," said Howard, "we need some help."

"I'm sorry but I don't have any money," said the young man, "there's a soup kitchen next to the church if y'all are hungry. I do have some beers and a little bit of whiskey left if you'd like some."

"No, sorry, we don't need any money," said Lorry, "we're kind of stuck."

"Oh," said the young man, "well, have a beer and tell me about it. My name's Greg, by the way. Take a load off."

Howard and Lorry introduced themselves and sat down next to Greg on the elevated bandstand. They each accepted a beer and the three of them drank quietly, sitting and talking. The Rubenstein's brought him up to speed with their situation and told him about the van, light details about Mary, and the fight in the restaurant and Tommy Mamaluke, of whom Greg knew all too well. When they mentioned that they were looking for a place to stay, the young man nodded and lit another cigarette.

"I might know somebody," he said, "lemme make a call real quick."

He started making a call before he interrupted himself to ask them a question.

"Are either of you allergic to cats?"

Neither of the Rubenstein's were allergic to cats so Greg continued with the call. There was approximately thirty seconds of conversation of which the Rubenstein's could only hear what he was saying. It seemed to promote a tone of positivity, but there was a sense of hesitancy in his voice. Greg was smiling as he ended the call.

"Ok," he said, "I have a friend who has a spare room. It's about a mile from here if you don't mind walking."

"Thank you," said Howard, "how much for the room?"

"No charge," said Greg, "she's funny like that."

The three of them walked to the house where the Rubenstein's would find shelter for the night, and not a moment too soon. A cold and heavy rain began to fall as soon as Greg knocked on the front door. A beautiful young woman answered and threw her arms around Greg as she pulled him tightly against herself. He smiled unabashedly and embraced her as she ushered them inside. Introductions were made and coffee was poured while the Rubenstein's settled into their shelter. The young woman's name was Jessica and she looked to be younger than Greg but acted like an old woman from the society pages. The only trait which betrayed her youth was a need to be presented on display.

The apartment itself was warm and it resembled one of the many antique stores that lined the main street except it had a cozy lived-in feeling. The art on the walls sported old travel posters of sailboats and art deco advertisements of cities like New York and Prague. Lorry did a double take when she realized that there was an authentic Kandinsky painting on one of the walls.

It was clear that Jessica was the kind of young eccentric that could only come from wealth. She lived more as an observer than a participant in the human race and said as much as she talked about herself. The Rubenstein's knew the type and generally held a small contempt for it, but they needed a place to stay. Howard and Lorry tried to keep their judgments in check while two calico cats roamed freely throughout the apartment. Sad jazz music from the nineteen-thirties droned on from another room.

"Thank you so much for letting us stay here," said Lorry, "are you sure we can't give you some money?"

"No," said Jessica, "no, nonsense, dear. I'm glad for the company and Greg said you were good people." She looked up at Greg with a strange light in her eyes. "I trust Greg more than I trust myself."

Jessica cackled at her own joke and sat down in a plush green velvet chair. The high back was upholstered with copper studs that kept the fabric pinned to the strapped leather binding. Jessica sighed and clicked her tongue as she pulled out a small box from the tableside drawer. She removed the lid and produced a bag of cocaine with a little silver spoon. She offered some to Howard and Lorry, who graciously declined, before taking some for herself. Greg thought about it for three seconds before happily accepting. He knelt beside Jessica and took a bump of cocaine in each of his nostrils.

"Anyway," she said while holding her nose. Her face twisted briefly in the discomfort caused by the drug. "Oh, fuck. Sorry. Anyway, I love to entertain, and it can be…difficult to find the right kind of guests who appreciate…well, anything."

"I'll bet," said Howard.

Lorry gently elbowed him between the ribs as Jessica continued.

"It's weird, but I really like this place. Winsted, I mean. It's such an honest town, you know? I love the truth of it all. It's like…nobody cares who you are or what you do. I mean, I lived in New York for a while, and let me tell *you*! People from New York are insufferable. They're just a bunch of stuck-up phonies. Who was it? I think it was Ayn Rand, or…was it Peikoff…oh, I give up. Either way, somebody said, and I do agree, that there is such a thing as having too much diversity. Wouldn't you agree, dear?"

Now it was Howards turn to nudge Lorry as she had begun to cut off his circulation with how strongly she was squeezing his hand. She loosened her grip and stared at the Kandinsky painting.

"And the conversations here are so real," said Jessica, "if someone doesn't want to talk to you, then they definitely let you know that they don't want to talk to you but in that non-verbal way, y'know? Like how when you're clearly not interested in what somebody is saying and you just kind of nod and say, 'Uh-huh'? Have you ever met someone like that? Just so clueless that they can't take a hint?"

"Uh-huh," said Howard.

"Well, that's not around here, not at all, dear! I mean, some of these people are simply charming little darlings, don't get me wrong, but it's so difficult to find a stimulating conversation about anything substantial. It was so simple at first, when I moved here, I mean. Finding anything of a social value here was just out of the question, dear. You'd have more luck training a bear to write prose. I remember there was a young man who had asked me for five dollars as he had just run out of gasoline for his car. Unfortunately, I didn't have anything less than a fifty with me and who am I to say what his intentions were? I didn't *see* a car and we were in the parking lot behind that...what was it? McDonalds, on Elm St. or some such place."

Jessica took another bump of cocaine and offered more to Greg, who graciously accepted. She teased him by pulling the spoon away at the last minute, but they both giggled at the game.

"After a few weeks of staying here, and I was so grateful when I found this darling little apartment, I must say. Oh, don't you just love it?! But it didn't look like this when I moved in. No, sir! There were all sorts of problems, but nothing I couldn't handle. Greg was a great help, too. I really couldn't have done it without him. But anyway, after a few weeks of staying here, I found that the spirit of hospitality had been lost to these people many years ago. It didn't take too long for me to realize their priorities. If someone doesn't want to talk to you then they just walk away. Yep! Just walk straight away and go fishing or work on their truck or see who can drink the most beer in their barn. Hah! I love this place, I really, really do."

Jessica fixed herself another bump of cocaine, pausing to offer some to the group. The Rubenstein's once again declined, but Greg accepted with enthusiasm. He genuflected again and pinched one nostril shut, inhaling sharply. Jessica laid her hand softly to pet the back of his head as he coughed. She pressed her forehead against his and said that Greg was such a good boy. There was a moment where Greg looked like he would go in for a kiss, but Jessica pulled her face away quickly and began to rub her eyes.

"Ugh, I hate myself," said Jessica, "I never get to talk to anybody interesting around here and here you are, complete strangers to the town, and all I do is talk about myself. You could very well be wild ax murderers, for what I know."

A thought crossed Jessica's mind as her whole composure seemed to shift. She looked at Greg seductively with her eyes half closed while she lit a black cigarette.

"You wouldn't do that, would you Greg?" she said, "Kill little old me with an ax? If I were bad?"

Greg began to blush and became visibly uncomfortable as he assured Jessica that he would never do such a thing. Jessica smiled and stared at Greg through her cocaine eyes.

"What if I wanted you to, Greg," she shifted her weight in the chair to face him, "would you chop me up if I asked you to? If I begged?"

Greg's face went a bright red at this, and he stuttered when he said that he never would.

"I know that he wouldn't," said Jessica, "he won't do it because he'd never hurt me. He's in love with me."

"Jess, please," said Greg.

"He's in love with me because he wants to be. Needs to be. Why? I have no idea. But I don't love him. Isn't that tragic? Pathetic, even? Aren't I the worst?"

Greg grabbed his guitar and walked straight for the door. He turned to say something when Jessica interrupted him.

"Jeez, lighten up, gorgeous," she said, "I was only joking. He's such a sensitive kid."

Greg slammed the door as he left, turning his coat collar up in the downpour and balancing his guitar case flat on top of his head. It shielded him from the rain, but he knew it would cause damage to the case. His efforts to light a cigarette failed and he cursed to himself, wiping his nose as he walked down the street while the rain poured all around him. Lorry and Howard sat stunned on the couch and expressed their concerns for Greg's reaction.

"He'll be back," said Jessica, "I hope he always comes back. Honestly, dear, I don't know what I would do if anything happened to him."

"So, you do love him," said Lorry.

"Oh god, absolutely! He drives me wild! Makes me feel all crazy when he's around me. Sometimes I can't even sleep when I think about what I want him to do to me."

"So, what the fuck was that?!" asked Lorry, "he looked like he was ready to die!"

"You can't let them know, dear," said Jessica, "once they know then they're useless."

"If you call me 'dear' one more time, then I'm going to,"

"Howabout a game?!" shouted Howard, oblivious to his unhelpful suggestion.

"No," said Jessica, "no, I'm not very much in the mood for games, thank you."

She stood up from her green velvet chair and wrapped herself in a golden silk kimono that had been hanging on a hook beside the bathroom door. She tied her hair up in a swift, fluid motion, suggesting that this action had been practiced in the mirror several times. Jessica's mood had dropped suddenly, and she began to move as though she were trying to swim through margarine. Each of her gestures became limp and half-hearted.

"There's a guest room down the hall," she said, "and please help yourself to anything that you'd like. There's more weed and coke. If you want any. It's in that top cupboard, there."

"Goodnight Jessica," said Howard, "and thanks again. We'll try to keep it down."

"Oh, I don't care," said Jessica, "I don't usually fall asleep until six in the morning anyway."

She made a pspspsps sound to her cats who obediently followed her up the stairs, but not before they turned back to stare at the Rubenstein's. One cat yawned while the other sat still. The two cats each made a grumble as they climbed the stairs to Jessica's room. After the Rubenstein's heard the door close, Lorry started pacing around the room in a huff while Howard poked around in the fridge.

"I hate it here," said Lorry, "do you think we should steal that Kandinsky?"

"They're only young," said Howard, "but they both ought to wise up, and quick."

"This place is so weird! I don't get it."

"Well maybe that's just it," said Howard, "we don't get it. But that doesn't mean that it isn't good for someone else."

"I can't stay here for four days," said Lorry, "and I'm definitely not staying *here* for four days."

"We'll find a motel tomorrow."

They sat on the couch and turned on the television. Charlton Heston and Roddy McDowall were discussing the societal rights of man on Planet of the Apes. Howard found a bottle of wine and two glasses for them to enjoy as they tried to relax and think about how to escape the town of Winsted, Connecticut.

22. It's Complicated

"What happened?" asked Mary, through a dry and sandy voice.

She rubbed her eyes and fought against the thin cotton curtain that lay draped across her face. The daybed that held her was dusty and a faded yellow velveteen with curled wooden legs that fit handsomely in the green and brown room. She, however, did not feel handsome. She felt thick as the dust floated in the morning light across the space that had been long since abandoned.

Mary remembered that this was once her grandmother's "resting room". Her grandmother would lock herself in if she was beginning to feel overwhelmed or confused. Mary had never been allowed in the room as a child so the thought of her now owning the space made her uncomfortable. Lately everything made her uncomfortable. After a night of binge drinking and pharmaceutical experimentation with Joey had led to a rambunctious exploration through the maze of a house, Mary had collapsed upon the daybed without memory. She was now waking up with a familiar feeling in an unfamiliar place at an unfamiliar time.

Joey lay sprawled on his stomach still wearing the wrestling singlet. He was lying on top of a large round ottoman of brown leather in an opposite corner of the room. Rolling onto the floor, he began a coughing fit so pronounced that he would mutter "Ow" sporadically between each hack and wheeze. He lay on his back and groaned in the revelation that he was awake and alive, much to his own regret. For Joey, there were two sensations in being alive: pain and pleasure. He swore on this philosophy that every sensation experienced was a gradation between the two and that sometimes the lines would blur. In his most recent comprehensions of the world, there was no pleasure in his being awake. Not currently.

"I'm dying," said Joey, "I'm dying a death."

"Then die already," said Mary, covering her eyes with her hands, "just please stop talking."

Joey's phone started buzzing on the floor beside him. The noises that left his mouth when he reached for the phone were pathetic, at best. They got even worse when he read what was there.

"Oh, shit," he said.

"What happened?"

"Oh, shit. Oh, God."

"Joey," said Mary, "use your words but use them lightly, please."

"I think evil Joey may have been texting Sam last night."

Mary snorted out a laugh and immediately regretted it as a sharp pain hit the back of her nose. She proceeded to cough up some phlegm and groaned through her laughter.

"Yeah, you did," she said, "I remember that. Did you write anything good?"

"No," said Joey, "this doesn't make sense. Listen to this: 'If there was something you could hold inside your hand (spelled wrong) and feel it move around you fucking idiot.' Then I called him a slug, blah, blah, blah. There might be a death threat here, and then I say I'm sorry."

"Makes sense to me," said Mary, "did he write back?"

"Yeah, there's like…a novel here. Mary, would you be so kind as to kill me?"

"I'm not that kind."

"Please," said Joey, "exaggerate my life when they put me in the ground. Tell them I was made of sex and gave the best head."

"But sweetie, you do give the best head," said Mary.

"You are such a delight. Please just kill me."

"Maybe after breakfast."

They both lay about the room groaning to each other for half an hour. Mary checked her phone for the time and was surprised to see that they had been either high or asleep for nearly seventeen hours. They had already spent their first night in the house and then some. Driven by a powerful recognition of hunger, Mary rose from the daybed only to fall back down onto it. She laughed in pain as Joey inched towards her like a broken ant.

"Ok," said Joey, "for real this time. We need to go to the store."

"Do we have any food?" asked Mary.

"Like…maybe a jar of peanut butter and some dried lentils. And drugs."

"We'll be fine," said Mary, "food accessibility is a privilege of the bourgeoisie."

"Well, two things," said Joey, "no, it isn't, and you're a homeowner with a trust fund there, friend. I wouldn't fly your red card just yet. I need to eat something. Where's the nearest store?"

"You wanna go back to the shamrock spaghetti place?"

"No," said Joey, "I have suffered enough."

"Never forghetti…the shamrock spaghetti…"

"I can't think of a threat," said Joey, "just know that I am threatening you. Like one of those weird lizards with the frill necklace."

"The screaming guys?"

"Yeah, the screaming guys. I may be more lizard than man."

"Ok," said Mary, "ok. Lemme get dressed and we'll head out."

The two friends could barely move, Mary on her daybed and Joey on the floor, while the dust kept itself in perpetual motion. Two minutes passed with the only sound being the rhythm of heavy breathing.

"You gonna get dressed?" asked Joey.

"Yeah, just...gimme a minute. You gonna change, or just go like that?"

"I'll change, yeah. I just can't blink too fast right now."

With a collection of grunts, and moans, Mary and Joey stood up and walked out of the room like newly born foals. It took some doing, but after changing back into their street clothes, and with their unsteady hands on the banister, they did their best to support themselves as they slowly stumbled down the stairs and into the kitchen. Rinsing out their mugs from the previous night brought a patchwork memory of indulgence as the lingering smell of whiskey hung around them in the air. They each took turns filling and refilling their mugs with the cold water that generously bubbled out from the tap in a thick flow. It tasted sweeter than the water in New York and Mary thought it might have come from a magic well deep in the earth's core. With any luck, she thought, the water would bring them supernatural restorative properties. Unfortunately, it did not. It still felt very nice.

Mary lit up a joint and passed it to Joey as they sat on the front steps and stared at the car. Loose Lips stared back at them in a mocking display of, *Oh, what? What's the matter? Too sick to drive? Waaah, waaah, waaah.*

"Shut up," said Mary.

"I didn't say anything," said Joey.

"Sorry, never mind."

"Can you just give me a heads up when you start to feel crazy?"

"Ok," said Mary, "I'm starting to feel crazy."

Joey put his arm around Mary as she leaned her head against his shoulder.

"So, you giving up city life," asked Joey, "gonna stick around here and grow some...chickens, or something?"

"Fuck, I don't know," said Mary, "I don't know what I'm gonna do. This place has kind of gone to hell, though."

"I dunno," said Joey, "I kind of like the Adams Family vibe. You would make a lousy Morticia, though. You're so cheerful."

"I feel more like Uncle Fester."

The two friends sat on the steps and listened to the breeze cut through the sugar maple branches. A spattering of bird calls scattered through the air with signs of invisible life saying all was well. Even in their state of recovery, Mary felt good to be back in the woods and she closed her eyes.

"Wasn't there a car, too," asked Joey, "Did I make that up?"

"Oh yeah," said Mary, "I don't know where it is."

The car was nowhere to be found and there was no garage to store it. Mary and Joey walked around the house twice in case it had been hiding in plain sight, but they only found more of the long grass and misguided bird nests that had fallen off the roof. They gave up their search and returned to the familiar interior of Loose Lips, along with all the aromas it contained.

Both of their bodies lurched forward with nausea as Joey did his best to slowly maneuver the car out of the driveway and into the real world. The weed helped them feel a little more settled as their appetites began to overpower their discomforts. Joey kept a steady speed through the sleepy day as the woods rushed around them symphonically. He turned the radio on low volume, and they caught the middle of a conversation on talk radio:

"...hundred found dead in the aftereffects of an earthquake that struck the city of Lima, Peru at three-thirty in the morning on Thursday. Emergency crew workers are still trying to sort through the debris in the hopes to find more survivors and to get an accurate tally of the casualties. The mayor had this to say:

"It is a great tragedy, naturally. We are doing our best to come together as a community and care for those who require assistance. We ask that if you have the capability to donate blood, blankets, or non-perishable food, please contact your local church or emergency red cross station."

"The mayor, who is currently under investigation for charges of embezzlement and manipulation of city funds, will be up for re-election this august..."

Mary switched the radio to a rock and roll station and the car continued down the road towards the city center. As they approached the outer lines of the downtown area, several streets had been blocked off for the continuation of the Fisher Festival. Anticipating the annoyance of navigating the streets which had been left open, they decided to park the car and walk to the nearest store to pick up some basic supplies.

Children were wearing weasel hats and running around the street fair that expanded down most of the city center. Brightly colored balloons and the smells of fried food were everywhere as the same live band from the day before played loose renditions of Steely Dan songs. Awkward teenage couples moved through the fair with their hands clasped and sweaty in each other's grip. Each pubescent wishing that the other would make the first move while also dreading what that would be like. Older couples who had most definitely outgrown their own hormonal inexperience sat along the sidewalks in folding lawn chairs. They would fan themselves with their hats and shade their eyes with magazines as they curled their lips in contempt for the youth of today.

Joey paused in front of a taxidermist booth who had made models of every U.S. president out of stuffed squirrels. He held one up posed on a small wooden horse as Theodore Roosevelt charging up San Juan Hill and showed it to Mary.

"Mary," he said, "can I please borrow two-hundred dollars?"

"No, Joey. That's so gross."

"You don't understand," he said, "it's Teddy Roosevelt. On a little horse. But it's a squirrel. I need it."

"Find me Taft in a bathtub and I'll think about it."

No sooner had the words left Mary's mouth when Joey turned to find the exact example that Mary had requested. A largely overstuffed squirrel had been given a curled mustache and a nervous expression on its face while lying in a comically small bathtub.

"Come on!" said Joey, "are you kidding me?!"

Mary rolled her eyes and walked away from the booth. Joey made one final attempt to change her mind but surrendered his requests, thanking the vendor for their good taste.

Mary walked down the line of craft tables and food before stopping in front of the taxidermist's shop window. She saw an old man behind the counter watering chrysanthemum while a cat slept peacefully in a sunspot on the windowsill. The room looked warm and inviting. Several stuffed birds and weasels were stacked along the wall behind the counter and a variety of taxidermy supplies were for sale along the shelves. Mary lingered in front of the shop window to watch the cat when she noticed the old man staring at her from behind the desk. There was a look of serious effort and confusion across his face as he furrowed his brow and squinted, looking as though he was trying to remember something important. He put down his watering can and walked to the door, opening it up to the brisk autumn day. Mary felt the dry radiator heat coming from the shop as he beckoned her over.

"I know you," he said, "I know you from somewhere."

Mary had no recollection of the old man, but she understood how it could be possible that they had met before. He rubbed his chin and scrutinized her face.

"Are you local," he asked, "or are you just in town for the festival?"

"I used to live here," said Mary, "but that was a long time ago. I inherited my aunt's house so I'm just checking out the place."

"What's your name?" he asked.

"Mary Rubenstein. It would have been Kirkland when I lived here."

"Mary!" he said, "Mary Kirkland! Oh my god, it is you!"

He clasped his thin hands around Mary's as he smiled a mouthful of brown and incomplete teeth.

"Oh, I haven't seen you since...oh, come in! Come in!"

He brought Mary inside the store and sat her at a table in the back of the shop. Mary sat, high and polite, as the old man scurried to prepare coffee and small butter cookies from an old blue tin. The cat remained unbothered.

"You don't remember me, do you?" he asked, handing Mary a cup of coffee.

"I'm sorry," said Mary, "my memory is a little...funny."

"Well, I can't say that you look the same, but that's time, isn't it? Time and fools, etc."

He ran his hand over his bald head and laughed.

"My name is Patrick. I was a friend of your grandmother. I was helping with her affairs after your grandfather's disappearance. She was very broken up by the whole thing. Lots of anger. We would exercise together, play games sometimes. Found ways to decompress some of her frustrations."

Mary felt a lump in her throat at the thought of Patrick existing as an extension of her grandmother. This was someone who knew her well. She had spent so many years pushing the thought of her biological family out of her mind that reestablishing a connection felt painful. She smiled and looked away towards the cat whose tail swayed lightly in the sun. A row of glass jars on a shelf above the window were filled with fetal pigs in a green liquid. She thought she saw one of them move.

"I haven't seen you since...yes, it must have been your grandmother's funeral. Oh, but you were so young and moody. You probably don't remember me. But this is a surprise, to be sure. And when we heard about your poor parents, oh, what a tragedy! We were all very worried about you."

"Thanks," said Mary, her head was swimming and the heat from the radiator was making her uncomfortable, "it's been hard...but it's good to be back, yeah."

Patrick took Mary's hands in his own and gave her a light squeeze.

"Mary, we were *all* worried about you. We were so glad that you got out of that house."

Mary paused in the statement. There were unspoken implications to Patrick's tone. For everything that a person could be worried about, she thought that her leaving and becoming an orphan would be the worst of it. If there was another factor that had been otherwise unknown to Mary, this would throw everything she understood into chaos. A fresh metallic taste crept up the back of her throat.

"What do you mean," asked Mary, "what are you talking about?"

Patrick took a deep sigh and folded his hands as he looked to the ceiling. He was choosing his words very carefully and speaking very slowly.

"How much do you remember of your grandmother? Of your parents?"

"Some. I remember playing in the woods a lot. When my parents were around, we used to watch TV together. Old movies and I Love Lucy. I remember that."

"We all knew...well, we *suspected* that there were some problems with your grandmother's health."

"She had dementia," said Mary, "she wasn't all there."

Patrick was quiet and stared at the table for thirty seconds. Mary was growing increasingly anxious as the silence carried the promise of new information. Of what, she was unsure, but she was beginning to understand that Patrick was becoming confessional.

"It's complicated," said Patrick, "well, no. Maybe it isn't. People say things are complicated when what they really mean is uncomfortable. It's uncomfortable, Mary, and I'm almost grateful that you're unclear about certain facts regarding your family. But it would be cruel to keep you in the dark for much longer. I...Mary, are you alright?"

Mary had entered a fugue state as she nibbled the side of her finger.

"I have to go," she said, "...I have to go."

Despite Patrick's insistence that she should listen to what he had to say, Mary could not hear him as she stepped out the front door of the shop. She walked down the street, nibbled her finger, and the cat stretched its arms and legs, yawning on the warm windowsill.

Mary was no longer in the world. She had become like a shadow, the impression of a person in the afternoon sun. She muddled down the festive streets filled with cotton candy and weasels while darkness surrounded her peripheral vision. Children danced around her in sing-song maypole fashion, growing longer, and wider, and thicker, and hollow. Through all of this, her eyes never drifted from off the horizon.

She walked without a destination or purpose beyond the motivation to keep walking. She wanted to walk to the edge of the world and throw herself down to be received by long-neglected stars. The desire was strong enough to convince Mary that it was possible. She had almost figured out how to throw herself into space when Joey grabbed her by the shoulder.

"Where'd you go," asked Joey, "I turned around for a second and you disappeared. You alright?"

Mary rubbed her forehead and shut her eyes. An incredible headache had begun to pulsate behind her temples.

"I don't know," she said, "I was talking to this old guy. Then I was here. I think there was a cat. Fuck, my head hurts. Do you have any water?"

"Let's go to the store and get some food," said Joey, "we'll get you back to the house and take it easy."

Mary nodded without saying anything and leaned on Joey, arm-in-arm, as they walked to the nearest market.

The market they found was a specialty store with boutique groceries like milk infused with lavender and flax seed encrusted figs. There were flowers of a sizable variety and scale to which the most jaded of lovers would have little choice but to abandon their apprehensions towards romance. A row of essential and non-essential oils lined the entrance beside a woman in burlap and sandals explaining how the moon affected the personality of your fingernails. An older man with a balding ponytail stood beside her and gave finger-guns to whomever walked past. If someone reciprocated, then he would become elated and play air-guitar while howling out some song that only he knew.

Shopping carts were considered too aggressive for the store, so handwoven baskets were provided. Each basket was selected by an unbiased committee and made by individuals that had proven their generosity to be non-performative. No conglomerated name brand items, just locally and ethically sourced products of economic uniqueness. The only artificial thing in the store was Albert Robinello's hearing aid.

Albert was a stocky Italian man who was born and raised in Boston. When the delivery trucks would arrive and drop off shipments of fresh produce and seafood in the middle of the night, Albert would be there to receive the goods with bloodshot frustration. He worked with a tall, lanky man named Ralph. Ralph was Albanian, I think, and had jaundice due to chronic bouts of kidney infection. It affected his eyes most of all; giving them the yellow quality that removed any whites from around his iris.

A lack of confidence and general self-abasement made it difficult for Ralph to look anyone in the eye in conversation. Incidentally, Albert was a close talker with a loose understanding of boundaries and personal space. The pair of them were not terribly popular and they may have had three friends between them, including each other. This is one of the many reasons as to why management primarily kept them both on the overnight third shift.

Ralph saw Mary and Joey enter the store before Albert did, but he quickly looked away and allowed them to wander about their business unobserved. He thought nothing of their arrival as the day had been busy with customers coming in and out of the store. Ralph was tired as he and Albert had already worked the third shift from the previous night but were now rounding off the tail end of a double without sleep. They would have eight hours of rest before they were expected to return in the coming evening. Albert nudged Ralph to get his attention.

"You think we're gettin' time and a half?" he asked.

Ralph scratched his head beneath his cap and stared at the ground as he wiped some dead skin cells on the leg of his pants.

"I dunno," he said, "I don't think so. Mr. Gleeson didn't mention anything about it."

"We better get time and a half," grumbled Albert.

The two men worked on, with Albert complaining about their work and their unpaid wages while Ralph did his best to hold a wooden crate steady.

They had already been through a string of odd jobs and unsuccessful scams that had failed to gain traction, so their time working at the market was not an ideal situation. Albert had been released from prison the previous year on a charge of petty larceny with assault and battery, but his criminal record was more successful than his variety of legitimate careers. He had often bragged about having gotten away with murder, but he talked so much that very few of his stories maintained any level of credibility. Ralph had never been to prison, but he had never been a saint, either. He was just a little more subtle with his sins.

Mary was still unnerved from the end of her most recent episode. The smells of organic cleaning products and oil diffusers were unpleasant, despite their advertised effect. She was beginning to feel sick when Joey asked if she had a preference between hemp-based corn flakes or fruity hippo chocolate holes.

"I have to sit down," she said, "I have to go outside."

"You wanna go to the hospital?" asked Joey.

"No, no I'm ok. I just need some air."

Joey returned to his handwoven basket with "Generosity" sewn into the handle when Mary promised that she did not need him to join her outside. She promised not to run away and left through the fully voluntary and gracious automated doors while Joey continued to scrutinize the market. Ralph watched with moderate interest as Mary left in an uncomfortable hurry. He was holding a wooden crate steady for Albert who was opening the lid with a crowbar. In his time of distraction, Ralph let loose his grip on the box, causing Albert's hand to run jaggedly along the split side of the wooden crate.

"Shit," shouted Albert, "shit, shit, shit!"

Albert's hand had slipped and scraped across a broken side of the wooden lid, leaving long strips of splintering pine sticking out from his hand. Ralph, who detested the sight of blood and gore, quickly turned his head in the other direction and did his best not to faint. Albert continued to wail until their manager came over.

"What's happened?" asked the manager.

"My hand," cried Albert, "my fucking hand!"

"Albert, we cannot use such violent language in a place of peaceful commerce," said the manager, "now you have been warned before about your aggressive energy. I am willing to accommodate your right to expression up to a point, but this is making me feel very anxious and sensitive."

The manager held an organic biodegradable non-GMO paper-adjacent synthetic towel beneath Albert's hand while he attempted to remove some of the shards of wood that had become embedded beneath his skin. As soon as the fabric touched Albert's blood it disintegrated and allowed the wound to bleed freely onto the floor. The manager removed a larger shard from Albert's hand and more blood began to flow from the opened wound. Ralph, after having peeked at the scene out of curiosity, collapsed. A small crowd had gathered and were kind enough to step over Ralph so as not to disturb his fainting spell.

"You asshole," cried Albert, "you stupid prick!"

"Albert this is your last warning," said the manager, "one more outburst like that and I'll have to consider thinking about terminating your employment."

The manager misjudged the length of a wooden shard and in his attempt to dislodge it forced it sideways, digging it deeper into a portion of undisturbed meat in Albert's bleeding wound. Albert howled and thrashed, punching his manager in the mouth with his good hand. Whether it was intentional or not he could not say, but a brief smile broke through the pain Albert carried on his face. His manager flew backwards into the crowd and landed on top of Ralph who had just begun to regain consciousness. They knocked heads together and were both out cold.

Another manager new to the scene arrived with two police officers who grabbed Albert and escorted him out of the building. Shortly after Albert had been removed, it was agreed upon between management that Ralph should also be terminated on the grounds of his implications towards the spread of what human resources referred to as "bad vibes". His unconscious body was decidedly tossed out of the front door of the market, landing next to Albert who was still picking shards of wood out from his bleeding hand. Albert barely flinched as Ralph bounced beside him against the ground.

"Well, there's another one for the books," said Albert, "some great help you are."

Albert kicked Ralph in the leg and his eyes fluttered as he returned to consciousness. He looked around the front of the market in confusion before dusting himself off and returning through the front door. He was immediately thrown out again and landed next to Albert, this time without bouncing.

"We've been fired," said Albert as he wrapped his hand in a handkerchief that he had tied around his neck, "no thanks to you."

"What'd I do?" asked Ralph.

"Oh, shut up!"

Albert and Ralph sat on the curb in front of the market. Ralph scratched the top of his head beneath his hat while Albert lit a short, stubby cigar. A small voice came from behind them asking for a cigarette. They turned to see Mary crouched on her heels and hugging her stomach. Ralph fished through his pockets and retrieved a half pack of cigarettes, tossing them to Mary.

"Thanks," she said, lighting a cigarette and throwing the pack back to Ralph, "what happened to you?"

She gestured to Albert's hand to which he made a face implying that it was just "one of those things". Mary nodded and pulled a long drag.

"I saw you come in," said Ralph, his yellow eyes fixed on a spot on the ground, "I saw you come into the store with your boyfriend. Are you sick?"

"He's not my boyfriend," said Mary, "he's my business partner."

"Oh," said Ralph, trying to work out the social mathematics, "I'm sick. Albert isn't sick, but I am. I have to take pills. Sometimes I can't piss right."

"Shame," said Mary, not wishing to continue the topic, "y'all just get fired?"

Albert and Ralph nodded their heads.

"I might need some work done at my house," said Mary, "I can pay."

Albert and Ralph looked at each other with suspicion as they were unaccustomed to good fortune. They had never met anyone that would be so willing to suddenly take them into employment. They considered her proposal to potentially be an exaggerated con where she could exploit them for their labor without paying them when the work was completed. Still, they had nothing better to do.

"What kind of work?" asked Albert.

"Yardwork, mostly," said Mary, "some painting and light construction. Maybe some plumbing and electrical if you could manage."

Albert and Ralph knew next to nothing about how to approach work like this, but they were desperate and figured that they could learn it as they went.

"Five hundred dollars a week each," said Albert, "we won't work for anything less."

Ralph nodded in agreement and Mary considered their proposal. She could afford it and it would be better than maintaining the house herself when she knew nothing of plumbing or carpentry. Besides, this would most likely be a short arrangement.

"Three hundred a week," said Mary. She had never haggled before, and the opportunity was too tempting to pass up.

"Four seventy-five, final offer," said Albert.

"Three-fifty," said Ralph, getting caught up in the moment.

"Alright," said Mary, "Three-fifty a week, plus meals."

Albert smacked Ralph in the chest with his bad hand and immediately regretted it. Having their terms set, the three shook on the arrangement. Ralph requested that they should have something put into writing and Mary agreed to draw up a simple contract when they got back to the house.

Joey emerged from the market with three bags of food and toiletries. He had been worried that Mary would be gone when he left the store but seeing her talking to Ralph and Albert brought different concerns to his mind. The two men took the bags from Joey, introduced themselves, and then they all got into Loose Lips to drive back to the house in which Mary had been raised. They rode with light attempts to learn as much about each other as was possible in fifteen minutes. It was becoming obvious that Albert had opinions about Joey's sexual identity.

"Yeah, I had a gay friend once," said Albert, "he was a good guy for bein' queer. Not real showy about it. Acted normal enough. Not that it was a problem, just, like, y'know, don't try nothin'. Queers don't bother me until they bother me, y'know what I mean?"

Albert made a familiar series of obscene hand gestures and continued to explain how tolerant he was, although this was debatable. Joey was hardly surprised but was becoming increasingly uncomfortable.

"So, Joey," said Albert, "you, uh, got a girlfriend?"

He snickered at Ralph and elbowed him jokingly. Ralph was about to say something when Joey flatly replied that no, he did not have a girlfriend.

"Right," said Albert, "well, uh, I hope you find the right kind of girl, y'know?"

Joey pulled the car around the front of the house and Albert whistled as he opened his door.

"That's some place," he said, "who the hell threw this together?"

"My great-grandfather," said Mary, "rumor has it he was insane."

"You don't say," said Albert.

Mary and Joey brought the groceries inside while Albert and Ralph walked around the property pretending to assess and measure the work they had to do.

"I don't know how to be a plumber, Al," whispered Ralph.

"Yeah, me neither. But a house this big has to have some antiques in it. We stay on for a couple of days mowing the yard and hammerin' nails. Once we get a good idea of what they got worth takin', we take it and split."

"So, you wanna rob 'em?" asked Ralph.

"Yeah."

"Ok, sounds good, " said Ralph, "I was just checking."

"What if they don't have anything worth takin'?"

"Place this big," said Albert, "guy that crazy? I'd bet you anything he's got something in the walls."

"Yeah," said Ralph, "probably mice. I don't like catching mice."

The sound of an engine coming up the road broke the train of thought that Ralph was struggling with. The two crooks turned to see a large maroon van coming up the driveway and kicking up a good amount of dust in its wake. The van pulled up to the house and brought a new sense of dread that their plan had just become more complicated. The sound of the '70s rock and roll machine was blasting an old song as the van came to a sudden stop, spitting small stones and dirt around its tires. The engine sputtered and cut and out stepped the largest man that Albert and Ralph had ever seen.

The Rubenstein's had managed to expedite the repair of their van in record time and had required no more shelter from the people of Winsted, Connecticut. They had left Jessica's apartment in a hurry the morning after they had arrived. They were halfway out the door when she offered to show them her collection of love letters she had received over the years from different men and women that had threatened to kill themselves for her affection. They never did see Greg again, but they hoped that he was doing ok and that he would smarten up a bit. The follies of youth can linger to plague the oldest of fools.

Howard and Lorry stepped out of their van to find Ralph and Albert staring at them from the front of the house. The Rubenstein's smiled and waved to them only to find no response from either man.

"Hi there," said Howard, "is there a Mary Kirkland living here?"

Ralph was about to speak before Albert nudged him to be quiet.

"Who are you?" asked Albert.

"We're Mary's parents," said Lorry.

The Rubenstein's approached Ralph and Albert with apprehension while the two men remained locked where they stood. Neither of them made a move to welcome or refuse the Rubenstein's. There was a tense minute before Albert spoke.

"You got I.D.?'

"Who are you?" asked Howard.

"Never mind," said Albert, "we're carpenters."

"And plumbers," said Ralph, "and sometimes gardeners."

"We also do security. What's your business?" asked Albert, feeling bolder in the face of Howard's mass. It was often stated throughout his life that Albert was too stupid to feel pain and too dumb to know fear.

"Where's Mary?" asked Lorry.

"She's fine," said Albert, "but she isn't taking company. You're gonna have to come back later."

"I don't have time for this," said Howard, "Mary! Mary, you home?!"

He strode towards the front door while Albert attempted to stonewall his gate. He stretched his arm straight-out with his palm facing Howard while Ralph slowly stepped to the side. Albert's hand remained locked until Howard grabbed him by the collar of his shirt and lifted him off the ground. Lorry and Ralph leapt into action as they did their best to dislodge Albert from Howard's grip. Neither of them had much effect.

23. Two Sheep Were Grazing In A Field

Joey was standing on a blue paint-chipped wooden chair with its back against the wall. He had just discovered a neglected bottle of wine that had been sitting on top of the kitchen cabinet but had rolled along its side and into the corner of the room. He was reaching as far as his arms would allow while simultaneously tilting the chair in the direction of the bottle. With his own legs knocking about from the rickety base, there was a passing thought, for an instant, of *This is how I die*. But with surprising skill and prowess, he managed to grab the long neck of the bottle and pull it out from its hiding place. He wiped off a layer of dust that had covered a label that read, Petrus Pomerol Grand Vin 2016. Joey smiled to himself for his ingenuity and began searching for a bottle opener.

"What's that," asked Mary, "bonus hooch?"

"I got a nose for this stuff," said Joey, "if there's free liquor within a ten-mile radius then that is where I shall be."

"Love that for you."

The sound of a car pulling up to the house broke their reverie and a curious expression came upon Mary's face. Joey nudged her with his elbow.

"Do you think it's *James*?" he asked.

"Shut Up."

"Do you think he *likes* you?"

"Fuck off."

"Oh," gasped Joey, "what if he's *naked* and...?!"

"Joey, I swear to god."

"THROBBING?!"

The raised voices in the yard brought the joke to an end as both Mary and Joey looked out the kitchen window to see what was happening. The thinly veiled silhouette of the Rubenstein van could be seen through the curtains. They both ran out the kitchen door and Mary stood in the kind of confusion when you see something familiar but out of place. It would have been as if she had gone to the moon and found an aquarium. She stepped out from the kitchen door with her head curiously tilted to the side while she watched Howard Rubenstein holding Albert up in the air by the front of his shirt. Howard was shaking Albert like a ragdoll as Lorry and Ralph did their best to pull Howard's arms away. The whole display was very silly.

"Howard quit it," shouted Lorry, "Howard?! Honey?! My darling?! Stop it!"

Ralph said nothing but would hop in the air and do his best to grip Howard's arm. It was impossible to gain leverage against the massive man, and to be clear, he gained nothing. He also kept losing his hat. Ralph would let go of Howard periodically to pick it back up before returning to his futility. Mary jumped into the fray and wedged herself between Howard and Albert.

"Dad! Stop it!" she shouted.

The sight of Mary threw Howard off his anger. His anticipation of seeing her had been temporarily clouded by the unexpected confrontation with Albert, but his priorities were snapped back into place upon Mary's intervention. He released Albert from his grip, causing him to fall to the ground in a crumpled mass of dust and limbs. Ralph, unable to recognize that the struggle had ended, continued to hang off Howard's arm. He was thrown through the air with a roll of Howard's shoulder. Howard engulfed Mary as he pulled her tightly against his chest. Neither of them spoke for a few seconds until Mary pushed away from her father.

"What are you doing here," asked Mary, "how did you find me?"

"We came to get you," said Howard, "we thought you might be in trouble. Might need help."

"Help?!" shouted Mary, "I don't need your help! It's nice to see you and all, but no thanks. What, did you think I was just going to jump in the van and head back to New York?"

"Mary," said Lorry, "Mary, what's going on? You haven't talked to us in months and then you just up and disappear completely?"

"Nothing," said Mary, "I don't have to report every part of my life to you. My aunt died and left me this house. Me and Joey were gonna fix it up and I come out here to find you beating up my gardeners. Some help you are!"

"We tried calling you," said Lorry, "but you never answered the phone. We left you so many messages, Mary. Please don't shut us out."

Mary turned to go back inside the house. She stood on the steps for a moment until she looked back over her shoulder.

"Well, are you coming in or not?"

The Rubenstein's followed Mary into the house, leaving Albert and Ralph lying on the lawn. The two thieves were still trying to center themselves as Howard shot them a dirty look from the front door.

"Too big," said Albert, trying to catch his breath, "what the fuck was that?"

"I think he might be a problem," said Ralph.

"No shit. We're gonna have to be careful. Easy-does-it, y'know?"

"I don't want to go inside," said Ralph, "maybe we should just forget the whole thing."

"We'll wait," said Albert as he rubbed his sore neck, "for now, we'll wait."

Joey was standing in the kitchen about to open the bottle of wine when the Rubenstein's came in with Mary. He had been trying, and failing, to chip away at the wine cork with a steak knife he had found in one of the drawers. Howard and Lorry were relieved to find Joey had accompanied Mary on her trip, but they also tore into him about not thinking to call them at any point in time. Joey was in the middle of an apology when the knife managed to push the rest of the chipped cork into the bottle. They would have to be careful about drinking it, but it was ultimately a success. Joey found a lemonade pitcher and did his best to filter the bits of cork from the drinkable wine.

Howard, Lorry, and Mary were sitting at the kitchen table as Joey brought the wine and four glasses. He poured himself a glass and leaned against the kitchen counter.

"Mary, listen," said Howard, "Mary, we're not going to force you to do anything or try to convince you to do something you don't want to do."

"You got that right," said Mary.

"You scared us, honey," said Lorry, "you drop off the face of the earth and then disappear completely? What are we supposed to do?"

"You could mind your own business," said Mary, her voice beginning to shake, "you...you could..."

Mary began to cry and fell into her mother's arms. Lorry held onto her with intensity, as though Mary would sink through the floor if she let her go. Howard and Joey said nothing but began to arrange light refreshments from the groceries that Joey had bought. Howard's face was turning red as he was still on edge about Albert. The hostile reception after their journey was enough to compromise his sensibilities. There were only a few times in his life when Howard had to resort to violence. Big as he was, there were times when violence had found him.

He was so tense that he accidentally shattered a wine glass in his palm, causing blood to run down the fresh cuts on his fingers. He ran his hand under the cold tap in the sink without saying a word. Joey took a towel from a kitchen cabinet and began to clean Howard's cuts, but none of them were substantially deep and they looked much worse than they were. After keeping his hand beneath the faucet for a minute, most of the bleeding had stopped. Mary's tears had subsided as she rested her face against Lorry's shoulder. Lorry stared at Howard as though her entire world were falling apart.

"It's a good house," said Howard, "your family build it?"

"Great grandfather," said Mary, wiping her nose, "I never met him, but he was strange."

"Hm. How long has it been since you been here?"

"Sixteen years. A lot of it's changed."

Joey placed a tray of apples, crackers, and cheese on the kitchen table. The four of them sipped their drinks initially without talking until Lorry spoke up.

"Well, this just isn't right," she said, "you're a homeowner now. It's bad luck not to toast a new house."

She stood ceremoniously and raised her glass, beckoning the others to do the same.

"To Mary," she said, "and the house that her family has built. Here's to many years of health and happiness."

"Na Zdorovie," said Howard.

They drank their wine and sat quietly, occasionally picking bits of cork from their tongues. Lorry's toast was meant to begin a sort of normal conversation, but there was still a lot of tension to be worked out. Lorry and Howard never produced a strategy for how they were planning to talk to Mary. An overabundance of anxiety kept Howard's mind clouded and unable to think of the right words while Lorry's own anxieties had only been amplified by Howard's. Most of their trip was spent talking about anything else.

"Oh wait," exclaimed Lorry, jumping up from her seat, "I have something for you!"

She darted out of the house and jogged to the van, returning with an authentic and recently stolen Kandinsky painting.

"I knew I'd forgotten something," she said, "just a little housewarming present."

Mary took the painting and examined it with minimal interest. Her knowledge of contemporary artists was not expansive, but she thought it looked nice. She wondered which of her parents' friends had painted it. Mary thanked them for the painting and left it leaning against a wall in the hallway whose length she used to run as a child.

The idea of Mary being a homeowner was still too alien for her to take seriously. The unique coincidence of returning home after so many strange happenings had befallen her was impossible to ignore. Mary felt like a stranger in her own house, and she was not sure how to adjust. It did not matter how old Mary was, she would always feel like a child in trouble. Even with all her anger, she was relieved that Howard and Lorry were there.

Mary returned to the kitchen and sat beside Howard. She elbowed him and gently headbutted his shoulder while Joey and Lorry talked about their own travel experiences. Joey told the story about the owl, of which his wound had nearly healed, and Lorry talked about the bizarre town of Winsted, Connecticut. Howard started to ruffle Mary's hair, but then thought better of it and simply smoothed it down.

There was a knock at the door and Mary opened it to find Albert and Ralph standing remorsefully on the steps. They apologized to the Rubenstein's for any misunderstanding and said that they hoped that they could become friends moving forward. There was not a clear indication of agreement, but Howard and Lorry passively accepted their apology. Howard sipped his wine without looking at Albert.

"Well, if there's nothing else, you'll be needing from us," said Albert, "Ralph and me will be heading out. You want us back here in the mornin'?"

"Oh, yeah," said Mary, "come by around...ten? Does that work?"

"We'll be here at nine fifty-five," said Albert, "sorry again for our misunderstanding."

With a wave to the Rubenstein's, Albert took Ralph by the arm and the two men left Mary's house. After a few moments, Albert poked his head back into the kitchen.

"If it isn't too much trouble," he said, "could we, ah, get a ride back into town?"

"Joey, would you mind?" asked Mary.

"Sure thing," said Joey, "yeah, sure."

The gentle sounds of Loose Lips' engine sputtered out concern as the car had seen better days than the previous few. With a cloud of dust rising from the tires, Joey drove Albert and Ralph back to the center of town, leaving Mary in the kitchen with Howard and Lorry. Now that the initial shock of seeing her parents unexpectedly had settled, Mary sat in the uncomfortable silence of accountability. The Rubenstein's were just as uncomfortable and were unsure as to how they should casually spend time with their daughter. Howard would occasionally clear his throat but resolved himself to deep sighs. His mind was struggling to express his feelings with words. Lorry poured the rest of the wine evenly among three glasses and handed one to Mary and Howard. They clinked their rims and Mary started to smile.

"Two sheep were grazing in a field," she said, "the shepherd had fallen asleep after a heavy lunch and his dog was taking a nap beside him. One of the sheep turns to the other and says, 'Hey Frank, we should make a break for it.'. Frank the sheep turns to his friend and says, 'Baaaaaa'."

Lorry chuckled and smiled out of the corner of her mouth while Howard rested his large hand on Mary's shoulder.

"It's good to see you," said Howard.

"I'm sorry it's hard," said Lorry.

"Louise sends her love," said Howard.

"Who's Louise?" asked Mary.

"Bigger French lady," said Howard, "used to work in the kitchen at St. Philomena's. She said she was sorry that she was late, but she wants to come visit soon."

It all came back to Mary; the kitchen, Therese and Louise, sinking Nazi U-boats in the sink. Mary laughed and rubbed her eyes to keep more tears from falling down her cheeks.

"Oh," said Mary, "oh, her. How, um, how is she?"

Howard and Lorry looked at each other, trying to decide how to explain their encounter.

"She's fine," said Lorry, "had nothing but good things to say about you."

"She's the one that gave us your address," said Howard.

"Good," said Mary, clearing her throat, "good. I'm glad she's still around. So, lemme give you the tour."

Mary led her parents through the house where she had grown up. She showed them her old room which was now filled with Aunt Coleen's junk. There was the usual head nodding and polite repetition of the word "nice" before Lorry's eye caught the framed vacation photos of Aunt Colleen's travels. She looked at them uncomfortably as she considered how to navigate Mary's potential feelings for her recently deceased Aunt.

"She was an asshole," said Mary.

"Ah," said Lorry, "I see."

Mary closed the door and took them to her grandmother's room. Howard and Lorry stood admiring what they saw as a time capsule from a forgotten era. The green plush decor and light blue walls brought a sense of calm to the collection of old furniture and antiques. Howard looked up at the hole in the ceiling and sucked his teeth. He ran his finger around its edge, examined it, and then wiped his hand on his pants.

"What do you think?" asked Mary.

"I think you got a hole."

Lorry had already found the small cupboard door built into the wall. She crouched in front of it and pushed on it a bit to see how much give was held by the latches and locks. Seeing that the door did not budge, she pressed it again and accepted it as secure.

"What's in here?" she asked.

"Not sure," said Mary, "waiting on a set of keys or a locksmith."

Finding enough satisfaction in the answer, Lorry stood up and walked to a rolltop desk that sat evenly against the wall. She began to look through old papers and drawers, finding old photographs and strange little trinkets.

'Please don't do that," said Mary.

"Sorry," said Lorry, closing the drawers and returning the papers as carefully as she could.

Walking back out to the hallway, Howard opened the door to Mary's parents' room before she could say anything about it. There was a sound that Mary heard as they walked into the place where her parents had slept. Whether the sound was real or not, Mary could not tell. It lasted only for an instant, but her bones felt like they were shaking beneath her skin.

It was bright in the room thanks to the large windows, and it looked just the same as it had always been except for some new additions to the art on the walls. The simplicity of which the Kirkland's had kept their room was somewhere between monastic and eccentric. The decor was sparse, but the furniture was a combination of art deco and there was the mirrored bed frame from the nineteen eighties where you can see yourself when you first wake up and think, *dear god, what time is it and why do I look like this?*

What hung on the walls were all the drawings that Mary had made as a child. Every crayon and paper that had touched Mary's hand was delicately maintained and preserved. Drawings of animals and monsters stretched from wall to wall as Dracula and the Wolf Man stared with their fire engine red eyes and goldenrod teeth behind clear plastic frames. Howard and Lorry examined each piece as though they were in a museum while Mary lingered in the doorway, unable to enter the room. A framed picture of her parents standing with Mary at the beach sat on a desk in a simple brown frame. Lorry lifted the picture and smiled.

"They look nice," she said, "do you remember getting this taken?"

Mary said nothing but shook her head as she lifted her finger to her mouth. The raw skin on her hand stung as she took the first nibble. She tried to focus on the pain. Lorry put the picture back on the desk and hugged Mary against her chest while she felt the shudder of hot tears soaking into the shoulder of her shirt. No one said anything for a long time until Howard made a declaration.

"We should get more wine," he said.

Once back in the kitchen, Howard set to work clearing the dishes and washing the glasses from the light lunch provided by Mary and Joey. He looked out the window to see Mary staring at a spot in the yard, sweeping her foot across the blades of grass as though she expected to find someone lying there. Lorry stood behind Howard and began to rub his back.

"This is hard," he said, "do you think she's ok?"

"Probably not," said Lorry, "maybe she won't be."

"What can we do?"

All the air left Lorry's body in a long sigh.

"Listen to her," she said.

"Are you ok?" asked Howard.

"Yeah."

Howard turned to face Lorry and he pulled her close against his body. She nearly disappeared into his arms.

"Why do you stick around with an idiot like me?" asked Howard.

"Because you make me look good," said Lorry, muffled in Howard's chest, "and you're a good lay."

Howard and Lorry left the house and walked to where Mary stood in the backyard. The afternoon was waning on to early evening and the breeze had picked up enough to be considered wind. It pushed the blades of grass against each other in sweeping ripples of breath while Mary kept her eyes fixed on the trees that bordered the edge of the yard. All of this was hers now.

"Come on," said Mary, "I want to show you something."

She took the Rubenstein's through the back yard and into the woods, passing the flowering dogwood tree. Mary kissed her two fingers and pressed them against the small branch that was growing from the broken limb. She decided that this would become a new ritual whenever she passed into the woods. Her woods. She felt more comfortable away from the house. In all the anxieties that came with the walls, there was none of that out in the wild. She thrived with the feeling of dirt on her hands and the smells that were surrounding them.

Under urban circumstances, she was just as much a part of life as she would allow herself to be. Sometimes, when she moved within the city, the world would come to her in bright sounds of admonition. In the dirt she found herself and moved in serenity. She kept a passive understanding that there were so many potential ways in which she could be killed in the wild that her reverence ran deeper than any law, be it from God or man. There were plenty of ways to die in New York, but none of them deserved her respect. Mary was an extension of the forest and had become its consort.

A different expression crossed over Mary's face as they stepped through the threshold of the forest. Howard and Lorry had not noticed it until Mary turned to tell them something about the ravine where she used to play. The Rubenstein's knew about the ravine from stories that Mary had told them in her youth, but when they saw Mary's face, they were both startled as her appearance had shifted into the features of mania. Mary now wore a rictus display where her lips had begun to curl, showing more teeth than the Rubenstein's had expected. Her footing held the certainty of one who had traversed the land with such frequency that they would face no difficulty in walking the trail under any circumstances. Howard and Lorry struggled with some of the upturned roots and stone footholds that had become slick with moss and moisture, but Mary scaled each obstacle as though she were a spider. She would look back periodically to match the Rubenstein's pace, but after a while she began to tease them.

When they finally reached the ravine, Howard and Lorry sat themselves on two small boulders and waited to catch their breath. Howard had nearly fallen on the incline and his stamina was not what it used to be. Lorry had her own difficulties, but she did maintain a stronger sense of balance. Mary stood at the water's edge and watched the small river flow intently as it traveled on its way towards an unknown destination.

"This is nice," said Lorry, "I can see why you came here."

"It's nice in the spring," said Mary, "everything starts to wake up. Personally, I think early fall is best. Sometimes there's so much life down here that...wait a minute."

Mary quickly turned and walked behind the Rubenstein's. Very gently she parted the branches of a milk thistle bush and revealed one of the small amphibian cemeteries that she had created when she was a child. The popsicle stick headstones that did remain after the years had developed a considerable lean, with some sunk down into the earth nearly up to their tops. She ran a finger over the dirt which crumbled beneath her touch, having become hardened by the coming cold. Mary smiled as she pushed the dirt back into place.

"There's another place," she said, "I don't think it's too far if you're up for it."

"Oh, sure," said Howard, "lemme just fix my bones."

Howard stood and stretched his back, which audibly cracked with enthusiasm. He let out a moan of satisfaction and jumped in place three times.

"OK," he said, "I'm ready to go. Lorry, you comin'?"

"I might stay here a bit," said Lorry, "I kind of like it here."

"Suit yourself," said Mary, "we'll swing around on our way back."

"Oh, don't worry. I can find my way back to the house. It's basically a straight shot, anyway. Enjoy your nature walk."

"Will do," said Howard.

Mary and Howard continued to the other side of the ravine. The path cut out by the small river allowed them to wind downstream until the incline became less formidable. Howard was grateful for this and seemed to have an easier time climbing what had now become a small hill. He sighed with a feeling of accomplishment as he reached the top. The path had all but disappeared as there was no proper trail that could lead them clearly through the woods. This did not appear to be a problem for Mary as she remained confident in her abilities to guide Howard through the terrain that had been such a reliable part of her childhood.

Howard struggled with his size at first, but he soon learned how to bend the brush and smaller branches out of his way without breaking them. There was something altogether pleasant about the place. They came to where there was a small break in the trees. The clearing was in an almost perfect circle, which could have held the entirety of Mary's body when she was younger but now had the capacity to contain her torso alone.

"Hold on," she said, "I want to show you something."

She lay on the ground with only her head entering the ring of trees while the rest of her body lay stretched into the woods. Howard copied her action and placed his large head between two birch trees that formed a part of the circle. They both lay with the sun and blue sky shining down on their faces.

"You do this a lot growing up?" asked Howard.

"Yep." said Mary.

"I could fall asleep like this."

"I used to," said Mary, "I'd wake up when it was dark. Didn't know what time it was. It was a little scary, but not in a bad way. Nighttime is different here. It moves different. I used to think it was evil or there would be werewolves or something. I thought I saw something once or twice, but who knows. There'd be all these lightning bugs flying around here. They made me feel better. Safe. Man, I'd get it when I got home though. My grandmother used to beat the shit out of me if I came back after dark. One time I was so scared to go back that I stayed out here all night. I slept in this little circle, and I thought it would protect me. When I went home the next day I got beat twice as bad."

Howard did not speak for a few seconds. He allowed the gravity of what Mary had told him to linger above his body before the weight could press down against him. After deciding that he should have something to say, he simply tilted his head towards Mary and said:

"I'm sorry."

"S'cool," said Mary, "over and done with."

"What did your folks think about it? Did they even know it was going on?"

"Let's just say that I fell out of trees a lot."

"Aye."

"She wasn't like that all the time," said Mary, "she worked in extremes. She'd be super sweet and lovely and then turn on a dime. I'd imagine there was some undiagnosed shit going on there, but therapy had never been big in my family. She ended up with dementia later, so that might have been a big part of it."

Howard and Mary lay with their heads in the circle for a few more minutes before Mary sat up and wiped her hands together.

"It's getting too cold for this," she said, "I almost fell asleep, too. Let's get movin'."

"Aye aye, cap'n," said Howard.

He winced as he pushed himself back up. He'd forgotten about the cuts on his hand and the weight of his body pushed his wounds against the twigs and small rocks on the ground.

"You ok," asked Mary, "how's the hand?"

"It's alright," said Howard, rubbing it and shaking it back to life, "not as bad as all that."

They continued into the woods with Mary running her palm across the trees that they passed. Howard was continuing to notice a change in almost every aspect of Mary's demeanor. Her face looked brighter, and she was smiling more than she usually did. For the first time since meeting her, Howard considered the possibility that New York had been choking the life out from Mary. He was having a good time, but he knew that the real test of Mary's health would be a process of grief and acceptance that may have been neglected for all this time since her parents had died. This was most likely the biggest piece of the unresolved trauma that she had experienced, but Howard was curious as to the number of other times Mary had been hurt as a child. The resolution may not come quickly or all at once, but Howard was determined to be there for Mary every step of the way. His inability to solve Mary's problems himself stood as one of the most painful experiences of his life. He had no say in the matter, but he could be present when necessary.

Walking in the absence of a clear path caused Howard a slight disorientation with where they were regarding the house. Howard had always admired nature, but from a spectator's perspective. Now that he was in it, he was beginning to feel a certain unease about his unconscious vulnerabilities. If anything were to happen to them out here, then there would be no one around to help them. A quiet anxiety crept about his giant body as Howard tried to convince himself that he was not afraid. The feeling of a forgotten memory formed in his mind, so he cleared his throat and tried to distract himself by telling a story.

"One time," he began, "I went on a camping trip with my dad. Did I ever tell you about him?"

Mary shook her head no.

"I don't know if you would have liked him. Sometimes I did, but most of the time he was…difficult. Hard man to know. Didn't really let you know what he felt until he hit you. Sometimes I had to avoid him. Mom did, too. I dunno. He had his problems I'm sure, but we never really knew about the specifics."

An owl screeched somewhere in the trees, causing Howard to startle. Mary was unaffected by the interruption.

"Jesus," said Howard, "anyway, he took me camping once, just him and me. We drove out of the city and went to the woods upstate outside of Poland. I remember most of the drive was quiet. He didn't even turn the radio on. So, we're just two guys in a car for four hours not talking. I was so excited to be spending time with my dad, but I didn't want to break the silence. Thought I might annoy him, and it felt like a special trip."

"Once we got to the campsite, we found a spot and set up the tent. There was still a good amount of daylight left so we decided to go for a walk in the woods. I felt so safe with him on account of him being so big. He was a giant to me. And as much as he scared me, I still felt safe with him. I guess I had convinced myself that I deserved it when he hit me. I must have done something wrong, even if I didn't know what it was I had done. I trusted my dad."

"It was summer and I wanted to go swimming in this river that we came across. My dad told me to be careful because the rain had made the water bigger and faster, but I was too excited, and I wanted to show off. Show him I was a man. So, I walk into the river, I was a skinny little guy, if you could believe it, and I make it maybe five steps before the current rips my legs out from under me and I'm flying down the river like a bastard. I was so afraid. I screamed for my dad to help, but every time I opened my mouth, I'd get river water straight down my throat. I could see my dad standing where he was, just not moving, arms crossed watching me float away. I managed to snag onto a huge log that stopped me. I crashed into it and hit my back so hard that it knocked the wind out of me. I mean, maybe I was already drowning, but I held onto that log for dear life. I started crying and screaming for my dad to help me, but he just kept standing there. Eventually I managed to drag my scrawny ass back to the shore just inching over, step by step. When I did get back to land, I was cryin' real hard and scared and angry, embarrassed, the whole thing. I cried so hard I threw up and when my dad walked up to me, he took his time, too, he walked up to me and looked down at me and said, 'I told you to be careful'."

"We spent the next two days not talking to each other, really. Four hours driving not talking, two days camping not talking, four hours driving back not talking. I was angry at myself for not listening to him. I was embarrassed that I didn't look like a man in front of him. This was my chance to show him, impress him, that I could be a man. I couldn't allow myself to be angry at him for letting me nearly drown."

Mary listened to Howard's story as they had both stopped walking at this point.

"How old were you?" asked Mary.

"Twelve," said Howard, "maybe thirteen."

"Well, I'm glad you didn't drown. Is he still around?"

"No," said Howard, "he died a couple of years ago."

"Did you ever get to talk to him about it? About the camping trip?"

"No," said Howard, "I never brought it up."

Mary wrapped her arms around Howard as best she could. She hardly even made it halfway around his waist, but he gently rested his hand on the top of her head. She felt the heat coming from his palm and it felt nice.

"I'm sorry," she said, "I'm sorry I haven't been around."

"We're not mad at you," said Howard, "we just got scared. We missed you."

"Come on," said Mary, "we're almost there."

They continued into the woods, where the sun was beginning to fall behind the top of a hill rising against the horizon. They were approaching a place where the ground began to transition into slabs of gray stone. The trees had begun thinning into patches of birch and large boulders had begun to sprout to replace the low bush and shrub of the forest's dirt floor. Howard recognized the absence of sound and the fear that comes with such a stillness. Mary stopped walking when the tree line was behind them, and they both stood on the beginning of a large cliff base ending at a precipice. Howard peeked over the edge and immediately regretted it. He felt his knees begin to buckle as he turned and walked back towards the woods.

"Oh, that's high," he said, "that's very high up."

"Something happened here," said Mary, "something I still don't understand."

"What happened?"

"One time when I was little, right before my grandmother died, she took me here to check on something. I'd never been this far out into the woods before, and I didn't understand what was going on. She seemed so angry, or maybe scared. Either way, she wasn't happy."

Mary walked towards a spot on the stone cliff that would be insignificant to anyone else, but she felt a magnetic draw. She lingered over the area and would not allow herself to take another step.

"There was a shed here," she said, "a big white shed. I remember it didn't have any windows. It looked so screwed up. My grandmother came up here to check on something inside it and she asked me to listen with her. We didn't hear anything at first and then this terrible sound came out of it. Like some animal trapped inside was trying to get out. It sounded so angry and then my grandmother started screaming at it. I was so scared."

A metallic flavor crept into the back of Mary's throat, but she coughed sharply to knock the taste back down.

"After that we went back to the house, but I never found out what happened. I came back here once after that, but the shed was gone. Then my grandmother died, and I never found out what was going on. Kind of made me crazy."

"Your grandmother sounds like a complicated woman," said Howard, "you said she had dementia, right?"

"Yeah," Mary paused as the memory of Patrick's information came back to her. She would return to him later and hear what he had to say.

"There was a lot of weird stuff with her. I didn't understand what it meant at the time."

Howard looked over the side of the cliff, although it made his stomach drop. He lay down to help himself feel closer to the ground as he peeked his head over the edge.

"Lotta junk down there," said Howard, "people party here a lot?"

Mary also got on her belly and inched her face over the edge of the cliff. There were piles of debris and scattered garbage that spread across the ground beneath them. The gorge was expansive with no clear design as to how a person would descend into the quarry. If not for the collection of splintered wood pallets, dried out campfires, bags of trash, and broken glass bottles, it might have been beautiful.

"Some people ain't got no culture," said Mary, "shit heads."

Mary and Howard stood from the ground and sat on different boulders as they watched the sun hang through a cloudy haze. There was no breeze or sound coming from the world around them, and it was making it difficult for Howard to think clearly. He had only just then realized how hungry he was and how badly he wanted several cheeseburgers.

"You want to head back," asked Howard, "we could pick up some food from town and make cheeseburgers."

"Yeah," said Mary, "that'd be nice."

24. I Don't Wanna Go Down To The Basement

Joey had returned from driving Albert and Ralph back to town, and he was already well on his way to being drunk by the time Mary and Howard got back to the house. Their departure had become tense when Joey refused to advance them their salary for the coming week, despite their production of several reasons as to why they needed it. Joey laughed at their suggestion and reminded them that he was, in his words, "broke as shit". He said this as he gripped the wad of cash that was stuffed in his jacket pocket. After dropping them off in the center of town, Joey made sure to stop at the liquor store on the way back to the house for a bottle of whiskey, and a case of beer. When Howard and Mary returned, there was a slight slur to Joey's speech when they asked about Albert and Ralph.

"Why should I cover their asses," said Joey, "I don't like how they talk to me."

"Did it get bad?" asked Mary.

"I'm just waiting for one of them to call me a faggott. I can hear it wantin' to come out."

"Joey, I'm sorry," said Mary, "just say the word and they're gone."

"Oh, totally. I don't trust them at all."

"Then they're gone," said Mary, "I'm not gonna put you in a position where you don't feel safe. Fuck 'em."

"Oh, so the owl in the motel was fine, though?"

"Hey, that wasn't me," said Mary, "I'm not the queen of owls."

Howard snickered to himself. A strong feeling of vindication for his earlier throttling of Albert spread throughout his heart and a sense of pride in Mary's judgment emerged. He poured four short glasses of whiskey and distributed them to Joey, Mary, Lorry, and himself. The group clinked their glasses to Mary's continued good health and her growing future. And to Albert and Ralph, fuck 'em. Mary and Joey were talking at the table when Lorry pulled Howard out into the hall.

"How was the walk?" she asked.

"It was good," said Howard, "necessary. She's been through a lot, but I feel like she's starting to talk about it."

"That's huge," said Lorry.

She gestured to Howard for a kiss. He obliged graciously and the Rubenstein's embraced for a few stolen moments of passion. Howard was blushing as Lorry pulled away.

"You're a good man," she said.

"Only for you," said Howard.

The two gave each other a few more kisses before they returned to the kitchen where Mary and Joey were sitting at the table in conversation. Lorry walked over to Mary and gave her a hug to which Mary playfully pushed her away.

"So, what's in the tower," asked Joey, "any weird family secrets? More skeleton bones?"

Mary coughed on the sip of whiskey she had just taken and gestured a negative response while she tried to catch her breath.

"Nothing," she said, "there's nothing up there, I don't think. Old junk and tarps"

"So, we're not going up there?" asked Joey, "not even just to see it?"

Mary was afraid to return to the tower, but she could not think of a good enough reason without explaining what she remembered from her childhood.

"There may be rats," she said, "I think we had rats up there."

"Listen," said Joey, "they can't be worse than what we got in New York.

Let's go check it out."

"I don't want to," said Mary, "you can go ahead."

Joey shrugged and rose from his seat.

"If I don't make it back, you know what to do," he said, "oh, you should show your folks the sex dungeon. Bye for now!"

Joey left the kitchen and began to climb the stairs that would lead him to the door of the tower. He let out an exaggerated shriek followed by a cackle as he opened the door. The liquor had provided him with the kind of Dutch courage that made every joke funny to the comedian. Mary shook her head and chuckled nervously while biting the side of her finger.

"Mary," said Lorry, "why don't you want to go to the tower?"

Mary had a moment of panic where she felt as though she could not explain herself. She flinched when a slip of raw skin ripped awkwardly off from her finger and a light cut produced an unexpected amount of blood. It was a great distraction. Mary cursed to herself and walked to the sink to wash the cut. Lorry and Howard looked at each other and spoke without words. After a brief psychic conference, Howard changed the subject.

"Sex dungeon?" he asked.

Mary laughed with her back to her parents and waved her hand away from them towards the red door built into the black wall.

"Help yourself," she said.

The Rubenstein's looked through the hallway and towards the red door that was built into the center of the big black wall.

"Well, if that just ain't obvious," said Lorry, "Mary, was this...I mean. Did your folks..."

"No," said Mary through a laugh, "no, nope. No, not at all. My folks were as vanilla as it comes. That was all dear Aunt Colleen. She was a lady who knew what she wanted."

Howard and Lorry looked at the door but decided to lean upon their better judgment and dismiss it as unnecessary. In his collection of conversational diversions, there was always the failsafe question that had yet to let Howard down.

"So, what's for dinner?" he asked.

"I believe there was some cheeseburger talk not too long ago," said Mary, looking out of the kitchen window.

"Indeed, there was," said Howard, "Lorry my dear, whaddya think?"

"Can you make me the burger that I love? The one you hate?" asked Lorry.

"Ugh," said Howard, "oh, man. Special occasion, I guess. Mary, what have you got for groceries?"

Mary poked through the shopping that they had brought back with them from town, but the food they had purchased was barely enough to accommodate two people, much less four. She did find two bottles of pills and a small sack of cocaine amongst the groceries which she quickly removed and stuffed in her jacket pocket. Howard committed to an executive decision that they would have to return to the town center for more appropriate provisions. He made a quick list with minimal arguments from Lorry and Mary, except for the question of preferred condiments. Ketchup can be wasted on the wrong people. After a detailed list was curated, Howard took the van out onto the street and rumbled down the road towards the promise of a bountiful harvest. Lorry and Mary remained at the kitchen table and sipped on their whiskey. Lorry rubbed her hand on Mary's shoulder, and it was met with the warmth of Mary's own hand.

"This has got to be so overwhelming for you," said Lorry, "I mean, this is where you're from. Heh. This is wild for me so I can't begin to imagine how you feel. Thank you for sharing your space with us."

"It's weird," said Mary, "it's definitely weird. But that's just a bullshit expression, anyway. 'It's weird'. People only say that to fill space. It's like calling something 'interesting' or 'random'. Doesn't mean anything."

Mary took another belt of whiskey and began to refill her glass.

"You wanna slow down a bit there," asked Lorry, "I doubt you've eaten anything today. Maybe get some water in you, too."

Mary rose and poured herself a glass of water without offering one to Lorry, who in turn rose to get her own glass of water after Mary returned to the table.

"Alright, so it's weird," said Lorry, "weird how?"

"It's hard to explain. So much of this place has changed. What I do remember is either falling apart or covered in dust. Anything new or clean here means nothing."

"Would you prefer new and clean memories?"

"Can't happen," said Mary, drinking her whiskey, "they don't exist."

"Right," chuckled Lorry, "why are they so important, anyway? Not just yours, y'know. I just mean in general. People build their whole lives around their memories."

"Can't see the future," slurred Mary, "don't know the future. People like what they know. What they knew. Try to do it again. Why people make plans. Or try to, at least."

Lorry lay her hand flat against Mary's back and began to rub in small circular patterns.

"What's your plan, Mary? What's your future?"

Mary laid her head on its side on the kitchen table. It felt cold and pleasant. Her head was beginning to hurt and overheat from the day. This happened sometimes when Mary drank, but she usually had precautionary actions to circumvent the outcome. Without access to her routine of supportive prevention, her drinking became a proper stinging. She let out a long sigh and played with her fingers under the table, being mindful of the fresh cut.

"I don't know," she said, "no plans for me."

"Well, are you going to keep the house? Sell it? Stay here, move back to New York? You should really try to start thinking about this stuff."

"Technically I wasn't supposed to leave the state," said Mary, "I'm still on probation. If they find out I left New York, then I could go to prison."

"What did you say?" asked Lorry.

"I'm...I kind of got arrested a while ago for fighting some guy. And stealing his car. And parking it on the beach at Little Odessa. Don't worry, he was a dick anyway."

Lorry rubbed her forehead and stopped herself from saying something she would later regret. Instead, she tried to keep her questions practical.

"So, you're coming back to the city then, right? You're gonna sell the house and come back to the city, right?"

"I dunno," said Mary, "I dunno..."

Lorry was doing her best to be patient with Mary's process, but the whiskey was making her feel more impulsive in how she supplied her guidance. The new confessional glimpse into Mary's delinquencies brought Lorry a strong desire to shake Mary violently and just scream at her in frustration over the past few years. Lorry wanted to hit her and hug her at the same time. She continued to rub Mary's back instead.

Joey returned to the kitchen and sat down at the table in a single fluid motion. He leaned heavily on his elbow and rested his head in his hand while he reached for the bottle of whiskey, pouring the remaining liquid into his empty glass.

"So," said Joey, "what are we talking about?"

"Nothing," said Mary with her face pressed against the table, "how's the tower?"

"Smells weird, but it's nice. A lot of creepy paintings and furniture up there. What are we doing about dinner?"

"Was there a big, white shed in the middle of the room?" asked Mary.

"Please, you and your shed. No, Mary, no shed upstairs."

"Good, just askin'."

"Howard went out to get stuff for cheeseburgers," said Lorry, "he should be back in a little bit."

"Beer it is, then," said Joey.

Joey stumbled as he left the table and nearly tripped on the leg of his chair when he walked over to the fridge. Lorry sucked her teeth and finished the whiskey that was in her glass.

"Ok," she said, "let's go, Mary."

Before Mary could say anything, Lorry had her up and standing. She hung her arm around Lorry and was guided through the hallways of her new house. Lorry did not say a word as she started up the stairs with Mary in tow but was only met with light complaints from her drunk daughter. They were both very tired. It was only when they had reached the second-floor landing when Mary realized what it was that Lorry was doing.

"Mom, wait," said Mary, "wait, mom, I don't want to do this!"

"We're not doing anything, Mary. Just going for a little walk. You have to show me the rest of the house."

Lorry held a firm grip on Mary's arm and walked behind her, guiding Mary to the door that would lead to the room at the top of the winding stairs. Mary was terrified but was too tired to protest in earnest. Instead, she just dragged her feet, as if it would do her any real good. This was not an ideal situation for Lorry, either, but having grown across the strangeness of parenthood had made her experience several examples of unpleasantness. She did not wish to cause Mary harm, but she also needed to feel as though she were doing something progressive. Maybe the whiskey was a bad idea. They really should have waited until after they had eaten a cheeseburger. Everything seems a little nicer after a cheeseburger.

They reached the door leading up to the tower and paused as neither of them really knew what to do. Mary reached out her hand and touched the brass doorknob from her childhood. The door at the bottom of the steps swung open slowly presenting them with a cascading invitation of polyurethane and the smell of dry heat from the pipes that were set in the walls. Mary looked up the stairs and her eyes followed the curve as it led to one of her many inevitabilities.

"It's smaller than I remember," said Mary.

Lorry gave her arm a little squeeze.

"I'm right here with you," she said, "every step of the way."

Mary bit her lip and nodded with her eyes on the ground. The two women began to climb up the passage leading to the door at the top of the stairs. They both had to duck a little as the ceiling that wound around and above the stairs seemed to shrink lower with each step. They were both nearly on their hands and knees when the stairs ended at the little door that would bring them into the heart of the tower. Mary opened the door, and it gave a little pop that startled them both. The height of the tower allowed the setting sunlight to glaze over the trees stretching out from the window. The diminishing light brought a dusky haze throughout the room. Much to Mary's surprise, when she did turn on the halogen floor lamp, the light shone brightly and removed all the shadows. She reminded herself to examine the breakers to see what was working and what was not.

Everything flooded Mary's mind in an instant; the dusty smell of old carpet and upholstery, tarps in humidity, and the prying eyes of so many old paintings stacked neatly against the wall. Lorry lingered against the door and watched Mary walk around the room. She moved slowly at first but began to explore with more curiosity. Mary walked to a stack of old paintings that were leaning against the wall and began to shuffle through them as she looked for some familiar faces.

There was one painting that she remembered most from her childhood. It was a portrait of a regal looking woman dressed in a bright yellow sundress holding a nervous looking dog in her lap. This painting had often frightened Mary as she had once been bitten by a nervous dog who was being held by a woman. Although it might have been more upsetting if she had been bitten by the woman instead of the dog, it was the woman in the painting who frightened her most. There was a specific tilt of her head which lent a subtle expression of judgment to the woman's face. It was a look that Mary had seen several times when she would play in the tower. She would try to mind her own business while the woman with the dog kept an immovable eye fixed upon her with contempt. Contempt for what? Mary could not say. Because the expression remained unchanging and unyielding to Mary, the idea that she was perpetually wrong and in a state of disgrace followed her. It was not until young Mary had covered the painting with a tarp that she could feel confident about moving around the room freely and without consequence. At least until all the unpleasantness began to happen. Looking at the woman in the painting now brought no feelings at all.

The couch was still there in the middle of the room and the boxes that lined the walls wrapped around the center with the promise of forts yet to come. Mary's eyes scanned the row of boxes until they fell upon the grandfather clock that stood against the wall by itself. Lorry walked towards the clock and stood beside Mary, crossing her arms as she scrutinized the piece.

"This is nice," said Lorry, "how old is this?"

"I don't know," said Mary, "we've always had it. The owl used to scare me when I was little."

"Does it still work?"

Mary found a small, latched panel on the side. She popped it open and there was a silver key hanging on a hook beside a small piece of paper glued to the inside of the door. Faded pencil scratches from so long ago were handwritten in script that read Crafted and Inspected by Charles Babbitt, Eighteenth of June 1821 Taunton, Massachusetts. Mary took the key from the hook and began to wind the clock. After a few turns, the mechanisms began to clunk and click and jostle and spin as the grandfather clock shook the dust from its bones. A few awkward bongs rattled atonally out from its chest as the eyes of the owl head sleepily tried to open. One eye remained closed, but the mice on the ends of the clock face arms began their merry chase without haste.

"Still works," said Mary, "funny."

The two women took a step back to admire the mechanical craftsmanship as Joey entered the room. He had a beer in one hand and two in the other.

"Hi gang," he said, "thought you might want one. Sorry, I didn't bring any for the ghosts."

He handed a beer to Mary and Lorry while the grandfather clock incorrectly sounded a chime of the hour. They three tapped the necks of their beer bottles together and Mary was beginning to feel less afraid. What she had previously experienced in the room all those years ago was no more real than the mice in the belly of the owl. Standing with her mother and Joey made her feel slightly less alone, if not just vaguely uncomfortable. There was still a lot of work to do before Mary could allow herself the vulnerability to trust them completely, but at that moment, she felt a growing hope and optimism. This was a unique sensation.

"There's a lot of potential up here," said Lorry, "I mean, with all this natural light! This is a painter's dream room."

"My grandfather was a painter," said Mary, "he'd spend hours up here just painting portraits and still-life's. He'd have all these friends coming up here to be painted. One time I'd snuck up here and watched my grandfather paint a naked woman."

"Dirty old man," said Joey, collapsing across the dusty couch.

"No, for real though," said Mary, "he was just painting her at first. She was beautiful. Much too young for him but then he walked over, and they just started fucking. Right there on that couch."

Joey carefully stood up and wiped the dust from his clothes while he contemplated his most recent life choices.

"Did your grandmother ever find out," asked Lorry, "I mean, this couldn't have been the only time."

"I don't know," said Mary, "he was definitely bringing a lot of models up here. Men and women."

"So, grandpa was just DTF," said Joey, "what an icon."

"Well, yeah," said Mary, "he was a weird guy."

"Hm," said Lorry, "is he still around?"

"No, he disappeared I guess," said Mary, "the way my dad told it, he just up and left one day. He must have run off with one of his models."

"Did he paint all these?" asked Joey, gesturing to the line of frames against the wall.

"I don't think so," said Mary, "He had some artist friends that he traded with."

"Do you think he's still alive?" asked Lorry.

Mary ruminated on this for a moment before returning to the door leading down the stairs. Lorry and Joey followed, filing down the narrow steps that would bring them back to the darkness that was swallowing the lower section of the house without power.

Two hurricane lamps were brought out of a closet and placed on the kitchen table. The wicks were small, but there was enough oil left to provide a soft glow in the otherwise darkened room. The conversation had taken on a gentler tone while Lorry and Joey caught up with each other's most current social events. Joey was beginning to explain his saga of Sam and Biscuit when Mary decided to investigate the basement in search of a fuse box. Mary turned on her phone's flashlight and made her way down the steps.

The unfinished basement had been an eternal project for Mary's father, but one that never formed past the planning stages. The uneven cement floor had poor drainage and was known to catch water, making it difficult for snakes and small animals to get out if they had found their way in. The skeletons of spiders from so long ago hung from the ceiling and had been knotted and tied with fresh webbing from those that were still alive. The white husks would camouflage the living, allowing for their movements to be sudden and unexpected. Mary descended the stairs with caution as the basement had already flooded with a few inches of standing water. When Lorry asked Mary if she needed any help, Mary suggested they try different switches to see which circuits were still functioning.

The light coming out of Mary's phone danced across the ripples of water that were caused not only by her steps, but also by the movement of unknown life that was becoming disturbed by her presence. Mary stood in the middle of the basement and turned slowly, allowing her light to sweep the darker corners of the room. The single beam provided limited visibility as no other light could make its way in. Mary suddenly had the sensation of feeling very small in the darkness.

The flicker of movement from behind the stairs caught Mary off-guard and made her hands shake as she tried to bring the light back to what she had seen. She found no definition of what form could have been behind the stairs, just the lasting ripples and small splashes to suggest its size. From what Mary had seen, it was big. She stood immobilized with the light shaking in her hand and her voice caught in her throat.

The circuit breaker was just beyond the space where Mary had seen the creature, but she could not find the courage to approach it. Somewhere the sound of a mouse crawling into the stone wall cut across the air, causing Mary to jump and drop her phone. It landed with a thunk, as the shallow layer of water was barely enough to cushion its fall. Fortunately, the light remained on which allowed Mary to find her phone quickly. When she brought the light back up from the floor, the form of a human face hovered twisted and frozen in the air above her head.

The creature stood quivering with an occasional spasm of the eyes and mouth without making any sound. It was as though it were dead, but the nerve endings were still working and trying to figure out how much pain it should be receiving. The length of the creature coiled around the basement ceiling and traveled in the form of shadow and smoke. A long pair of thin oily arms were bent at the elbow, bringing its hands up to its mouth and then back down to its navel, wringing them all the while. The fixed grimace on the face resembled St. Sebastian, or that of a child who had lost its favorite toy because it had misbehaved. The eyes darted from side to side in an unblinking search for the valued possession. Its hair lay flat, limp, and greasy across its pale forehead stained with grime while its tongue, both long and gray, flicked itself out like a lizard failing to moisten its lips. Its eyes fell upon Mary as the creature reared back its spine and spoke.

"This is not your home," it said, "it might have been once, oh, so very long ago, but you haven't the right to belong here."

The creature's voice had a sound like it was speaking underwater or from the inside of a very large bell. It reverberated through Mary's mind, but the mouth loosely hung open without moving. The childlike face maintained its grotesque dissatisfaction while its eyes darted in all directions.

"So brave, to run away," it said, "so brave to let him die."

A wet cough gurgled with laughter out of the creature's mouth as the eyes twitched compulsively. Its tongue retreated behind its lips while the hands began rapping their fingers against its own cheeks. Once the hands moved up to its face, only the eyes remained visible through the smokey knuckle digits. Mary was angrier than she was frightened, but not by much. Her hands and knees shook uncontrollably while a tremor ran through her words.

"I'm not afraid of you," she said, "get the fuck out of my house."

The creature continued to laugh as it stooped down to match Mary's gaze. Its twisted face was inches from her own. The smell was terrible.

"I don't want you to be afraid of me," it said, "don't you know how much I love you?"

The creature reached out with its long oily hands and held Mary's face.

"I've spent my whole life...trying to protect you..."

Mary struggled to breath as the stench of the creature was overwhelming.

"You don't...understand yet," it said, "...but he's still here...and I'm not going...anywhere."

....

Mary was lying on her back in three inches of standing water. The creature was gone. She was almost getting used to these episodes at this point. Mary lay awake staring at the skeletons of dead spiders hanging from the ceiling and wondered when she would officially lose her mind. There must be a scale somewhere to measure how crazy a person can get. Mary was almost looking forward to the progress. The skeletons above her head gently dangled and twitched on the strands of old webs.

Feeling the implications of a powerful headache just around the corner, she got to her feet and tried to shake as much of the water from her clothes as she could. There was no satisfaction in being soaking wet with cellar water. Mary trudged back up the stairs by the light of her phone and tried to ignore the heartbeat she felt in her temples.

"What happened to you?" asked Joey, opening another beer.

"I slipped," said Mary, "probably unwise to mess around with a circuit breaker when you're standing in water."

"You want me to take a look?" asked Joey, "I can probably figure it out."

"Naw, it's fine. I'll get my dad to look at it when he gets back. I'm going to get changed."

As if on cue, Howard entered the house from his trip to the store with his arms loaded with groceries. Bags and parcels were carefully placed on the kitchen table as Mary and Joey began to help unpack the groceries.

"You guys been to that hippie market yet," he asked, "bunch a nut jobs around here."

"This is too much, dad," said Mary, "we're not even sure how long we're gonna be here."

"Well, *I'm* hungry," said Howard, "what happened to you?"

He eyed Mary up and down as she was patting the back of her head with dry paper towels.

"I went to look at the circuit breaker, but I slipped. There's a lot of water down there."

"I'll take a look," said Howard, walking back out the door, "come on, there's more in the van." Joey and Lorry followed Howard out to the van while Mary went upstairs to change out of her wet clothes. She felt for the small bag of cocaine, still dry in her jacket pocket. Mary saw this as an opportunity for a small treat while she had some alone time.

There was a new jovial nature to his motions as Howard began to deposit the groceries in the pantry and refrigerator. Whether it was due to his opportunity to provide a bountiful harvest for his family, his lingering elation towards the absence of Albert and Ralph, or both, he sang a little song to himself as he put away the beans. There were already a few things worth celebrating, but that was a bonus. Howard returned to the kitchen with two cases of beer, one bottle of whiskey, a bottle of gin, and some juice and soda for mixers. Lorry found some frying pans and started to get to work preparing the food to make a cheeseburger buffet. Howard was asking about the electricity when Joey interjected.

"Might not be a good idea. Maybe we need some rubber gloves or something."

"At least the gas works," said Lorry, "and we have some of these lamps goin'."

She was melting butter in a pan by the light in her phone as she said this. The light from the lamps was fading quickly as the wicks were not long enough to last the night.

"Lemme take a look," said Howard.

He could barely fit through the door leading down to the basement, but after a series of grunts and the sound of snapping wood, he disappeared into the darkness. They could hear him sloshing around and cursing to himself as he bumped and jostled through the wet and cluttered room. There suddenly came a loud and hollering yell as the lights returned to the house. This was met with a triumphant chorus from Joey and Lorry in celebration.

The smell of meat frying in the pan seemed to get stronger as Howard returned from the basement. There were traces of smoke coming off his body and many spiders in his hair, both living and dead. Some looked as though they had fused to his skin while the livelier spiders began to drop down clumsily from strands of new silk. They scattered across the floor and Howard looked unwell.

"Oh god," said Lorry, "oh god, Howard!"

She ran to him and began to wipe the spider carcasses from his face and out of his hair. He seemed in a daze and was passively smiling at her as she proceeded to stomp on the living spiders that were trying to escape. Bringing Howard to a chair, she had him sit while she poured him a glass of water.

"Are you ok," she asked, "oh baby, what happened?"

Howard looked at Lorry with a stupid smile on his face. The smoke coming off his clothes smelt like burnt cotton and ozone.

"I don't wanna go down to the basement," said Howard, smiling, "bad things in the basement."

"I know, baby. I know. You don't have to go down there."

"I don't wanna go down to the basement."

"You want to lay down for a bit?"

"I don't wanna go down to the basement."

"Let's go lay down for a bit."

"Are we having soup?"

"No, Howard. Would you like some soup?"

"I don't wanna go down to the basement."

Lorry and Joey helped Howard over to a couch in the hallway. They laid him down with a blanket and a glass of water while he nervously looked around the room.

"Too many spiders," he said, "I don't like spiders."

"Should we take him to the hospital?" asked Joey.

"Probably," said Lorry, "let's check on him in a few minutes. Howard, sweetie, do you want to go to the hospital?"

"I don't wanna go down to the basement."

It was agreed that Howard would no longer be required to go down to the basement. Joey and Lorry left him on the couch to finish cooking in the kitchen when Mary came back downstairs. She had changed her clothes and was returning to the kitchen when she passed her father in the hallway. Her mood had taken an upswing from a fresh bump of cocaine.

"Thanks for fixing the lights," she said, "Hey, are you ok? What happened?"

"Bad things," said Howard, "bad things in the basement."

Mary was not willing to discuss what she had seen in the basement. If Howard had seen the same thing, then that would bring about a different kind of crisis. Mary had convinced herself that these episodes were psychological in nature, but that did not make them any less real. She needed that separation.

Howard lightly touched Mary's hand and smiled at her with an expression between joy and regret.

"I wanted to do my best...trying to protect you..." he said, "I'm sorry, Mary. I'm always going to love you. I don't want you to hurt this much."

An echo of coincidence from Howard's words ran through Mary's mind while his emotions overpowered the composure he tried so desperately to maintain. Howard shut his eyes tightly and allowed a few loose tears to roll down his cheeks. Mary knelt beside her father and put her hand against his large head, thinking about what she might have been putting them through.

"You don't have to protect me all the time," she said, "I'm sorry I made you worry so much."

Howard wiped his nose on the blanket and rubbed his eyes with his free hand.

"Anything you need," he said, "we're here for you. I'm sorry if you ever felt like we weren't."

Mary hugged her father around his neck and stayed there until she noticed that he had begun to snore. Letting go of her father, she gently rested his head against the arm of the couch, and he fell into a deep sleep, mumbling something about spiders. Dinner was served at the kitchen table with cheeseburgers, fries, salad, and all the fixin's. Mary was still thinking about what she had seen in the basement and what Howard had said, wondering if there was a real connection or if it was an extension of her mental health. She ravaged her first cheeseburger as Joey was getting up for his second. Lorry had moved on to water while Mary and Joey opened more beer.

"How's spider man?" asked Joey.

"He'll be ok," said Mary, "he should get checked out, though."

"Let him sleep for a bit," said Lorry, "I've seen him in worse shape."

"Like the time when he tried to build his own super radio and nearly set the apartment on fire?" asked Mary.

"Which time?" said Lorry.

"Every time," said Mary.

"Or the time that he tried to make pork ceviche," said Joey, "he was sick for a week."

"That's my man," said Lorry, "simply perfect."

"What did you see in dad, anyway?" asked Mary.

"I'm not even sure," said Lorry, "I just knew. He was funny. Kind, you know? He didn't try to be somebody else. I dated a lot of artist types because they were clever or handsome or…whatever. Your dad was just unapologetically himself. Even when he did try to impress me it'd come out so goofy and awkward that I couldn't help but love him."

They sat at the table in the kitchen while Lorry tried to make a circle with the ring of water that had developed beneath her glass.

"Yeah," said Lorry, "he's always been my favorite."

Not having realized how hungry she was, Mary ate a second cheeseburger and decided that it was time for her to lay down. She walked up to her grandmother's room and climbed into the bed that she had not known since her childhood. It still smelled of stale cigarettes and body powder.

25. Not Much Further To Go

Albert and Ralph returned to the house around ten-thirty the next morning. Joey and the Rubenstein family were themselves just waking up and shuffling towards the idea of coffee. A fresh bird's nest had fallen off the roof from the previous night and Howard was feeling good as new, if not just a little rattled from his surviving electrocution in the basement. He was in no rush to return downstairs if it could be helped.

Joey was manning the stove and he insisted on making his famous sausage gravy and biscuits with scrambled eggs and roasted red peppers. It was a recipe that he had learned from his grandmother, but it was also the only meal he felt confident in making. He could cook most things fine, sure, but this meal, to him, meant welcoming comfort. It was good luck. With everything that they had each encountered over the past few days, a little luck and comfort would go a long way.

There was a knock on the door as Mary was pouring her first cup of coffee. She answered it to find Ralph and Albert standing on her front steps and wearing their best smiles, although Ralph could not lift his eyes from the ground. They had no tools, cans of paint, or ladders, but they were dressed in clean white overalls and had decided to treat themselves to a morning bath.

"G'morning, miss," said Albert, "apologies for being late. We had some trouble finding a ride. Now we wouldn't wanna disturb your breakfast. Kinda late for breakfast, isn't it? But we were wondering if we could sit down and draw up that contract."

Mary sipped her coffee for dramatic effect, but she was also buying time. She was not in the mood for confrontation, and she still had a headache from the day before.

"I'm sorry guys, but we have to reconsider the offer," she said, "new developments have, uh, developed."

Albert fiddled with his hearing aid and asked Mary to repeat herself. She raised the volume in her voice, although it was unnecessary with Albert's adjustment. Ralph stared at the ground and dug into the dirt with the toe of his boot.

"We can't hire you," she said, "we're gonna fix the place ourselves."

"We had a deal," shouted Albert, "we came all the way out here and we had a deal!"

"Well, I'm sorry," said Mary, "turns out we made a mistake. We don't need the help after all."

"You made a mistake alright," said Albert, "and you're gonna pay for your mistake."

The growing shadow of Howard began to cover Albert and Ralph as the gigantic man of imposition stood behind Mary. He silently placed a hand on his daughter's shoulder. Ralph had already begun to walk back up the driveway, but Albert stood his ground.

"Someday you're gonna have to learn how to talk to people," said Albert, "I hope that day don't come too late for you."

With his words hanging in Mary's mind, Albert spit on the ground and followed Ralph up the driveway that led back to the main road. Mary and Howard watched them leave until they were well out of sight.

"You ok?" asked Howard.

"Yeah. You?"

"Yeah. Let's get some eggs."

Joey and the Rubenstein's finished their breakfast with the leisurely tone of a Sunday morning. Joey's comfort cooking was a resounding success and left everyone ready for an early afternoon nap. Howard returned to the hallway couch with the intention of folding up his bedding from the night before, but then he made the critical mistake of sitting down. It was nice at first and led into a substantial lean. Leaning on your elbow can lead to all sorts of dangerous situations. In Howard's case, his body began to slide into a naturally horizontal position. Curling his arm beneath his head, he thought to himself:

Maybe just five minutes.

Whether this was vocalized or not, he felt secure in the knowledge that everyone else would know what he meant.

Lorry had begun to clear up the breakfast dishes, which are often more than you would expect, but she did not mind the work. She turned on the radio to see what the local college stations would be playing and found delight in not being able to recognize anything that she heard. Lorry did her best to keep up with pop culture media as it developed, especially new music. She did, however, find it difficult to sift through the layers of tired rhythms that seemed to come in abundance. She would spend weeks filtering through the genres that she enjoyed in search of new music. Most days she could find at least two examples of unfamiliar songs that she enjoyed, but there was a great deal of filler that she had to wade through to get there. When she did find something that struck her interest, she would obsessively collect whatever she could of their catalog. Her most recent discovery was a South American punk band called Las

Salchichas. She was expecting two of their records in the mail and was now worried that they may have already arrived while her and Howard had been away. A song by Serge Gainsbourg crackled through static on the radio and Lorry considered leaving the country after all this was over.

Joey had taken a moment to sneak away and privately masturbate while everyone else remained occupied.

Mary sat on the front steps of her house in a moment of reflection. This was a new practice that she was trying to allow herself. These were not calculated attempts to rationalize what it was that continued to affect her, but more of an attempt to draw a psychic map of understanding. She thought that if she could allow herself enough time to recall her episodes chronologically, then there may be a recognizable pattern.

After the party in New York, the guy in the bathtub, went to Ruth's (have to talk to Ruth), Joey and Bosco's, bad thing, Aunt Colleen died, get back house, other bad thing...what am I missing.

There was something she was missing. She thought that it must have been an obvious oversight on her part because this was her series of hallucinations. She thought of her personal history of psychotropic experimentation and narcotic enthusiasm. Could it be possible that all those years of indulgence and downright fun had left a lasting impression on her perception of the world? This brought forth the desire to get high while the following thought of practicing sobriety arrived as an undesirable option. She decided to fall back on her only known effort to figure this out on her own. It was her battle, after all. She just felt like she would be able to handle it all better if she had a little chemical intervention.

Mary was grateful for her parents' intrusion into her situation, although she would be the last to admit it. Even with the discomfort of accountability and guilt that accompanied unwanted attention, she was afraid to be left alone. Having had little to no support in her developmental years, Mary had learned that her ability to rely on help from other people was non-existent. This was a fallacy, of course, but some behavior learned in the crucial stages of growth can adapt into an individual's perception of themselves. Sometimes change is hard. Growth sucks.

Joey sat down beside Mary and lit a cigarette. Offering one to Mary, she took it quietly and they sat smoking together. When Joey looked at Mary's face, he could see that she was a million miles away.

"Where are you right now?" asked Joey.

"I am on the front steps of my once childhood home. I can barely recognize or remember a lot of it and what I do remember is either falling apart or terrifying. I don't know why I'm here and I don't know what to do."

"...great!"

Mary laughed and shook her head as she looked at her feet resting on the stone steps. She took a long drag from her cigarette and let the smoke slowly leave her nose. The burning smell that lingered in her nostrils made her feel good.

"What am I missing, Joey," asked Mary, "what am I forgetting?"

"Beats me. That's between you and the walls."

"I hate this place," Mary said, sadly, "I wish I'd never come here. What am I even doing here?"

Mary's hands started to shake so hard that she dropped her cigarette. She moved as though she wanted to pick it back up, but she changed her mind and laid her head in her hands. Joey stamped it out and put his arm around Mary's shoulders as he gently rocked her from side to side.

"We'll figure it out," he said, "we always do."

Mary kissed Joey on the cheek and put her head against his shoulder.

"You wanna get fucked up?" she asked.

"Noooooo," said Joey, "no. Not right now. I mean I do, yeah. Your folks would kill me though."

"Us," said Mary, "they'd kill us."

"Bullshit," said Joey, "they love you. They tolerate me. Although if your dad ever touched me, I'd die a happy man."

"Gross, Joey!"

"Oh, come on," said Joey, "he's not even your real dad."

Mary got quiet at this remark as it hurt her more than she thought it would. Joey, recognizing his blunder, did his best to backpedal.

"I mean, you know what I mean. It's not like you're related."

"Right," said Mary.

"I'm sorry," said Joey, "I'm sorry, bad joke."

"Right."

She got up to leave, walking down through her backyard and into the woods that surrounded her house. She could hear Joey yelling after her but refused to acknowledge what it was that he said. He had hurt her feelings and she wanted to be alone, which was her favorite place to be when things got hard. Seemed as though things were always hard. Mary kissed the new branch of the flowering dogwood tree and continued into her woods.

She walked past the ravine as the thought of stopping never entered her mind. She walked through the late-morning sun as it cut through what leaves remained on the trees. Her steps were as though she were moving on clouds in how effortlessly they remembered everything. The song "Have You Ever Seen A Dream Walkin'" was stuck in her head, but she could not make it past the first few lines.

The stone ground leading out of the woods to the precipice carried its ambivalence as Mary walked to the edge and investigated the gorge decorated with garbage. It was a long way down and there was a moment where she considered doing something foolish. It was only a passing thought and not so unusual. She had had similar thoughts and contemplations while standing on bridges or subway platforms. They never came with enthusiasm and left almost as soon as they arrived. For Mary it was more of an intrusive curiosity. She knew there was a name for the feeling, but she could not remember what it was.

Looking into the gorge, Mary spotted someone moving through the garbage and stones. There was a person rooting through the trash and carefully moving smaller rocks as though he were looking for something. Mary lay down on her stomach and wrapped her fingers around the cliff's edge as she poked her head further than her normal comforts would allow. She was elevated in such a distance from the man that it was difficult to make out his features clearly, but she saw that he was old, bald, and moving with care. After a few minutes of scrutiny, Mary recognized him to be Patrick, whom she had met in town.

It looked as though his cautious need to sustain his physical health was balanced evenly with the importance of his search. He moved with calculated intentions, stepping from stone to stone while he walked patiently towards his next move. Mary felt as though she were a hawk watching a mouse move through the prairie underbrush. Her eyes were nowhere near as good, but she needed the playful distraction. She lingered over this fantasy in her mind for a little while. She even let out a small "caw" that would have barely been audible had you been lying beside her. It was curious to Mary how Patrick came to be down in the gorge. There were no convenient trails or roads that led into the quarry. Considering the fragile nature of the man, she would be impressed if he had scaled down the rock face.

How the hell did he get down there, Mary thought to herself.

She watched Patrick with interest for a few more minutes before she turned to lie on her back and stare up at the sky.

Mary considered several things. She always joked that she did her best thinking on her back, but that was more of a knock at the years of crummy sex she had experienced. Her mind wandered to thoughts of David and her parade of disappointments that took the form of her previous lovers. There were several partners who had been both kind and terrible towards Mary. There were also several partners to whom Mary herself had been kind and terrible. For each relationship that had disrupted the natural order of Mary's life, there were just as many instances of her own actions taking their toll on a person for whom she had cared. As she looked at the sky and reflected on her romantic history, a small bird landed on the low branch of a thin birch tree. This was the first time Mary had seen any wildlife in this area of the woods and it was a curious sight.

"Hello, David," she said to the bird, "you still a dick?"

Mary took out her phone and lingered over David's last message. He had sent it at a time when she was otherwise occupied. The message was brief. Two words.

"We good?"

She read it three times, put her phone away, and then picked it up again and read it five more times. She thought about texting him. She wanted to tell him that it was whatever. His leaving hurt Mary more than she would admit, and she had not allowed herself the time to acknowledge it, either. There was already too much aggravation in her life now to consider her feelings towards David. The choice of silence would take priority towards her approach to his inanity. If he was gone, then so be it. She would try to keep this in mind if an unforeseen spike in sentimental memory may occur. Those moments were never well-designed or well-intentioned. They could spur up from nothing in times when the task at hand is imperative in its need for accuracy. You could be balancing a marble between two vials of sulfuric acid and then, before you know it, you start to think about ol' what's-his-name or whoever. After that you're all thumbs, heh heh.

With her phone turned off and stored in her pocket, Mary turned to lie on her stomach and look for Patrick to see what he was up to. There was no clear sight of his presence among the stone and gravel landscape. He had disappeared.

The garbage must have taken him. He is now of the trash. Where the hell did he go, thought Mary.

The afternoon was allowing more daylight to produce the illusion of time when Mary decided to find a safe way into the gorge. She thought that if Patrick had lost his footing, slipped, or had hurt himself, then she could not just leave him alone to die. She also had several questions for Patrick that would hopefully help her piece together her own history. Patrick was the only remaining person with any insight into Mary's childhood.

She stood up to take in a lay of the land but could not find a clear path to lead her down the cliff safely. She decided to walk along the edge in the hopes that it might connect to a trail. This was also an enticing and familiar energy in the knowledge that she was beginning to investigate a previously uncharted area. She felt like an explorer for the first time in a long time. It was a good feeling, but it made her realize that she had left her grandfather's compass back at the house.

Mary walked for about half a mile before she found a small set of rusted metal stairs leading down to the gorge. They were rickety with holes in some of the steps from the years of elemental exposure and neglect, but they did lead down to a trail that looked as though it would cut back to the quarry. This was an opportunity that she could not ignore. Turning her feet sideways, Mary descended the stairs carefully. She tried to feel for each step and test the durability with the knowledge that they could potentially give way to a nasty fall. From this height it may not kill her, but there would be no hope for a soft landing. Slow and steady, stupid.

The single railing that ran the length of the stairs wobbled freely in her grip. After a tense collection of minutes, the time at which Mary's descent had two near falls and one unsuccessful attack from a wasp, Mary left the final step and stood with her legs shaking on a slab of stone. She turned to look back up the stairs and they appeared smaller now that she had reached the bottom. Climbing back up would be less enjoyable than climbing down, but she would worry about that later. For now, she had to walk half a mile back to the point where she lost sight of the little old scrounger.

Unlike the cliff that Mary had known, the inside of the gorge was teeming with signs of life and sound. Snakes and lizards lay on top of stones to catch sun-lit rays for warmth. Soon they would be off to hibernate after having eaten their fill of mice, voles, and other prey that never stood a chance. Trees grew out from the cliff walls, leaning sideways at first before curving up to where they would catch the most sunlight. The sounds of birds still yet to be found came down from the trees in little spurts of song. Mary thought of herself as a frog in her own ravine, now to scale.

She had walked for so long in wonderment that she had almost forgotten her mission. Once the ground began to show signs of light trash, her mind returned to finding Patrick, of whom she hoped to be in one piece. She entered what appeared to be a centralized spot from where she had been looking over the cliff. It was hard for her to tell where she was in relation to her point of origin, but after recognizing some shapes and shadows from this new angle she settled on the area with the most campfire remains. The amount of trash that was spread across the ground was both impressive and depressing.

The abandoned tents and campfires from over the years laid by twos and threes around the ground. Broken bottles of every size and shape were scattered all around her, as well as beer cans, newspapers, and dented tins of food. Mary had an impulsive desire to begin cleaning up the place, but the scene was all too dire. She knelt to pick up an opaque glass bottle that was no bigger than her ring finger. It was one of those small bottles for antique capsules that had been made one-hundred years ago. She wiped the dirt from it and stuck it in her pocket to bring it back with her. It felt as though she were saving a life.

Beside the campfires was a collection of broken wood and pallets that had been gathered over the years. Mary walked towards the wood that lay so close to the wall of the cliff and found large, splintered pieces that may have been painted white at some point but had become worn and chipped from exposure to the sun and the elements. Some broken pieces fit together enough to form part of a door to a shed.

"Son of a bitch,' whispered Mary.

The sound of falling rocks caught Mary off guard as Patrick stepped out from behind a small pile of stones. They stood and stared at each other for a moment. Patrick's face looked frozen in the grimace that sometimes comes with being old. His expression switched in an instant to a shy smile as he rubbed the top of his head and began to sheepishly laugh.

"Looks like you found me," he said, "I was hoping I would have more...more time."

"Time for what," asked Mary, "what are you doing here?"

"Ah, right. Well...you...oh boy..."

Mary felt angry. The balance of anger and fear became such an overwhelming sensation that she imagined, for a moment, smashing Patrick's head against a stone. She knew it would collapse much like a stuffed cabbage. The thought fizzled and left Mary's mind as Patrick continued to speak.

"There's something I think you should see."

Patrick led Mary over the trash and stones into the small entrance of a cave that was hidden behind a boulder. The rock formation had created an optical illusion that caused the opening to be nearly imperceptible to the naked eye unless you were really looking for it from the right angle. Mary considered the likelihood of an escape route as Patrick was becoming increasingly more nervous. There was nothing about Patrick that Mary could trust. Any information that she could get from him would have to be filtered through whatever incentives he was working through. Her justification for this was that she had no other alternatives.

"You usually take young women into caves?" asked Mary.

"Mary, please," said Patrick, "I'm too old for that business. Now follow me. This is important."

There were several scenarios in which she could overpower him if she needed to. He did not look particularly strong or sinister, just nervous. Mary lingered on the potential danger for a few moments before agreeing to follow Patrick into the caves. Her need for answers outweighed the threat of harm.

The cave was shallow at first and looked more like a shrine built onto the side of the rockface. After turning a corner that was covered by a separate sheet of stone, there was a path that led further underground. Three mining helmets hung on wrought iron spikes that had been hammered into the rock many years ago. Patrick lifted two helmets from the wall and handed one to Mary.

"It gets dark," said Patrick, "follow my steps."

They put their helmets on, and Mary did her best to mirror Patrick's walk. His footing was sturdy and cautious as he moved, but it looked as though he had known these caves for many years.

"This used to be a clay mine in the nineteen-twenties and thirties," he said, "after a couple of years, the mine was abandoned. I don't really know why, but some folks claimed ghosts, etc. Monsters. The Dover Demon was said to have made an appearance. They blamed him for a decapitation when one of the foremen was probably just drunk. The company went under after a while. I've always been a cave nut. When I found this place, I wanted to see where it would lead. Probably foolish to do it alone, so I would bring friends around here when I could."

"You bring a lot of dates around here?" asked Mary as she lightly kicked some garbage out of the way.

"Oh, no," laughed Patrick, "romance hasn't been a priority for me in a long time. However, I did date your grandmother. Before she was married."

"Oh really," said Mary, "what was that like?"

"She was lovely," he said, "if not just a little impulsive."

"So, grandma was always nuts?"

"She was insane," said Patrick, "but so was I. We had a lot of fun. Watch your step."

There was a dip in the path with a two-foot drop that came abruptly. It would be easy to break an ankle if you were distracted or lost in thought. Patrick took Mary's hand and helped guide her down the step.

"Thanks," said Mary, "what did you mean when you said she was insane?"

Patrick stopped walking and turned to face Mary. They both shielded their headlamps to minimize the light in their eyes.

"She didn't have dementia," he said, "she knew exactly what she was doing at all times. Your grandmother was a very calculated woman."

"What?"

"They called it dementia because she committed suicide," he said, "drank poison."

Mary took a moment to receive this information. The words came over and over as a loop in her mind, but she could not make sense of them on a real level. More answers led to more questions.

"Wait a minute," said Mary, "so everybody knew it was suicide?"

"Yes, but we weren't about to tell you that. Your parents certainly weren't. They thought telling you something you wouldn't understand would be easier than the truth. When I say that your grandmother was insane, I'm not trying to exaggerate. She was out of her mind. Prone to violence, manic episodes, hallucinations. She was a mess."

Patrick removed his helmet and wiped his forehead with a handkerchief.

"How much do you remember," asked Patrick, "about your grandmother?"

"I remember she was kind of a dick, but in a fun way. Does that make sense? I mean, she scared me, too. She hit me a couple of times, but only when I acted up."

"Uh-huh," said Patrick. He walked further down the path with his back to Mary. "...do you remember a boy?"

Mary was struck dumb by the question. A million images flashed across her mind, and she began to feel faint as she steadied herself against the wall. She tried to look as casual as possible, but her knees betrayed her, knocking against each other.

"He would have been younger than you," said Patrick, "but not by much. Short mop of brown hair. Very serious eyes."

"He came into our yard," said Mary, "he said he was playing hide-and-seek, and he just came out of the woods. That was real?"

Patrick closed his eyes painfully and shook his head in shame.

"I was hoping you wouldn't remember it," said Patrick, "we hoped that you'd just forget."

"That was real?! This whole time I've been losing my mind over some ghost kid that follows me around and talks like a fucking wizard and you're going to tell me that that was real?! What the fuck is wrong with you?!"

"Mary, please calm down."

Before there was enough time for Mary to think about it, she punched Patrick in the mouth as hard as she could. He made a ghastly sound. The old man fell backwards and landed against a wall of the cave while Mary rushed to help him. She had not meant to hit him, but she did. Her rage that had been building into an unmanageable force without release had become unleashed. To be fair, he should not have been standing there.

"I'm sorry," said Mary, "I'm sorry! Are you ok?"

Mary reached down to help Patrick up, but he shook her off his arm and slowly pushed himself back up to standing. He held his hand across his mouth and looked down momentarily to check for blood. There was a small cut on his lip that felt worse than it looked.

"Do you feel better?" asked Patrick.

"Not really," said Mary.

"Pity. Anyway, I'm sorry you've had to remember all that. I can't imagine what that must have been like as a child."

"I don't remember much," said Mary, "I remember I made him a sandwich. Grandma got mad and she said he wasn't real. She got so angry. I'd see him all the time, though. He'd talk to me and follow me and sometimes I still see him. Am I insane? Why am I still seeing him?"

Patrick turned his head and hesitated.

"Is that all," he said, "you don't remember anything else?"

"She took me out to the woods one day. Right on the top of that cliff, there. There was this white shed that was all old and beat up. Something was trapped in there. Sounded like it was trying to get out. I got scared and grandma got angry. I tried to go back there after that, and the shed was gone."

"You never looked inside?"

"I don't think so."

"Are you sure?"

Mary was unsure. So much of that time had been blurred by nightmares and illusions, chemically induced or otherwise. She had flashes. Sometimes she thought that she could have remembered something, but the sensations that accompanied her memories were filled with such immaterial expression that the closer she came towards revelation seemed to simultaneously push her farther away. The orbital sway of push and pull became too heavy for her mind to maintain its focus. If she thought about it for too long, she would get headaches. She was beginning to get one now.

"Come on," said Patrick, "not much further to go."

They continued down into the cave, far beneath the light and life of the world. They pressed on, walking slowly with great care not to trip or fall in the darkness. Different shadows of inconsistency jumped and danced along with the jostling light coming out from their helmets. Patrick would make Mary stop occasionally so he could test the next few paces, only to nod back to her in confidence that the path ahead was safe.

It felt as though they had been traveling through the tunnel for hours before it suddenly opened into a larger cavern. The air felt different and there were slivers of light that were entering through cracks in the stone ceiling high above where they stood. It was a dim collection of light, but their eyes had adjusted to the dark so well that they no longer needed the head lamps. Patrick switched his off while Mary removed hers altogether. She breathed in the air that was slightly less stale. A shy hint of the outside world was falling within the cavern.

"This is beautiful," said Mary, "I was starting to think that we'd never get out of that tunnel. How much farther is it?"

"This is far enough, I think."

The sound of a pistol's hammer being cocked back echoed off the stone walls. Mary turned slowly to find the steady hand of Patrick gripping a revolver. It was pointed at her head.

"I'm sorry," said Patrick, "I was really hoping you hadn't remembered anything. I believe you when you say that you don't remember everything, but I can't take the risk."

Mary froze. With so many things that she wanted to say, there were no words that could leave her mouth. Patrick moved to the side and Mary matched his pace, keeping him in her line of sight. He held up his free hand to signal that she should stay put.

"You should have stayed away, Mary," said Patrick, "you shouldn't have come home."

Mary threw her mining helmet at Patrick as hard as she could. It struck him in the face, and he fell backwards against the stone wall while his pistol fired into the air. Lifting a large stone from the ground Mary pounced on Patrick, knocking him to the cavern floor. She had his face bashed into his skull before the reverberation of the shot had ended. It happened so quickly that Mary had barely noticed what she had done. She also had not noticed that she was still smashing the rock against the paste that had formerly been the skull, skin, and gray matter of Patrick's head. One of his eyes remained beside the body, staring cold and blue against the ground. Mary's breath was shaking, quick and broken as the last rings of the pistol shot faded away. Then there was nothing.

Mary sat straddling Patrick's dead body with the stone held tightly in her hands. There was a driving desire to keep smashing the stone against him for fear of his somehow being able to survive his demise. As the silence surrounded her in the cavern, she threw the stone as far away as she could. With her arms shaking beneath the weight, it flew about five feet from her before it landed and rolled to a stop.

The cavern had no pools in which Mary could wash herself clean. There were drops of dew and condensation that were falling from the ceiling, but they were barely enough to fill a teacup, much less relieve Mary of Patrick's remains that were now covering most of her torso, face, and hands. She held her arms upright like a surgeon while she looked for anything that she could use to clean herself. She was not sure what it was that she was looking for, but she needed something else, anything else, then what she had just seen and done. Finding nothing, Mary fell to her knees and wept as she wiped her hands on the ground, trying not to touch her face.

"That was disgusting," came a small, familiar voice.

Mary felt a hand on her shoulder, but she already knew who was speaking to her. The boy was wearing his brown corduroy pants and blue buttoned shirt.

"Go away," she said, "please go away."

"That's not how this works," said the boy, "I wish it were that easy."

A second, longer, fouler hand rested on Mary's other shoulder now. The long neck and grease grimace face of manipulation sidled up to Mary's, remaining inches away from her ear. A voice of malignant despair gurgled from the bottom of its self-indulgent well.

"You've come up a murderer, Mary," it said, "oh no, oh no, now what will you do next?"

The voice laughed through an oil slick.

"He was gonna kill me," said Mary, "I had to…"

"You had to *what*," said the greasy voice, "what did you *have* to do? Nobody ever *has* to do anything. Ever."

"He was gonna kill me!" said Mary.

"Wouldn't that be for the best," it said, "wouldn't that be just grand?"

"Oh, shut up," said the boy, "she's been through a lot."

A hissing laugh came gurgling out from the darkness.

"And there's still so much more," said the voice, "so many distractions to enjoy."

"Please go away," said Mary. She sat on her legs, alone in the cavern beside Patrick's body, and covered her face with her bloody hands.

"Please go away…"

26. Is This Real?

"Call her again."

"I just called her five minutes ago."

"And?"

"Straight to voicemail. Again."

"Well, when did she leave?"

"She's been gone for over two hours."

"And?"

"And she's probably chilling out in the fucking woods or something! She probably wants to be left alone!"

"Being alone may not be the best thing for her right now."

"Oh, because you know what's best for her?"

"More than you do, you little asshole!"

"I said I was sorry!"

Lorry, Joey, and Howard had been arguing for the better part of forty minutes. Mary had gone into the woods after Joey had hurt her feelings and had yet to return to the house. It took them some time to notice that she was missing, but when it did become apparent, there was no way of knowing where she had gone. They were, for lack of a better term, concerned.

"Why did you let her go off on her own?" asked Howard.

"Because she wanted some space," said Joey, "yeah, I said a dumb thing. She's just pissed. She's been pissed at me before."

"Hard to imagine that," said Howard.

"Listen," said Lorry, rubbing her eyes, "we're all upset. It's going to be dark soon. I say we take what daylight we have left, go look around the woods. If we can't find anything, then we'll drive into town. Maybe she's just at a bar somewhere."

"Fine," said Howard.

"Fine," said Joey.

"Do we have any flashlights?" asked Lorry.

"There's one in the kitchen drawer," said Howard, "I don't know how old it is, but it's one of those flashlights that are supposed to last forever."

Howard took the flashlight from the kitchen drawer and was already rehearsing what he wanted to say when they found Mary. He had a penchant for fabricating different scenarios that would never match the reality of any given situation. Whether he was going into an argument or even a casual conversation, Howard's anxieties would often overcome his optimism. This had never truly been a devastating habit, but there were instances of unfair assumption that caused an imbalance in his social follow-through. Lorry had to sometimes interject and pull Howard out of conversations if he started to get a little too excited. He often felt big emotions.

Lorry had found another flashlight in an upstairs closet, but Joey had to go without. They organized a rudimentary plan for how to approach Mary when they found her and what that could look like. Howard took point while Joey walked behind him. Lorry took up the rear and it was decided not to use their flashlights until it became dark.

The three members of the search party were each distracted by their own thoughts and the late afternoon sun was already setting as they reached the ravine. The water which would usually push down the stream looked still with a lazy current. Howard knelt on the bank looking for signs of Mary not because he was trained in any kind of tracking skill, but because he did not know what else to do. Any footprint could be helpful, but he found none. They decided to press on towards the direction that Mary had taken Howard the previous day.

There was a feeling that all the woods were looking for Mary. Small animals that were usually reserved as night approached became more active and social. Each step brought life out from under Howard's boots while critters of various forms scurried around them as they walked. Lorry had a passing thought of remembering this moment for a future piece that she would work on, but quickly dismissed it as her mind returned to Mary. If anything had happened to Mary, then she would never be able to forgive herself. There was a strange comfort when she considered the amount of support that Howard would need if such a loss should occur. It would be enough of a distraction to keep Lorry occupied for the rest of her days. Sometimes she selfishly loved Howard's sensitivity because it kept her too busy to think about her own troubles. She also found it to be fundamentally endearing.

Joey was struggling to keep up with the Rubenstein's. He had been working through a hangover/bender for the better part of, well, years. He was not accustomed to long bouts of exercise and did not find peace within the woods. What he did find were shadows that moved without reason and the calls of unfamiliar birds. He was startled by the unexpected rustling of shrubs and low branches while gripping a walking-stick he had found as though it could be used as a possible weapon, if needed. His thoughts would jump between the guilt for having upset Mary, concern for her safety, and his getting out of this alive. Periodically he would catch Howard looking back at him and see murder in his eyes.

Joey thought about how he could have been back in New York by now and having fantastic sex in the basement of an illegal speak-easy. The specific location was irrelevant if they had good music and a loose definition of security. His mind drifted back to Sam and Laura and whether his leaving New York had been a good idea or the results of a manic episode. Mary needed his help, and he acted as any good friend would, but there was also a plaguing doubt that his intentions may not have been entirely sincere. He pushed these thoughts out as absurd and primarily the result of his guilt for having upset Mary. Sam would pop up in his mind, but after recalling their last conversation, and his own jumbled threat that he had sent while very fucked up, Joey found some peace in the thought of letting it all go. He knew that Laura would require a more delicate conversation. Joey was planning on returning the drugs eventually but knew that he would have to speak very carefully when he explained why some were missing without any money to show for it.

They were coming to the point where Mary had shown Howard the nearly perfect circle that had been formed by a ring of trees. He stopped and considered showing it to Lorry and Joey but began to feel sick with the memory that had happened less than twenty-four hours ago. He knew that if he lingered for too long at the place then he would become lost in dark emotions. For the sake of the search, and to protect his own sanity, he decided against the stop and allowed himself a painful sigh.

Lorry began the call for Mary as her voice echoed through the woods. Joey and Howard followed her example and soon the calls for Mary were mixed with the birds leading up to the tops of the trees. As there was no response to their calls, the sun itself abandoned the search as daylight quickly snuck away. Soon it became too dark for the group to see without the aid of flashlights.

"We should head back," said Lorry, "we can drive into town and check the bars."

"There's still light," said Howard, "I think we're close."

"If we don't head back to the house now, then we're really going to be lost," said Lorry, "and that won't help Mary."

Howard knew that Lorry was right. He wanted to continue the search, but he suspected that he was thinking irrationally. Reluctantly, Howard agreed to return to the house. They found their way back with only a few stumbled missteps and minimal confusion. Breaking out through the tree line and into the backyard, Lorry looked at the house with confusion.

"Did we leave a light on?" she asked.

The upstairs light of the halogen lamp was shining through the tower window. Lorry and Joey had thought to have unplugged it when they left the other day but were unsure. There was rustling in the bushes a few yards from where they stood and the sound of running steps. Howard flashed his beam of light in the direction with just enough time to see a few of the branches moving as though they had been pushed aside.

"Mary?" said Howard.

Nothing. He was about to go after the sound when Lorry darted into the woods with more speed than Howard had ever seen her produce. It frightened him when she re-entered the woods and a silence grew around them. Joey stood with his hands shaking and his heart beating in his throat. After a few tense minutes of waiting, Lorry calmly walked out from the woods and back into the yard. Twigs were stuck in her hair and there was a good-sized scratch across her cheek.

"What happened," asked Howard, "was it Mary?"

"I don't know," said Lorry, "I thought I saw someone, but it was too dark. Might have been a bear."

She removed the twigs from her hair and wiped some blood from her face.

"I'm going to wash this cut and then me and Joey will drive into town. Howard, you check the upstairs and stay here in case Mary comes back."

Howard thought to protest this decision for a moment but agreed. He and Joey went to check on the tower while Lorry washed her face in the bathroom. The cut was shallow, but it stung when Lorry applied some alcohol from the medicine cabinet. Her bag was in the bathroom, with her wallet and travel necessities. Lorry liked to travel light, so she never brought too many things with her. When she looked in the mirror, Lorry saw the face of a tired woman staring back at her. The cut had stopped bleeding but left a clean little line that traveled up beneath her cheekbone. It would heal in a day or two and leave nothing more than a faint shadow. Even that would fade in time. Lorry splashed more water on her face and leaned her hands against the sink while she searched for the strength to continue looking for Mary.

Howard had not completely forgiven Joey for upsetting Mary but had realigned his priorities to focus on finding his daughter. The stairs leading up to the tower were too narrow for Howard to climb, so he sent Joey up alone to see if Mary was hiding in the room. Joey did not stay to argue despite being nervous to go to the tower by himself. There was nothing out of the ordinary when Joey opened the door to the tower, and none of the boxes were big enough for Mary to hide behind. He poked around the room and called out to her once but was met with no reply. Joey unplugged the halogen light in the tower and the two men returned to

Lorry with the confirmation that Mary was not upstairs. Howard said he would stay and wait for Mary while Joey and Lorry drove Loose Lips back into town. Howard stood in the driveway and watched their headlights disappear into the night, allowing the seclusion of the woods to surround him.

He was alone.

The cicadas had hatched from a long seventeen years beneath the ground and their drone of tymbals resonated through the darkness. Howard sat down on the steps with his flashlight pointed at the sky, watching the beam dissipate with the altitude that it tried to reach. Shadows of bats were quickly swooping down to catch the insects that had become attracted to the light. Howard thought he was doing a service for the bats, so he kept the light on for a few minutes while simultaneously apologizing to the bugs.

He had a memory of being a child and throwing balls of aluminum foil up into the sky at dusk. The aluminum would reflect the sonar of hungry bats, causing them to dive at the balls of foil thinking that they were prey. It delighted Howard as a child, but in retrospect he could see the argument that it may have been a little cruel. He had tried to be nicer to bats since then. A possum waddled across Howard's line of sight and startled him so intensely that he jumped to his feet. The possum hissed and moved a little faster into the tree line. Howard was not inherently afraid of possums, but the sudden and unnatural movements in the dark played heavily on his nerves. Howard coughed and stretched his back with an audible groan to show the world he was present and not afraid, but he also refused to turn his back on the darkness as he entered the house. He nearly tripped over the threshold as his heel caught the door frame. Howard stumbled, but he did not fall.

He closed the door and locked it behind him out of habit but then decided to leave it unlocked in case Mary should return to the house. He took the bottle of whiskey off the shelf and poured a tall glass for himself, something he suspected would cause regret as it would certainly go straight to his head.

Placing the flashlight back in the junk drawer, Howard walked through the first floor of the house by himself to see if Mary had fallen asleep somewhere. He also wanted to examine the design of the interior more closely. It confused him, but not in an unpleasant way. He had often fancied himself as a handyman, although he knew very little outside of his collection of radios. They would also stump him at times, to which he would grumble and say that the damn thing was busted. A few of those busted radios were lying around their apartment, waiting for the day that they could become unbusted.

The door to the sex dungeon was left open and Howard's curiosity had momentarily gotten the better of him. He poked his head inside and looked at all the clothes and devices that he had only seen or read about through magazines and pornographic websites. He got a kick out of some of the items until he saw a large and bulbous rod on the end of a long leather strap. The purpose was unclear as he was not sure if it was for flogging or insertion or both. It made him feel a little intimidated. He cleared his throat and quietly shut the door. With no sign of Mary to be found on the first floor, Howard called down to the basement to be certain that Mary was not there. He was hesitant to investigate any further after his last trip down, so Howard called out twice to be sure. The only sound was the smaller scurrying of critters that had found their way into the basement but could not find their way out. Howard closed the door and decided to search the second floor of the house.

The stairs creaked beneath his weight as he brought his full figure up to the second-floor rooms. He observed them in greater detail than he did on his initial tour. There was something rushed about the first walkthrough as it felt more ritualistic than personal. Now that he was by himself, he felt privileged to have a glimpse into the previous life of his daughter

He was entering the room of Mary's grandmother when he thought he heard a bump coming from downstairs. It was only a small sound, but small sounds can be very big in an empty house, especially at night. Howard poked his head back from the top of the stairs and called out Mary's name. It was met with no reply. After telling himself that it must have been the house settling, he returned to the room and closed the door behind him.

He tried to look out of the window that faced down and into the backyard where the woods began, but it was impossible to see with the light on in the room. After he turned out the light, Howard was able to take in the limited sights of a deeply wooded night and the illusions that the eye and the mind produce with each other. Every movement felt devious and there was the sneaking suspicion that he was being watched. After having lived in the chaotic noises and momentum of city life, Howard found the calm peace of rural living to be deeply disturbing.

How could anything be so quiet, he thought to himself.

He was beginning to feel uncomfortable, so he turned the light back on in the room. He assured himself that it was done to let Mary know someone was home, but it also made him feel safer.

Howard was about to leave when he saw the small, padlocked door that had been built into the wall. He knelt to examine the locks that had carefully been put in place to secure the small closet. They stood fast in their installment when Howard gave them a light tug. The need to respect the privacy of others and the desire to abate his own curiosities had been a practice for which Howard was trying to hold as a virtue. With his recent breach of Mary's privacy and all that that entailed, he was re-evaluating the guidance of such a philosophy. He still felt guilty for having betrayed Mary's boundary, but the result had been relatively harmless, all things considered. It was still not enough to justify Howard's invading Mary's personal space, but he found some consolation there. These were the thoughts that were dominating his mind as he forcibly removed the latches from the wall with his bare hands. Howard was feeling violent. He thought it better to vent his frustrations against an inanimate object than a living thing. If it could provide some insight into Mary's past as well, then all the better.

 The panel ripped off its hinges with ease, along with the latches. Large portions of the wall came with it and there was a fleeting moment of panic as Howard looked around to see if anyone had witnessed the act. He quietly apologized to whoever had built this house. Howard removed a lamp from the bedside table and plugged it into the outlet beside the small opening. He had seen small rooms like this before in other houses and apartments. They were utilized mostly as additional storage or held water heaters, electrical panels, etc. This was no different.

 The first box that Howard removed was filled with photo albums and 8mm film reels. Holding the film up to the light allowed Howard the presumption that they were home movies from long before Mary was born. Possibly longer than her parents were born. There were small snapshots of people at a beach and what looked like a birthday party in someone's backyard. Howard thought it curious that old photographs and films with young people still made them look older than they had been. He sat and looked through the photographs, none of which had been taken after the nineteen seventies.

 Howard thought the idea of preserving incidental moments in time was what gave them value. Everything smelt old. Many of the photographs contained the same woman, whom Howard assumed was Mary's grandmother in her younger days. There were a variety of different men in the pictures at first, but the further Howard flipped through the albums, the more he began to recognize the same man. He was young and skinny with thick black hair. He looked like a nice enough guy, but there was something in his eyes that made Howard stop and look a little deeper into his expressions. His smiles became nearly cruel and presented a certain callousness to whomever was taking the picture. He was prominently kept in clean sleeves of the album until he was replaced by a larger man with glasses and a beard. The following pictures were from her and the bearded man's wedding day and these concluded the album.

Howard continued to rummage through the crawlspace and found all sorts of different things. There was an accordion that worked for the most part, except for a few keys that stuck and a tear along the bellows. The upper half of a mannequin was missing a hand and looked as though a portion of its face had been chewed off. A set of boxing gloves and a deflated basketball were in a box along with blankets. There were a surprising number of items that Howard kept removing from the crawlspace. He had almost emptied it out when he reached into the very back, with more than half of his body in the wall, and carefully removed what felt like a large glass cylinder that had been carefully wrapped in a sheet. He had almost gotten stuck when he started to back out from the hole, but with some light chest compression and patience he managed to squeeze through without jostling the item in his hands. He removed the sheet to find the preserved remains of a human head suspended in a green viscous gelatin. Its skin, hair, and teeth were all in place and its bloated eyes stared out into the world. There was a striking resemblance to the bearded man in the wedding photographs.

Someone grabbed a mass of Howard's hair and pulled his head straight back. A calloused hand clasped over the front of his mouth, and he heard the voice of Albert hiss in his ear.

"Surprise, fucker."

There was a brief stinging sensation in the side of Howard's neck, and then he felt cold as a white light flashed in his mind. A strong flow of hot blood was leaving the arteries as he clasped his hand against the wound and tried to stand up. He could not speak, but even if it were possible, he was unable to think of anything to say. There were flickering thoughts that ran across his mind, but they were happening too quickly for him to understand them. Howard made it to one knee before he lost his balance and fell face first onto the floor. His body lay across the rug as it became engorged with the blood of Howard Rubenstein.

"See," said Albert, "nothing to it."

"There's so much blood," said Ralph, as he began to feel faint.

"Well, he was a big bastard. Come on. Help me get him in the wall."

It took all their strength to move Howard's body into the crawl space that he had so carefully emptied. The blood that was still flowing freely from his body created a lubrication that made any kind of grip difficult. However, this also helped to slide Howard's frame through the hole. The floor had lost its traction as they both began to slip with each step and pivot. Ralph had nearly managed to commit the act without vomiting, but unfortunately lost all composure at the tail-end of his duties. Albert curled his lip and shook his head at Ralph's reaction.

"Disgusting," said Albert.

Ralph wiped the vomit from his mouth, but the blood on his hands smeared it across his face and made a kind of jelly. He then gagged and dry heaved from an empty stomach.

"Go clean yourself up," barked Albert, "I want to be long gone before anybody gets back."

Ralph obeyed with his head slumped between his shoulders. He did not feel well at all and did not enjoy being yelled at. He knew that he was stupid and that he probably did something to deserve it, but it still hurt him all the same.

The bathroom light brought Ralph's reflection staring back at him from the mirror. His eyes looked better today, he thought. They still carried the jaundice which he had become accustomed to seeing, but if he looked very hard, he thought he could see some white coming through. This made him smile as he began to wash his face. The cold water hurt his teeth as he rinsed out his mouth. Decades of neglected dental hygiene had left his gums in a sorry state. They were barely equipped to hold his teeth in place, and his temperature sensitivity was so severe that there were few instances where he was without pain. Ralph had accepted this as a reality long ago and barely flinched anymore. It still hurt him all the same.

Lorry's bag had been left on the bathroom sink where Ralph was washing his face. He had not noticed the bag at first but became delighted at the prospect of providing Albert with proof that he was not as much of an idiot as presumed. Ralph had been raised to know not to rummage through a woman's bag, so his initial inspection tapped into an organic guilt that came from the knowledge that he was doing something wrong. Lorry's wallet was filled with business cards, a small drawing of a flower, some ideas scratched on strips of scrap paper, and two credit cards that Ralph put into his pocket along with two hundred dollars in cash.

He was feeling proud of himself until he came upon a photograph of the Rubenstein's together when Ruth and Mary were still young. It was a simple picture. Howard and Lorry had taken the girls to Coney Island shortly after they had adopted Mary. She and Ruth were still inseparable at this point. Before their lives crept up around them.

Ralph examined the picture with his dull eyes and began to feel an overwhelming sense of remorse for the murder that he and Albert had just now committed. When Ralph saw Lorry's face in the photograph as she was looking up at Howard, he asked himself why nobody had ever looked at him that way. In an unusual display of self-awareness, Ralph looked at his reflection in the mirror and imagined what it would be like to have someone love him like that.

It was difficult to imagine at first, but then his mind went into a sprawling fantasy where he had found love young, it flourished, and he was transported to his wedding day. He would look so handsome and smart in a top hat and tails while his love would look beautiful in whatever she wore. Ralph promised himself at that moment that he would always remind his love of how beautiful she looked whenever he could. He and his love would then grow old and raise a large family who, in turn, would go on to raise families of their own. His mind then leapt to his sitting at his love's deathbed, trying to think of everything he still wanted to say and everything he still wanted to do. His love would look upon his face with the radiant glow of understanding and simply put her palm against his cheek. She would hold Ralph's face and say, "I love you", and Ralph would know that she meant it. In that moment when his love would die, Ralph himself would have lost his own will to live.

In this instantaneous projection of what had never been, Ralph felt gutted at the picture of the Rubenstein's at Coney Island. He looked at the photograph through blurred vision as his yellow eyes began to flood with tears. There was no way for Ralph to take it back. He was an accomplice to murder, and he would never forgive himself. There were no words of comfort that he could provide to anyone else in the photograph. Ralph shut the bathroom door and sat in the tub, crying harder than he ever had in his life.

"What are you blubbering for," shouted Albert from the hallway, "I need your help out here!"

"Just a...a sec...second," replied Ralph, washing his hands and face in the sink. He did his best to calm himself, but it was more difficult than he thought. After a few tense minutes, he managed to regain his composure as his sorrow turned to rage. Ralph wanted to kill Albert. He exited the bathroom after returning Lorry's money and credit cards back in her bag. Albert was standing in the hallway holding the cylinder containing the human head.

"Look at this shit," said Albert, "is this real?"

Ralph inspected the cylinder with the scrutiny of someone who would know the answer, although he would be the first to admit that he was no expert in biology. He nodded a few times and confirmed Albert's suspicions.

"Jesus," said Albert, "we're dealing with some sick people here. Who do you think this is?"

Ralph was too angry to answer the question. He was shaking with a mix of every possible negative emotion that a person could experience at once. As his mind went blank, a certain calmed detachment fell across his demeanor.

"We should put it back," he said, "we should take what we need and get out of here."

"That's the first sensible thing you've said in a long time. Come on. We'll do a quick sweep and then we're gone."

"What about the blood?" asked Ralph, although he would not look at it.

"Fuck it," said Albert, "none of its yours or mine. We'll let it be a mystery, heh."

Ralph imagined Albert on fire and stabbed by a thousand swords in a thousand different places. He would find the world's strongest horses and have them rip Albert apart, starting with his fingers and toes. Ralph smiled at the many ways he wanted to hurt Albert. He decided that when the time came, he would take care of it.

They ransacked the house, producing two large duffle bags that they had brought with them. Albert was going through Mary's bag when he found the compass that her grandfather had given to her. He examined it for a moment before he shrugged and put it in his jacket pocket, deciding to keep that for himself. Any loose cash or jewelry was immediately thrown in the bags while anything antique was considered up for the taking. Ralph came across Joey's collection of cash and drugs, deciding that he would keep those for himself. Ralph had never sold drugs in his life, but he figured they would practically sell themselves. He opened the window and gently dropped the bundle of weed and narcotics to the soft ground below. He would collect it later after making sure Albert was dead. With their bags filled and their pockets strained at the seams, Ralph and Albert began to walk back down to the first floor. As soon as they took the last step, they heard the door opening in the kitchen.

"Fuck," said Albert.

"What do we do?"

"The basement," said Albert, "we'll wait in the basement."

The two burglars tried to run quietly through the first floor of the house and down the stairs that led into the basement. They ducked their heads beneath the hanging skeletons of spiders as best they could, but some did get entangled in Albert's hair. He scratched the remains into his scalp, unaware of the eight legs that fought in vain against his fingertips. They whipped around the corner, dropped their bags as gently as they could, and stood in the damp darkness, trying their best to catch their breath. The sound of footsteps above them knocked slowly across the floor. Ralph and Albert sat crouched beneath the stairs as they scanned the ceiling, trying to figure out where the person was and who it could be. They strained their ears until they could recognize the sound of Mary's voice calling out to her family.

"That bitch," said Albert, "I'll kill her just like I killed her old man."

Ralph felt his skin tighten around the thought. He would not allow any more murders to occur unless it was his own hands around Albert's throat.

"Let's wait," said Ralph, "we'll wait until she falls asleep."

"What if the rest of them come back before then, genius?"

"Then we'll wait some more. We'll cut the power when everyone goes to sleep and then we'll do what we have to."

Albert's eyes were still adjusting to the darkness, but he could vaguely see the features on Ralph's face. He wore an expression that Albert found to be disagreeable. For the first time in their relationship, Albert felt intimidated by Ralph.

"Right," said Albert, "right."

An hour passed while they waited in the basement. There was no way of knowing if the others had returned home, but Albert was getting impatient. Ralph, having no way to change Albert's mind, agreed to expedite their plan. Albert and Ralph tried to move as quietly as possible through the standing water, doing their best to ignore the creatures that moved in the darkness. The sounds of small chittering and ripples made them both feel jumpy. Ralph had spent the past hour deciding in what way he would end Albrt's life. He could easily strangle him. That would be the cleanest method. It was too dangerous to try and take the knife away from him and the thought of seeing more blood was already making Ralph feel sick. He could bludgeon Albert in the head with something in the basement, but if he missed then the retribution would be devastating. As the time for action drew near, he found himself conflicted in his resolve.

Albert felt tight and wound like a spring that had been coiled to its limit. He was still running on adrenaline from having murdered Howard and now that he had a taste for it he wanted more. He had only killed one other person in his life and that had been an accident. There were times when Albert would brag about the murder as though it were intentional, but he knew the truth of it.

He was in a college town at the time, although not having gone to college himself, and was caught in a barroom fight that ended poorly for the other person. Albert had managed to land a lucky punch in the brawl against a stranger who may not have even been involved in the conflict. It can be difficult to tell who's who in a brawl. The punch from Albert knocked the individual against the windowsill and he cracked his skull on his way to the floor. Albert managed to slip away unnoticed, but he was the cause of the only death in the fight that night. Having gotten away with the crime, he had often thought about murdering again. A lucky shot for Albert, not so lucky for the stranger.

There was some light fumbling in the dark as they looked for a circuit breaker or something to cut the power to the house.

"I can't see anything," said Albert, "I keep stepping on mice."

"I think I stepped on a snake or something," said Ralph.

"This place is a mess. Look! Here we go."

Albert had his hand on the lever that controlled what he presumed to be the fuse box for the entire house.

"Are you ready?" asked Albert.

"Yes I am."

Ralph had his hands at his waist, waiting for the opportunity to strangle Albert and leave him to die in the basement. Albert would be found with the murder weapon and would take all the blame while Ralph could escape to find the lover that he did not know he needed. Albert flipped the lever for the fuse box when a sudden explosion from the circuitry knocked both Ralph and Albert back ten feet across the unfinished basement. A sudden smell of fish filled the room, and a strong black smoke began to flow from the wall. The electricity ran through the pine boards that lined the basement and found a collection of half-filled gasoline cans beside an old lawnmower. The standing water that spread across the basement floor became a flammable pond and a vessel for the fire to spread to the other areas of the room. Albert and Ralph regained consciousness just in time to find the basement engulfed in flames.

27. I Found You

Mary had been sitting in the cavern beside Patrick's body for half an hour. She had not spoken or moved in that time, but neither had Patrick because he was quite dead. The dead tend to be much less ambitious and certainly much less opinionated. Unless you become a ghost. Ghosts seem to have a lot of opinions, if I do say so myself. But Patrick was not a ghost, only dead. It was for the best.

The cavern was echoing small sounds that came from unknown places. The space in which noise traveled allowed the sounds to take on an ambient tone that stretched out to thin waves of dissipation. Under different circumstances this could have been beautiful. Mary was not feeling beautiful as the blood and gunge of Patrick was beginning to dry against her skin and seep in through the fabric of her clothes. She was amazed at how such a frail old man could hold so much blood. She scratched her head and removed a small piece of brain and skull fragment that had landed in her hair. There was a passing thought to eat it, but she threw it away before the notion could be entertained.

Mary thought about how long it would take someone to starve to death. She remembered hearing somewhere that the human body begins to break down after five days without food, but she had forgotten the source to base it. Maybe she was just hungry. Hunger, however, was not the dominating force which was weighing on Mary's mind. She was not feeling well.

"Get up, stupid," she said to herself, "get up get up get up get up."

Mary slowly rested on her hands and knees as a test to see if she could go further towards standing. It seemed like a possibility, so she pressed her hands against the ground and straightened her body upright. She felt taller than she ever had before. Her eyes had now become well-adjusted to the darkness, but much of her visibility was still manipulated by shadow and stone. Mary felt blind in the sense that as far as she could physically see, there was nothing that she could focus on without her vision becoming distorted. This was not caused by the darkness as much as by the attempt of her mind to comprehend what had just happened. She thought a little light may help.

The mining helmet that she had thrown at Patrick had broken its lamp when it landed on the ground, but Patrick's was still in full working order. Mary put the helmet on and cringed as the blood in her hair had gone cold and created a dense spongy sensation. She continued into the cavern in the hopes of finding a different way out other than the tunnel that had led them to this point. A little further in, not at all far from Patrick's body, was a tarp fastened to the ground with stakes and covering something large.

The light from Mary's helmet shone with a tremor as her body went cold and began to shake. She could only stare at the shape hidden beneath the tarp and the thought of walking towards it was met with numb receptors. The anxieties of both commands to investigate and avoid were pressing against each other. There seemed to be a stalemate.

Mary glanced back at Patrick's body, looking more deflated than it ever had, and thought about the questions she wanted to ask him. By the time Mary made up her mind to investigate the tarp, her body had already begun moving towards the bulky shape. The corners were tied to metal stakes that had been driven deep into the earth between the stones. Some of the fabric had eroded so much in the corners that they gave no resistance and ripped almost instantly when Mary tore at the seams. A large wooden chest fastened by padlocks and rust was revealed. The locks on the chest were dense and it would be impossible for Mary to remove them with her hands. She flipped them front to back as though it would make a difference, but they stood strong in their bindings.

It's such a simple thing, a lock, thought Mary, *something so small and so strong. I can't even budge the wood on this thing.*

Try as she might, Mary could not get the wood to break apart. Time should have rotted it away, but the lid remained formidable against Mary's attempts. After several tries with muscle, stone, wet cloth, and erosion, all of which were unsuccessful, Mary picked up the gun that was lying next to Patrick's body. She had never fired a gun before, but this had also been her first murder, so comparatively it seemed like a very possible thing to do. Closing one eye, Mary did her best to take aim at one of the locks. She was mindful not to shoot the crate for fear of damaging what was inside, but she was about to find out whether she was a good shot. Truth is when she fired the gun, she had both of her eyes closed.

She missed, screamed at the noise of the gunfire, and dropped the pistol when she was startled. She stood with the noise bouncing off the walls and felt her stomach drop down to her bowels. Mary was scared to fire the gun again, but she picked it up without thinking. She did her best to keep at least one eye open, aimed, fired, and missed again. Mary managed to hold onto the pistol this time without dropping it and made another quick shot after the second attempt. The third bullet struck its mark and one of the padlocks flew across the cave. It made a gratifying noise and Mary laughed, feeling proud of herself. She was starting to get the hang of this. She fired twice more but only hit one of the other locks before she ran out of bullets. With the two locks having been shot off she was able to pry the lid of the chest open, allowing a cloud of foul dust to fly out from the inside.

A large portion of the condensed air and debris entered Mary's mouth, giving her a flavor of ash and old death. She coughed, sputtering out from her already dry mouth as she did her best to catch her breath. The dehydration from her hangover and lack of fluids caused the remnants from the chest to thicken and cake against her tongue. She did her best to scrape it out with her hands. Only when her hands were in her mouth did she remember that they were covered in blood. Once she made that connection, Mary proceeded to vomit against the wall. When she finished expunging her sour stomach, the dust had all but settled around her. Mary was gasping for air, but the cold rock wall of the cave helped to make her feel a little better. Spitting what she could on the ground and wiping her mouth with the neck of her shirt, Mary turned to see what was inside of the chest.

The lid of the chest was open to show a collection of photographs of different people with no connections to her memory. They were old pictures and judging by the clothes worn by the people in them, she presumed that the pictures were taken some time in the nineteen seventies. She started thumbing through them until she found what appeared to be a photograph of her grandmother and Patrick, albeit with a full head of black hair, arm in arm at a carnival somewhere. More photographs showed Patrick and her grandmother in different locations, each one looking more and more intimate than the last.

Mary found a photograph where Patrick was standing in front of a white shed that he had just freshly painted. His coveralls were stained, and he had a smear of paint across his cheek. He looked like a proud idiot. Her hands were shaking as Mary choked on the lingering taste of bile and dust. After a time, it looked as though Patrick had been replaced by Mary's grandfather and her grandmother's disposition had also changed. She was smiling less in the pictures with her grandfather. When she was smiling in the photographs it looked insidious. Pictures from their wedding day were bundled together with twine and when Mary began to shuffle through those, she found pictures with Patrick and her grandmother looking at each other from across the room at the reception.

Mary moved more stacks of photographs out from the chest to reveal a book titled The Rules of Hide and Seek. It was a simple notebook with a cardboard cover that was mostly eroded by damp and mold. The first section of lined pages was torn and incomplete, having compounded together to form a kind of mush brick. Any attempt at separating the pages was met with their immediate disintegration.

Towards the back of the notebook there was a legend next to a crudely drawn map showing different locations around Mary's house and the surrounding woods. The tower on top of the house was marked as well as the circle of trees that Mary loved, the basement was designated by a black spot in the legend and highlighted in black on the map, the cliff overlooking the gorge was marked by a red circle and the cave, presumably where Mary stood, was marked with the word "Home".

Mary carefully flipped through the final pages to read the broken phrases and half sentences that were collected in different sections. Most of it was illegible, especially in the darkness, but there were three names beside numbers that stood out on one of the last pages. The names were Lisa Hawthorne (5), Arthur Burgess (8), and Felix Asher (8). Mary looked back from the names to the map. There was no immediate connection between the journal entries and the names, but Mary was beginning to piece together a dark plot.

Burgess..., thought Mary.

Looking back in the chest she found a thin floral sheet covering a plank of wood that rested across the length of the center. Mary attempted to lift the plank of wood with the sheet, but it felt as though it had been fastened or bolted inside of the crate. She pulled and jostled and tried her best to remove the wooden plank, but in her miscalculated physical exertion managed to tip the whole thing over. The plank snapped loose as three glass cylinders came rolling out from beneath it. Mary fell backwards and landed hard on her hip, which made a sharp popping noise and began to sting and swell. She grunted in pain as her eyes tightly closed and her hands tried to softly examine where she had fallen. It did not feel like she had broken anything, thankfully, but the fall had enacted a nasty sprain to her ligaments.

Her mobility was becoming limited and there were few motions which did not cause her intense amounts of pain. Mary gritted her teeth as the ripples of agony filled her body. She tried to get up twice but fell both times. Carrying her weight on the other side allowed her the ability to crawl across the ground. The plank of wood was a good distance from where she was, and the three cylinders had rolled away down an incline from the chest. One of the cylinders had broken on the ground and was leaking a green and foul-smelling gelatin which had encased a spherical and bulbous object. It was difficult to see what it was in the dark, and even with the light from her headlamp it was almost unrecognizable. She inched her way closer to the object as the light from her helmet bounced from side to side.

When she managed to reach the broken cylinder, she had to cover her mouth because the smell had become unbearable. Closing her eyes as though it would help to eliminate the stench, she carefully rolled the remnants of the cylinder towards herself, being mindful not to cut her fingers on the broken glass. When the cylinder was close enough for Mary to see the object clearly, she opened her eyes to reveal the severed head of a child.

Mary did not scream. Mary did not say anything. She stared into the open eyes of the young corpse who looked back at her without judgment. The blank expression sealed on the face resembled a drunk old man who had laid his head on the bar to settle a nasty case of the spins. The gelatin, or whatever it was, had managed to preserve the skin, hair, and teeth of the head almost perfectly. There was a green tinge to the skin and some bloating as it had been kept in fluid for so many years, but the signs of decomposition had hardly taken its toll. Mary turned the cylinder over to examine the back of the head, but it fell out and rolled a few feet away from her. The slow drip of condensation and the sound of ethereal chittering filled the cavern once more.

Mary crawled towards the other two cylinders that had rolled in a different direction. They had both remained intact from the fall and the first cylinder she reached contained the head of a young girl. Her hair was dark and cut short with small curls floating above her forehead. Her eyes were closed, and she looked like a wax figure. Mary ran her finger over the glass in front of the girl's mouth and quietly apologized. She was not sure what she was apologizing for or why, but she felt that someone had to, and she was the only living person there. Mary crawled closer to the third cylinder and found the familiar head of the boy she had known since her childhood. It was as though he had never aged.

"I found you," said Mary, weakly. She lay next to his head and felt hot tears falling down the sides of her face.

It all came back to her at that moment, in the time that it would take for a heart to break. She flashed to the memory, a memory thick and stinking of unusual autumn heat and the wild. Her grandmother was watching her and made her promise not to leave the house while she went to visit a friend. Mary had promised with her fingers crossed as she had just seen the trick in a movie, and she wanted to know if it would work. She was not trying to disobey her grandmother, but she wanted to play outside and not waste an afternoon. It was a beautiful day and there were adventures to be had.

Mary watched her grandmother leave that morning and waited for a good long while before she decided to make any big moves towards escape. She had a little breakfast, brushed her teeth, took her grandfather's compass out from one of her many hiding places, and ran out the back door into the woods. The idea that she was breaking a rule by leaving the house had added such joy and excitement to the day. In this first moment of pure rebellion, she pretended to be so many things.

It was a fact that as soon as she learned of something new, she would pretend to be whatever it was. Why would anybody want to be themselves when there are so many other things to be? She instinctively started walking towards the ravine but stopped before she had reached it.

Why should I spend all my time at that old place, she thought to herself, *there's a whole world out there!*

Mary decided to see how far it would take her to walk until it got dark. She had visions and hopes to visit faraway lands where mysterious strangers could search for buried treasure and fall in love on a boat in the Mediterranean Sea. There were odd jobs she could pick up on the way like a railyard operator or a private detective. She had been walking much further into the woods than she ever had before and as excited as she was to sail the seven seas, she was starting to feel a little frightened. Mary began to imitate a helicopter because anyone with common sense would tell you that helicopters are never frightened. The propellor that she had crafted out of leaves was nearly finished when she heard two voices further ahead past the trees.

Quietly she crept behind some bushes that encircled a cliff jutting out from the woods and into the rest of the world. It was very quiet and very gray as the grass receded back into the forest from which she came. She lay on her stomach and watched as her grandmother and a man she did not know walked up to a white wooden shed. Her grandmother carried a brown burlap sack in her arms, and something was moving inside of it. Mary thought it might have been kittens, so she ran out from her hiding place to surprise her grandmother and maybe get a kitten out of the deal.

Mary's grandmother was very upset upon seeing her. At first Mary thought that she was angry because she had broken her promise to stay in the house, but she became confused when her grandmother began to smack her in the face. Her grandmother started to yell and say terrible things. It was like she had the ability to become gigantic in a fit of rage. Mary tried her best to block her face from her grandmother's blows, but her arms were too small to make much of a difference. She started to shake with terror.

"Go home, Mary," said her grandmother, yelling and shaking her by her shoulders, "you have to get out of here!"

"What's that little bitch doing here," said Patrick, "you told me she was out of bounds." He looked at Mary hard and smiled without using his eyes.

"You want to see our game?" He said, "let me show you how we play."

Patrick opened the door to the shed and threw the burlap sack inside of it. The sound of a child crying immediately cut through the silent world. It confused Mary as it was an unexpected noise. A little boy wearing brown corduroy pants and a blue button-down shirt emerged from the burlap sack and pleaded with Patrick to let him go. He was not wearing any shoes.

"Please," he screamed, "please! I don't wanna play anymore! I wanna go home!"

The boy broke down in howling fright as he shook in the terror of an uncertain fate. Patrick stood grinning above him with a knife in his hand. He flicked it to shine flashes of light across the boy's face and chuckle as the boy whimpered with his eyes closed. Mary was too frightened to move.

"Please," screamed the boy, "I wanna go home!"

The boy begged Mary for her help. She could do nothing more than stand and shake as Patrick chuckled and started scraping the side of the knife against his jeans. He ignored the boy's tears as he knelt in front of the child, brandishing the large hunting knife and softly singing.

"Who's...a...fraid...of...the big...bad...wolf..."

"Patrick, wait" shouted her grandmother, "not in front of Mary!"

Patrick spun on his heels and shot straight up to full height. Mary's vision was becoming clouded by flashing jolts of light that seemed to stab her eyes from every angle.

"Oh, so *now* you feel bad," said Patrick, "now, all of a sudden, *now* you have a conscience?"

"Patrick," said her grandmother, "I swear to God if you don't stop this right now then I'm going to kill you."

"I fucking dare you," said Patrick. He took three long steps to face Mary's grandmother and grabbed her by the hair as he held the blunt side of the knife to her throat. "I thought we were having fun, darlin'. I thought you loved me."

Mary's grandmother said nothing, but she held Mary tighter against her body. She would do anything to protect her, despite her own homicidal tendencies. Patrick released Mary's grandmother and knelt on the ground, taking Mary's chin in his hand.

"You got a good memory, Mary?"

Mary was shaking from fright and did not answer. The strength to stand was quickly leaving her body and a dark metallic taste began to linger in the back of her throat.

"I sure hope you don't," said Patrick, "you ever think about this again...what you see here...then I'm gonna kill your grandma here. After that, I'm gonna kill your folks, and your friends, and anybody else you even think about knowin'. Once I'm done with that, I'm gonna kill you, Mary."

Patrick stood up as silent tears fell down Mary's face. He smiled, took his pointed knife, and plunged it into the boy's chest. The boy tried to scream but there was no air left in his lungs. He muttered weakly and then silently slumped forward. The boy looked at Mary coldly and without expression as the brief life he had known left his body and spread across the stony ground. Mary backed into her grandmother's arms and buried her face in her waist. Her shaking had become so pronounced that it transitioned into a grand mal seizure that knocked her onto the ground. After what felt like an eternity, Mary lost consciousness and lay still upon the stones.

The expression which she saw on the boy's face when he died was the same that he wore in the glass cylinder. He looked sad and blank. Scared and alone. Mary gently rubbed her hand across the front of the glass as though she were trying to comfort the boy in his time. The action brought little more than repetitive motion without any relief. After lying on her side and staring into the eyes of her lifelong friend, Mary began to violently sob while she held her answers in both hands.

She screamed and cursed until her throat hurt, reverting to the helpless feeling of childhood. It was far too late, years too late, for Mary to do anything to save the boy. She could not save him. Instead, she wanted to bury him. The idea that he had spent so much time locked in a chest without anyone knowing what had happened to him was altogether too painful for Mary to consider. He had spent more time buried in the cave than he had been alive. Mary tied up the floral sheet around the boy's cylinder and made a kind of bindle to carry back to the house. With the cylinder and sheet slung over her back, and a rudimentary crutch made from the broken pieces of wood, Mary began to limp back up the tunnel by the light of her miner's lamp. By the time she made it out of the cave and back to the quarry, the sun had already gone down.

Getting back to the house was an arduous task, starting with the walk back from the quarry through the gorge. The walk back to the staircase was difficult in the dark. Mary's footing was more confident in the daylight but with the minimal help from the miner's helmet, most of the walk back to the staircase was filled with stumbles and the fear of stepping on snakes. Half lame and toting a severed head in a jar, Mary pressed on.

There were times when Mary would fall to the ground and convince herself that it was impossible to continue. The cylinder gave Mary a sense of duty, as difficult as it was to carry. He needed a proper burial. With all her left side burning in pain, and the cylinder growing heavier by the minute, Mary reached the rusted and wobbly staircase that would bring her back up the cliff-side.

Impossible, she thought to herself, *this is impossible.*

Mary tucked her crutch under one arm and used the railing to support her weight as the entire staircase shook with every move she made. She had to place the cylinder on each sequential step in order to climb the stairs, but it was a system that seemed to be working. Everything would be fine if absolutely nothing went wrong. If she could make this ascension without any miscalculation, then she could proceed through the woods and towards the security of her home. There was still a long way to go and no easy road to take her there, but Mary was too determined to quit on the boy. She had already failed him once and she felt as though she had given up on herself years ago. She had no need or want of ambition and the simple pleasure of existing in an indifferent world was enough to keep Mary satisfied, as long as she could remain medicated. She stumbled and fell so many times that her hip and leg had begun to go numb.

Once Mary had reached the ravine, she stopped to wash in the cold water that had always made her feel better. This time was no exception. It was a shallow current, shallower than Mary had ever seen. Her hands brought small splashes of water across her face and arms as she did her best to scrub herself clean of all traces from killing Patrick. She tried not to think about it as a murder, but the images kept flashing through her mind and replaying over and over again. Mary had killed Patrick in self-defense, but after remembering what she had witnessed as a child, she felt it just as appropriate to call it revenge. There was some peace in the thought.

There was no real way of telling whether she had cleaned herself thoroughly, but her wet hands moved vigorously over her face and through her hair. Hopefully the water would wash away any lingering guilt that she could have felt for her actions. Mary felt a little better, but her left side was still numb. She was tempted to just lay down and sleep in the ravine, but it was getting colder, and she knew that her family was probably looking for her. There was one small hill left to climb before Mary could find her way back home. After a final push through incredible pain from walking, Mary could see the light of her house up ahead just a way.

She was approaching through the woods when she heard voices and saw a flashlight moving from side to side. Mary crept as quietly as she could to the tree line and hid behind a large bush across from where her family were standing. Joey, Lorry, and Howard were in the backyard with flashlights, talking frantically among themselves. Mary nearly called out, but after a moment of self-awareness she remembered that she was still covered in blood and carrying a severed head. With her history of crisis and their presumed suspicion of her unpredictable behavior, Mary thought that they would put her away in some kind of asylum.

In her haste to leave, she accidentally disturbed her hiding space enough to get the attention of her family. She knew that they would catch her if she ran, so she hid behind a large tree under the cover of darkness. Footsteps were sprinting into the woods after here, but she kept perfectly still in her hiding place. Clutching the cylinder close to her chest, Mary held her breath and waited for whoever it was to go away. Her leg and hip were throbbing, and Mary began to whimper in pain. After a few minutes of staying perfectly still, she heard the footsteps slowly recede back out of the woods. Mary heaved a sigh of relief and began to rub her injured leg.

It was difficult for Mary to tell if her family had gone inside or if they were still in the woods looking for her, so she stayed hidden until she heard the sound of Loose Lips leaving the driveway. Mary was grateful because it would give her enough time to bury the boy's head in the yard and clean herself up before they got back. She would have to be quick, but it was possible.

She found a spot beside the flowering dogwood tree where they had first met. Using her hands and the broken piece of wood that she had been using for a crutch, she dug a wide hole deep enough to bury the cylinder. After she had finished digging, she took a moment to say goodbye to the boy she had known all her life.

"I'm sorry," she said, "I'm so fucking sorry."

Her heart was beating heavily from her chest and her breath was caught in her throat. Mary gripped a low hanging branch from the tree for support as she broke down completely. It was over. She had found the answers she was looking for and they brought her no comfort. She wished her grandmother were still alive so that she could kill her. She wished her parents were alive so she could kill them. She lost any remorse for having murdered Patrick. She wondered if she would ever murder again. The murder was such an automatic response that Mary was concerned with how easy it was. All the thoughts that had been running through her mind suddenly came to a standstill. What had been existing as inescapable panic over the past week had now dissolved into a blankness. Mary felt sorrow more than anything else.

A light came on in the house and she saw the image of Howard standing in her grandmother's room, looking out the window. Mary instinctively crouched and backed into the woods, hid beneath the underbrush, and wondered why he was home.

Probably in case I came back, she thought, *now what am I going to do?*

The answer came to Mary as the light in the window went out. She could still see an image of her father's silhouette, but he soon turned his back and retreated into the room. After a few moments, the light turned on again. Mary was flooded with the urge to run inside and tell him everything that had happened. She felt foolish for being ashamed to ask for help. Throughout her life she had never felt comfortable asking anyone for anything. If there was ever a time when she needed help, this most certainly hit the mark.

Mary returned to her funeral after waiting in the bushes for a few minutes. She gauged the measurement of the hole by placing the cylinder inside of it and it was a perfect fit. This made Mary terribly sad because it meant that there was only one thing left to do. It was time to say goodbye.

"I hope you find your shoes," she chuckled, "not gonna do you much good now, but anyway…"

She felt a sting behind her eyes that told her more tears would come if she were to continue.

"I'll tell your brother," she said, "I'll tell him about it tomorrow. Oh, God! What am I going to tell him? Maybe I'll wait on it. Fuck. I'm…I'm sorry I didn't do anything. I'm sorry you were so sc-scared. I'm…look, it wasn't my fault. I was scared too, y'know? I was just a kid…and so were you…I…I'm sorry. I'm sorry."

Mary filled the remainder of the hole and buried the cylinder beside the flowering dogwood tree. Standing up and brushing the dirt from her knees, Mary laughed as she looked at the rest of her clothes that were covered in dried blood and filth. She stood silently for a few moments before kissing the sapling branch that was growing out from the limb she had broken so many years ago. With nothing more to do, Mary returned to her house with a new hope that Howard would be there to listen.

Of course he'll be there, she thought to herself, *he's always ready to listen. Dad'll understand. Christ, I need a drink.*

Mary walked into the house and stood in the kitchen. She thought she had heard someone moving in the house, but it sounded strange. Rushed.

"Dad," she called out, "Howard? Is that you?"

The call was met with silence as Mary continued through the first floor. Looking at herself in adequate light allowed her to see just what a mess she had become. She stood before a full-length mirror and examined her reflection. There was no recognition of the person staring back at her. Mary's upper thigh and hip were noticeably swollen, but she had become accustomed to the pain which had evolved into more of a dull throb. Her short lemon hair was still dyed brown with blood and dirt, even with her attempt to wash it out. Her face was cut, smeared, and tinted with a thin blood mask of Patrick's former fluids. Washing her face in the dark seemed to yield minimal results. The rest of her clothes and exposed skin were deeply stained. For the first time that night she could smell herself just by standing still.

Mary grabbed the bottle of whiskey and headed upstairs. She was unable to find the bag of Joey's drugs but decided to search her grandmother's room for any more of Aunt Colleen's prescriptions. Sobriety was now something that felt intolerable.

A new sensation of clarity swept over Mary's mind. She decided then and there that she would get drunk, get high, have a bath, and go to the hospital. Spending time in the hospital made sense for several reasons, but she would not be arriving sober. She was walking through the upstairs hallway thinking about this when she nearly tripped over the large jar that was left to the side of the stairs. Mary recognized the cylinder to be the same construction that had housed the heads of the three children. Turning it into the light allowed her to find the head of her grandfather perfectly preserved in a jar filled with the green gelatin that was used for the others.

So much of her childhood was coming into focus in a way that brought a certain numbness to the front of her mind. She looked at her grandfather's head as though it were no more than a film prop and placed it on a table that stood at the end of the landing. Mary entered her grandmother's room and immediately stepped in a large puddle of blood that had seeped into the carpet. She jumped back instinctually but remained unbothered at the sight.

"Oh good," she said, "the floor is bleeding."

After she walked around the puddle, she opened her grandmother's medicine drawer and found a box containing a large supply of Aunt Colleen's painkillers and benzodiazepine. She took the bottles, set up a little buffet on a small plate and made her way to the bathroom for a soak. Passing her grandfather's head, she kissed her fingers and pressed them against the glass.

"Hi, grandpa. Been a long time."

The head of Mary's grandfather lay slanted inside of the cylindrical glass. His face remained unchanged in a frozen world.

"You sure can pick 'em, huh?"

The water was hot right out of the tap. The bathroom had an old claw-foot porcelain tub that lay next to a window looking out to the front of the house. It was the tub of her birth and although she had no personal memory of the event, she had been frequently reminded of it by her parents. Mary had stripped off her clothes and let them fall on the bathroom floor. They had begun to crust over and were stiff with the remnants of the day. Mary was trying hard not to think about that anymore. There was nothing that Mary wanted to think about. She took two pills and poured a short glass of whiskey to start because she had no intention of accidentally killing herself.

With all that had happened and been brought to light, Mary was experiencing a new period of what felt like spiritual enlightenment. It would take a long time before she would be able to appropriately communicate what she had seen or what she had done, but there was hope. There had to be hope. A sense of independence that had once been relied upon to defend her vulnerabilities was now becoming a desire to grow. She was nowhere near healed from what she had experienced, but she was approaching the idea that she wanted to heal. She wanted to feel better about herself and her life. Despite everything, despite her best efforts, Mary was beginning to feel good. In fact, she felt very good.

In about an hour, enough time had passed to where Mary sat gleefully in the tub. The whiskey had filled her with a warm kind of glow while the pills she had taken were making her feel as though she were floating through the vastness of space. She felt a heat form around her that was not unpleasant but resembled what she imagined it would feel like to be inside of a womb. The water around her had turned a ruddy brown as the blood and dirt had dissolved from her skin. Looking out the window and onto the front driveway, she thought she could see Ralph sprinting full speed away from the house.

Get out of here, Ralph, she thought, *look at him run. What a knucklehead.*

The ground behind him looked like Christmas with a massive flickering light coming from downstairs. Mary waved goodbye to Ralph from the window, although he never looked back.

They must be having a party, she thought, through her haze, *just ten more minutes and I'll go downstairs. It would be good to see everybody. Smells like they lit up the fireplace.*

Mary closed her eyes and drifted off to sleep. Her dreams were woven through forests of smoke while the flames from the basement had made their way up the stairs and were licking at the bathroom door.

Epilogue: How Showing Up Is Overrated

The Museum Ludwig was buzzing with guests who had traveled from across Europe to witness the premier of an interactive exhibit called "Ego Nunc Abibo". International press from across the globe were sent to cover this sensational new performance art that had been kept, for the most part, under wraps. No one was certain as to what kind of performance was to be displayed, but there had been speculation about who would be performing and what they would be doing. The most popular theory was that it would be a final concert by a prominent rock and roll band from Ireland who had a history of exaggerated vanity and showmanship. This was not the case, but it is fun to disappoint people. That can be an art form all its own.

Three cameramen from Czechia were leaning against their news van as they performed the final preparations and checked their equipment. Two were older men named Dominick and Filip who had worked for the city capitol newspaper for over fifteen years while the third was a young man named Jacob who had recently been hired as an apprentice. The two older men were rapidly smoking cigarettes while the young man was wiping camera lenses.

Translated from the Czech

"Look at him wipe," said Filip, "I'd imagine he has the cleanest ass in town."

Dominick laughed and spit on the ground.

"Even that would be a better time than standing here starving," said Dominick, "we're not going to get anything to eat inside and we're probably going to be finished here around three in the morning."

"And then back to the office at six."

"Exactly."

"Would you like me to find us some sandwiches?" asked Jacob.

"Keep wiping," said Dominick, "we don't have time for sandwiches. All the restaurants are full, and the vendors have lines around the block."

"Just think of your hunger as a sacrifice to our lord Christ," said Filip.

"Should be easy enough," said Dominick, "Christ hasn't eaten in two thousand years."

"Do not mock our savior," said Filip, "you're not exactly on the fast track to heaven, friend."

"No, but I don't speak from my ass either."

"I'll be right back," said Jacob.

"Where are you going?" asked Dominick.

"I'm going to find some food. You two can starve if you'd like."

Jacob placed the lenses carefully in the foam case that he would later carry over his shoulder. Dominick and Filip continued to make fun of Jacob, calling him lazy, but he did not care. He was hungry and thought them both to be fools.

He made his way through the parking lot behind the Museum Ludwig. The whole city square was alive with street performers, food vendors, pickpockets, and music. What was scheduled to be an event held exclusively at the museum had grown to be more inclusive for those who were not of the proper social status to receive an invitation. The party outside would later prove to be much more fun.

There was a man selling currywurst and spaetzle in a pushcart and the aromas of grilled meats and fried potato were enough to drive Jacob to the brink of lust. He removed an envelope from his pocket that contained a few dozen Euros that his mother had given him for the trip and made his way to the food vendor. He was passing along the square when a drunk woman knocked into him and sent him falling to the ground.

"Oh," she said in English, "Oh, I am so(hic)orry. Are(hic) are you al...alright?"

"Watch where you go, you ugly old drunk!" said Jacob. His English was not spectacular, but he knew how to either start a fight or start a relationship. His conversational English was...it was ok.

"Who you ca(hic)alling ugly you HEY! OLD?! I am no(hic)ot old. What are you anyway, like...(hic) ten?"

"I'm twenty."

"Well, hello Twenty. I'm Ruth."

Ruth reached down her hand to help Jacob back to his feet. He nearly pulled her down to the ground as her footing was insecure. She laughed at this when he finally stood up.

"Are...are you hungry," asked Ruth, "I've got plenty of money."

Jacob looked at the large wad of Euros that Ruth pulled out from her pocket. He quickly covered her hands and looked from side to side.

"Are you crazy," he said, "you're going to get robbed."

"Then let's get out of here. I have to find Alex. ALEX?!"

Ruth continued to shout Alex's name and laugh as she turned in circles looking for her friend.

"Well, shit," she said, "let's get out of here, Twenty."

Ruth took Jacob's hand and walked into a restaurant that was attached to the side of the museum. She pushed against the doors expecting them to open, but unfortunately, they said Pull. Her momentum was held with such enthusiasm that her face bumped hard against the glass.

"Fuck," she yelled, holding her nose, "shit-ass door!"

Ruth kicked the glass, and it made an audible pang as it smacked against the metal frame. The bottom corner of the door cracked, and the glass splintered into spiderwebs against her boot. Jacob had an impulse to run away from this crazy drunk American woman, but he was too hungry. Besides, she had a firm grip on his wrist. He knew this was foolish, but he was not so foolish as to reject a free meal. Jacob gently pulled the door open, and they stepped inside.

The restaurant had been closed to the public for the event, but Ruth walked through the kitchen as though it were her own. Jacob trailed behind her reluctantly as the gravity of his situation was becoming clearer. He was certainly hungry enough to accept Ruth's generosity, but not if it meant him spending a night in jail. The threat of losing his job was not a luxury he could afford, so he decided to attempt an escape.

"I have to go," he said, "I have to go to work."

"Here," said Ruth, "I'll rent you for the day."

She pushed two-hundred Euros into Jacob's pocket. He did not protest the donation, but it did not ease his mind.

"I am no prostitute," said Jacob.

Ruth cackled and said, "Don't worry, honey. You're not my type."

The chefs barely blinked as Ruth and Jacob walked through the kitchen. They had their minds on their work as they prepared appetizers, salads, soups, entrees, desserts, and hors d'oeuvres for an expected two thousand people. Ruth picked up a plate of small sandwiches and tossed three back at Jacob. He failed to catch any of them but managed to be hit in the face by all three. Thankfully none of them had toothpicks, but a slice of ham did land inside of his shirt-front pocket.

They exited a door leading to an industrial stairwell that was primarily utilized as an emergency fire exit. The door was marked red with the words "ALARM", but thankfully remained silent as they rushed through. Ruth descended two flights of stairs with Jacob trailing behind her. She lost a boot in the process but was not bothered by the inconvenience. Ruth sat down at the bottom of the second landing and tried to catch her breath while Jacob began to take some of the sandwiches from the plate. They were a combination of cured meats, cheese, and cucumbers so Jacob took a few and put them in his jacket pocket for later. He handed one to Ruth and she ate the whole thing without expression. Reaching into her pocket, she produced a pack of cigarettes. She offered one to Jacob who shook his head while he held a sandwich in each hand.

"I didn't used to smoke," said Ruth, "not in years, anyway. I used to hate cigarettes."

"You should quit then," said Jacob, "they'll give you cancer."

"You know what," said Ruth, "No one in my family has ever died. You should come by around Christmas. It's terrifying."

Ruth laughed at her own joke and began to cough deeply.

"That's not the smoke," she said, "I'm just out of shape."

The sound of heavy steps grew louder as two large men in black suits charged them from the stairwell above. They were shouting in German, but Ruth and Jacob had a general understanding of what they meant. Ruth threw the rest of the sandwiches at the security team as they sprinted down the final flight of stairs and into the underground garage. Nearly every parking space had been taken by the guests and staff who had arrived much earlier in the day.

Ruth and Jacob darted and ducked between cars to escape while the two men increased their pursuit with expedition. Whenever Ruth and Jacob felt they were getting closer to escaping, they would turn around and see the tops of their assailants' heads closing in from behind. Jacob, seeing an opportunity to be freed of this American lunatic, suddenly turned right when Ruth turned left.

"Sbohem, ty bláznivá svině!" he shouted as he ducked through a pair of compact cars and made his way up the exit ramp.

The two security guards let him go and focused their efforts on Ruth. She was halfway beneath a large SUV when they grabbed her by the ankles and dragged her out from under the car. She had a few choice words for them, considering her position. She was brought into an elevator and up to the security center that monitored the entire museum. They sat her down in a chair before a clean-shaven man in a dark gray suit. He looked pleased with himself, as though he had just caught a burglar. For all that he cared to know, that was what Ruth amounted to.

"So," he said, "I've been told you are American?"

"So, what," said Ruth, "I'm not allowed to be American?"

"If only that were a crime, then the world may find some peace. No miss, your being an American is not your fault, it is simply your misfortune. What we cannot abide is theft and the disruption of the operations of this facility. We have a very important artist performing here tonight and...what are you doing?"

Ruth was going through her pockets and trying to find her wallet. She wanted to show them that she was the artist who was supposed to be performing that night. In doing so, she put all the cash that she had on the table. It equaled about eight-hundred Euros. She realized in her search that she had forgotten her wallet in the hotel room. She had also left her phone behind so that she could focus on the performance.

"I left my damn wallet back at the hotel," she said, "I'm Ruth Rubenstein. I'm performing tonight."

"That is not the name that we have," said the security chief, "the name we have for the artist is Alex Hernandez."

"That's my agent. I've been looking for them."

"Ms. Rubenstein, have you been drinking?"

"I dunno," said Ruth, "have you been…sucking balls?"

Ruth cackled and fished another cigarette out of her pocket.

"You can't smoke in here," said the security chief.

"Well then you can't suck balls in here, either. Looks like nobody gets to be happy. What a sad state of affairs we find ourselves in."

"Get this drunk out of here."

Two security guards picked Ruth up by her shoulders and escorted her out of the room. The security chief began to collect the money that Ruth had left on the desk.

"Hey that's my money, you Nazi prick!"

The security chief chuckled and waved goodbye to Ruth as she was taken out of his office. The two security guards held Ruth's arms tightly as they brought her to a door that led out to a side street. The guests for the event were beginning to enter from the front of the museum and the security guards wanted to avoid any more of a scene than had already happened. Ruth did not go quietly.

"Hey," she screamed, "Hey! Somebody get these, you fucking dick, Hey! HEY! Alex! Fucking…ALEX!"

The side door to the museum flew open as the two security guards pushed Ruth onto the street. They said nothing as they closed the door, locking it behind them. Ruth banged her fist against the window and continued to berate them from outside the museum. All that they heard was the muffled profanity of a drunk American. Penniless, drunk, alone, and missing a boot, Ruth sat on the curb and lit a cigarette. She had no idea how to continue the night, but she wanted to keep drinking.

There was a small cafe across the street, and it looked as though no one there had been paying attention to Ruth's expulsion from the Museum Ludwig. Ruth stood up, wiped the dirt and wrinkles from her dress, and tried to look as normal as possible as she crossed the street and entered the cafe. She tried to stand in such a way that no one would notice that she only had one boot on. It was busy enough inside for Ruth to remain relatively unnoticed. This suited her fine.

A young woman in a stylish black dress greeted Ruth at the door. She did her best to remain neutral but definitely noticed the sour smell of alcohol and cigarettes that had lingered around Ruth. She became immediately suspicious when she saw that Ruth was also missing a boot.

"Hi," said Ruth, trying to sound sober, "can I get a booth?"

"Yes, certainly," said the hostess, "are you American?"

"Yes, but apparently that's an unpopular condition."

"Perhaps you would like to sit outside?"

"No, thanks. Just a booth. Somewhere in the back."

"Why don't you sit outside? It's such a beautiful day!"

"I don't wanna sit outside. Gimme a booth."

"Please sit outside."

"Listen, you stuck-up..."

Another woman entered the conversation with the characteristics of an authoritative personality. She had to be a manager.

"Wo liegt das problem," she asked, "Ist diese Frau betrunken?"

"Sie ist nur eine betrunkene Amerikanerin," said the hostess.

"Hey, I understood that, Eva Braun!" said Ruth, "never mind, I don't need this bullshit."

Ruth turned to leave the cafe but had caught her single boot on the lip of the doorframe. The speed with which she had begun her departure had been so great that her body was launched out of the door of the cafe and onto a table occupied by an older couple. The table flipped beneath Ruth's weight while the food and drinks went flying and splattered onto the ground.

Covered in beer, wine, knoephla soup, and apfelkuchen, Ruth looked up to see the grimacing face of Martin, the security guard from the Algonquin Hotel. He had been saving up for years to take a vacation to Germany with his wife and they had only just arrived the previous night. Well, how do ya like them apples? Martin did not, in fact, like them apples. Get it? Apples? The apfelkuchen? It's a...

Never mind.

In the amount of time it took for Martin to recognize Ruth, she was already on her feet and hobbling across the street. Now that she looked like an authentically deranged street person, there was no chance in hell that she would be allowed into the museum. Sitting on the curb outside of her own event, about half a block up the road, some of the arriving guests threw spare change at her feet out of pity. Dejected and utterly exhausted, Ruth collected enough change to afford the bus fare back to her hotel. Thankfully she still had her room key in her pocket.

After a shower and a few small bottles of wine from the mini-bar, Ruth found her wallet and her phone on the bed where she had left them. She looked at her phone and found three missed calls from her mother, two missed calls from Alex, and an email from Julia. She did not listen to the voicemails but instead jumped straight to Julia's email. It read as such:

Hey Kiddo,
    I don't want to start anything and I'm not looking to pick a fight. I just wanted you to know that I'm ok. In fact, I'm better than ok. This might be the happiest I've ever been in my life. Sometimes I think about what could have been. With us, I mean. I still think about you late at night. Sometimes I talk to you when I'm by myself. I've been seeing this guy and...you know what, never mind. It doesn't matter.
    I hope you're doing good! I mean that, ok? I got your email and I still read it sometimes. I hope you're happy, y'know? I want you to be happy. I read about your new performance art, and I think it's just wonderful. Wonderful. Please know that I'm rooting for you and...well, take it easy. God, that sounds so dumb.
    See you in my dreams.
    -J

    Ruth read the email two more times before she threw her phone against the wall as hard as she could and screamed. Her throat was raw by the end of it. She went on to set a new personal record for alcohol consumed in a single night.

    Ruth woke up the next afternoon to the frantic voice and frantic knocking of Alex coming through her door.
    "Ruth," yelled Alex, "Ruth, are you in there?! Open up! You have to see this!"
    Ruth attempted a groan, but the sensation of small needles slid through her throat from the previous night's screaming. She rolled out of bed, coughing through her pile of small empty bottles, and moved just close enough to open the door without leaving the bed. She already began to regret her decision as Alex came into the room with an energy that Ruth was not prepared for. Even in her most sober state of mind, Ruth had never enjoyed an abundance of enthusiasm.
    "Ruth, you fucking genius," said Alex, "why didn't you tell me you were gonna go off script?! No. You know what? I'm glad you didn't tell me. It was so...authentic. Ugh, we are going to make so much money!"
    Ruth tried to find the strength to open her eyes while Alex was speaking. She understood a few of the words, but their order was confusing. She managed to get the word "water" out of her mouth before she felt too sick to say any more. Alex ran to the sink and got a glass of water for Ruth.
    "Turn on the TV," said Alex, "you're not going to believe this!"

Alex grabbed the remote and turned on the television before Ruth could process their request. The news channel was dubbed in English, and it had begun to explain the innovative new performance art from the previous day that had been received as a resounding success. The newscast told of the critics and journalists who have coined the newest art movement as "Absent Art" and have credited Ms. Ruth Rubenstein as its founder and matriarch. A prominent member of the board of trustees from the New York Metropolitan Museum of Art, a Mr. Carter Davis, had this to say:

"Well of course I had found Ms. Rubenstein to be a fledgling artist at the time, but it was clear that there was something different about her technique and understanding of the world around her. I knew from the very first exposure to her work that there were great things in store for her. No, I don't take credit for discovering Ms. Rubenstein, but I will be forever grateful for my consistent ability to recognize genius."

Another critic from the London Times had this to say:

"While the guests of Ms. Rubenstein's curated performance piece, Ego Nunc Abibo, had entered the Museum Ludwig for an evening of Avant Garde entertainment, they were instead met with a revolutionary approach to the art world: the Absence of Art. While the anticipation for performance grew around them, the guests began to discuss their own ideas and concepts for what the performance would be. In doing so, some critics have claimed that the audience was then transformed into the art. Living art. We are waiting with anticipation for an official manifesto from Ms. Rubenstein, but the Absent Art movement has already been hailed as the greatest contribution to the art world since postmodernism. Ms. Rubenstein, who has maintained a reclusive air of anonymity, has already begun to receive multiple requests from Museums across the globe. The art world itself seems to be clamoring for their own experience with what Ms. Rubenstein will bring, or not bring, to their galleries."

"Fuck a duck," said Alex, "you're Andy Warhol! You're Van Gogh! You! Are! Ms.! Ruth! Rubenstein!"

Alex took Ruth's hungover and puffy face in their hands and kissed her on the lips.

"Baby," they said, "you're a fucking superstar!"

Ruth fell back onto the bed and wanted to die. The news of her guaranteed success was irrelevant compared to the hangover that wanted to kill her. She had a vague understanding of what was going on, but it would only feel real when she could call her parents and tell them all about it. She hoped that with her newly found fame she could possibly help her sister Mary, too.

Acknowledgments

Whew! Golly, that was somethin'. Thank you very much for reading through the story. If you skipped ahead to this part, well I don't blame you. You missed the Annual Henry Kissinger Rhino Orgy Clown Hunt, though. Might be worth thumbing through.

Anyway
Thanks again for stopping by
Sorry about the bad French
This was fun.

With gratitude and admiration to:
Nicholas Adams, Daniel Gursky, Todd Davis,
Michael Flowers, Rachel Koelsch, Nina Alexander, BiL, PRC,
Brian Halligan, Ad, William and Anita Panagakos,
and Yanira Kilgore

A special thank you to Allen McRae who refused to publish this which provided me more time to work on it and fix several discrepancies. At the time of this release, he has still refused to publish the book.

Until next time.

N.J.P.
04/04/2024

Printed in the USA
CPSIA information can be obtained
at www.ICGtesting.com
LVHW090901060924
789777LV00010B/107